HADES

ALSO BY RUSSELL ANDREWS

Gideon

Icarus

Aphrodite

Midas

HADES

RUSSELL ANDREWS

NEW YORK   BOSTON

Mysterious Press
Hachette Book Group USA
1271 Avenue of the Americas
New York, NY 10020

Visit our Web site at www.mysteriouspress.com.

Mysterious Press is an imprint of Warner Books. The Mysterious Press name and logo are trademarks of Warner Books.

Printed in the United States of America
First Edition: March 2007

10   9   8   7   6   5   4   3   2   1

Library of Congress Cataloging-in-Publication Data
Andrews, Russell.
    Hades / Russell Andrews. — 1st ed.
        p. cm.
    Summary: "Russell Andrews returns with another large scale political, conspiratorial thriller featuring East End Harbor's police chief, Justin Westwood"—Provided by publisher.
    ISBN-13: 978-0-89296-021-7
    ISBN-10: 0-89296-021-3
    1. Police—New York (State)—Long Island—Fiction.   2. Murder—Investigation—Fiction. 3. Hamptons (N.Y.)—Fiction. 4. Political fiction. gsafd I. Title.
PS3551.N4525H33 2007
813'.54—dc22
                                                                    2006035316

Over the years, in real life while using a real name, or in my pseudony-mous thriller-writing existence, I have worked with wonderful writers, editors, directors, agents, and various colleagues. Whether they know it or not—and whether they want to admit it or not—every one of the following has taught me how to write and how to think like a writer: Dave Anderson, William Bayer, Henry Beard, Edward Behr, Roy Blount, Jr., Lorenzo Carcaterra, William Darrid, the late William Diehl, Bill Duke, Jack Dytman, Jason Epstein, Joe Eszterhas, Joni Evans, Jackie Farber, John Feinstein, Colin Fox, Joe Fox, Nicholas Gage, Peter Gent, Steven Gethers, William Goldman, Gerald Green, Linda Grey, Lewis Grizzard, Michael Gross, Pete Hamill, Wil Haygood, John Helyar, Sy Hersh, Carl Hiaasen, Robert Hughes, Susan Isaacs, Marc Jaffe, Bill James, Ricky Jay, Penn Jillette, Pat Jordan, Stefan Kanfer, Kitty Kelley, Daniel Keyes, Joe Klein, Naomi Levy, Bob Loomis, Mike Lupica, Eric Lustbader, Sonny Mehta, Walter Mosley, Leona Nevler, Esther Newberg, Roman Polanski, Roberta Pryor, Bob Reis, Tom Robbins, Stephen Rubin, Hank Searls, Roger Simon, Teller, William Thomas, Alex Witchel, Audrey Wood, Alan Zweibel.

ACKNOWLEDGMENTS

The usual list, with a few additions and subtractions as the case may be: John Alderman at Trellus Management Co., Eric Pessagno and D. B. Lifland at Trellus, Mike Takata at Soros Fund Management, Ron Malfi, Janis Donnaud, Esther Newberg, Jack Dytman, Colin Fox, Jamie Raab, Hilary Hale.

PROLOGUE

Favignana, Italy
May 22

It was nearing the end of May, in the middle of *la Mattanza*—the tuna killing. During these few weeks, the tuna follow the currents from the Atlantic Ocean into the warmer Mediterranean to deposit and fertilize their eggs. For centuries, the fishermen have known this secret, and in mid-April they begin to set up a series of net barriers in the water. The tuna become trapped, forced to follow the direction of the barriers, and are obliged to swim straight toward those who patiently wait to slaughter them.

The boats were coming in now. They were driving the tuna, thousands of them, toward shore. Soon the water's rolling waves would be red; the islanders would be cheering; and all the nontourists who made their living on this speck of land just off the coast of Sicily, a short ferry ride due west from the city of Trapani, would be secure again. The restaurants would have no empty tables, the stores would sell their trinkets and T-shirts, and the poor box in the church in the Gothic square would be filled to the brim.

One of the most beautiful islands in the world, Favignana is speckled with coves, into which creeps the clearest water in the sea. Thin slices of white sand and finely pebbled beaches glisten and gleam in the summer sun. The island's main attribute is tufa—an almost-translucent-looking rock, formed over centuries as water gradually evaporated from the abundant amounts of lime that form the cliffs and caves. Remnants of ancient excavations are everywhere, the sites abandoned seemingly in mid-dig. Thick blocks of the stone are discarded and left to turn even more yellow and red from rust. Four- and five-hundred-year-old villas built out of that tufa are still standing, though, and dominate the coastline, giving the ancient stone a productive as well as ornamental life in the modern world.

Narrow strips of road cut into the hills and the rock, winding east and west, north and south, forging an impossible maze. Primitive and lovely, the island is mostly unspoiled by foreign tourists (except for the stray German here and there and the Italians from up north who come to lounge and tan and eat mounds of pasta with *bottarga*, the pungent tuna roe). Favignana is paradise for most people. But Angelo Tornabene was not most people. Angelo Tornabene hated the small island on which he had spent his entire life. He couldn't wait to escape. He didn't care that the great tuna hunt was described and revered as far back as *The Odyssey* or that the tufa could be linked to the building of the great pyramids. He couldn't get away fast enough from the foul-smelling fish; the bland, monotonous rock; and the tourists from the north who came for the weekends and the summer and bicycled around the maze from one bar *ingresso* to another. Angelo wanted to escape. Anywhere. Anywhere that wasn't this goddamn island. He didn't care about the great Roman naval battle with the Carthaginians. He didn't care at all about the past. Favignana was only about history. It was about things that no longer existed. Dead things. Dead stone, dead fish, dead people. Angelo wanted to live.

It's why he'd spent the last three days talking to the sailors on the huge ship. They were from South Africa. He didn't know where exactly. He'd never heard of the city whose name they kept repeating, but he understood the word "Africa" and knew they weren't Arab and knew they weren't black, so he decided they must come from the white part, which he knew was south, and all he really cared about was where they

were going, which was far, far away from here. The Africans were waiting for the tuna to come in so they could load up on fresh fish for the
next leg of the journey; they were excited that the wait was almost over,
that it was almost time to leave. The sailors heard the cheering and they
ran to look, to see the bloody spectacle, as Angelo knew they would. He
ran with them, pointing out the oncoming boats, celebrating, slapping
as many white Africans as he could on the back; and while everyone was
cheering it wasn't hard for him to disappear, to slip below, and wander
through the ship. As he wandered, a thick metal door opened and a
man came through the opening. He was not in a uniform; he wore
a dark business suit and a thin tie. He looked at Angelo but did not
seem to care that a stranger was exploring places he shouldn't be. Angelo
smiled to show that he belonged, but the man didn't smile back—he
just walked slowly back to join all the commotion. The man looked serious and important, and Angelo wondered if he might be the captain. Or
even higher up than the captain. The thought made him nervous, and as
the man passed by, Angelo knew he had to be quick; so he darted ahead,
caught the heavy metal door before it could close, stepped forward and
found himself in a passageway that led to many rooms. He began moving slowly, tried several doors, all of which were locked. And then he
tried one and it opened. Now he was in another maze of rooms, and
without knowing what else to do he began trying more doors, examin-
ing more rooms. After perhaps fifteen minutes, he was standing in a
doorway that led into a small dark space, a nearly empty room of seemingly little importance. There were wooden crates stacked up. Many of
them. Still holding the door open, Angelo inched his leg in front of him
and put his foot against one stack; it felt solid, as if filled with canned
goods. Maybe it was a room for storage, but it didn't look as if it was
used much. That was good, Angelo thought, it meant he'd have more
time to remain hidden.

He stepped farther into the room and let the heavy iron door close
behind him. He heard a lock click into place. Angelo tried to open it,
found that he couldn't, but that was all right. He didn't mind. At some
point, when they were far out to sea, someone would open the door and
come into the room. They would see him and they would be angry, but

what could they do? It would be too late. They would shrug and kick him off at the next port and that was just fine with Angelo. It didn't matter what that next port was. He'd be someplace else. He was sixteen years old, and he would no longer be on Favignana. He'd be free.

So he took off one shirt (he was wearing three—he was prepared for this journey; he'd brought shirts and nuts and raisins and bread and cheese, all hidden away in deep pockets); crumpled it up into a kind of pillow; and he sat on it, leaning against one corner of the room, and decided he was comfortable enough to wait. He knew he could wait now as long as he had to. He had already waited a long, long time, his whole life, really. He could certainly wait a little while longer.

He did not know how many hours later it was when the ship began to move. All he knew, all he cared about, was the movement itself. His voyage had begun.

He did his best, after that, to keep track of the time but it was difficult. It was pleasantly warm in the room and a bit stuffy and Angelo kept getting drowsy. He slept many hours, so he could only guess at the time or even if it was night or day. He guessed that it was already two days later when he'd finished eating some of his hard Parmesan cheese. As usual, he wasn't aware of the moment when he had fallen asleep that day and he didn't fully realize when he'd awakened, only that something had awakened him. A loud noise. Like an explosion. Or maybe a gunshot. He heard another loud noise. Yes, this was definitely an explosion. And then the ship was moving. But this was a strange movement. Not as if it was leaving port, it was moving as if something was wrong. The room was tilting, and the boxes of things, he didn't know of what—he had not yet looked inside the boxes that were in the room—were sliding and falling. Angelo stood up, wondering what was happening, and then he realized his feet were wet. There was water in the room. A lot of water. Angelo went to open the door, remembered that it was locked. He pounded on the thick steel, yelling, knowing that no one would understand his Italian but surely someone would hear him and let him out. He pounded again and again, and then he couldn't pound because he could not stand up. He was down in the water, and the water was getting higher and higher. It was almost to the ceiling. Angelo was a good swimmer, but soon there was no place left to swim. There was no place to keep his head above the water, and soon he was holding his breath, praying that someone would open the door because he couldn't hold his breath forever, couldn't even hold it for another minute. Not one more second.

He felt the water rush into his mouth. Tasted the salt and the fish. He waved his arms and kicked his legs because his body was filling with the sea, but however much he raged, it did no good. He tried to spit the water out but the water was all around him. Inside and outside. He was like the tuna he had hated all these years: defeated by the sea, driven toward his death with nowhere to turn away.

From under the water, another explosion filled his ears. And then Angelo Tornabene was not raging. Or struggling or spitting or moving at all, except to bob up and down in the turbulent water, rolling with the sinking ship.

He was finally free.

He had finally left Favignana.

Alice, Texas
June 8

It wasn't so long ago that Teddy Angel figured out that, when he really thought about it, he liked four things in life.

Not *just* four things. There was plenty of other stuff he was pretty fond of. Pussy, for instance. That was always good. And one of the guys on *American Idol*—he could never remember his name—the fat black guy whose stomach shook like crazy when he sang. That dude was pretty fuckin' amazing. Teddy also liked really hot, humid days, the kind that made everyone else uncomfortable; it was pretty awesome just standing in the sun and wearing a muscle shirt and dripping with sweat, watching the little drops gather on his triceps and then stream down to the sizzling sidewalk. And he had to put frozen grapes right up there. He was crazy about frozen grapes; they almost made it into his top four. Whoever invented that was one motherfucker of a genius. But when you got right down to it, there were only four things he really, *really* liked. That he considered *essential*.

He liked having money in his pocket, that was number one. And he had some right now—did he ever—almost five thousand dollars. Well, really about forty-two hundred because he'd pissed away four dimes in a card game last night, most of it coming when he'd had nines over sixes but lost to a bigger boat, queens over eights. He'd also spent a hundred on a used .38, a really nice piece, good weight, comfortable fit in his hand (he liked guns, too, liked the way they made him feel, although not as much as frozen grapes; guns were maybe sixth or seventh on his list). The other two or three bills he'd spent buying drinks, tipping heavy, showing off. All well worth it. Especially because he had plenty more. And even more coming when he got to Mexico; and that wouldn't be too long now—maybe another couple of days, tops—till he got to the town he was supposed to get to, dropped off the truck, picked up his plane ticket, and got the hell back to Detroit where he belonged. He was in Texas already, had crossed the state line about half an hour ago. Teddy decided he didn't like Texas, not that he'd ever been there before, but what the hell was there to like? Been pouring rain ever since he'd arrived, raining so hard it was steaming up the highway. Huge drops of water were banging into the windshield like they were gonna bust it open. It wasn't just the rain, though. He knew it could rain anywhere. But Texas was still a fucked-up state. Bunch of cowboys and rich white men, that's what was in Texas. It's why he'd bought the .38, in case one of those cowboys called him a nigger. He almost wished someone would. He'd just saunter up to the guy, blow the asshole away, toss the gun, and get back in the truck and keep on driving.

He liked being called Teddy Angel. That was probably number two on his list. He wasn't sure when it had started. He thought maybe when he was a kid. Always in trouble. Always getting picked up by the police, getting in fights, talking back, stealing something. His real name was Anjule. Edward Anjule. His grandmother was the one who used to call him Teddy. He wondered if she'd tagged him Angel, too. Maybe she thought she was being funny. Such a nice name for such a bad boy. If it was her, he decided he owed her one. He wondered if she was still alive.

If she was, he thought maybe he'd drop in on her when he got back, buy her a drink, maybe lay a hundred on her, thank her for the cool name.

Teddy also liked being drunk. He put that third. Drugs were okay, too. Weed, coke, X—he wouldn't turn none of that down. But he mostly liked liquor. Tequila, scotch, bourbon, any of it straight up. A nice cold beer when he was hot. He didn't just like drinking, he loved it. Did it pretty much all day and all night long. Was doing it now while he was driving. Swigging from a bottle of Jack. The bottle was almost empty, now that he looked, but that was okay because there was another one, this one full, sitting right next to it. And beside that was a six-pack of Bud. Probably not real cold by now, but that was okay, too, the air-conditioning in the truck was on and working pretty well, so Teddy Angel wasn't too hot or too thirsty. If he felt like a brew, a slightly warm brew would be just fine.

The fourth thing that Teddy liked was music. All kinds of music. He was into 50 Cent pretty heavy, hard not to be. That motherfucker spoke some shit. But he liked older stuff, too. The classic stuff is how he thought of it, early Puff and Jay-Z and Tupac—those were good days for sound. He liked all the way back to Motown. Had to appreci-ate the Berry Gordy shit when you came from Detroit. The Four Tops, Supremes, Stevie Wonder. That's what he was listening to now. On his iPod, 'cause there wasn't a CD player in the truck and the radio was for shit and the speakers were even worse. So it was Stevie and *Talking Book*. A classic. Some major phones clamped on his ears, the little touchy white dial thing fingered all the way to the right, as loud as it'd go. Drivin' along at eighty-six miles per, "Superstition" blasting into his brain.

Teddy Angel was a happy man.

And he was happy right up until the very moment he died, when he was reaching for the second bottle of Jack and the truck started to skid on the wet, slick road. He tried to grab the wheel with his left hand, never letting go of the bottle with his right—tried to turn himself out of the spin—but his reflexes were slowed by the alcohol and his hand slipped, banging into the dashboard, and the truck rumbled over the divider. It just missed a Caddy coming from the other direction; then it rammed into a shiny green Taurus that couldn't get out of the way;

and then it jumped off the shoulder, toppling, turning over twice, the second turn breaking Teddy's neck.

The truck was on its side, the wheels still spinning, when the police arrived, maybe ten minutes after the accident. A couple of state troopers. One of them, Wade Turner, was thirty-eight years old, had seen plenty of accidents, been next to his share of dead bodies. His partner, though, Morgan Lanier, was only twenty-four, and this was his first.

The Caddy had never stopped, the driver didn't even slow down and think about it—just tore the hell out of there to wherever he was headed—but the Taurus was damaged, and sat sideways on the road, half in the right lane, half on the narrow shoulder. Turner went to check on the driver, a woman in her late twenties who had used her cell to call in the accident. She was not at all bad looking, could've been a cheerleader—maybe UT, not the Cowboys, not that good-looking—and luckily she wasn't hurt. She'd been wearing her seat belt and was a little hysterical but no serious injuries. Turner assured her that she was fine and that everything would be all right. "Just a little accident," he said, "and you're fine." Then he went to the trunk of his car, got a flare and lit it, stuck it on the road side of the car—if anyone else drove by they wouldn't hit the Taurus again by mistake.

The woman in the car had been too frightened to check on the driver of the small truck—she hadn't even gotten out of her car—so Turner nodded in that direction and he and Lanier left the woman and went to see the extent of the damage.

Wade Turner didn't pay much attention to Teddy Angel. There wasn't any question the guy was stone-cold dead. As Turner bent down over the body, he recoiled at the stench of bourbon. And he shook his head when he removed the headphones that were still covering Teddy's ears, startled by the music blaring. The older trooper reached over Teddy's body, picked up the white iPod, lowered the volume. He put the headset on his own head now, smiled, and nodded at his younger partner.

"Stevie Wonder," he said. "Great fucking album."

Lanier, partly to get away from the dead body, partly to get away from his partner, walked away from the cab and crawled into the back of the truck. A minute or so later he heard Turner say, "Anything back there?"

"Not much," Lanier answered. "Looks like he was logging sporting goods. Baseball gloves, team shirts—shit like that." He reached into a box that had split open, picked up a leather outfielder's mitt. "How the hell'd Matt Lawton get his own glove?" he asked, but his partner didn't answer. Turner wasn't into baseball much. Just college football. He probably didn't even know who Matt Lawton was.

If it was possible, the rain seemed to be coming down harder now. It made Lanier feel claustrophobic in the back of the truck, as if someone were hammering on the walls, telling him to get the hell out.

"Ambulance'll be here in a few," Turner said from outside. "Probably catch pneumonia by then with my luck." He started to head to the Taurus, check back on the second-rate cheerleader, but he stopped when he heard Lanier call out, "Hey, Wade?"

"Yeah?" Turner said.

"I think maybe you should take a look at this."

"I'm fuckin' drownin' out here, Morgan. What is it?"

"I don't know," Lanier said, "but you better come here."

Turner sighed; felt the heavy rain pelt against his neck and down his back despite all the weather gear; and then he climbed into the back of the truck and pulled out his flashlight, pointing it toward his partner, who was crouched in the far corner.

"Check this out," Lanier said. "It's like some kind of secret compartment thing. Built-in."

Turner crawled over to the boxes, pushing aside the loose sporting equipment and clothing that had spilled out. He shone his light where Lanier was pointing. His partner was right. Some kind of wooden cabinet had been built into the paneling in the truck. Turner moved the light, saw that the cabinet went around three quarters of the space. The wood had splintered in several places, the result of the accident. Lanier reached inside, started to slide out what looked like some kind of lead weight.

"Jesus Christ," Lanier said. "It weighs a ton."

"Looks like a gold bar." Turner spoke quietly now. Almost reverently. "Like what they got at Fort Knox."

"Isn't gold kind of . . . you know . . . yellow or . . . *gold* . . . or something?"

"I think so," Turner said. "I've only seen it in the movies. That James Bond movie, the one with Sean Connery."

"*Goldfinger,*" Lanier said.

"Yeah. It was yellow in *Goldfinger.*"

"Maybe it's silver. Silver bars. It ain't yellow, so maybe it's silver."

"Maybe," Turner said. "But I'll tell you one thing. Whatever the hell it is, this nigger sure as shit shouldn'ta had it."

Two ambulances arrived, about ten minutes later. One took the blond woman to the nearest hospital, the other carried Teddy Angel's body to the nearest morgue. A local tow-truck service arrived another forty-five minutes after that and, after getting the truck upright, towed it back to Turner's and Lanier's station.

It took the Texas State Police three days to prove Wade Turner correct in his assessment. Teddy Angel sure as shit shouldn't have been carrying his cargo. In those few days, they were able to determine that Teddy's truck had been reported stolen three months earlier in Cincinnati, Ohio. It had been refitted completely—repainted and given false license plates. The name stenciled onto the side of the truck—Hirshey Sporting Goods—belonged to a nonexistent company. The permit found in the glove compartment, the one that would have allowed the truck into Mexico with its sporting goods cargo, was a forgery. The Mexican company listed as the recipient of the goods, El Sportiva Mexicana, was also nonexistent.

Teddy Angel's driver's license was not in the name of Teddy Angel. Or even Edward Anjule. It had been issued in the name of an Easton, Pennsylvania, male who had died at the age of two, just over eight years ago. Teddy's fingerprints had been "interfered with"—those were the words used by the forensic expert who worked on Teddy's body. It meant that someone had operated on Teddy's hands, cut the tips of his fingers so he could not be identified using his prints. Teddy had also clearly never had his teeth so much as cleaned, so nothing came up when a search for his dental records went through the computer. The Texas police had no clue to his true identity.

As near as could be determined, there was absolutely nothing real about either the truck or its driver. At least nothing that the police—or the FBI, who had been called in—had much hope of finding.

The contents hidden in the built-in wooden compartment of the truck *were* real, however. The metal bars.

Wade Turner's and Morgan Lanier's captain called them into his office four days after the truck had driven off the side of the highway. He told them that he figured they deserved to know the result of the investigation up to that point, not that the result was going to add up to much because they were pretty well stymied. But the captain told them all about the stolen vehicle and about Teddy Angel's nonexistent fingerprints. And about the bars they'd found just sitting in the back of Teddy's truck.

They weren't gold. They weren't silver.

They were platinum.

Solid, pure, unidentifiable and untraceable platinum bars.

Three million dollars' worth.

PART ONE

1

Justin Westwood was experiencing a combination of emotions he was not particularly used to, and he wasn't sure exactly how he felt about it. For one thing, he was relaxed. For another, at least for the moment, he was content. If push came to shove, he realized, he might even describe himself as happy. He was well aware this was not his normal state of mind, and he couldn't help but wonder what the hell was going on.

The good feelings came partly from the very cold Ketel One vodka martini he was sipping, his second in the past half hour, each with two spicy jalapeño-stuffed olives filling up the bottom of the glass. He'd also indulged in a few hits of a superb joint. He wondered what would happen if one of East End Harbor's young police officers happened to walk into his house sometime to find him happily getting stoned. Probably nothing, he thought. It was one of the few advantages of being the chief of police.

Things had been quiet in the small Long Island resort town for nearly a year now. And quiet was good. Teenagers had gotten drunk and turned over a few garbage cans. Three houses had been broken into: someone had stolen food out of one refrigerator; another master thief had broken a window to climb into a bedroom and had cut himself so badly he called the hospital to send an ambulance; and the third break-in was an ex-boyfriend trying to get a piece of jewelry back, an earring. It turned out the earring had cost all of forty-seven bucks—not quite the expensive diamond that had been promised in happier times—so the victim was more than willing to let it go and forget about pressing charges. And even more determined to keep the "ex" in any references to the would-be burglar.

Justin was getting used to the peace and calm. He had had enough turmoil to last several lifetimes. One of the things that had helped him put the turmoil in the past was the naked woman on the bed next to him. She was lying on her right side, propped up on her elbow, also sipping her second martini. Justin would have settled for straight vodka— he probably wouldn't have even bothered with the ice—but she had insisted on bartending. She'd shown up with the dry vermouth and the olives and even supplied the martini glasses, divining that his kitchen cabinet stock went only as deep as four or five Kmart water glasses, if that. She'd also shown up with two thick sirloin steaks, saying that if she had to settle one more time for pizza or the dreadful East End take-out Chinese food he usually ordered, she wouldn't be held responsible for her actions. She also made it clear that she provided groceries when needed, but she hadn't actually cooked anything since she was twelve years old and had no intention of starting now. Justin had looked through his cupboard and asked if spaghetti with garlic and oil and hot red pepper flakes would satisfy her as a side dish, and she had said absolutely, as long as they got to do certain things close up before the garlic took over. He was happy to oblige. They didn't make it halfway through the first martini before her clothes were off and he was putting Sticky Fingers in his CD player—he was really in the mood for the driving beat of "Moonlight Mile" and the sweaty feel of "Can't You Hear Me Knocking"—and she was pulling him onto his bed, and they were making love about as well as love could be made. No, not exactly accurate, he thought. What they had really done so far that night was screw their brains out. And that was definitely satisfactory.

Justin smiled at the memory of what had transpired maybe twenty minutes ago, realized she thought he was smiling at her, and then he *was* smiling at her. She was something to smile at.

He'd met Abby Harmon four months ago. In Duffy's, not a bar where you'd expect to meet someone like Abby. She confessed later that she'd come in looking for him. She knew it was where he went to drink, and she'd heard so much about him she decided she had to see the real deal for herself. For a stretch of quite a few months, she couldn't go to a party where people weren't talking about Justin Westwood. His background. His aloofness. His lack of interest in just about everything that everybody at those parties was interested in. She wanted to see him for herself, see what made him tick. So she pulled her Mercedes CLK550 convertible up to the old-fashioned blue-collar hangout at ten-thirty at night, walked in, and ordered a glass of their best red Bordeaux. Their best red Bordeaux was six months old, from the North Fork of Long Island, and cost three-fifty a glass, so she went instead for a Sam Adams on draft. Donnie, the bartender, nodded in silent approval when she'd switched her order. A much better choice.

Justin had recognized her as soon as she'd walked in, of course. It was not hard to recognize Abigail Harmon. There were plenty of rich women coming in and out of East End Harbor. And there were plenty of sexy women. But there wasn't anyone who was quite as rich and sexy as Abigail. Certainly no one who also had her kind of reputation.

Justin knew a horse trainer, a fairly placid guy, who'd done work at the stable where Abigail kept her two horses. "The meanest bitch I've ever met," is the way he had described her. Justin had seen her once, striding out of the mayor of East End Harbor's office. When Justin walked in, the mayor, Leona Krill, looked as if she'd gone ten rounds with the young Mike Tyson; when he'd asked her if she was okay, Leona had said, "Jay, I feel like I've just been bitten by a rattlesnake."

But he also knew that Deena, his ex-girlfriend, gave Abigail Harmon private yoga lessons. Deena went up to the Harmon mansion—the only way to describe it—three times a week. She was very well paid, but she wouldn't go there just for the money. Deena would never do anything just for the money. She liked Abigail Harmon. She told Jay, during their once-every-three-or-four-months lunch date, that Abby—it was the first time Justin had heard anyone refer to her as "Abby"—was "incredibly smart and really comfortable in her own skin and about the only person I teach around here who doesn't treat me either as the help or as if I'm some kind of kook. And she's incredibly nice to Kenny." Kenny was really Kendall, who was Deena's now twelve-year-old daughter. Justin was once the love of Kendall's life. Of course, she'd been nine years old then. Now he was almost but not quite yet just a grown-up to be tolerated. He took Kendall out to lunch every three months or so, too. And every so often out to dinner. He figured he had until she was fourteen for the dinners. Then she'd dump him for some pimply-faced teenager who, sooner or later, Justin would have to talk to about getting drunk in public and knocking over garbage cans.

That night at Duffy's, Justin had been drinking with Gary Jenkins and Mike Haversham, two of the young cops who worked for him. When Abby walked in, Gary and Mike stared in awe and disbelief. When she sauntered over to their table and asked if she could join them, they looked as if they might faint. After a few sips of her beer, she leaned over in the direction of both young men and said softly, in that voice of hers that somehow managed to be both fire and ice, "Could I ask you guys a real favor?" When they nodded, she said, "What I really want to do is have a drink with your boss. Would you mind giving us some privacy?"

The two cops practically fell over themselves to comply with her wishes, and suddenly Justin felt as if he and she were the only two people in Duffy's wood-paneled room.

She didn't say anything for a fairly long while and neither did he. Not speaking was one of Justin's better things. He was comfortable with silence. More comfortable than he usually was with conversation. He'd seen something once, when he was a kid, still in college and traveling for the summer in Europe. It was some ancient aphorism—his memory told him it was Turkish—and it said, "With language began all lies." He had liked the thought then, and now that he was grown-up and a cop, he liked it even more. So he was in no rush to interfere with the quiet that settled in over the table at Duffy's. Finally, Abby just introduced herself. And smiled. He thought he'd never seen anything quite as perfect as her white, sparkling teeth. Unless it was her shoulders, which he could see because she was wearing a sleeveless shirt; and they were tan and perfectly round and so smooth he thought someone must have oiled and polished them before she stepped out. Her eyes weren't too shabby either, he had to admit. They were big and almond shaped, brown with tiny specks of yellow. It was the floating specks that were so hypnotic, and they made him think of a song lyric he'd heard long ago, when he was a teenager and his parents had taken him to Manhattan to see Bobby Short sing at the Carlyle. He didn't remember all the songs he'd heard that night, but he did remember Short crooning about a woman whose eyes were open windows and when you looked in, there was a party going on inside.

Sitting at the table with her, he decided he wouldn't mind an invitation to the party that was going on inside Abigail Harmon.

"Is there something in particular you wanted to talk to me about?" he asked.

She shook her head. Her straight brown hair moved in sync with the motion, rolled left and right, then settled back easily, still and soft and glistening. Her hair was pretty damn perfect, too.

So they started talking about the town. She told him about her dealings with some of the younger cops, one of whom—she thought maybe it was Mike—had once tried to give her a speeding ticket.

"What do you mean 'tried'?" he asked.

She waved her hand, as if brushing aside a gnat. "Oh, I talked him out of it."

"How fast were you going?"

"Eighty-five."

"And what was the speed limit?"

"Twenty-five."

"Jesus Christ." He rolled his eyes. "What the hell did you say to him?"

But she just smiled and shook her head. "Sorry," she told him. "I might have to try it on you if you ever give me a ticket."

Then they spoke about the Hamptons and a little bit about Rhode Island, which is where Justin was from. Abby had spent time there. In college she'd dated someone who went to the Rhode Island School of Design. The fact is, he didn't really remember much of what they'd talked about. It wasn't her words that were so beguiling. It was her voice and her manner and her legs, which kept crossing and uncrossing, and looked so muscular and firm and inviting. And it was definitely her eyes, which hinted at all sorts of pleasures and an equal number of dangerous things. And which were vulnerable. And even a little bit sad.

They talked until he looked around and realized that almost everyone else in Duffy's was gone. There was one drunk regular, who had passed out at a table and was left to fend for himself, and Donnie, who was busy wiping the scarred wood bar down with a damp cloth.

"Look—" Justin said, not exactly sure where the rest of the sentence was going, but it didn't matter much because Abby cut him off.

"I know," she said. He wasn't sure how she managed to interrupt him. She didn't speak loudly and her words weren't rushed. Somehow, though, when she spoke, the right thing to do seemed to be quiet. "I know about your wife and I'm sorry. I know about Deena, too. Well, enough to know that there's something inside you that frightens her, which is why she broke it off, and she feels as bad as a person could feel about that. And I know about that woman police officer who was here last year. I don't know what happened—I've just heard rumors—I figure it was bad and complicated and now she's gone. All I want to say is what happened to your wife happened a long time ago, and maybe one of these days you'll let go—or maybe you won't. But, just so you know, I don't frighten so easily. And I don't want any complications in my life. And, best of all, I'm not gone. I'm right here. So you wanna go someplace a little nicer than this and have a real drink?"

Justin hesitated just a split second before he nodded. He didn't know why he hesitated. He was never going to say anything but okay. "Got somewhere in mind?"

"How about your place?"

"The bad news," he said, "is that my place isn't any nicer than here."

"What's the good news?"

"There isn't any good news."

"Let's go," she said, "sweet talker." And it was the "sweet talker" that did it. He saw her sense of humor and her toughness and her soft spot at exactly the same moment.

That first night was sensational. He wasn't at all surprised at how sexy she was, how uninhibited and demanding she was in bed. He *was* surprised at her tenderness and the way, after sex, she kind of rolled into him, collapsing, drained, as if it wasn't just about the pleasure and the physical relief but also about getting rid of anger and shaking off the outside world and all sorts of things that didn't have anything to do with him or what they'd just experienced together.

After that, they began seeing each other. Not constantly. Sometimes once or twice a week. Occasionally even three times. They'd have dinner, usually in his small, Victorian house on Division Street at the end of East End Harbor's historical district. They watched a few DVDs, mostly old movies. They drove into Manhattan one night, had dinner at Barbuto, way west down in the West Village, and spent the night at the Soho Grand Hotel.

And now here they were sitting on his bed, eating the steaks and pasta he'd cooked up, finishing off their martinis. He didn't even mind that he knew one of the reasons she was smiling and shaking her head affectionately was because she was enjoying the fact that he was a clumsy oaf.

He'd come back into the bedroom with the food and a pained expression on his face, and as soon as he'd set the plates down, he began looking at his right hand with his eyes narrowed. She didn't have to say a word, just gave him that look, that cocked head, and he said, "I have those stupid electric burners on my stove. You can't tell if they're on or off—"

She'd interrupted him, saying, "You mean *you* can't."

He gave her a mock scowl and said, "Okay, *I* can't." And then he said, "But what I *can* do is burn myself every damn time I go near the stove because I can't even remember to turn the thing off."

She'd laughed—laughing at the big tough guy who couldn't handle a small burn—and she'd taken his hand and softly kissed the blister that was forming, letting her tongue linger and gently lick the heel of his hand until he didn't really care about the minor burn.

Yes, it was safe to say that right now, right this minute, in this woman's presence, Justin Westwood was reasonably happy.

When they were done eating, Abby picked up both plates from the bed, saying, "Nobody'd believe it, me clearing the table." Then she said, "I'll be right back," and wearing only his light cotton summer robe, she made her way down the stairs, dropped the plates in the kitchen sink, then half walked, half ran to her car, which wasn't in his driveway but parked about a quarter of a block away on the street. She was back in his bedroom in less than a minute and in her hand was a red cardboard box. She handed it to him.

"Open it," she said.

Justin cocked his head a bit to the left, looked at her curiously, and did as he'd been told. He pulled out a small, perfectly round cake. With one candle sticking up in the middle.

"Happy birthday," she said. Then she reached for a match, struck it, and lit the candle. "June twelfth, right? Think I'd forget?"

"I didn't know we'd ever even discussed it. So I didn't think there was anything to remember. I—"

"I know. You haven't celebrated your birthday in years. I figured it was about time to start again. I mean, since this is the last time you'll be able to say you're in your thirties."

"Thirty-nine's the prime of life," he said. "Everybody knows that."

"Uh-huh. You gonna blow that out?"

"In a minute."

He put the cake down on a small end table by her side of the bed and then he kissed her. Slow and nice, a lingering kiss that told her a lot more about how he appreciated the gift than he'd ever put into words.

"*Now* I'll blow it out," he said. But as he took one step toward the cake and leaned over, the phone rang.

"Other women hoping to shower you with gifts?" Abby asked.

He didn't answer, just walked over to the phone, which was sitting in its cradle on the end table on his side of the bed. He looked at his caller ID and frowned.

"It's the station," he said.

"Now?"

He nodded, let the phone ring twice more. Then he picked it up, against his better judgment.

"I hope it's important," he said into the mouthpiece.

It didn't take him long to realize that it was.

2

It was a magnificent house. There was no other way to possibly describe it. The house of his dreams. Built to specifications with seven bedrooms in the main house and a guesthouse with three more. There was an Olympic-sized swimming pool that was barely visible from the French windows, almost lost amid the Japanese sculpture gardens, and an angular glass pool house and a man-made freshwater pond that was stocked with an endless supply of koi; and perhaps his favorite thing: the outdoor redwood Jacuzzi and sauna.

There was nothing cheap in this house, from the crystal doorknobs and chandeliers in almost every room to the original Warhols on the walls to the walk-in closets in the master bedroom suite that were filled with three-thousand-dollar men's suits and even more expensive designer dresses and women's shoes. The carpets were plush and virginally white, the curtains the most delicate silk. Even the kitchen was magnificent, with a professional Wolf eight-burner stove, a stainless steel Sub-Zero refrigerator the size of a New York City studio apartment, and gleaming copper pots that seemed to glow as they hung on the walls.

Best of all was its location. In the glorious Hamptons. On the border of chic Bridgehampton and the more blue-collar but charming East End Harbor. The best of all possible worlds. The glamour of the Bridgehampton and Sagaponack beaches and the Calvin Klein and George Soros parties, combined with the small-town simplicity of the village of East End, where the shopkeepers knew you by name and the woman at the post office would ask how your pets were and knew if you were a Mets or a Yankees fan.

He had dreamed about living in a place like this, in a house like this, and now that he was here, alone for the moment, he suddenly wasn't sure what to do. Maybe strip off all his clothes and take a moonlight swim in the heated pool. That sounded good. It was unseasonably cool outside, so a nice swim, then a quick dash through the chilled air to the sauna. Then open a splendid red wine, an '85 Mouton Rothschild—he knew there were several bottles in the cellar, he'd checked the very first thing after he'd entered and reset the alarm system. Then, after one glass of the Bordeaux, taken in the living room, perhaps an omelet, something simple, with some caviar on the side. Slowly finish the bottle of wine—in the den might be nice, with the very manly oak paneling and the cracked leather easy chairs. Then slip on a robe and put some Mozart on the stereo and stretch out on a freshly ironed linen sheet, under a goose down quilt, and read Evelyn Waugh. *Brideshead Revisited* was the book he'd selected for tonight. It just seemed so apt.

But first, there was something he needed to do. The urge was too overpowering.

He climbed the stairs to the master bedroom, went through to the walk-in closet on the left, the one that led to the slightly smaller of the two bathrooms in the suite. He stood before the elegant, conservative suits—he estimated there were fifty, maybe seventy-five—and crisply starched shirts that hung on wooden hangers as firmly as if they were being borne on perfectly formed shoulders. He opened one drawer, then another, and then a third, each one filled with the softest, smoothest cashmere sweaters. He selected a powder-blue cardigan, tenderly removed it from its bag, and wrapped it around him. He loved this sweater and it fit him as if it had been handmade for the contours of his body; plus the color went divinely with his dark blue eyes. He moved to stand in front of the full-length mirror and couldn't help admiring his looks and his sophistication, reveling in his luck and the unlimited upside that was surely waiting for him in the future.

The noise behind him startled him, and he turned suddenly. Even as he turned, he was aware of how gentle the cashmere was against his flesh. What he saw, standing in the doorway, however, made him forget about the pleasure he was feeling. He was suddenly uncertain about the upside in his future. He touched the hem of the sweater—he couldn't help himself, tugging at it for a moment of security.

"I thought . . ." he began but didn't know how to continue, because he wasn't sure exactly what it was he thought. He was startled at the sight that greeted him, standing in the bedroom doorway, and a little panicky, too. And then he realized what he wanted to say, or at least what he should say, so he tried to finish his thought. He got out the words "You weren't supposed to—" and that was all he got out before he saw the rise of an arm, and he felt a terrible sting in his left shoulder. His right hand moved to the pain, as if covering it with his palm would somehow help, but then there was more pain in the right side of his chest, this one even worse. Everything slowed down then; the world seemed to turn hazy and dim. And then he realized he wasn't standing anymore, he was on his knees, tumbling onto the thick Persian carpet that covered the bedroom floor. He heard another pop, and another, then he really couldn't hear much more. He tried to speak, tried to ask what was happening, and why, but his tongue didn't work, and his mouth made sounds that even he could tell were not real syllables, that expressed no thought. Through the haze, he saw something rise and fall, felt a horrible jolt in one leg, then the other, then his hip and his arm, and then the worst pain of all in his head, and then he felt nothing.

His very last thought was that he'd put on the wrong sweater. He had wanted the powder blue. But somehow he'd selected the red. Wine red, he thought. Then realized no, he was wrong.

Bloodred.

3

Justin held the phone to his ear as Mike Haversham talked. The young cop told him about the call that had just come in and exactly what the hysterical caller had said. Justin listened quietly, trying to keep his expression stoic and flat. As he listened, Abby jumped onto the bed, one graceful leap, gently put her hands on his shoulders, softly kissed his neck, teasing as well as tempting him. His robe was loosely tied around her and her bare leg was directly in his line of vision. He stared at the only piece of jewelry she usually wore, a diamond ankle bracelet that sparkled against her lightly tanned skin.

When Mike had finished with everything he had to say, Justin just said, "Call Gary, tell him to get there ASAP. I'll leave here in two minutes and meet him. You wait at the station."

He hung up, shifted his body so he could face Abby.

"Is everything okay?" she asked. She gave him an evil little grin, an invitation to forget about whatever it was he'd just heard and hop back into bed with her.

"No," he said. "Things aren't okay."

"What's the matter?" She edged the robe off her right shoulder. And then, vamping, "What could be so bad on your birthday?"

Justin put his right hand up to his face and rubbed the middle of his forehead. He exhaled a long breath, took both her hands in his, and said, "A body was just found. There's been a murder."

She looked at him, still smiling the sexy, inviting smile, waiting for the punch line. When she saw no punch line was coming, the smile faded.

He nodded, because he saw the question she was asking with her eyes.

"It's Evan," Justin Westwood said. "It's your husband."

The silence lasted until he realized he couldn't let it go on any longer.

"Get dressed," Justin said gently. "I've gotta go to the house. And you should come with me."

She didn't say anything. Didn't cry. Didn't make a sound. She simply shook her head in tight little motions, as if what she'd just been told couldn't be true. Then she slid off the bed, not slowly but listlessly, all energy drained from her body, and she began to pull on her clothes.

Justin watched Abby for a second, then he found the pair of jeans he'd tossed onto the floor and the black short-sleeved polo shirt that had been discarded near them. He waited for her to finish dressing and watched as she grabbed what was left of her martini, downed it in one quick gulp, and then walked down toward the living room.

So much for contentment, Justin Westwood thought.

So much for happiness.

Then he blew out the candle on his birthday cake and followed her downstairs.

The Harmon house was only a ten- or twelve-minute drive from Justin's. Sitting in his beat-up '89 BMW, he let the first two or three minutes pass in silence. Then he said, as delicately as he could manage, "I should ask you some questions before we get there."

She turned to him, her eyes still dull, and she nodded.

"Where were you before you came over?"

"To your house?"

Justin nodded. He realized that Abby's silence wasn't just due to the shock. He heard the tremor in her voice, understood she was fighting back tears. Knew she was, even more than that, struggling not to reveal any weakness.

"I was looking for your birthday cake," she said.

"Where did you get it?"

"What does that have to do with anything? How stupid is—"

"Abby, please."

"Why do you care—"

"Answer the question," he said. "Please. Just answer the question."

"At that giant supermarket in Bridgehampton. In the mall. King Kullen."

"What time was that?"

"I don't know. What time did I get to your place?"

"Tell me approximately what time *you* think you were there."

"Jay, what difference does it fucking make what time— Oh my god." She shifted in the bucket seat of the convertible so she could face him. The anger biting through her words was both palpable and remarkably restrained. It was the restraint that surprised him, not the hurt or the bitterness. "Do you think I killed my husband?"

"No." He didn't hesitate or stumble over his response.

"Then what the hell are you doing?"

"They're questions that have to be asked. Someone's going to ask them—I thought it would be better for you if it was me and I asked them now." When she didn't respond, he said, "Look . . . Abby . . . I'll know more when I see the crime scene. Evan's death is going to have repercussions. He's rich. And I assume you'll have been left a lot of money."

"That makes me a murderer?"

"No. That makes it a situation cops have to investigate."

Now he hesitated again, and Abby picked up on it.

"And I won't exactly be perceived as the grieving widow, will I?" she said.

"You were having an affair. And I'm not egotistical enough to assume I'm your first."

He didn't say it as a question, but she knew she was supposed to give an answer. "No," she told him. "You're not the first." She chewed on her lower lip for a few moments. He made a right turn now off South Hole Road, the road that separated East End Harbor from Bridgehampton, and drove up into the hills. The charming little houses were no more, replaced by imposing gates, long driveways, hedges, and unseen mansions.

"When was the last time you were home?"

"This afternoon."

"What time?"

"I don't know." She bit off the words, speaking through clenched teeth.

"Approximately," he said. "Two? Three? Six?"

"Three. Maybe four."

"And what were you doing between three or four and . . . birthday cake shopping?"

"Errands."

"What kind of errands?"

"I don't want to do this anymore, Jay. Stop it."

"Abby, was anyone at the house when you left?"

"No."

"No maid?"

"No. Sara and Pepe were there this morning. Evan gave them the rest of the day off."

"Was that normal?"

"No."

"So why'd he do it?"

"I don't know." She hesitated. "He knew I'd be out tonight. I guess he wanted to be alone."

"Why?"

"Jay, I don't know! I don't know *what* he did when I went out!"

"Did he know what *you* did when you went out?"

She opened her mouth, but no words came out. Her hands were clenched tightly, and he realized she was shaking. He couldn't tell if the shaking was due to fear, anger, or sadness. "What is it you're trying to get at?" she said finally.

"Some of this is conjecture on my part, but I've done this before. I know the drill."

"And what is that drill?"

"A lot is going to depend on what time Evan was killed. We'll know that fairly soon. The timing is going to make things complicated."

"Complicated how?"

"You have to understand, I'm talking about appearance now, not reality."

"Just talk."

"I might be your alibi. Depending on the timing. I'm also your lover. And I'm also the fucking chief of police."

"So?"

"If the time line shows that he was killed while we were together, there are going to be several possibilities that have to be covered. One is that I'm lying to protect you. Two is that we're both lying to protect each other."

"It's crazy. They'll think *you* killed Evan?"

"Maybe. Or that you were using me and you hired someone to kill him while you could get me to vouch for you."

"Nobody could think that."

"Yes, we will."

"We?"

He nodded and cleared his throat uncomfortably. "I don't know how this is going to play out, Abby. But I'm going to be involved in this investigation one way or the other. Either as a suspect or because it's my job."

"Do you think I'm capable of doing that, Jay? Do you think I'm capable of doing what we just did in your bedroom while I knew someone was murdering my husband?"

He couldn't help himself. The tiniest hint of a sad, regretful smile crossed his lips. "I'm a cop, Abby," Justin Westwood said. "I think almost anyone is capable of doing almost anything."

Abby Harmon shifted in her seat again so she faced forward. She didn't say another word as he made a left and drove through the open gates, ornate enough that they looked like they should lead toward a stairway to heaven but only led up the driveway toward her house where her murdered husband's body awaited them.

4

Justin had been in similar situations often enough to know that for many people death turned the world upside down. The secure became insecure. The satisfied were suddenly morose, and the complacent were lonely. Murder took things to another, surreal level. Truths were often shown to be lies. Strength was revealed as weakness. The mundane could prove crucial. Things that seemed so impregnable suddenly crumbled at the merest touch.

His life had disintegrated when death had hit his family. His lovely little daughter had been murdered and, never being able to cope with the loss, his wife had committed suicide a year afterward. It was only now, so many years later, that he felt as if his life was being stitched back together. And Justin was very cognizant of how quickly that stitching could unravel.

Watching Abby walk up to the home she'd lived in for over four years, Justin understood that she was uncertain now about how to do something as simple as open her own front door. He took her arm as they approached the steps, and she didn't flinch or shake him off. He saw her shoulders sag just slightly in relief, and her muscles relax, grateful for any support. When they got to the door, she stood frozen. She didn't know if she should reach for her keys or knock or just go right in. He'd noticed that, although she hadn't said a word, her eyes had narrowed at the gate to her driveway, in recognition of the fact that it was open and that it was unnecessary to use the various security precautions that normally kept people off the property. Invasion was not normal for her. She was used to controlling her surroundings, dominating her environment. But things were no longer normal. Even walking into her own house had become disorienting. She didn't know who'd be inside. She didn't know the protocol. She didn't have any understanding of the world she'd just entered so unwillingly.

"It'll be open," he told her. And when she didn't move, he took the door handle and pushed. When it swung open and she still didn't move, he said, "I'll be with you every second you want me to be with you. Okay?"

Abby nodded, and Justin acknowledged the briefest of grateful smiles, and then she stepped forward. *Death brings things to a grinding halt,* he thought. *But life starts moving around you again pretty damn quickly.*

As they stood in the Harmon foyer, Justin saw that Gary Jenkins was waiting nervously in the living room. His leg was jiggling and his right hand was flapping against his thigh. With him was a man Justin didn't recognize. He looked to be about forty, rail thin; his hair was cropped close, probably to hide the fact that he was losing it. The man's face was angular, almost gaunt, but at the same time there was something soft that shone through. He had a runner's body, and Justin, sizing him up quickly, couldn't help but think that he was running away from some kind of weakness. He glanced over at Abby, saw that she most certainly did recognize the man. And wasn't all that crazy about him.

Gary made his way quickly over to meet them. He turned to Abby, shifted his eyes so he could look everywhere but directly at her, and mumbled that he was sorry for what had happened. She nodded graciously. Justin touched her elbow lightly and guided her forward until they and Gary were back in the living room with the thin man.

"Forrest," Abby said. She did not do a good job of disguising her distaste.

The gaunt man took one step toward her, holding out a hand and saying, "I'm so sorry," but he had to stop because he was tearing up and could no longer speak.

Justin gave him a few moments to compose himself. The man tried to stop his sniffling but wasn't having much luck. Shaking his head, embarrassed by his lack of control, he put out his hand to shake Justin's, and Justin saw just how badly the hand was trembling. "Forrest Bannister," he said. "I—I—"

"He found the body," Gary said. "It's upstairs." He saw Abby's expression and immediately said, "I'm sorry. *He's* upstairs. Jesus, I'm really sorry. It's just that—"

"Gary," Justin said to the young cop.

"What?"

"Shut up."

"Right. Sorry. Oh, I'm sorry. I shouldn't be saying I'm sorry. I'll—I'll just stop talking."

Justin shook his head and let a small sigh escape from his lips. "Why don't you sit down, Mr. Bannister," he said. And to Abby: "Do you want some water?" She shook her head, but he followed up his question by saying, "I need to go upstairs to see Evan's body. I'd like you to come with me and identify him." When she managed a deep breath and a nod, he followed it up with, "Are you sure you don't want water?"

She was looking wobblier by the second. She didn't nod or shake her head at his second question. She just went to a cabinet beneath an ornate mirror at the far end of the living room. Abby opened the cabinet door to reveal a bar and she reached in to grab a bottle of vodka.

Justin thought about telling her she should stay sober, that she had important decisions to make, and then he decided what the hell difference did it make; she needed a drink and she should have it. He waited for her to pour a long one, then he motioned to Gary to step into the foyer with him. There he asked a few questions about the condition of the body, about any disturbance of the crime scene, about anything he should know that might await him upstairs. Gary gave him a solid, professional briefing, and Justin thanked him. He told Gary what he wanted him to do next—call one of two stations within an hour's drive that could put together a crime scene unit, get another officer from the East End station over here as quickly as possible, get an ambulance to come take the body when the CSU was done. Then Justin stepped over to the archway, looked into the living room, and nodded at Abby. She walked toward him, continued past him, drink tightly clutched in her hand; and he let her lead him upstairs.

At the top of the landing, she stopped.

"He's in the master bedroom," Justin said. Before she could step forward, he took her hand. "It's not going to be pleasant," he said. "He was beaten to death."

Confused, trying to comprehend: "Beaten how? Punched?"

"No," Justin said softly. "It was with some kind of implement. A club, a bat, I don't know. Gary said his face is . . . well . . . like I said, it's not going to be pleasant."

"I can do this."

"Are you sure?"

"No. But stop asking me questions, 'cause I won't even *think* I can do it for very much longer."

"All right. Let's go."

He walked in ahead of her, his body momentarily shielding her husband's corpse. He took in the sight of the mangled and bloody body of Evan Harmon. Justin had to close his eyes for a moment, but that didn't cause the horrific image to go away. He knew the image would now be fixed in his memory forever; this was not the kind of picture one could remove merely with wishful thinking. Every bone in Evan Harmon's body seemed to have been crushed. His face was particularly gruesome. Even his eye sockets were shattered, and his nose was flattened and formless. Under his light brown hair, part of his skull was visible where the skin covering his forehead should have been. His teeth were scattered on the floor near him, looking as if they'd tumbled from a collector's jar. On his neck and forearms were round, deep burns. Justin heard Abby moan behind him, turned to see her eyes widen in shock and horror and the excruciating awareness of the pain her husband must have endured before his life ended.

"That's Evan?" he asked, his voice low and hoarse.

"His face," she said. "His face . . ." Her breathing was heavy now, coming in short, heavy bursts. "What are those burns? Why does he have all those burns?"

"Is it Evan, Abby?"

She nodded. Made a coughing noise and a thin stream of vomit escaped from her tight lips. She immediately wiped it away with her hand.

"Are you sure?"

"Yes," she said. "His hands. Our wedding ring. Those shoes . . . he just bought those shoes yesterday. No, two days ago. Maybe yesterday . . . I don't know . . ."

"It's all right," he said softly. "It doesn't matter."

She was breathing quickly now, unable to tear her eyes away from the devastating scene. "And his sweater," she wailed. "Oh god, I gave him that sweater."

The glass of vodka dropped from her hand, landing softly on the thick carpet. She looked down, watched the liquor spread into the fibers, but made no move to pick it up.

"It's his favorite sweater." Abby looked up at Justin in bewilderment. It was what murder did. She understood that her husband was dead. She understood that some sick fuck had been in her house and committed an unspeakable act of violence. She understood that life as she'd known it had now changed forever. She didn't comprehend how a favorite sweater had somehow been defiled. Didn't see how something so delicate and beautiful had become a part of the tragedy, had been changed into something ugly and unusable. Something repellent.

"His favorite sweater," she said one more time.

"I know," he told her. And then he said, "Let's go back downstairs."

After getting Abby settled onto the living room couch, and putting another glass of vodka in her hand, Justin went back to the bedroom, and spent twenty minutes there, alone. At one time, he had considered himself a truly good homicide cop. Not now. His skills had been dulled over the years. But certain memories remained, memories that told him he had to trust his instincts and his feel for the crime. So for the first few minutes he just stood there, forced himself to look at the violence that had been inflicted upon Evan Harmon, made himself take in the aura of the room, the sense of space, some kind of physical feel for what had occurred.

He knew that CSU would have to go over everything with a fine-tooth comb. But still, those were just facts. And selective facts. He wanted to remember everything. There had been too many times when something supposedly unimportant had been overlooked or ignored, but his memory had come into play and dredged up a solution. There was one case up in Providence. He had been a young cop, working on one of his first murders, and he wasn't the lead detective. A twelve-year-old girl had been battered and beaten to death. Her hands had been cut off and placed next to the corpse. The parents were suspects, but their grief seemed real and there was nothing to tie them to the murder or to any sort of motive. But Justin remembered, at an early interview, that he'd noticed something odd: he'd been in several rooms—the kitchen, a bathroom, the living room, a front porch—and every single room had an ashtray with a nail clipper in it. CSU had paid no attention to that, neither had Justin—it just seemed like a quirk. But at a second interview, the mother of the girl had begun to bite her fingernails and her husband had suddenly and violently swatted her hand away from her mouth. The woman had shrunk back in fear when his hand had moved. Justin realized the nail clippers were no longer on view, so he went to the lab, had them blow up one of the photos that had been collected of the dead girl's hands, and he saw that the girl had bitten her fingernails down until her cuticles had bled. He went back to the house, arrested the parents, and at the station he separated the man and woman, eventually got the woman to talk about the fury that erupted from her husband whenever she or their daughter bit their nails. She saw her husband repeatedly hit the little girl when she bit her nails in his presence, knew that this last time she'd put her hands in her mouth he'd hit her hard enough to knock her unconscious. That's when her husband had banished her from the room. Later, he'd told her that the girl had run away. But she knew that was a lie. She knew he'd killed her . . .

Justin could still picture those nail clippers, sitting in their ashtrays.

Unassuming, unimportant items that held the key to a deep-rooted sickness and to death.

Looking around Evan Harmon's bedroom, he didn't see anything that struck him as an oddity. The splatters of blood on the walls, the carpet, and the bed had to be seen as normal, considering the brutality of the murder that had taken place. Everything in the room was extremely ordered. The bed was made, the bathroom spick-and-span, the clothes in the closets undisturbed. It looked as if the room had been tidied and made pristine by a maid prior to the murder. There was no sense that the room had been lived in that night. No shirt tossed on a floor, no book laid aside, no speck of toothpaste spit onto the side of the bronze bathroom sink. It looked like a hotel room.

He reached into the dead man's right pants pocket and pulled out a wad of cash. Justin flipped through it, over two thousand dollars in hundreds. So much for robbery. He shifted Evan's body, pulled a wallet from the back pocket. Driver's license, two different American Express cards, one MasterCard, all platinum. An ID card for Harmon's money management company, Ascension—it looked like one of those treated IDs that allowed you to open lobby doors and pass through turnstiles so you could get into the right elevator bank of a large building.

Justin spent two minutes just crouching over the body, staring at it. The strange, multiple burn wounds on the arms and legs and torso. The bloody sweater. The bloodstained pants. The highly polished black loafers, worn without socks. Two minutes was long enough for what he needed. He had the mental picture in his head. From here on in, the CSU guys could come in and gather their facts. And he was happy to let them do so.

Justin was a big believer in facts. But he knew that facts were only part of what composed any kind of final truth. He wasn't sure he could define what the rest of the composition was. Only that, like those damn nail clippers, it was, on the surface, usually unimportant, overlooked. But underneath that surface, it was usually the key. And the key fit a door that led to places most people would never want to go.

*   *   *

Downstairs, in the living room, Abigail was sipping another vodka. A dull glaze was starting to cloud her eyes.

Forrest Bannister sat where Justin had left him, the color still drained from his face. He kept making the effort to sit up straight but didn't seem to have the strength, so he'd move, without warning, from a rigid position, staring straight ahead, to slumped over, head in hands. Occasionally, he made a sound that was somewhere between a sad, lonely sigh and a strangled sob.

"Mr. Bannister," Justin said. He thought the man might be nearing a state of shock, so he spoke firmly, trying to get him to snap to attention.

Bannister slowly turned to face Justin. For a moment, he registered confusion, as if they'd never met, then he seemed to remember where he was and who was speaking to him. He nodded as a response, an indication that he was able to understand that his name had been spoken aloud.

"Mr. Bannister, I'd like to know what you're doing here."

"Excuse me?"

"Why are you here?"

The man didn't seem to understand the question and shook his head as if to clear it. "Because Evan told me to come."

"Told you to?"

Bannister seemed to realize how the phrase must have sounded so he emended it. "He asked me if I could."

"What time was this?"

"What time did he call, you mean?"

"Yes."

"I guess around seven. Maybe a little earlier than that. A quarter to. Six-thirty."

"And what time did you get here?"

"Around ten."

"Why the delay?"

Bannister seemed even more confused. "What delay?"

Justin cleared his throat and twisted a crick out of his neck. "What were you doing for the three hours in between the call and the time you got here?"

"I was driving. I took a shower and had to change my clothes, then I had to get the car—"

"Where were you driving *from*?"

"The city."

"Manhattan?"

He nodded. "The Upper East Side."

"What was so urgent or private that Mr. Harmon couldn't discuss with you over the phone?"

"Nothing. He just wanted me here."

Justin glanced over at Abby. The look on his face said, *What the fuck is going on here?* The look on her face gave him nothing in return.

"Forrest," Justin said, "were you in the habit of dropping everything and driving a hundred miles just because Evan Harmon asked you to?"

"Yes, I was."

"And why do you think he wanted you here tonight?"

Forrest Bannister allowed a thin, sad smile to curve his lips only after he gave a long, hard look at Abigail Harmon. "I think he was just lonely," Bannister said.

"You're a heartless prick," she told him.

"And you're a selfish bitch," he spat right back.

In the silence that followed, Abby put her drink down on the table. "Jay," she said slowly. "Excuse me . . . Chief Westwood . . ." Now her voice betrayed the tiniest slurring of words and syllables. "Forrest worked for Evan. He made a lot of money off Evan. So he, like many people, was at Evan's beck and call. Also," she said, picking her drink back up, "he was a little bit in love with Evan."

Bannister swiveled to stare at Abby. "More in love with him than you were, that's for damn sure!"

Abby ignored Bannister now. She was staring at Justin, giving him an answer to his what-the-fuck-is-going-on-here look.

Bannister realized that his outbursts were inappropriate. He did his best to look dignified, and said, "I'm Evan's CFO. We've worked together for over ten years. Starting at Merrill Lynch. I didn't go with him to Rockworth and Williams. But when he started Ascension, his hedge fund, he called and I came."

"Do you think there was a reason he wanted you here tonight? Other than loneliness? A business reason?"

"Maybe. He was very concerned about Ellis St. John."

"Who is . . . ?"

"Ascension's prime broker. He's at Rockworth. He may have wanted to talk about Elly."

"And what was the problem with . . . Elly?"

"I don't know. I just know that Evan was unhappy with him. I believe he was thinking of making a change."

"Changing brokers?"

"Changing his primary broker. We use quite a few different brokers."

"But you have no idea why he'd want to change?"

"I don't know for sure that's what he wanted. It's just a guess on my part." He shrugged in a strange kind of false modesty. "An educated guess."

"He never discussed this unhappiness or this desire to change?"

"Not in any great depth. Just hints. Bits and pieces."

"How about giving me some of the bits?"

"It wasn't anything major. Evan felt Elly was a tad . . . well . . . ambitious."

"And that's bad?"

"It was a question of personal ambition compared to ambition for the good of the company."

"He steered Evan toward bad investments for his personal gain?"

"I don't know that. As I said, Evan never got that specific with me." Forrest bit his lip, as if debating whether to speak further. It was the kind of gesture a flirtatious teenage girl would have made. "Frankly, I think some of it was that he just didn't like Elly."

"Thass not true." It was Abby speaking now. Facing Justin, she said, "Evan liked Ellis. Really did." She turned to Forrest. "Liked him a helluva lot more'n he liked you."

"I'm not going to get down in the mud with you," the CFO said.

"I'm just not. I know what Evan thought about me. And I know what he thought about you, too."

Justin stepped in between them. "How big is Ascension, Forrest? How large is the fund?"

"I don't think I should be giving out that kind of information."

"Almost two billion dollars," Abby said. The word "dollars" came out as "dollarsh." "Give or take a few hundred million."

Justin kept his eyes on Forrest. By the aggravated look on the man's face, Justin thought Abby's estimate was probably accurate. This was clearly a man who liked to control information. It was the only power he had. "What happened when you got here?" Justin asked the CFO. "Walk me through it."

The thin man nodded. He seemed to be regaining strength from being the sudden center of attention. "I got to the driveway and the gate was open . . ."

"Was that unusual?"

"Yes. I usually had to punch in the code to open it. Most people had to use the intercom, but I had the code." He was obviously proud of this access.

"That's good," Justin said quickly. He spoke up because Abby was rolling her eyes at Forrest's misplaced smugness. He wanted her to keep quiet for a bit so he could get what he needed from this strange and strangely sad man. "So the gate was open. What then?"

"I came up to the house."

"Was it unlocked?"

"Yes."

"Do you have a key? Just in case."

Now Forrest Bannister looked pained and slighted. "No," he said. He started to make some sort of explanation or excuse, stopped himself, shook his head, and just said, "No key."

"So what then?"

"Well . . . it wasn't normal for everything to be so . . . open. I had kind of a sixth sense that something was wrong. Because of the gate and the door and Evan's tone when he called."

"What tone? I thought you said he just seemed lonely."

"Yes. But it seemed more urgent than usual. More pressing than usual."

"But you didn't ask why?"

"No. It didn't matter. I figured I'd find out when I got here."

Justin nodded, then nodded a second time for Bannister to continue with his story.

"When nobody answered the door, I opened it and went inside."

"No one was here?"

Bannister shook his head.

"The couple who worked here?"

Bannister shook his head again. "No. The house was empty. At least I didn't see anyone. I called Evan's name a couple of times, then I thought that maybe he was taking a shower or something. So I—I went upstairs. And saw him."

"How long before you called the police station?"

"Immediately. Well, I don't know how long I stood there. I mean, I couldn't believe what had happened, what I saw, but I don't think it was more than a few seconds. And I didn't call the station, I called 911."

"Did you ask for an ambulance?"

Bannister looked startled at the question. "No. The police. I said there'd been a murder."

"Did you check Evan to see if he was alive?"

The same flash of confusion—Justin thought that this time it might have been embarrassment—crossed Bannister's face. "No," he said quietly. "I . . . He was dead. He was clearly dead. My god, it was so horrible. I couldn't bring myself to touch him, to get close. I just couldn't."

"I understand," Justin said. "What did you do until Officer Jenkins arrived?"

"Nothing. I came downstairs . . . I couldn't stay in that room . . . and I just sat. I felt dizzy—I may have even passed out for a few moments."

"You didn't move around the house?"

"No. I just sat on the couch."

"Were you planning on going back to the city tonight?"

"No. I was going to stay here."

"In the house?"

"Yes." He glared over at the ever more inebriated widow. "I stayed here sometimes when she was . . . out. I don't know what I'm going to do now."

"I'd appreciate it if you'd stick around until tomorrow morning, in case we have some other questions."

"But I can't stay here."

"No. Officer Jenkins'll find you a hotel in East End Harbor. I don't think it's a good idea for you to drive tonight anyway."

"Yes. I mean no. I mean, yes, I'll stay and, no, I don't want to drive back."

"An ambulance should be here soon. So will another officer who works with me. And I'm going to get a crime scene unit over here as quickly as I can get one. As soon as the officer arrives, Officer Jenkins will get you settled. I'd appreciate it if you'd come to the station by nine tomorrow morning so we can see if there's anything else you might be able to help us with. It's possible that the media'll get hold of this story very quickly. They'll probably want to talk to you. I'd appreciate it if you didn't talk to them. At least not yet."

Bannister nodded. He'd used up whatever strength he'd regained and looked ready to slump over again. Justin stepped over to Abby, touched her lightly on the elbow, quietly said, "Let's go. I'll get you settled, too." But before he could steer her to the door, Gary Jenkins cleared his throat, looking uncomfortable.

"Um," the young officer said, "could I just talk to you for a second, Chief?"

The two men walked over to the foyer and Justin waited for whatever Gary had to say, but the younger cop just looked more and more on edge. Justin finally had to say, "What is it?" and Gary turned a slight shade of red.

"I'm trying to learn, you know? Learn what to do, I mean. Although, Christ, I hope I never have to deal with anything like this again."

"What do you want to know?" Justin asked.

Gary lowered his voice, almost to a whisper. "Taking Mrs. Harmon upstairs . . . to see the body . . . couldn't that have waited? Until he'd been cleaned up, I mean. Did she have to see him like that?"

Justin scratched under his chin, felt the stubble that had grown back since he'd last shaved. "No," he said. "She didn't have to see him like that. It could have waited."

Still speaking just a shade above a whisper, Gary said, "Then . . . Jesus . . . why'd you make her do it?"

"Because I needed to see how she'd react."

"You think she killed him?"

"No. But she might've. So I wanted to watch her when she saw the body, see if she was calm or surprised or sickened."

The two men faced each other. Gary nodded his understanding. Justin turned to return to the living room, but Gary reached out and grabbed his arm.

"It was kind of a cruel thing to do, what you did." It wasn't a statement, more like half a question. The younger cop knew the answer but wanted to hear it said.

"I thought it was necessary," Justin told him.

"And you like her, don't you? I mean, you—you know . . ."

"Yes, I know. And, yes, I like her. I like her very much."

Gary didn't say anything else, but Justin knew he wasn't quite through. There was still another question hanging in the air and Justin decided to deal with it before it could even be asked.

"You want to know what I think my job is?" Justin asked. "And your job? What a cop's job is?"

Gary didn't even nod this time, but his eyes answered yes.

"It's to find out what happened," Justin said. "That's all. Everything else after that—justice, lack of justice, punishment, revenge, everything else—all depends on us doing our job, finding out what happened, finding out the truth. Without that there's nothing."

"But—"

"There's no but. There's only the truth."

"And once we know the truth?"

"Then we're on our own. Then it's every man for himself."

"I understand."

"Do you?"

"Pretty much."

"Then you want to ask the question you really want to ask?"

"What's that?"

"If I could do something that cruel to someone I like, what could I do to someone I don't care about? Is that your real question?"

"Yeah. More or less."

"You want me to answer it?"

"No," Gary said. "I don't think so."

"Good," Justin said. "Make sure that skinny little creep gets put to bed and get him to the station by nine tomorrow."

"Yes, sir."

"I'll see you in the morning," Justin said.

And with nothing else to say, he took Abigail Harmon out to his car and drove her back to his house. As he made his way around the circular driveway, he saw her peering out the window at a black Lexus.

"Evan's car?" he asked. When she nodded he said, "His only one?" And she nodded again.

He didn't say anything else to her during the ride, let her fall asleep in the silence, her head resting on his shoulder as he drove. The only thing he made sure to do was not look in the rearview mirror. He didn't want to see his own eyes. Not because of the Bobby Short song. Not because there was a party going on inside his head. It was because of something else someone once said: that the eyes were the mirror to the soul.

If that was true, that was the one place he definitely did not want to peer at.

5

One more vodka and an Ambien—no self-respecting wealthy Hamptons woman was without a supply handy at all times—and Abigail was sound asleep in Justin's bed twenty minutes after they got back to his house on Division Street. He helped her get undressed, made sure she was securely between his almost clean sheets, and gently pulled his light wool summer blanket up to cover her. He leaned over and, although she didn't feel a thing, he kissed her gently on the top of her head. As he went downstairs, the sweet smell of her shampoo filled his nostrils. He quickly shook it away. He didn't need any distractions now.

Downstairs, he went straight to the telephone and dialed the home number of Leona Krill, the mayor of East End Harbor. A woman's voice answered on the fourth ring, and when Justin went, "Leona?" the half-asleep voice said, "No." Justin could hear the rustling of sheets, some mumbled words, and then Leona was speaking into the receiver.

"Whoever it is," she said, "do you know what time it is?"

"Maybe if you didn't stay up all night sleeping with strange women, you wouldn't need so much rest."

"Jay?"

"Yeah."

"Melissa is my wife, in case you don't remember. You were invited to the wedding but didn't show up."

"I've met Melissa. She qualifies as strange."

"Why are you calling me in the middle of the night?"

"Because there's been a murder and I thought you'd want to know about it right away."

"Good Christ. Who is it?"

"Evan Harmon." There was a long silence from the mayor's end. "Leona? You still with me?"

"Yes. And I'm wide awake now, thank you. I have so many questions, I don't know where to begin."

"That's probably good because I don't have too many answers."

"Are you sure it was murder?"

"As compared to what?"

"Natural causes, suicide—I don't know, how else does someone drop dead in the middle of the night?"

"He didn't exactly drop dead," Justin said.

"How was he killed?"

"Beaten to death. And from the looks of it, tortured, too."

"Was it his wife?"

"Who killed him?"

"Yes."

"No," Justin said.

"Are you sure?"

"Reasonably sure. Why do you ask?"

" 'Cause she's capable of torturing just about anybody. And isn't it almost always the spouse?"

"Well, this one's got an alibi."

"A good one?"

"Pretty good," Justin said.

"Any other suspects?"

"Not yet. I'll have more info in the morning, I hope."

"I hope so, too." Another silence. Then Leona said, "Jay, you understand—"

"I understand."

"Christ, the papers. And TV reporters."

"They'll be sliming all over the place."

"Who else knows?"

"From me? Gary Jenkins. He called Mike Haversham. The CSU guys know, assuming they're there by now, the ambulance driver and EM workers . . ."

"Have you called Larry Silverbush?"

Silverbush was the DA for the East End of Long Island. He was based in Riverhead, about forty minutes or so from East End Harbor, and had been involved in several high-profile trials over the past five or six years, winning them all. Three years earlier he'd put a British nanny away for poisoning the baby daughter of a well-known record producer—that's what had made his reputation. It was a tough case to make, but Silverbush had made it brilliantly, slowly reconstructing for the jury a history of the woman's carelessness, thoughtlessness, arrogance, and lack of warmth. There were no witnesses and no real forensic proof, but Silverbush showed the jurors—and the media—that she was *capable* of murder. That was enough to swing them over to the fact that she'd committed this particular murder. The nanny was still proclaiming her innocence and still trying to build a valid appeal, but she was serving twelve and a half to twenty-five years in prison.

Silverbush's other attention-getting case was a year ago. A famous—and famously obnoxious—public relations diva had gotten drunk and driven her SUV into a Hamptons club. No one was killed, but several patrons and two doormen were injured. The case had turned into a class war—blue collar versus rich summer interlopers. The PR queen was an interloper—and not a Mid-Island voter—so Silverbush was able to put her away for eighteen months. Justin had met him once, just a handshake really, not enough to get a sense of the man. His reputation was as a no-nonsense, no-bullshit guy. Instinctively, Justin didn't buy it. Word was that Silverbush wanted to run for state attorney general and already had some major financial backers. And AG was not a bad stepping stone to governor. So he was a politician at heart, which Justin thought pretty much eliminated the no-bullshit possibility. "No," he told Leona. "I haven't called him. I thought it might be better coming from you."

"Thanks," she said, not bothering to hide the sarcasm. Then: "Hold on a second." There was the slight rustling of bedcovers. Justin was fairly sure that Leona put her hand over the phone because he heard a very muffled, "No, it's all right, sweetie, I'll be off in a minute." The hand was then removed because Justin next heard very clearly, "What about Harmon's father?"

"No," Justin said. "I haven't notified anyone yet. Other than Mrs. Harmon."

"Thinking it's her responsibility to tell the old man?"

"My brain doesn't work on that many levels, Leona. My thinking was that my only responsibility was to tell *her*. She's the next of kin."

"Well, sometimes there are things other than legal responsibilities to consider."

"You're worried about the moral thing to do now?"

"Don't be an asshole, please. I'm being practical. I don't want him hearing about this from the outside."

"It's too late to make the morning papers—the deadline's past even if they get the story now. And I don't think the Internet or TV'll get it until the morning."

"So that's your plan? To keep things quiet and hope no one hears about it until they're having their egg-white omelets for breakfast?"

"My plan is to keep things quiet until morning. That'll give me enough time to try to figure out what to do. I don't think it'll help anything if we wake people up in the middle of the night to spread the news."

"Except me, you mean."

"The only advantage we have right now is that we're the only ones who know about it—except for the killer. I don't know how to use that advantage yet, but I don't see the value in having H. R. Harmon trying to tell me how to run this investigation at three A.M. And if it'll make you feel better, I don't think I'll be getting much sleep either."

He could practically hear Leona's brain working as she tried to figure out the political and PR ramifications of the crime she'd just been alerted to. He figured she didn't come to any satisfactory conclusions because all she said was, "I have to let Silverbush know. I can't keep him out of the loop for something like this."

"All right."

"I know you don't like it, but this isn't something you can run as a one-man show."

"I understand."

"I'll sell you to Silverbush, Jay, don't worry about that. You won't be left out of this thing, if that's what you're worried about."

"That's not what I'm worried about, Leona. I'm worried about solving a murder."

Again, he could almost hear her thinking, figuring out what she was going to say to the attorney general, deciding how hard she was going to push her own chief of police. "Jay, we're going to have to trust Silverbush now, and I think we can. But I can trust *you* on this one, right? You know what you're doing?"

Justin couldn't help himself, his eyes shifted to glance toward the stairs. The whiff of Abby's shampoo still lingered. He shrugged, said, "Sure, I know what I'm doing," and hung up the phone.

For the next four hours, he did his best to prove that he did indeed know what he was doing. He programmed his iTunes library on his computer to play two Tom Petty albums, *Wildflowers* and *Greatest Hits*, Patti Smith's version of "When Doves Cry" four times in a row, and then *Mingus Plays Piano*. He turned the volume on low so he wouldn't disturb Abigail, but he needed music right now. He worked better with the right music, thought better with the right music. Music helped him focus at the same time it could keep his mood constant. Right now he wanted to keep his mood unwaveringly somber, and he had to stay as focused as he'd ever been. Definitely Petty, Smith, and Mingus.

Sitting at the computer set up in his living room, he signed onto PublicInfoSearch.com, a pay site he'd authorized all EEHPD cops to use. There were nine categories of available searches: Background, People, Criminal, Bankruptcies & Liens, Sex Offenders, Property, Marriage, Death, and Divorce. He went to "People," typed in "Evan Harmon," and printed up anything he thought might be relevant about the man's background and activities over the past few years, professional as well as social. There was material quoted from a biography of Evan's father that talked briefly about Evan's school years. He'd grown up in New Hampshire and gone to two New England prep schools. The first was one of the elite academies in the country, Melman Prep. Evan had transferred out of Melman when he was a junior in high school. Curious. Justin was not unfamiliar with that world and he knew that "transfer" was another word for expulsion. Or failure. People like Evan Harmon did not transfer from a top school to a lesser one unless they were forced to. The writer of the book also had the same suspicion—but Evan's records were sealed and the biographer could not get them. There was speculation about getting some girl pregnant, something about a violent episode with another student, but neither could be validated. Justin dismissed both things as rumors, stuck in to sell a not very commercial book, but he made note of the school change. And he made a note to check it out. Patterns. Even those from twenty years ago counted.

Evan's college years were uneventful. He didn't get into an Ivy League school, went instead to a small private college in Connecticut, Connecticut University, which Justin knew was mostly populated by rich kids who couldn't study their way or buy their way onto better campuses. Justin remembered that in his day the college was known as FUU—Fuck-Up University. But Evan hadn't seemed to fuck up too badly. He graduated with a decent average and no more possible scandals.

Going chronologically, there was some simple information on Evan's early career at Merrill Lynch, some bare-bones material about four years he spent working at Rockworth and Williams, the same money management firm that Ellis St. John worked at. Justin began jotting down a few names, nothing in depth, nothing that gave him a great feel for what was going on, but connections were being formed and he was a big believer in patterns and connections. If there was one thing he'd learned since he'd become a cop, it's that the world might function in random and unpredictable ways, but within that disorder people managed to impose their own repetitive behavior. The world made no sense, Justin had long ago determined, but people did. Or at least their patterns were remarkably consistent. In a crazy world, everyone—the good guys and the bad—attempted to bring some sanity, usually in the form of regulation, to their actions. And it was that attempt that got the bad guys caught every time. So Justin looked for patterns. Even before he searched for motives.

Justin was beginning to get a vague feel for Evan Harmon. Again, nothing substantial, and of course he knew a bit about the man from Abby. He instinctively didn't like Harmon. He didn't seem connected to something that Justin cared very much about—productivity. A picture was slowly forming of someone distant and cold, someone removed from the give-and-take of everyday human relationships. He thought about Abby's relationship with her husband, about her constant attempts to avoid and escape from that relationship. He wondered how much she knew about Evan's past. For that matter, he wondered what she could possibly know about Evan's present. Well, he didn't actually have a present any longer. As of last night, Evan Harmon existed only in the past.

There was a decent amount of information on Ascension, Harmon's hedge fund company. Justin scanned the company's history, jotted down a few key names, and printed the whole thing, knowing he'd eventually have to pay closer attention to the details. In these details, he was certain, were the answers to many of his questions.

The last thing he saw was a photo of Evan Harmon, dated two years earlier. It showed Evan playing in the yearly Hamptons celebrity softball game. The game was played every July in East Hampton. Writers, artists, musicians, and rich people who had muscled into the celebrity crowd got together to raise money for medical research into leukemia. Each year the game raised about fifty thousand dollars, but it had become a competitive sports event. The rich and famous slid hard and ran fast, and the occasional fight even broke out over an umpire's call. The photo showed Evan at home plate, swinging at a pitch. His stance was good, his balance looked professional. He looked like an athlete. Most of all he looked alive.

Justin didn't feel great about it, but he also ran a search on Abby Harmon. Most of the clippings had to do with Abby's impact on the social scene—raising money for charities, being seen late at night in clubs without Evan but with some rich or famous tabloid star, hosting politicians busy raising money and wooing votes in the Hamptons or in

Manhattan. He knew some of her history but read carefully what was on the screen. He knew the reason for his scrutiny, and he felt a little guilty about it—he wanted to see how much of what she'd told him of her past jibed with what was on the record in front of him. He told himself that he was just looking to verify that she'd been honest with him about the past as a way of justifying his trust in the truthfulness of her version of the previous night's events. But somehow that didn't make him feel a whole lot less guilty.

As he read, he nodded, pleased, because there was nothing in print that went against what she'd told him of her history. Abigail Marbury had grown up in Chicago and had come from money. Her family probably had more money than the Harmons but not nearly the same social standing. Abigail's father had started as a salesman, working the floor of a small store that sold household appliances. The owners were elderly and no longer interested in increasing their fortune so, after a few years, they sold the store to Regis Marbury and happily retired. Regis was anything but satisfied with his lot. Aggressive and savvy and educated about the latest advancements in the field, he made a minor name change and turned one Appliance Heaven store into a string of Heaven Hardware outlets. It took him a little over a decade to have the biggest hardware chain in the Midwest. It took him two years after that to have a massive coronary and drop dead at the blue-ribbon opening of his latest store in St. Louis. He was forty-nine years old when he died; his only daughter was seventeen. Abigail tried college after her father's death, the University of Michigan, but lasted only two years before she dropped out and came to New York City. She was beautiful and adventurous and didn't have much trouble getting work as a model. She spent those years doing drugs and hanging out with rock stars and actors and getting photographed in every hot spot imaginable. Justin and she had talked about those days because she'd been reminiscing with a mixture of fondness and distaste. He'd asked her how she could have spent so much time doing little but fucking and drugging and being mindless. She'd looked up at him and said, "I liked fucking and drugging and being mindless. I still like it," and Justin had to agree that it wasn't all bad. But then he said, "But that's *all* you were doing," and she said, "I know. It's why I stopped. My life got boring. My friends got boring." The way she said it—a distance and coldness in her eyes and voice—made Justin wonder when it would be that she looked at him and said, "You bore me now, too." He decided that she probably would say that to him at some point. And he also decided he didn't really care; he didn't bore her now and that was fine with him.

The material on her marriage to Evan was fairly standard: the ceremony was tabloid fodder and the honeymoon was bliss, and Justin knew from their talks that within six months they were both having affairs and going their own separate ways. Evan Harmon and Abigail Marbury never seemed to actually be in love with each other. They'd crossed paths at a moment when both were bored with the lives they were leading and both thought the other person would provide some combination of excitement and stability. Neither happened. But neither did divorce. It was easier to stay together. And Abby told him once that, no matter the arena or the situation, she and her husband were both people who tended to do whatever was easiest.

Remembering that conversation made him feel on edge. Sometimes people thought that murder was easy.

Justin closed out the windows on Abby and moved on to Evan's father. There were probably a thousand pages of available material on Herbert Randolph Harmon. Justin printed up just some of the highlights. H. R., as he was often referred to, had used his family connections—his wife's money and his father-in-law's business, a leather tannery that he ran after the father-in-law's retirement—to become both wealthy and a political force in New England. He had never been perceived as being interested in the public at large or being interested, in fact, in anything but adding to his own wealth and prestige, but he surprised everyone who knew him when he turned thirty-five and ran for the New Hampshire congressional seat being vacated by the Republican who'd held it for eighteen years. H. R. served two terms in Congress, neither distinguishing himself nor embarrassing himself, then his higher aspirations took over and he ran for the Senate. It was a close race and, in the end, one that turned bitter and nasty. What public reputation H. R. had was largely based on his seemingly unshakable decency and civility. But when it looked as if he was going to lose the election, he had no compunction about diving into the political sewer. Or, rather, getting his handlers to dive in for him and take care of the dirty work. The tough-guy strategy backfired, however. As the campaign grew mean, H. R.'s jovial facade crumpled and a nastier foundation was exposed. That didn't sit well with voters. It also exacerbated the fact that underneath that facade was very little substance, at least when it came to issues that mattered with the voters. The voting was close, but H. R. lost the election. As 1982 ended, at age forty-seven, he was back in the private sector, but it didn't take long for him to become one of those hard-to-define political hangers-on. For years he had no real connection to Washington other than his ability to rouse other rich political hangers-on and spur them into financial action. He supported conservative candidates who came up to campaign in his state; raised money for national figures; began to be quoted in local newspapers and then national magazines, espousing conservative causes; and eventually emerged as a party spokesperson. By the mid-eighties he was back in the inner circle and in 1985 was appointed the U.S. representative to the United Nations. For three years he threw elegant parties and was briefed on the politics of many countries he'd previously never heard of, and then in 1988 became the president's choice for secretary of commerce. His main order of business was helping to develop trade relations with China, which he did efficiently and seamlessly. In 1992, when his party was voted out of office, H. R. returned to the business world. He was lured to Wall Street by Lincoln Berdon, the venerable head of the even more venerable firm of Rockworth and Williams—there it was again, Justin noted—which is where H. R. was ensconced for most of the next decade, his wealth quickly soaring to another level. While he was reading, Justin couldn't help but think of John Huston's line in *Chinatown*, about buildings, whores, and millionaires all becoming respectable when they get old.

In 2001, H. R. Harmon left his cozy corner office and became the U.S. ambassador to China. In 2003, while he was in Beijing, his wife, Patricia—Evan's mother—died. She succumbed to a several-year battle with cancer at a Boston hospital. H. R. had not seen her in four months.

He returned to Boston for the funeral, stayed three days, went back to China.

Herbert Harmon stayed in his ambassadorial position until mid-2005, when he suffered a minor heart attack. And thus ended his political career and globe-trotting ways. Since the attack, he'd been based in New York City and been a consultant for his son's hedge fund company, Ascension. His name stopped appearing in the papers on a regular basis. His face stopped showing up on television interviews. The only thing he seemed to do consistently was play golf. Every afternoon, weather permitting, at his Westchester country club, he teed off at 4 P.M. The time rarely varied because he was both punctual and a creature of habit and because the course was empty then. Sometimes he would take a business associate, sometimes a friend. But mostly he went by himself. H. R. Harmon didn't like to play with friends. He liked to play alone, with just a caddy. *It's easier to cheat,* Justin thought, *if the only person watching you is someone you're paying to walk along beside you.*

And that, Justin decided, was all he was going to learn that morning. He didn't know exactly where he was headed, but he had some names and places with which to start. And he had a few patterns. They were vague and tenuous at best, but they were there. Now he just had to figure out what they meant.

At 6:30 A.M., Justin Westwood left his computer and stretched out on the living room couch. At 6:35 he was sound asleep. He stayed asleep for all of twenty-five minutes. As tired as he was, he couldn't ignore the urgent ringing of his telephone. And at 7 A.M., when he stumbled back toward the small table that served as his desk and spoke to the person on the other end of the line, he wasn't tired anymore. He was, in fact, as wide awake as he could be.

6

Li Ling waited in the shadows without moving.

It was not difficult for her to wait. She had long ago been trained to view time as something that could be mastered. That was unimportant. Time was something that, for her, did not really exist except as a way to put chains around anyone weak enough to bend to its will.

It was also easy for her to stay completely still. The position was called Silent Oak. They had taught it to her when she was three years old. It had been torture to remain so unbending at such a young age. Her tiny body had wanted to wiggle and squirm and run free. But with every little spasm, every minute tic, came punishment. By the age of five, she could remain perfectly rigid for four hours at a time. At seven, she knew she could stand without moving all day and night if need be. When she reached the age of ten there was no longer even a thought of movement or of freedom. Restriction *was* freedom by then. Freedom from her body. For with her training came the knowledge that the body was merely a tool of the brain. It was there to do what it was told. By itself it could feel nothing: no pleasure, no discomfort, no pain. It felt only what she decided it would feel.

She had worked with her master before she could even walk. He taught her many variations of the martial arts, always making sure she understood that it was indeed art she was learning to create. The art of movement. The art of power. The art of violence. The ultimate art of both life and death.

The discipline she gravitated toward was shin yi, for she loved its short, precise moves. There was no waste of motion or energy and no room for error. Much of its art was in knowing when *not* to move. It reinforced what she had, nearly from the beginning of her life, instinctively understood: in stillness there was also beauty. And it was beauty, above all, that she learned to crave. Beauty in any form. Beauty that could match her own.

She had known that her appearance was not ordinary from the time she was able to stand so silent and unmoving. She saw the looks in men's eyes when they stared at her. In women's eyes, too. The eyes of others revealed all: desire, envy, submission, rage. She saw all that when people looked at her. She saw it and she began to crave it the way she did beauty. She wanted all of it.

As she grew older, her form became even more exquisite. Her body lengthened and became lithe and hard. Her fingers could flutter like graceful butterflies, her hair was thick and dark and seemed alive in its own movements. Her skin was smooth and unblemished. Her eyes—light brown—were captivating, capable of overwhelming and luring others into her lair as irresistibly as any siren, capable, too, of cruelly dismissing anyone who dared to venture, unwanted, into that same lair. As she went through her teens, her expertise in shin yi became even greater. She exalted in the most difficult moves: The Pouncing Lion, The Twisting Grasshopper, The Stinging Wasp. She mastered it all. Everything she touched, everything she tried, she mastered. And when her own master decided that she had become arrogant, that she was not in proper control of her pride and her emotions, she mastered him, too. She remembered the movement she used to break his spine: it was her own creation, her first work of original art, and she named it Shattering Glass. She could still see the look of surprise on his face. And she could still conjure up the enormous feeling of pleasure it gave her when he pleaded silently for her to end his pain by ending his life. She obeyed him one final time. A quick jab: The Kiss of the Scorpion.

No, Silent Oak was not difficult at all. Not for her.

She was Li Ling.

She could do anything.

Several hours before dawn was due to break, she felt the breeze rustle past her. She smiled—and only her lips moved; even her forehead did not crease—because she knew it was not the breeze. It was another perfect and beautiful form of nature. It was Togo.

Ling had not seen him, but she had felt his presence. He would not be seen unless he wanted to be seen. Togo lived in the shadows. He moved as if carried by air. So she waited, knowingly, confidently, to see how he would reveal himself. And then the shadows moved and he appeared before her, as if created from a sliver of smoke.

She looked into his eyes. There was no need for words. They did not communicate with words. They communicated with their souls. Sometimes with their bodies. Always with love. But rarely with words.

They had been trained together. Neither ever knew their parents or where they had come from or why they had been picked for such an honor. They were taught that the past did not matter. Nor did the future. All that mattered was the present and their training and their obedience. When she was a child, she thought of Togo as her brother, but when she turned fourteen, she looked at him as if seeing him for the first time and realized he was as beautiful as she was and as well trained. Their minds had been as one for many years, and then one day she no longer thought of him as a brother and their bodies joined together as well. She loved Togo fully and completely; he was the only person in the world to whom she was truly attached. Sometimes the mere thought of him caused an onrush of desire that could make her dizzy. At night they would lie together naked, entwined, and he would whisper how great their power was, how magnificent their strength was now that it was combined. He would tell her that the two of them made one whole being. That they were equal halves forming something perfect.

She knew that what he said was, in part, true.

But she knew one other thing, too: They were not equals. *She* had no equal.

She knew well that she would never love anyone the way she loved Togo.

And she knew even better that one day she would destroy that love when she revealed her superiority. The time would come when she would kill her other half to prove that she was indeed a whole all by herself.

Ling saw Togo's eyes move now, just a shift—no one else would have even noticed—and then he was gone again. For a moment she thought she had only imagined his presence, that he hadn't ever appeared, but she could sniff his fragrance lingering in the wind, and she knew that he had not been an apparition. He had been real.

The smile was gone from her face now and she was all but invisible again in the shadows. Time was once more standing as still as her rigid body.

And then she knew she had to move.

The door to the house was opening, just as they had been told it would. It was hours before the break of dawn and the only brightness on the street came from the stars above. When the man stepped out of the house, a crack of light escaped from inside. She saw his features for a moment, the pale skin, the glint of rust in his brown hair. She saw the fear in his eyes and the weakness he wore like a mask.

He had an overnight bag strapped over his right shoulder and as he stepped toward the street, he looked left and then right, as if this cursory search would somehow guarantee his safety. It was safe to smile again, silently, so she did, knowing that he would see nothing and that his safety was far from guaranteed.

He crossed over onto her side of the street, was only a few feet away from her. He stopped, as if sensing something. But still he saw nothing. She willed herself to be invisible and her will was strong because he looked right at her, shrugged as if taking himself to task for imagining things, took one more step forward . . .

And that was when his world melted.

Pain did that to people, she knew. Although she couldn't imagine the kind of pain he was experiencing so rapidly and unexpectedly.

Togo came up behind him, unheard and unseen, and his right leg kicked out in an exquisite variation of The Hissing Cat. His heel connected just above the man's right heel and Ling knew bone and tendons were immediately shattered. The man had enough strength left to scream and he began to, but that's when she moved, one elegant, long finger jabbing down into his carotid artery. It was a graceful movement, and she allowed herself to feel pleasure from its perfect execution. She took satisfaction, too, in his immediate silence. The scream that was going to force its way through his lips was strangled in his throat, unable to escape. His eyes bulged, and for a moment she felt like giggling because he looked like a frog about to explode. Ling whirled and her foot snaked out, a foot as sculptured and lovely and smooth as her perfectly shaped hands. And just as deadly. It was a wondrous quick jab the foot made, clipping the man's back. If she had kicked harder, he would be paralyzed. Instead, he was just filled with white-hot flashes of extraordinary pain. She could render men helpless with her beauty, she knew. But she much preferred doing it with pain. She gloried in his agony.

It didn't take long for Togo to pull the van alongside the man's prone body. She was able to lift him effortlessly into the back. Togo questioned her with his eyes: *Is he still alive?* The wordless question hurt her. And made her angry. *Of course he is still alive*, her eyes answered back. *I do not make mistakes.*

They'd been told to take him alive.

There were questions he needed to answer.

So she would make sure he lived until he answered them.

Then there were no more instructions. Then she could do whatever she wanted.

Then she could smile and giggle and laugh and let her body experience all the pleasure she allowed it to have.

Once the questions were answered, the fun could begin.

If there was one thing Li Ling loved more than her lifelong companion, Togo, it was when she could stop standing still and start having fun.

7

Justin was surprised to hear his father's voice on the other end of the telephone. He looked at his watch, but his eyes weren't focused yet. He rubbed them with his thumb and forefinger. It didn't help. The room looked as if it were swaddled in gauze. When he spoke, it sounded as if his vocal cords had rusted.

"Are you hungover?" Jonathan Westwood asked.

"No," Justin said. His sight was coming back. He could make out the numbers on the telephone. He glanced at his watch, and a faint groan escaped through his lips. He hadn't even slept half an hour. "I was working all night."

He could feel his father's hesitation. To ask about his job might somehow signal that he approved of it, which Jonathan Westwood most certainly did not. But because their relationship had relatively recently been repaired—after having been strained, even nonexistent for quite a few years—to avoid any comment at all might be perceived as too hostile. In the end Jonathan went for civility. "I hope things are all right. With your work, I mean."

Justin couldn't help but grin just a little bit. Times had certainly changed. "There was a murder here last night," he said. "The investigation's going to start this morning."

"So what were you doing last night?"

"Thinking. You know that's the tough part for me."

Jonathan Westwood didn't respond. He certainly didn't argue the point.

"Big family reunion coming up?" Justin said. "A Westwood outing to Disney World?"

"Excuse me?"

"I was just wondering why you called, Dad."

There was another pause from the Rhode Island end of the phone. For a moment, Justin thought he was going to receive bad news. Then he realized that couldn't be it. His father would not have hesitated giving bad news. He wouldn't have liked it, but he wouldn't have shrunk from it. Justin wondered what in the world would make his father hesitate. And he realized immediately. The elder Westwood needed his son's help.

"Is something wrong?" Justin asked.

"There might be."

Again the long silence. Then Jonathan broke it with the words "Victoria needs your help."

Justin's head was suddenly clear. But his chest was just as suddenly so full he could barely breathe. "She asked for my help?" he said.

"No. She has no idea I'm calling you."

"What would she say if she knew?"

"What do you *think* she'd say, Jay?"

Justin decided it was better not to answer that question. He knew what her response would be: She wouldn't say anything. She would just stare at him accusingly. Bitterly. "What is it she needs my help for?" is what he said instead.

"Ronald's missing."

"What do you mean?"

"I mean he's missing. When Victoria woke up this morning, he was gone."

"Maybe he went to the office."

"She woke up at six o'clock."

"Did he come home last night?"

"Yes."

Justin gave a half laugh. "So he left early. Maybe he went to the gym. Why do you think something's actually wrong?"

"Because Victoria *says* something's wrong."

Now it was Justin's turn to be silent. When he spoke, all he said was "Yeah. Okay." After the next silence he said, "Look, there's nothing I can do yet. You have to give this twenty-four hours. People just don't go missing from six to seven in the morning. You can't send up a flare when he's been gone for an hour."

"He was gone before six."

"Okay, *two* hours. Or three. It's crazy."

Jonathan Westwood didn't have to say anything for his son to tell the deep level of his disapproval. Justin sighed.

"What would you like me to do, Dad?"

"I don't know. This is what you do for a living."

"No. What I do for a living is get involved when a crime is committed. There's no crime here. There's *nothing* here."

More silence. Justin was beginning to understand where he got his own poor communication skills from.

"Have you called Billy?" he asked. Billy DiPezio was the chief of the Providence police force. He'd been Justin's rabbi when Justin was a young cop. Billy was, in fact, the *reason* Justin became a cop. He'd watched Billy in action—a friend of Justin's had been murdered and he saw Billy hunt down the killer, refuse to give up until he'd brought the man to justice. It had been amazing to watch—someone who did exactly what he set out to do, who let nothing interfere with his ultimate goal. As Justin got to know him better over the years, he discovered that Billy DiPezio never let anything interfere with his goals. The complications came because Chief DiPezio's goals were often a tad hazy. "Hazy" being the nicest possible interpretation. Justin always described his mentor as either the most honest crook in the world or the most crooked honest man there was. Billy was a great cop. He just didn't see any reason why, whenever he did a good job, he shouldn't get something out of it, too. Which he almost always did.

"No," Jonathan Westwood said into the phone. "You're the first person I've called."

"Here's what I can do. Billy would laugh if you called him about this. But he won't laugh at me. Well, he wouldn't laugh at you either, come to think of it—you're too rich. But he wouldn't do anything after he hung up on you. I'll get him to do something."

"What?"

"Whatever he can. Talk to Vicky for one thing."

"I don't think Victoria will have anything to say."

"Well, it's going to be very difficult to find out anything if the only person who thinks there's something wrong won't talk about it."

Another moment of silence. Jonathan was not used to being chastised. But Justin's words had their desired effect. "I understand," Jonathan said. "I'll tell her to talk to Billy. Thank you."

"Dad," Justin said. And before his father could say a word, he finished with, "I'm glad you called me. I know it wasn't easy. I know what you think of what I do."

"I hate what you do."

"Yes, I know."

"But you're very good at it, aren't you?"

"Depends who you talk to," Justin said.

Father and son hung up the phone at almost precisely the same moment. Justin held the cordless receiver in his hand. He thought about the relationship he had with his father, the years they hadn't spoken to each other, the pain they'd caused each other, the pleasures they'd each received from their rapprochement. He thought about his mother, how thrilled she'd been when he showed up on their Providence doorstep three years ago, Deena and her young daughter in tow. He thought about how helpful his father had been the year before, when Justin had been in the midst of searching for the solution to the mystery of Midas. He thought about how strange families were, how tenuous their ties, how mutually destructive and supportive. Mostly Justin thought about Victoria LaSalle. His wife's younger sister. He closed his eyes and pictured the expression on Vicky's face at Alicia's funeral. He saw the look of scorn that burned in his direction. A look that, over the course of the service, turned to cold fury and then to deep hatred. It was a look that made it very clear the younger sister blamed Justin for the death of the older sister. Blamed him and would never forgive him.

Justin understood the look very well.

It was the same look he saw on his own face when he looked in the mirror.

He'd spent years running away from that look. He knew he would never truly forgive himself. But he'd learned to live with the guilt and the loneliness. To compartmentalize it so it no longer took up the biggest share of his emotions and his life.

He wanted to help Victoria. After all these years, he wanted to change the expression in her eyes and on her lips.

But Justin knew he couldn't help her. At least not right now.

He had a job to do first.

So he put the phone back in its base and prepared a pot of coffee. Then he went upstairs to wake up the woman in his bed, gently kiss her good morning, and begin to make his plans to find out who had murdered her husband.

8

Larry Silverbush, Mayor Leona Krill, Justin, and Abigail Harmon met in Justin's office at the East End Harbor police station. Silverbush went to the chair behind Justin's desk as if it were his own and waved at the others to sit down. Justin decided to let the slight go unmentioned. He also decided not to bring up the subject of the DA's comb-over. When it came to hairstyles, Justin had not seen too many even remotely in the same league. It looked as if Silverbush had been walking down the street and a dead squirrel had been dropped from a twelfth-floor window onto his head.

As oblivious as he was to Justin's displacement, that's how solicitous the DA was of Abby. He was a politician after all. And dead husband or no dead husband, she was still an important member of a rich political family, so she was going to see law enforcement at its absolute best. Or, at the very least, at its absolute politest. Silverbush began by thanking her for coming in and offering his condolences, which she accepted passively but graciously.

"I spoke to your father-in-law a little while ago," he said, after her quiet murmuring of thanks.

"I spoke to him this morning, too," Abby told him.

She had. She hadn't wanted to but Justin insisted. She did her best to explain that Herbert Harmon would not want to hear from her, had never in his life wanted to hear from her, but Justin said very quietly that Herbert Harmon had also never lost a son before. He said that it was her responsibility to call him. She was as close to a child as he had left. So she called, reached him at his apartment in the city. She spoke to him from Justin's bedroom while he remained downstairs to give her some privacy. When she came down the steps, she was crying. Justin had never seen Abby cry before. He'd seen her angry and peaceful and bitchy and happy, but he'd never seen anyone come close to wounding her the way H. R. Harmon had in a five-minute phone call.

"He's very concerned about you," Silverbush said. "I assured him we'd do everything we could to help you get through this . . . situation. And I assured him, as I will now assure you, we will find the person who did this to your husband. You have my word on that."

"Did my father-in-law tell you that he already knows who's responsible for my husband's murder?" Abby asked.

This threw Silverbush. Justin tucked away in his mind the fact that this man didn't have much of a poker face. The best the DA could come up with in response to Abby's information was, "Um . . . no, he . . . um . . . didn't say anything like that."

"I'm surprised. He's convinced *I* did it."

"I'm sure you're incorrect about that, Mrs. Harmon."

"That's what he told me this morning."

Silverbush was definitely rattled, although he now did his best to hide it. A little late for the poker face, but at least he recovered for the betting round. "I assure you," he said, "the senator never mentioned anything remotely like that."

"It's funny. Everyone calls him that—the senator. But my esteemed father-in-law only *ran* for the Senate. He never actually won, so it's not really the proper reference. Well, maybe it's not really so funny. More pathetic."

This seemed to push the DA into a deeper state of confusion. The newly widowed Mrs. Harmon was being neither difficult nor cooperative. Those were the only two types of behavior that Silverbush knew exactly how to deal with. So, not on firm footing, he fell back on what he knew best: legal officiousness.

"There was no discussion at all about your involvement." Silverbush spoke as if he were talking about a parking ticket.

"My father-in-law blames me for almost everything bad that has ever happened to the Harmon family," Abby said. "And this morning, he made it very clear that this was no exception."

"I'm sure he was just upset."

"Have you ever met H. R. Harmon, Mr. Silverbush?"

"I have, as a matter of fact. At several charity dinners and fund-raisers."

"Then you know that he spent almost his entire life learning what to say and when or when not to say it."

"I don't really know him that well," Silverbush said.

"You will by the time this investigation is over. And if you want some advice, believe him whenever he makes a threat. Any other time, take things with a grain of salt."

Silverbush had exhausted his patience. He'd paid his respects to the powerful family as best he could; now it was time to move on. Justin was impressed by the man's ability to stick to his agenda while still maintaining a high level of obsequiousness. "We'll be investigating every possible angle," he said. "I promise you we will have a satisfactory outcome for both you and your father-in-law." Now he turned to Justin. "I assume you've prepared an initial report."

"Preliminary," Justin said, looking down at the folder clasped in his right hand. "I'm waiting for the ME's report and a summary from Southampton CSU."

"I can still start with that. Do you have anything at all to go on yet?"

"I have a few thoughts after seeing the crime scene. And I spent the entire night preparing for the investigation. The first few steps are outlined in the report. Once we're done here, I'll be going to the city to talk to people who worked with Mrs. Harmon's husband. And I'm hoping to see Evan's father while I'm there."

"That won't be necessary. Mr. Harmon will be coming here. This afternoon."

Abby spoke up now, surprised. "To East End Harbor?"

Silverbush nodded. "He wants to see his son's body. He's already on his way."

Abby said, "Jesus," and after that there was an uncomfortable silence in the room until Leona Krill spoke up for the first time.

"Larry," she said, "from what Justin has told me, that might not be a good idea." Leona looked at the woman sitting next to her, said, "I'm sorry, Abigail," then turned back to Silverbush and finished. "Apparently Evan was greatly disfigured."

"H. R. won't be seeing his son," Abby said quietly. "He won't be seeing anything that even looks human."

"I understand," the DA said. "I suggested that might be the case, but . . ."

He didn't finish the sentence, so Abby finished it for him. "But H. R. didn't take the suggestion."

"I'm afraid not." Silverbush inhaled deeply, said to Abby, "Are there any questions you have about what we're going to be doing?"

She shook her head.

"Anything you need, I'm available twenty-four seven." The DA then handed her his card, which she accepted with a nod. "I appreciate your coming to meet with me," Silverbush went on. "I know how difficult this must be. But I want you to know that Chief Westwood has an excellent reputation. We've never worked together, but I have the highest confidence in his abilities. I hope you'll be as cooperative with him as possible."

"I don't think I could be any more cooperative with Chief Westwood," Abby said and smiled for the first time in the meeting. Justin made a point of not smiling.

"Excellent," Silverbush finished. "I'll have someone drive you home."

"I'm not staying at home," she told him.

"Of course. Understandable. Just tell my driver where you're going and he'll be glad to take you."

"I'd rather walk, if you don't mind," she said. "It's not very far and I need the air."

"By all means," Silverbush said. Then he turned to Justin and Leona and said, "I'd like to talk to you both before we disband."

*   *   *

When Abby was out of the station, Larry Silverbush spoke quietly to Justin, although he never glanced in his direction while his lips were moving. "You do know how fucking important this is?"

"It's a murder," Justin said. "On a scale of one to ten, pretty high."

"I don't need any smart-ass shit. This isn't just a murder."

"Oh, that's right. It's a high-profile murder that'll get you lots of headlines."

"I know about you, Westwood."

"My excellent reputation, you mean?"

"Believe me, I fucking know all about you."

Leona reached over and put her hand on Silverbush's arm. "Larry, I don't know what you've heard, but Jay is a superb—"

He didn't let her hand rest on him for more than a moment, immediately shaking it away and cutting off her words. "I know how superb he is. I also know what an asshole he can be."

Justin shrugged, as if he'd been caught with his hand in a cookie jar. "Nobody's perfect," he said.

"Look," Silverbush said, "I really don't want this to get nasty. But I want you to understand I know what you're capable of, good and bad. I know the way you work. I know the trouble you've been in and the trouble you've caused in the past. This is an important case. It's highly visible, the media's going to be all over it in about five minutes, and it's got political ramifications."

"For you, you mean."

"Fuck yes, for me." He turned to face Leona. "And for you. It ain't like you're mayor of New York City, Ms. Krill, but I'm sure you like what you do. Running a cute, little town like East End has its perks. You're already on thinning ice thanks to your choice of sexual partners." She started to interrupt, but he barged ahead without letting her speak. "Hey, I couldn't give a shit who or what you're banging. But some voters do, so you better make it up to 'em by making sure we find out who killed Evan Harmon. You're in charge of the police department. This drags on, nothing gets solved, you look foolish, incompetent. Out here you can get away with being a dyke, but a dyke who can't get the job done, that doesn't fly. Am I right?"

Leona's head drooped and her voice was barely above a whisper when she said, "Yes, you're right. You're astoundingly offensive, but you're right."

Silverbush allowed a faint gloat of a smile to cross his lips, then pursed them and looked at Justin. "Same goes for you, too. Whether you want to acknowledge it or not, cowboy, we live in a political world. I know you think you make it up as you go along, but you live by the rules, same as the rest of us. Maybe you bend 'em more than most, but you've built up a life here. Got a nice little house; I haven't been able to find too many friends but I'm sure you got one or two; got the occasional girlfriend. And you took this job, which I know you didn't have to do, so it must mean something to you. You care about what you do; you care about the people in this town; you care about the results you get. In this instance, I care about the results you're going to get, too. We got the same goal—make everything come out all right so our happy little lives just keep rollin' along. So, you see, we're not all that different, you and me."

Justin didn't hang his head and his voice wasn't close to a whisper when he said, "You'll be good on the stump when you run for governor one of these days. But what is it you actually want from me?"

"I want you to work with me. I want you to work with my men. I want full cooperation. I don't want you going off half-cocked, and I don't want you to talk to anyone in the media."

"Anything else?"

"Yeah. I don't want you messing around in places you shouldn't be messing around in."

"Any specific places you have in mind?"

"H. R. Harmon."

"He's kind of relevant to the investigation, don't you think?"

"Obviously, he might be helpful. It remains to be seen just how much."

"But you'll be doing the seeing."

"That's right. I think a slightly more delicate touch than yours is required here."

Justin didn't answer immediately, not that Silverbush was looking for an answer. He was merely looking for acquiescence, which Justin gave him when all he said was "Okay."

"Good." Silverbush smiled at them both now. He stood as if waiting for them to leave.

"Can I just point out one thing?" Justin asked.

"Of course."

"You're in my office. You're the one who's actually got to make the graceful exit."

Silverbush laughed. It was almost an affectionate laugh—almost, but not quite. Justin handed him his preliminary report when the DA's laughter stopped. "You might want to read this sooner rather than later."

"I'm not big on reading. I'm big on action."

"Well," Justin said, "as you made clear, you're the boss." He nodded toward the report now in Silverbush's hand. "All I can do is tell you what I know and make my recommendation."

"Would you like my recommendation?" Silverbush asked. "Don't fuck up. Or I'll have your balls for breakfast."

"If the whole governor thing doesn't work out, try football coach," Justin said. "You've got that inspirational touch."

Silverbush laughed once more, this time with genuine good feeling, and left the East End Harbor mayor and chief of police alone in the office.

"Charmer, isn't he?" Leona said.

"You might want to read my report," Justin said, handing her another copy, "before Mr. Charm does."

"Something you didn't mention just now, Jay?"

"Hey," Justin said, "I'm not big on mentioning. I'm big on action." And then he said, "But read it."

9

The Rockworth and Williams offices were on the fifty-sixth floor of the World Financial Building. The expansive windows in the even more expansive lobby looked out, on this remarkably clear day, over what seemed to be the entire world. Directly east was Ground Zero, its presence still jarring. Looking north you could see almost all of Manhattan—Tribeca, midtown, Central Park, all the way up to Harlem, and even the distant specks of traffic inching along the Triborough Bridge. The view west took in the Hudson River and well into New Jersey. Looking south at the smooth expanse of the Upper Bay, you stared down at the Statue of Liberty and Ellis Island. Justin had the feeling that if he had a better sense of geography and knew which way to look, and if his vision were substantially better, he'd have a decent shot at viewing the jutting shores of Cornwall all the way across the ocean.

He was kept waiting for twenty-seven minutes, three minutes less than he'd expected. He could have barged in, flashing his badge, but he decided to keep this friendly. If the secretary had exceeded his thirty-minute waiting limit, however, his friendly demeanor would have gone out the fifty-sixth-floor window. Luckily for all concerned, she came in the nick of time to lead him back to Daniel French, the Rockworth executive who'd been picked to talk to him.

"I'm not quite sure what I'm supposed to be able to tell you," French told Justin. They were sitting in a conference room, which Justin figured was roughly the square footage of his house in East End Harbor. French offered water—cold or room temperature, which Justin declined; coffee, which Justin accepted, black. French had water. Cold.

"I'm gathering any information that might be helpful in the investigation," Justin explained. "I'm looking for help so I can find out who killed Evan Harmon."

"I still can't believe this happened," French said. "You never think . . . well . . . It's just so shocking."

"Shocking because Evan didn't have any enemies?"

"Everybody in our business has enemies. I'm sure Evan had his share. No, I meant shocking because people go broke all the time in our business, or people wind up in prison because they embezzle funds. People don't get murdered."

"Sometimes murder can even reach such rarefied air," Justin said.

"I'm not being some kind of prima donna asshole," French said. "I know it happens. It's just never happened to anyone I know. Or anyone quite so rarefied as Evan."

"How well did you know him?"

"Fairly well. We were approximately the same age; we moved in somewhat the same circles, at least professionally."

"Not socially?"

"No, not really. I mean, I'd see him around. At clubs or at a tennis match or something like that. But mostly we knew each other through business."

"I'd like a list of the people here who dealt with him regularly."

"Almost everybody on a certain level dealt with Evan. He was a player. I can get you the list, but it'll be fairly long and I don't know how helpful."

"You don't have anyone who's primarily assigned to Ascension?"

"As I said, we have a few—"

"How about Ellis St. John?"

Dan French was good. He barely missed a beat. "Ellis certainly spends a lot of his time on the Ascension account. He probably could be—"

"He was Evan's primary broker, wasn't he?"

"He is *Ascension*'s primary broker, not Evan's. He's been one of our main connections to people there for the past three or four years."

"One of?"

"Yes. Although I suppose he would be considered the main—"

"If he was the main contact, why did so many other people here need to be in touch with Evan? Or with other people at Ascension?"

"Because we have a lot of different departments, and sometimes it's easier for people to simply talk directly to the person who can best address a specific need. If Ascension wants some research done on a particular type of investment, they deal with someone in that department. Ellis might coordinate it but not always."

"Is that Ellis's main job, coordinating?"

"No. It's just a by-product of his link to Ascension. And to other companies, by the way. Ascension's hardly his only account."

"What exactly is his link to Ascension? Can you define it?"

"I suppose. It's not as if it's a unique job—it's fairly standard for any company of our size. As I said, R and W is the primary broker for quite a few funds."

"So let's go with the basics and explain to me what that really means."

French smiled broadly. Justin didn't know if he was smiling because he liked teaching people what he did or whether he just liked talking about how much money his company made. "The prime brokerage business is a direct beneficiary of the growth of the hedge fund business. And the hedge fund business has become, by far, the most—how shall I put this—active segment of the asset management business."

"Active meaning lucrative?"

"When it works," French said. "When it doesn't work, it results in the biggest losses."

"So it's the most unstable."

"We don't really use that word around here. Let's just say it's the most volatile."

"Okay. Keep going."

"Twenty years ago, money that was managed by hedge funds was probably somewhere around thirty, thirty-five billion dollars. Now it's substantially over a trillion. There's no other segment of the financial world with anywhere near that kind of growth and profitability. But, as a result, there's more and more competition. That's normal and it's probably healthy, but it also means you have to be more aggressive and you have to be good. You have to be better than your competitors, which means you need every edge you can get. So a lot of hedge funds hook up with companies like ours who can provide prime brokers, which helps give them the edge they need. We provide securities to cover short sales, make margin loans, clear trades, provide reporting services and custody assets, provide research. And we even help hedge funds raise money. As a prime broker, we probably execute twenty-five to thirty percent of a hedge fund client's transactions. We also provide a daily NAV—"

"Sorry," Justin said. "I'm a little rusty with my financial acronyms."

"Net asset value."

"That it? No free tennis lessons and shiatsu massage?"

"If need be. We provide whatever is necessary. We can set up a rudimentary risk management system for our clients; we'll find office space as a hedge fund company expands; we'll find someone an operations officer and traders; and, if necessary, we can even provide the accounting system."

"I assume you're not doing this out of the goodness of your heart."

"That's a phrase that no one even understands on the Street."

"So explain to me how you make enough to justify this extremely impressive office and your suits that cost more than most people's rent."

"We get commissions from every single trade and order flow."

"At no risk."

"We handle the transactions; we're not putting our own money in. And hedge funds probably account for a third of our trades now."

"You want to tell me how much that might come to a year?"

"We don't give out our financial figures," French told him.

"But if I say 'a lot' I'm not going to be far off," Justin said.

"No. That would be extremely accurate. But we also do a lot of margin lending, and that's at least as profitable."

"So you did all of that for Ascension?"

"As I said, and quite a few other hedge funds. We have many resources that smaller firms, money management companies and funds like Ascension, don't have. We can get better deals, get in earlier than other companies, sometimes get in on an investment opportunity when other firms can't get in at all. One of our jobs, one of the key aspects of Ellis's job, is to bring money in to those deals. Let's say one of our clients wants to raise three hundred million dollars in an IPO. We'll certainly have a share of that, if not the entire thing. We might need to raise half, a hundred and fifty million. So we go out and get it."

"And you might get it from Ascension? Telling them this is a good investment."

"Sure. But as I keep saying, we go to many other hedge funds like Ascension. We don't put all our eggs in one basket. Or even a hundred baskets."

"So Ellis is a salesman in a lot of ways."

"Yes. He's a salesman and an adviser and an investor and a deal maker."

"Can you walk me through a typical day-to-day deal?"

"I don't think it's appropriate for me to give you real cash numbers—"

"Just hypothetical. I want to make sure I understand the relationship."

"Is this really relevant to your investigation?"

"It might be. I can't say for sure until I know a lot more of the facts. And the background."

"You don't think Ellis has anything to do with what happened to Evan?" French asked. He didn't seem particularly horrified or shocked at the thought. More curious.

"I didn't say that. I'd just like to understand the kinds of relationships Harmon had with people who he worked with. It's very unlikely that Evan was killed by someone he didn't know. The odds are it was someone he knew extremely well."

"All right," French said. "Let's say the head of research into new media comes up and says we should invest in . . . oh . . . companies that are working on technology to make it easy to download original product into iPod-like devices. Got that?"

"So far."

"Let's say they've come up with a way to do it for audiobooks."

"Don't listen to them. I like to read the real thing."

Justin watched as French did his best not to roll his eyes. The executive stayed polite, and he barely hesitated before continuing his explanation. Justin was impressed. It was one of his best things: annoying people to see how they responded. French must have spent a lot of his days being annoyed by a lot of people because his response was to simply keep going. Didn't change his demeanor when caught in a lie, didn't flinch when aggravated by stupidity. No wonder he was a success on Wall Street, Justin decided.

"We have the resources to research which companies have the best technology and the greatest upside. Which companies are most likely to survive some very strict competition. We make our call; Ellis goes to Evan Harmon, says we think this is an area you want to invest in, here's the result of the data we've put together; Evan comes back to us and says, 'Okay, we're in, we're good for X dollars.'"

"X being a substantial amount of money."

"Very substantial in some instances," French said.

"That three hundred million you mentioned earlier—that's not way out of line."

"It can be less than that. Certainly for a company like Evan's. But the total overall can be more."

"And if Evan Harmon says no?"

French shrugged. "Then he says no. We move on to someone else."

"But a rejection could hurt St. John's pocketbook, right?"

French thought about this for a moment, then shrugged noncommittally. "It's possible. Our salespeople are expected to bring in a certain amount of money, and their bonuses are based accordingly. But for it to affect Ellis, it would have to be a lot more than one turndown."

Justin wondered if Daniel French's brown hair ever got mussed. Or even moved. Or if his three-piece suit ever got a little tight. Probably not, he thought. He wondered if French was wondering right now if he, Justin, ever wore a sport coat that actually fit.

"What if Ascension took its business elsewhere?"

"It happens all the time. People move around. Hell, we're not the only broker used by Ascension. They have several sources." French looked at his Rolex. Still no sign of impatience, even when he said, "Is there anything else I can do for you? I do have a substantial amount of work to do."

Justin nodded, determined to be just as polite as his corporate host, and he said, "I'd heard that Evan was not exactly thrilled with the job Ellis has been doing."

French looked surprised. "Where did you hear that from?"

"Is it true?"

"Not remotely."

"So he wasn't thinking of firing him."

"That's absurd."

"How can you be sure?"

"Because it's the kind of thing I'd know. I'd have to know it. We do a lot of business with Ascension—a lot of buying for them and a substantial amount of consulting and partnering. If Evan had any problem with any relationships, I'd know about it."

"But you didn't."

"No."

"Would anyone else?"

"Know about any problems? It's possible. Several executives might be aware if they existed. Possibly Lincoln might know about it because of his relationship with Evan's father. But, again, if I didn't know about a problem, it didn't exist."

"Lincoln Berdon? That's who you were referring to?"

"Yes."

"He's the CEO."

"That's right."

"He very friendly with Evan's father?"

"Yes. H. R. was part of this firm for a while."

"Why'd he leave?"

"H. R.? Because he went back into government. Happens, you know. He made his money here and went back to public service."

"Why didn't he come back here when he left public service?"

"You'd have to ask him. But if I had to guess, I'd say he just didn't want to work as hard. He'd had a heart attack, and even though his job here was fairly cushy, it was still work. A lot of meetings, a lot of socializing. Plus, Evan had started Ascension by then and I think H. R. wanted to help him out, lend his presence over there. Now, I really should—"

"Just another minute or so. This is very helpful. What does that mean, exactly? Lend his presence?"

"It's not a secret. People like H. R. hook up with companies like ours or Evan's because of their Rolodex. H. R.'s international relationships are priceless. Like the Bushes with the Saudis. Bush One was like a member of the royal family, and it paid off for them big-time. H. R. is as tight as it's possible to be with the Chinese, and since they're taking over the whole goddamn world, it's a valuable connection."

"How valuable?"

"Does his father's role at Rockworth have anything to do with Evan's murder?" French asked.

"Probably not. I'm just trying to get the big picture. Anytime this kind of money is involved, it's possible there's some connection."

"I'm not going to get into specifics, but H. R.'s role was essential to our doing business over there. We had access to investment opportunities in China we might not have normally had access to. Everything from financial markets to car manufacturers."

"Chinese cars?"

"Get used to it. The wave of the future. Chinese cars, Chinese televisions, Chinese everything. We're steering a lot of money their way."

"Makes sense. I like their food, why wouldn't I like their cars?"

The possibility that Justin might now discuss different types of egg rolls finally seemed to exhaust Daniel French's goodwill. Justin could see the helpful light go out of his eyes.

"What are the chances of my talking to Lincoln Berdon?" Justin asked.

"I doubt he's going to be of much help. He also may be the busiest man on the planet, so good luck getting in there."

"He's not around now, by any chance, is he?"

"He's in London today."

"How about Ellis? He in London, too?"

"No, Ellis is domestic only."

"Then where do I find him?"

There was a moment of silence from Daniel French. He looked down at his shoes, uncomfortable, before twisting his neck a bit to the side and saying, "He's not in today."

"Where is he?"

"I don't know."

"Sick?"

"I don't know," French said quietly. "He didn't come in today."

"Is that standard operating salesman procedure? To not come in on Fridays?"

"Sometimes," French said. "During the summer."

"And he doesn't need to tell anyone?"

"He told his secretary that he wouldn't be reachable today."

"Dan," Justin said slowly, "the guy is the key contact in your company for someone who was murdered last night, and you didn't think it was worth mentioning until now that he's missing?"

"He's not exactly missing. He's probably at a meeting somewhere."

"How about his assistant? Would she know what meeting he's at?"

"I checked with her before you got here. I assumed you'd want to speak to Ellis."

"And?"

French sighed quietly. "And she doesn't know where he is, either."

"Can I ask you a question, Dan?"

French was looking down at his shoes again. "Yes."

"Did you Google me before we met? Or have your people check me out?"

"Yes."

"Find some pretty interesting stuff, did you?"

"Yes, we did."

"Found some fairly violent episodes in my past?"

"Yes."

"I hope you don't think this is out of line," Justin said quietly, "because you've been very nice and very helpful and I appreciate it. But you should have paid more attention to your research, because I'm not someone to fuck with and you just fucked with me. I'm not sure why and it doesn't really matter. But my advice is don't do it again." He smiled brightly. "*Was* that out of line?"

"Is there anything else I can do for you?" Daniel French said.

"You can tell me who Ellis St. John's assistant is and you can take me to her. And then get the fuck out of my way."

They were given a small room down the hall from the big conference room. Ellis St. John's assistant was an attractive if somewhat husky young woman named Belinda Lambert. She had large, round, brown eyes that seemed to be pleading for someone to take her away from all this. Anywhere. Although preferably anywhere that included a bedroom. Justin didn't take the plea personally. He had a feeling that request had been made many times before.

Belinda wasn't overly helpful once Justin made it clear he wasn't taking her anywhere, although she was polite and her concern about her boss seemed genuine. When Justin had ascertained that she really didn't have any idea where Ellis St. John might be—she'd tried calling his cell phone several times as well as his apartment and had e-mailed his BlackBerry, all to no avail—he tried to get her talking about St. John in general terms. She was evasive about delving into his personal habits. She did say that she was sure he wouldn't stay away too long because of his two cats.

"He loves those cats," she told him. "Binky and Esther, that's their names. I mean, you wouldn't believe the way he treats them. Buys them presents and cooks for them. It's kind of crazy. But sweet, too, don't you think?" He agreed it was very sweet, and when he asked who fed them when he was away, she said, "I do. They don't like me as much, though. I'm more of a people person than an animal person. But I'll feed them tonight and for the weekend. Well, I guess I'll feed 'em as long as he's away."

"You know he won't be home this weekend?"

"That's what he said. That I wouldn't be able to reach him today and he'd be gone all weekend."

"When he told you this, did he sound upset?"

She thought for a moment. She had on a strange reddish-purple lipstick and her thought process involved licking the lipstick with her tongue and then leaving smudges of it on her white, white teeth. "No," she said. "I'd say he sounded kind of happy. You know, excited. I got the feeling it was a hot date or something."

"Does Ellis have a car?"

"No," she said. "You know, I told him he should, I mean he goes away all the time on weekends. Fire Island, the Hamptons, Bucks County. He says he'd rather rent."

"Do you make his reservation for him when he rents?"

"I don't have to," she explained. "At least during the summer. He has a standing reservation at Hertz on Thursdays. The one that's just a couple of blocks from here. If he doesn't want a car, then I cancel the day before."

"Did you cancel on Wednesday?"

"No. So I guess he picked it up."

"You have his cell phone number, Belinda?"

She nodded and rattled off the number. He picked up an office phone and dialed it. After several rings, a recorded message came on, a man's voice saying, "You've reached Ellis St. John. I'm not available, but if you leave a message I'll call you back as soon as possible." When Justin heard the tone, he said, "Ellis, this is Justin Westwood, I'm chief of police for East End Harbor in Long Island. Please call me as soon as you get this message. It's very important." He gave his home number and his cell number, and hung up. And he made a note of St. John's cell number.

"I'm sure he'll call you back soon," Belinda Lambert said. "He's very good about calling back."

Justin nodded. Then he asked about Ellis's relationship with Evan Harmon. There was a noticeable hesitation and a slight off-center smile on her lips, so when all she said was, "It was fine," Justin couldn't let it just stop there.

"Can you elaborate?"

"On what?"

"On their relationship." He knew that even assistants on Wall Street made six-figure salaries. Justin decided that Belinda was overpaid.

"What is it you want me to say?" she asked.

"I want you to tell me the truth. Did Ellis and Evan get along?"

"Sure."

"How do you know?"

"Because they spoke on the phone constantly. And they got together all the time. And . . ."

"And what?"

"Look, Mr. Westwood—"

"Chief Westwood. I'm a police officer, Belinda, and this is a homicide investigation—do you understand?"

"Yes, it's just that Ellis can be . . . well . . . he won't like it if I tell you certain things."

"Such as?"

She gave him an I-may-be-dumb-but-I'm-not-dumb-enough-to-fall-for-that look. Justin didn't change his expression, just waited.

"Look," she said, "I could get fired."

Again, Justin stayed quiet. Apparently silence was the one thing Belinda couldn't bear.

"I think Ellis is in love with Mr. Harmon." She shook her head as if she couldn't believe she said it out loud. But now that she had, it made it easier for her to keep going. "I mean, he never said that or anything, but you can just tell that kind of thing."

"How could you tell?"

"He would get so excited when Mr. Harmon called. You know, he'd, like, spruce up, fix his hair or something, like Mr. Harmon could see him, even though he was just on the phone. And Mr. Harmon could ask him to do anything. I mean, like anything. You know, run an errand for him or take someone to dinner, and Ellis would just get so excited."

"Ellis is gay?"

"Well, yah," she said. "I mean"—and she lowered her voice to finish—"you know, this is a weird place. It's kinda like the army, you know—don't ask, don't tell. It's a real guys' place, so Ellis isn't like some queen or anything. I mean, I don't know if everyone knows."

"But you know."

"I work for him. But even if I didn't, I'd know."

"Because you can just tell?"

"Just like I can tell you're straight." She maneuvered her breasts just a bit so they seemed to jut ahead a little straighter and she smiled at him with her abnormally white teeth. "You know, I kind of like the fact that you're, you know, maybe not in such great shape. I'm not big on the gym rat types. I'm a little bit zaftig myself. Maybe you noticed."

"Belinda, let me ask you something . . ."

"Sure, you might as well take advantage of me while I'm feeling so blabby." The white from her teeth flashed even brighter. The dark lipstick stain on the upper row made it look as if she'd just bitten into an extra rare and bloody steak.

"Was Ellis ever violent?"

"Ellis? With me?"

"With anyone."

"God, no. Well . . ."

"What?" he said.

"I never saw him violent. But once he couldn't come into the office, he said he was sick. I went to his apartment to bring him some work and he wasn't sick, he was pretty marked up, you know, like a black eye and some cuts and stuff. I figured it was, well, you know, a rough trade or something like that, but he'd definitely been in a fight."

"Does he have a temper?"

"Oh yeah. He does a lot of yelling and slamming the phone down and stuff like that. But that's not so weird around this place. I mean, you should hear Mr. Berdon sometimes, when he reams somebody out. It's unbelievable. But, you know, I don't want you to get the wrong impression. I mean, Ellis is a fantastic boss. He can be really generous. Like, they don't give assistants BlackBerrys here—it's really weird what they'll cut corners on, you know—and then they'll spend, like, a million dollars on some golf tournament thing . . ."

"Belinda . . ."

"But, anyway, Ellis got me a BlackBerry. Like, out of his own pocket, you know. He decided it would be more efficient so, I mean, he paid for an R and W techie to, you know, make all of his stuff work on it and he pays for the monthly bill and everything . . ." She stopped suddenly and lowered her voice again, this time to a hissing whisper. "Do you think Ellis killed Mr. Harmon?"

"Do you?"

"I don't know. I told you I think he was kind of in love with Mr. Harmon. Why would you kill someone you love?"

Because that someone was married, Justin wanted to tell her. Because that someone didn't love you back. Because that someone was capable of using love to get what he wanted, no matter the cost.

Because it's what people did.

Every minute of every day.

But he said none of that. Instead, he just told her, "Good question."

She nodded, as if acknowledging that her boss was now officially off the hook. Justin realized he wasn't going to get much more out of her, at least for now, so he started to make his move out of the small room but she reached out and put her hand on his arm. He looked down and saw a piece of paper in her hand.

"It's my card," Belinda Lambert said. "It's one of the cool things about this place: even the assistants get business cards." She produced a pen from nowhere and scribbled something on the card. "It's my home number," she told him, "in case you get, you know, some kind of inspiration at night and think of something, you know, you might want to ask me. Even late at night, that's okay with me. I won't mind."

"That's good to know," Justin said.

"Anything I can do to help," she said. "*Anything.*"

When Justin left the Rockworth and Williams building he felt as if he needed a shower. It was a place that was built on secrets and desperation. Not his favorite combo.

But a combo that definitely was capable of leading to a murder, he thought. So as he headed down the street, he called Mike Haversham at the East End station, told him to see if Ellis St. John had picked up a rental car for the weekend. If he had, he told Mike to get the make and plate number and to see if anyone around town had seen it yesterday.

He hung up, thought about Belinda's question to him.

Why would you kill someone you love?

Justin shook his head. He wondered if he'd ever been naïve enough to ask such a question.

He didn't think so. But if he had been, it was so long ago that he couldn't remember.

10

Larry Silverbush dreamed about being governor of the state of New York.

He had all sorts of reasons for wanting the job: he had very strong beliefs about certain things and he knew he could be effective in moving those things—as he liked to put it in his speeches—from the theoretical column over to the reality column. He believed in the death penalty and knew it should be applied in many more instances than it was being applied now. He thought the federal government wasn't doing shit for post-9/11 New York City, and as governor he was determined to get what he knew was not only due but crucial. He had programs to bring business back to the state, and he had well-thought-out plans to reduce taxes and reprioritize social programs and feed money to state schools. Oh yes, Silverbush knew he would make an excellent governor and knew, from deep within himself, that he deserved to hold that office. But mostly when he daydreamed about presiding over the New York state legislature, spending much of his time in Albany, and coming home on weekends to bask in his glory, he always wound up fixating on one thing: a car and driver.

Silverbush hated to drive. His mind wandered; he didn't concentrate, which he knew was dangerous. And he had a terrible sense of direction. He got lost when he was on his own, even when going to familiar places. He had trouble remembering landmarks and street names and, if truth be told, left from fucking right. When he became governor he'd never have to get behind the wheel of a car again. It was a thrilling thought. He'd have someone in a nice black uniform driving him wherever he went. And when he finally stepped down from office, he'd make a fortune in motivational speeches and he would be able to afford a chauffeur all on his own.

That was what he wanted and, all in all, he thought it was a pretty reasonable goal—better schools and someone to drive him to the goddamn grocery store—and that's what he was thinking about as he was stuck in traffic, behind the wheel of his own three-year-old Lexus, on his way to Southampton Hospital to meet H. R. Harmon and get a firsthand view of Evan Harmon's mangled body.

The drive should have taken fifteen minutes, but it took nearly forty as the Montauk Highway was bumper to bumper the whole way, and he had just decided that he wanted his driver's name to be Matthew—not Matt, definitely Matthew—or possibly Roberto; it might be smart to go ethnic—when the district attorney finally pulled into the hospital parking lot. Harmon was already in the lobby, standing by the admissions desk. Not the ideal situation, keeping H. R. Harmon waiting to see his son in the morgue, but the aging politician was relatively gracious about the inconvenience. Silverbush began mumbling something about the traffic, but Harmon waved the apologies away, just saying, "I'd like to see my son as quickly as possible."

The hospital staff was on high alert, and the two men were ushered into an elevator and taken down one floor to the basement. Silverbush could feel the tension and the hesitation in the older man. As they stepped into the morgue room, he instinctively took hold of Harmon's elbow. Harmon didn't acknowledge the support, but he didn't pull away. He stepped forward as if part of a military parade: stiff and erect, his face an expressionless mask.

The morgue attendant was already standing by a body that was covered by a white cloth. The attendant had clearly been through this routine many times. He looked neither interested nor bored by the proceedings and he did absolutely nothing until Silverbush nodded that they were ready for the viewing. The attendant then pulled the cloth back in a firm, steady movement, revealing the upper half of a man's body.

The district attorney had seen more than a few dead bodies over the years. But as this corpse was revealed he couldn't help himself, he had to turn away. He recovered quickly, forced himself to turn back. He glanced over at old man Harmon, who still remained ramrod straight and unemotional. After several seconds—seconds that seemed like several hours to Silverbush—Harmon stepped over to his son's body. He stood, hovering over him as a parent might over a sleeping child. The father didn't touch the son, just stared down at him as if trying to convince himself that what he was seeing was real—or perhaps unreal—then turned slowly on his heels and walked out of the room. His gait going out was not as commanding as it had been coming in. He looked weaker, as if the sadness he was feeling and the loss he was experiencing had sapped most of his remaining strength.

Silverbush nodded to the attendant, who quickly drew the cloth back over Evan Harmon's body. The Long Island district attorney turned and headed after H. R. Harmon. The sound of his hard shoes echoed through the room. It was the only sound. Everything else in the room was still and silent.

In the hallway, Silverbush waited as Harmon caught his breath and composed himself. The DA once again held his hand out to grab the older man's elbow, but this time Harmon shook off the aid.

"You have children?" the man known as the senator asked.

"Yes, I do," the DA answered. "Two. The boy's twelve and the girl's nine."

"I've lost two now. Two children dead."

"I—I didn't know . . . I didn't know you had—"

"A daughter? Jeannie. We called her J.J. 'cause she was such a hot little number it seemed like there were two of her. One *J* wasn't enough."

"How long ago . . . ?"

"Long time ago. Long, long time ago. She was five. Evan was two, somewhere around that. She had leukemia. Suffered like a sonuv-abitch. They told us we should just let her die, that we shouldn't make her go through the treatment, that it would be too painful for her. But we didn't listen. Billi—that was my wife—she said doctors don't know everything. They don't know how much that little girl wants to live. So we took her wherever we had to, did whatever we could. Kept her alive maybe a year longer than otherwise. Maybe. You know what I did the day she died?"

"Got drunk as hell I'd imagine."

"Went to work, played nine holes of golf in the afternoon. She was dead, her suffering was over. Nothin' I could do to help her, no amount of mourning was going to make a damn bit of difference to either one of us. So I did what I always did—went to work and played some golf. It's how you gotta deal with death. You do what you usually do, 'cause nothin' you do's gonna change a goddamn thing."

Silverbush knew it was cold in the hallway, the air-conditioning was on high, but he still found himself sweating. He rubbed his right hand along the back of his neck, felt the dankness. When Harmon spoke again, Silverbush still had moisture on his fingers. It felt undignified and he did his best to wipe his hand, unnoticed, on the back of his sport jacket.

"He looked like he suffered a lot," Harmon said. "Evan."

"It's hard to say exactly, sir," Silverbush answered.

"I don't like bullshit, son. I much prefer truth."

Silverbush nodded. "Then I'm sorry to say that your son probably suffered a great deal. It was a very sadistic murder." Harmon didn't seem to have anything to say in response. The DA did not want him to fall back into silence, so he went on. "Do you have any thoughts . . . Do you know anyone who might have wanted to do this to your son?"

"Abby—my son's wife—she saw him? She saw him like this?"

"She saw his body at the scene of the crime."

"That must have been even worse," Harmon said. "Those marks all over him . . . they looked like burn marks . . . What are those?"

"I'm waiting for the final coroner's report, sir. But I spoke to him earlier today and his initial inclination is that they're the result"—he hesitated, but the senator had said he wanted the truth—"they're the result of contact with a stun gun. That's what the coroner thinks."

Silverbush saw something change in H. R. Harmon's eyes. Just a minor shift, a brief hint of recognition.

"Sir?" Silverbush said.

"Yes?"

"It's just that . . . it looked as if that meant something to you—the fact that a stun gun might have been involved."

"It's not a phrase that one hears very often."

"Does that mean you've heard it used recently?"

"What the hell's your name again? Silverberg?"

"Silverbush. Lawrence."

"Larry, you said. People call you Larry."

"Either one is more than fine."

"Well, Larry, I have heard something about a stun gun recently. But I don't want to be throwing around wild accusations."

"With all due respect, Mr. Harmon, I don't think accusations can be too wild at this particular time. Someone has brutally murdered your son, and we need to investigate any possible lead. I can assure you that no one will be treated unfairly."

Harmon nodded a few times, as if digesting that information. Then he said, "I never answered your question, did I? The one about knowing if anyone might want to harm my son."

"No, sir, you didn't."

"Will you give me a little bit of time? Not much, just an hour or two. I want to figure out exactly how to answer that question. Both questions, really, because they're connected to each other."

"All right. I suppose that's fair."

"And if I decide I do have an answer for you, either I or someone else will call you and give you the information you need."

"Someone else?"

"It's a delicate issue. It might be necessary for me to step back a bit. There are entanglements. Family entanglements."

"Do they have to do with your daughter-in-law?"

"Why do you ask that?"

"Because when I spoke to her, she said you'd accused her of murdering your son."

"As always, she got it wrong. I told her she was responsible."

"I'm afraid I don't understand the difference," the DA said.

"I was speaking philosophically, referring to a much grander sense of guilt. Do I believe that Abigail literally did what I just saw was done to my son? I doubt it very much."

"But you won't say for certain?"

"I won't say anything until I look into the matter we just discussed."

Silverbush nodded, although he wasn't satisfied. But he knew that H. R. Harmon didn't give a damn about his satisfaction. "Then I'll wait to hear from you."

The two men stepped into the elevator, took it one flight up, walked together back outside to the parking lot. They shook hands at the door, and Silverbush watched as a chauffeur in a dark suit opened the back door of a black Mercedes sedan and H. R. Harmon stepped inside.

Silverbush wondered what the chauffeur's salary was, if it was possibly higher than his own.

Sadly, he decided it probably was.

They were not more than a few feet out of the hospital parking lot when H. R. Harmon leaned forward and spoke to his driver. Harmon spoke quietly, as if there were someone else in the car whom he didn't want to disturb.

"I'd like to use your cell phone, please, Martin."

Keeping his left hand on the wheel, the driver handed his phone back to the senator with his right hand. He was not surprised when the old man in the back told him to close the glass partition that separated the front seat from the back. Harmon often made calls and had conversations he did not want the help to overhear. What wasn't usual was that the old man was not using his own phone. There was a permanent phone built into the armrest in the backseat. Martin thought about reminding the senator about the phone, then decided he'd be better off keeping his mouth shut. H. R. Harmon did not much like being reminded of anything. And particularly today, Martin thought. He was probably just a tad disoriented. After all, who wouldn't be on the day you found out your own son had been murdered. No, Martin thought, he should just keep quiet.

As a result of his deference to his employer's whim, Martin did not hear the brief conversation that took place on his own cell phone. He did not hear H. R. Harmon say to the voice on the other end that he'd just left the Long Island district attorney behind. He did not hear Harmon say that the DA had identified the wounds on the body as having come from a stun gun. Nor did he hear Harmon say the words "The source is solid?" And then, "You're absolutely sure?" Glancing in the rearview mirror, the chauffeur did catch a glimpse of old man Harmon nodding his head. He did see the senator close his eyes for a moment before tapping on the glass and indicating that Martin could now open it back up. As he took his phone back, he saw the senator's eyes in the mirror. He thought he saw a deep sadness in those eyes, a sadness that was startling in its scope and strength.

Only natural, Martin thought. Only appropriate.

What could be sadder than outliving your own child?

The DA watched H. R. Harmon's limo disappear down the street, then he walked slowly over to his Lexus and got behind the wheel.

To absolutely nobody, he said, "Home, please, Roberto," and then he turned the key, listened as the ignition came on, and began to wend his way in and out of traffic on his way back to Riverhead. After twenty minutes of moving probably less than four hundred feet, Silverbush couldn't stand it anymore. He pulled his car onto the highway's shoulder and sat for a moment, staring straight ahead and sweeping his head clear of any thoughts whatsoever. The peace and quiet didn't last long—Silverbush was incapable of letting it last for very long—and when he came out of his brief reverie he reached for his briefcase and pulled out the report that the cop Justin Westwood had given him.

Larry Silverbush's reading experience lasted just slightly longer than his quick moment of nonthinking silence. Before he finished the second page of the police report, he was honking his horn furiously, maneuvering his car into the middle of the highway, driving across the grass divider so he could head in the opposite direction from which he started, and began speeding back toward East End Harbor.

Now there were no thoughts of Roberto or Matthew or any other fantasies about drivers and wealth and power. The only thought he had as he sped back was: *I hope some damn fool cop decides to pull me over for speeding. Oh god, I hope someone tries because I really want to rip somebody a new one.*

But no one pulled the district attorney over. No one interfered with his drive back to East End Town Hall. He didn't slow down until he reached the town limits, at which moment his cell phone rang. He eased his foot off the gas pedal, and he listened to the man on the other end of the phone. He said nothing until the man had finished, and then all he said was "Thank you, sir. Thank you very much, I can't tell you how important this is" before hanging up. And by the time he'd stormed into Leona Krill's office, he wasn't even thinking about ripping anyone a new one. He was way beyond that.

Way beyond.

Justin was on his way to midtown and the Ascension office when his cell phone rang. It was Leona Krill.

"Where are you?" she said. Her tone was brusque and formal. It was as if she was talking through clenched teeth. She wasn't really asking a question—it was more of a demand.

"I just left Rockworth and Williams. I'm on my way to Ascension."

"In the city?"

"Yes, in the city."

"Get back here immediately."

"Leona, let me just go to this meeting at Ascension, then—"

"That meeting's canceled. Get back here immediately, Jay. Be in my office in exactly three hours."

Justin hesitated. Leona rode roughshod over the brief silence.

"Did you hear me? And do you understand what I'm telling you?"

"Silverbush read my report, huh?"

"Three hours, Jay. Do you understand?"

Justin told her he understood. And unfortunately he did.

11

At 6 P.M., exactly three hours after speaking to Leona, Justin arrived at the East End Harbor Town Hall on Main Street. Reporters—maybe ten or twelve of them—crowded around the front of the building. Justin had driven past his house before coming into town but hadn't bothered to stop there. Inches outside his driveway—just off the official property line—was another group of reporters. Also two news vans parked across the street, one of them with a satellite dish perched on top of it. A helicopter hovered overhead, circling the house. So he just kept driving, found he couldn't park at the station because there were more reporters there, too, tucked his car in an illegal spot behind the old-fashioned five-and-dime, the one that had the 1960s mechanical horse ride in front of it—put in a quarter and it rocked back and forth, holding a small child on its back, for several minutes—and headed up Main Street on foot.

Justin pushed his way past the reporters at Town Hall and walked into the mayor's office. Leona was waiting for him, along with DA Silverbush and a uniformed police officer. No one looked very happy.

"You goddamn piece of shit" was how Larry Silverbush greeted him. "You were balling the victim's wife?! You were fucking one of our key suspects?!"

Justin kept his voice steady and low. "If you want to be technical," he said, "my relationship with Mrs. Harmon was prior to anyone being either a victim or a suspect."

"I don't want to be fucking technical," the DA screamed. "I want you to know that you are *this* close to being indicted!"

"On what charges?" Justin asked.

"Obstruction of justice, aiding and abetting a homicide, possible conspiracy to commit murder—how many fucking charges do you want?"

"I understand you're a little pissed off, but what the hell are you talking about? Who am I aiding and conspiring *with*?"

"Abigail Harmon."

"Don't be an asshole. I put the whole thing in my report. How can you turn that into a conspiracy?"

"I told you not to fuck with me, Westwood. I told you to play along. But no, you had to go on being a stupid cowboy. You let her spend the night in your own goddamn house last night?!"

"It's what I would have done for anyone in her position. She couldn't spend the night at home, so she stayed upstairs and I slept on the couch. There was nothing improper about it."

"Bullshit."

"There's nothing about our relationship that would hinder me from doing my job the way it should be done."

"You've already screwed up your job, you asshole."

"Since when is Abby a real suspect?" Justin asked. "What is it you think you know?"

"I don't *think* I know anything. While you were out screwin' around and pretending to be a cop, my men solved the whole goddamn thing already! And guess what, cowboy? You were played for a sucker. Big-time. At least you better hope that's all we find out was going."

"What are you talking about?"

The Long Island district attorney turned to the uniformed cop who, up until this moment, hadn't uttered a word or changed his expression. "This is Captain William Holden of the Riverhead PD. Captain Holden. If you don't mind . . ."

The captain turned to Justin. "We've ascertained that Mrs. Harmon was having an affair . . ." He didn't let a smirk cross his face, but the sense of satisfaction was unmistakable when he continued, ". . . *another* affair with a man named David Kelley. I believe you know him."

Justin's face was blank for a moment. Then he said, "Dave Kelley? The contractor?"

Holden said, "That's right. He operates here in East End."

Justin nodded. "I know who he is."

"You've never met?" This was Silverbush jumping back into the conversation. His tone made it clear that he felt he knew about every moment that Justin had ever been in Dave Kelley's presence.

"We've met."

"You spent time with Abigail Harmon and Kelley together. At Sylvester's Restaurant."

Justin started to shake his head. Then he remembered. Maybe a month ago, he and Abby had had lunch at Sylvester's, a kind of general store that served good sandwiches. They'd sat at the small counter and, while they were eating, Kelley had come in. He saw Abby, sauntered over, and said hello. Justin picked up a strange vibe. He'd met Kelley before, seen him around town, nodded to him at Duffy's, but didn't really know him. Abby had said that Kelley was a contractor, was doing some work on her house. Justin remembered now because she'd said "my house," not "our house." He always noticed when she went out of her way to avoid any mention of her husband. Kelley had looked on edge when he'd come over, seemed uncomfortable in his presence. At the time Justin wasn't sure why. Now he was.

"Yeah. I was with Abigail having lunch and Kelley came over and sat with us for a few minutes."

"A few minutes? That's all."

"That's all."

"What'd you talk about?" This was Silverbush again, not Holden.

"Nothing very interesting. Something about the work he was doing for the Harmons."

"Anything about the security system?"

"What?"

"It's more interesting than you think. Or at least than you're

pretending to think. That's one of the things Kelley was doing, overseeing the security system that was being installed in the Harmon house."

"That didn't come up."

"Did Mrs. Harmon ever talk to you about it separately?" This was
Holden. His tone was less hostile than the district attorney's. In fact, it
showed no emotion whatsoever. Justin decided that Holden could go
one of two ways: Either he was probably a very good cop, capable of
digging up the truth, or he could be in Silverbush's pocket, in which case
he was a very good cop capable of doing a lot of damage.

"No. Never."

Silverbush sneered. "So, you being a supercop and all, she never
even asked your advice about it?"

"No."

"Hard to believe."

"I can't help that. It's true."

"When you were with Kelley," the Mid-Island police captain said,
his tone still calm and smooth, "having lunch—"

"We weren't having lunch together. He sat down for two minutes,
that's all."

"Uh-huh. In those two minutes, did you talk about Evan
Harmon?"

"No."

"Never came up?"

"No."

"It never came up, let's say, how to set up various ways to establish
alibis for all three of you while Harmon was being murdered?"

"Are you out of your fucking mind?"

"No," Larry Silverbush said, jumping forward to stick his finger in
Justin's chest, "he's not out of his fucking mind. And you want to know
why?"

"Okay. Why?"

"Because you know those burns that were all over Evan Harmon's
body? Well, they came from a stun gun. And when we searched David
Kelley's house, you want to know what we found?"

"Can I take a wild guess?"

"You got it, cowboy. A stun gun."

"How'd you know to search Kelley's house?" Justin wanted to know. "How'd you know about his relationship with Abby?"

That threw Silverbush for a moment. His eyes shifted from side to side, and he wasn't sure exactly how to respond. Holden saved him the trouble, stepping in, quietly saying, "We had a tip."

"From who?"

"Doesn't matter who it was from. We're not ready to reveal that. It proved accurate. Kelley even used the stun gun in front of both Evan and Abigail Harmon. There's a witness. The son of a bitch liked to use it on animals. I guess your part-time girlfriend figured out if it worked on them, it'd work like a fucking charm on her husband."

Justin started to say something, realized he didn't have all that much to say at this point. He decided he was better off being quiet and listening.

"You want to know what else is gonna prove accurate?" Silverbush asked. And without waiting for Justin to answer, he said, "Kelley's fingerprints all over the crime scene. And phone logs that show Kelley talking to your girlfriend the morning of the murder. And another witness who heard Kelley say that that same girlfriend of yours had talked to him repeatedly about killing her husband."

"And what has Kelley said about all this?"

"So far nothing. But we're confident he'll roll. And when he does, he'll give us the lovely Mrs. Harmon as the one who planned the whole thing."

"You thinking of giving him a deal?"

Holden spoke up now. "We're thinking of doing whatever it takes to put two murderers in prison. Maybe three."

"Three?"

Silverbush's eyes flashed angrily. "That's right. 'Cause you want to know what else we're thinking, cowboy? We're thinkin' she couldn't have gone through with this unless you were involved. We think you helped her plan it."

"Do you have even the remotest shred of evidence to back that up?"

"Not yet. But we will."

"Where's Abby now?" Justin wanted to know.

"Over at your police station. Behind bars, waiting for her lawyer."

"And where's Kelley?"

"Mid-Island," Holden said. "In one of our jail cells."

"You have anything else to say to me before I go talk to Abby?"

"Yeah," Holden said. "If you have a weapon, surrender it now."

Justin looked at the police captain curiously, but Silverbush was the one who answered the silent question.

"You're suspended from your job as of this moment."

"You're making a mistake. You don't even know what I learned—"

"I'm not interested. We'll need your firearm."

"I'm not carrying one," Justin said.

"What the hell kind of cop are you?"

"In my experience, especially in a town like this, carrying a gun doesn't solve too many problems, it just causes them."

"Well, you do *have* a gun, don't you?"

Justin's eyes didn't waver as he took Silverbush's sneer head-on. "Yes, I have one."

"Where is it?"

"In my office. In the desk. Upper right-hand drawer. It's locked, but Officer Haversham'll have a key."

"I'll take your badge, as well," Silverbush said. "Or you keep that under lock and key, too?"

Justin looked at Leona Krill, said, "Leona? You have anything to say? I work for you."

She sighed. "I don't have much of a choice here, Jay. DA Silverbush is in charge of this investigation."

Justin didn't look over at the district attorney, just said to Leona, "I'm telling you he doesn't know what he's doing."

Silverbush snorted. "I'd say the evidence proves I know a helluva lot more than you do. Now, you gonna hand over that badge?"

Justin reached into his left pant pocket, withdrew his EEHPD badge, handed it to Silverbush, who said, "Captain Holden will accompany you over to the police station. As a courtesy we'll let you talk to your lady friend for a little bit. But after that, I'm telling you to stay away from her or we'll have you locked up for obstruction of justice faster'n you can scratch your rapidly diminishing balls. You got anything to say to that?"

"Yeah," Justin said and turned to the police captain. "Is your name really William Holden?"

When the officer didn't answer, and Silverbush just snorted in disgust and anger, Justin decided it was better if he didn't say another word, so he just turned to the door and headed out. Holden had to hustle a bit to catch up to him. Neither spoke during the two-block walk to the police station. Even if they'd wanted to, they couldn't have—the swarm of journalists was upon them, peppering them with questions and taking photos. Justin looked straight ahead and kept walking. There was usually a reasonable amount of traffic on Main Street—typical summer resort town traffic: cars driving slowly while their drivers desperately searched for a place to park—and what traffic there was now stopped cold as mass rubbernecking took hold. Pedestrians stared and people started coming out of shops to check out the commotion. Justin thought the whole scene looked like something out of a bad comedy: two stiff-as-boards cops, striding as fast as they could; a jabbering group of reporters surrounding them like a cloud of dust; the whole town watching in astonishment. Farce or slapstick, he thought. Hard to tell which.

When they reached the station, the reporters were barred from coming inside and Justin welcomed the sudden silence. He didn't much welcome the gaping stares from the young officers working the station, though. And the staring eyes only bulged farther as they watched Justin go to his desk—escorted by Captain Holden—pull out his gun, and hand it over, barrel first.

"I'd like to see Mrs. Harmon. And I'd like a few minutes of privacy."

Holden thought it over for a moment, then nodded. Mike Haversham led Justin to the one jail cell at the back of the station. As he did, he slipped a piece of paper into Justin's hand. The paper was carefully folded. Justin didn't acknowledge the exchange, nor did Haversham as Justin slipped it into his pocket.

Justin peered through the bars at Abby. She looked remarkably calm. Haggard, a bit drawn, but still cool and in control. It was hard to look as if you were in control when you were behind bars, Justin thought. He knew that from personal experience, when he'd been imprisoned and had been anything but in control.

Haversham opened the door to the jail cell and Justin stepped inside. Mike closed the door behind him, eyes aimed at the floor rather than at his now-suspended chief. The young cop shuffled back toward the central room where all the cops except Justin had their desks. He looked as if he were in mourning.

"We do meet in the strangest places," Justin said. It got a brief smile from Abby. "You all right?"

She nodded. "My lawyer should arrive soon. I'll be better when I'm out of here."

"You should probably stay in the city for a while. It'll be a lot easier on you than being out here."

Abby nodded again. "That's my plan. I'll stay in our apartment for a while, until this gets cleared up."

Justin couldn't help but notice the word "our." Now that Evan was dead, she was sharing her possessions with her husband again.

"Are you in trouble?" Abby asked.

"Depends on how you define trouble," he said. "If you mean, do I care what people think and how they're responding, no."

"Must be why we get along so well," Abby said. "We've got so much in common."

"With a few differences," Justin said.

"A few."

He reached out, took hold of both her hands. She relaxed at his touch, then tensed a bit when she realized he wasn't holding her strictly for affection. His hands felt for her forearms, and his thumbs pressed down lightly just above her wrists. She tried pulling back, but he held tight.

"I want you to relax," he told her. "And I want to ask you a few questions."

Her eyes narrowed, but she nodded.

"Did you kill Evan?" The question was casual, as if being thrown out in cocktail party conversation.

"Jay, what are you—?"

"Answer me, please. Did you kill Evan?"

"No."

"Did Dave Kelley?"

"I don't know."

"Take a guess."

"Will you let go of me, please?"

"No. Take a guess. Did Kelley murder Evan?"

"No."

"Did you know that Kelley had a stun gun?"

"What?"

"Just answer the question."

"I don't actually know what a stun gun is, but, yes, I know he had one."

"How?"

"Because he talked about it a couple of times. And he showed it to me. But it was before—"

"Before what? Before you began sleeping with him?"

She sighed. "Yes."

"How did it come up in conversation?"

"Oh, god, I have no idea. I think we'd been having some problems with animals or something—you know, digging up plants or doing something with the compost heap at the back of the property, I'm not sure."

"And?"

"And Dave said something about how he liked to take care of whatever they were, those big things with masks and ringed tails."

"Raccoons."

"Yes. Dave said that he had a stun gun. He said it was fun to use it on the raccoons."

"He had a strange idea of fun."

"Yes. He used it in front of us once, me and Evan. He showed us how it worked."

"Did *you* think it was fun?"

"No." She looked directly in Justin's eyes now, not flinching. "Dave could be extremely cruel sometimes." He met her stare. Finally she turned her head away and said, "Jay, what does this have to do . . . Oh my god . . . those burns. Those burns on Evan's body."

"Yes. It looks like they were from Kelley's stun gun."

"Oh my god."

"Do you still think he couldn't have done it?"

Now there was a real hesitation. This wasn't defiance, this was confusion, maybe even a touch of panic. "I don't know."

"Did you ever tell anyone you wanted Kelley to kill Evan?"

"For god's sake! No!"

"Even joking?"

"No!"

"Was Evan gay?"

"What?!" He had pushed her over the edge. Abby tried to stand up and jerk her hands away, but he refused to let go. He pulled her back down beside him, waited until she stopped resisting.

"Was he bi? Did Evan have homosexual affairs?"

"That's ridiculous."

"So you think it's impossible?"

"Jay, I'm starting to think that nothing's impossible. How can I know if Evan was doing something he didn't want me to know about?"

"Guess."

She pursed her lips and composed herself. "My husband was many things, but I'm fairly sure that gay was not one of them."

"Do you think you would know if Evan was having an affair?"

"Yes."

"Would he have told you?"

She shook her head. "Not in so many words. But he would have let me know, dropped some not-so-subtle hints. He derived a strange kind of pleasure from things like that."

"You handled it differently?"

This time she nodded. "I don't particularly like to go out of my way to hurt people."

"So you never told Evan about your affairs."

"No."

"Did he know?"

She didn't answer right away. Then slowly, she said, "I think that two people who know each other well always know when secrets are being kept. They may not acknowledge them, and they may not know the specifics, but they know."

"Did he know about me? About you and me?"

"I don't think so."

"How about you and Kelley. Did he know about that?"

Again, she took a long time before answering. Then: "I think he might have, yes."

"But you don't know it for a fact?"

"No. But I would say that he did."

"Why?"

"I don't know. I'm not sure. Just . . . things he said. His tone. I overheard him while he was talking on the phone once . . . I wasn't even sure he was talking about me, but I think he knew."

"Abby, why did you say you think Kelley didn't kill Evan?"

"Because he's not smart enough."

"It doesn't take a lot of brains to kill somebody."

"Okay, he's not tough enough."

"He acts tough."

"You pegged it. It's an act. He can torture animals. People are different. They can fight back."

"They've got a witness who says Kelley told people you asked him to kill Evan."

She looked genuinely shocked. "That can't be! I would never— It's a lie! What witness?"

"I don't know; they didn't say. But they've got a pretty strong case against Kelley, at least that's what it sounds like. It's possible he'll roll and peg you as the one who planned the murder. That might get him murder two, or at least take the death penalty off the table."

Now Abby turned a shade paler. Not completely white, but a definite change in pallor. "But it's not true."

"A lot's going to depend on his lawyer. And how willing he is to deal."

Abigail's breathing came a little heavier now, a bit faster. She seemed to want to say something but suddenly didn't have the strength to say it.

"So who *is* tough enough to have killed Evan?" Justin asked quietly.

"You are," she said.

"Who else?"

"I am."

"You're not helping your cause," he said.

"H. R. is."

"Evan's father?" When Abby nodded, Justin said, "Do you think he did this?"

"No. But is he capable of it? Yes. If he had to. You didn't ask me who did it. You asked me who was capable of doing it."

Justin suddenly remembered the folded piece of paper in his pocket. He fished it out and unfolded it. Mike Haversham had gotten the info Justin had wanted. Ellis St. John had rented a car on Thursday afternoon, the day he disappeared and the night Evan Harmon was killed. Haversham had gotten the make—a blue Mustang convertible—and the license plate number. Justin made a mental note to thank Haversham when William Holden wasn't around. He reached for Abby's wrists again.

"Is Ellis St. John capable of murder?" he asked her.

"Oh god, no."

"Why not?"

"He's just"—she was unable to come up with the right words—"he's just not. Why would you even ask about him?"

"Because he's missing."

She looked confused. "Missing? You mean he's run away?"

"Or someone's taken him away. I haven't been able to find him."

"Does that have something to do with Evan?"

"I don't know. I think it might."

They were both silent for a moment. Justin knew that Holden wouldn't give him much more time.

"Abby, is there anything you know about Evan's murder? Anything you're not telling me?" he asked.

"No."

"If there is, tell me now."

"There isn't. I don't know a thing."

Now he slid his hands off her forearms, and her arms fell to her sides. Abigail swallowed. A hard swallow. "Do you want to know anything about Kelley?" she asked quietly. "I mean, about me and Kelley?"

"No." And when she looked at him curiously, he said, "That's personal. That can wait."

"This is business?"

"This is business."

"I think I'm going to need some help here, Jay."

"I think you are."

"Will you help me?" When he didn't answer, she said, "I didn't do it. I didn't do it, and I don't know anything about it."

Again, he didn't respond, sat stoically, not dismissing her claim, not embracing it. Just wondering if he could believe the woman standing next to him. And what the ramifications were if he decided he could.

Abby cocked her head, spoke as if she weren't the one whose life was on the line, as if she was genuinely curious about his decision, as if whatever he decided would tell her what she wanted to know about him. "Will you help me?"

"I'll find out what happened. Whatever it is, whoever it is, as long as you understand that."

"I understand," Abigail Harmon said. "Business, not personal."

"No," Justin Westwood told her. "This one's personal, too."

12

Li Ling was naked.

And she was always happy when she was naked.

Having no clothes on was freeing to her. It was like shedding an outer skin. Like discarding some final form of repression and restraint. Being unclothed was exhilarating to her.

Togo also wore no clothes. He was lying next to her on the bed, his perfect body half visible, half hidden by the tangled sheets. They had made love three times, and she knew she had exhausted him. Drained him. Even astonished him, after all this time. She was not drained, though, not yet. She watched him sleep, gently put her hand over his heart, felt his chest move up and down. She traced a silver-painted nail across his chest, shuddering with delight as she felt his smooth skin and the tautness of his muscles. She moved her hand between her own legs. Watching Togo sleep, she pleasured herself. Her expression didn't change. She barely moved, but she came quickly and suddenly and whatever tension remained in her body and her mind was now gone.

Ling swung her legs out of bed and in one motion was standing. She enjoyed the feeling of the rough carpet on her bare feet, took a moment to spread her toes and rub them against the coarse fiber. She walked across the room to where the man was sprawled. He, too, was naked but he was not feeling any pleasure. Ling didn't even know whether or not, at this point, he was even feeling pain. He was probably beyond feeling anything.

She nudged him with one toe, and his body moved ever so slightly. She stood above him, put her bare foot on his neck. She stayed still, feeling the faint pulse from his neck vibrate against her sole. The vibration seemed to pump life into her body. Her touch seemed to stir him, too; his eyes fluttered but she couldn't tell if he could see her. She hoped so.

She bent over, her foot pressing down a little harder on the neck, the pulse feeling stronger against her skin, and she jabbed her finger downward, one quick movement, and then the pulse was gone. She straightened up slowly, luxuriously, as if coming out of a bubble bath, enjoying the way her spine curved upward, one vertebra at a time until she was upright and rigid. She jostled the man with her toes, but this time there was no movement, no fluttering of the eyes.

The man's name had been Ronald LaSalle. It was a meaningless name to her, a meaningless life. She did not know why his words had been important nor did she care. She cared only that he had talked, as she knew he would. And that he had told the truth, which there was no doubt he had. He had, very quickly, told them what they had been required to find out. There had been no need to put him through the agony he had endured before he died.

But sometimes, Ling understood, one did not do things strictly from need.

And with that, she smiled and went back to the bed. She stood on the mattress, her weight barely making an indentation, and this time she put her foot on Togo's neck. When his eyes slowly opened, he saw her standing above him in the position of power and dominance. He did not change his expression, but she saw that he instantly grew hard.

"We have time to make love one more time," she told him. She nodded toward the body of Ronald LaSalle. "And then we must finish our job."

His head moved, a slight nod, she could feel the movement under her foot. She clenched it slightly, gripping his neck with her toes, and she wondered when the day would come when Togo, too, would be as helpless and powerless as the dead man on the other side of the room.

She watched as he finally smiled up at her. She smiled, too, and then she dropped down next to him, straddled him, clenched her legs against his sides as tightly as she could squeeze. She leaned over, her bare breasts lightly grazing his smooth chest.

They made love once again while she thought of life, and the joy it brought, and of death, and the exquisite pleasures that could bring as well.

And she thought of the fact that because of what this man, Ronald LaSalle, had told them, she and Togo now had more work to do.

And sometimes work could be the best thing of all.

13

At 9 P.M., Justin was slouched in his living room on Division Street. The news vans and reporters had disappeared, as had a quarter of a bottle of Jack Daniel's and two bottles of Pete's Wicked Ale. The reporters had given up and stopped loitering around his property about forty-five minutes earlier. The JD and brew were still available. Justin was trying to decide now whether or not to go for a third bottle of Pete's.

He'd been online and seen the way Evan's murder was being treated, so he was prepared for the onslaught of publicity that was sure to break the next morning. AOL news, running a story from the Associated Press, was playing it up big. The assumption was that Abigail had set up her two lovers to murder her husband, and that was made clear by the headline: THREESOME NOT ENOUGH FOR MILLION-AIRE MURDERESS. The story went on to detail her affair with Kelley: how he had been hired as a contractor to redo part of the Harmon mansion—that was clearly the official description of the home from now on, "the Harmon mansion"—and how Abby had gradually succumbed to Kelley's charms. Justin learned details he had not been privy to, some relevant to the case against Kelley and Abby, some not. Kelley had worked on the house for the better part of a year. The job was supposed to take four months but had stretched to twelve. Abby was receiving credit for the extension; the story said that Evan had wanted Kelley to stop working, but that his wife kept finding more and more for him to do. The AP made it sound as if the extra work was sexual. Justin supposed that was possible, but he also knew that contractors had a way of overstaying their welcome. It was their nature. Start one job, get money up front, get partway through the work, take on another job with more money up front, spend less and less time finishing up the original job as the back-end money becomes less and less important. He dismissed the idea of Abby keeping Kelley around for sexual purposes. It didn't make sense. If she wanted to have an affair, she wouldn't want him hanging around her home. She'd want Kelley close by but separate—just the way she'd had with him.

Justin realized he'd mentally put their relationship in the past tense.

Well, he thought, a murder indictment does tend to put a damper on relationships.

Still, the connection between the affair and Kelley's work at the house didn't ring true. Abby had never seemed vindictive toward Evan; she did not seem anxious to spend his money or in any way financially punish him. And knowing Abby the way he did, she did not seem the type to go out of her way so someone like Kelley should make money off her husband. It just wasn't the way her mind operated. He'd be on his own when it came to business. Of course, Justin did have to consider that it was possible he didn't really know how her mind operated. If she'd been playing him all this time, manipulating him toward his complicity in this scheme, then all bets were out the window. But he didn't really believe that. He had never thought of himself as all that easy to manipulate. And he didn't think Abby could have faked some of the things he took for real: the fun, the passion, the intimacy. Even the bitchiness. He thought she'd revealed an awful lot of herself if she was merely acting.

One of the things that came up in the online article and that Silverbush had also mentioned was something Justin could not dismiss: Kelley had been responsible for installing a new security system in the Harmons' house. It was an extremely complicated system. It was run by computer, and it could be disabled from Harmon's desktop computer in his den; but, if someone knew how, it could also be disabled via an outside computer. Kelley did have that knowledge. He would know how to knock out the system and how to erase any photos and records from the hard drive. Justin learned from the article that it had been determined that the system had not been disabled from inside the Harmon house, it had been done from the outside. Kelley's laptop had been impounded, but there was no word yet if there was a link between it and taking the system down. Justin figured if that link was established, it would be a matter of only minutes before the plea came.

The most damaging evidence was the stun gun. It was found in David Kelley's garage. Silverbush and Holden gave out no statement about having received a tip. The discovery was being credited only to superb police work on the part of Holden and his team.

As compared to the work done by Justin Westwood.

The take on Justin was devastating. He was having an affair with the widow Harmon; he clearly must have known about her involvement both with Kelley and with the murder; the police were moments away from linking him to the crime. In the meantime, he'd been suspended from the force. He was the sad cop with the tragic past who'd obviously been taken in by a coldhearted siren. But his heart had to be equally cold to have gone along with the brutal scheme.

There was a statement from H. R. Harmon saying that he hoped and prayed his daughter-in-law hadn't done this terrible thing, but he would not be surprised to learn that she had. He said that his son had talked to him about her adultery, that it had broken both their hearts. Evan had not divorced her because he loved her. H. R. Harmon said that he, too, loved his son's wife . . . but he wasn't feeling love right now. He was feeling only the anguish of loss.

Justin decided to go for the third bottle of beer.

Standing in the kitchen, he suddenly felt incredibly weary. Holding the cold beer in one hand, he leaned down, put his other hand on the stove for support, suddenly jumped up, swearing. He stared at the tiny blister that was already forming on his palm, swore again, and turned off the knob for the right front burner. He'd made himself an omelet and, once again, had forgotten to turn the damn electric burner off. He suddenly missed Abby, wished she were there to put her lips to his hand, but he knew that wasn't going to happen anytime soon. Or possibly ever again.

Justin took a deep breath, shook his head to clear it, went back to the living room with his beer. When he'd nearly drained it—it hadn't taken more than a few gulps—he had an idea. He considered it a moment, playing it out in his head to see just how crazy it was. He decided it *was* crazy—but that it would also work. So he picked up the phone and dialed. His father answered the phone with a neutral "hello," and when Justin matched it, his father said, "I was just going to call you."

"Does that mean Ronald has shown up?"

"In a way," his father said.

"You want to explain that?"

"He's dead. The police found his body."

"Jesus Christ. Where?"

"Near Warwick, by Green Airport."

"By Rocky Point?"

"Yes."

"Off Tidewater Drive?"

"Yes." This time, the word was drawn out and there was a strong sense of wonder as well as annoyance in Jonathan Westwood's voice.

"Are you sure?"

"How could you possibly know that?"

Justin didn't answer. He just said again, "Dad, are you sure that's where he was found?"

"Yes. I just got off the phone with Victoria. Billy DiPezio was at the house to tell her in person. He might still be there."

"LaSalle was murdered?"

"From what I was told, yes."

"How?"

"Justin, I don't know. It wasn't really appropriate to—"

"I'm sorry, I'm sorry. I'll talk to Billy and get the details."

Justin said nothing for a quite a while after that. But that didn't mean his brain wasn't racing. There was an old construction site off Tidewater Drive, close to the Providence River. It had been abandoned probably thirty years ago and was one of the few blights on the landscape in that area. But the property, still referred to as Drogan's lot—Drogan being the developer who had gone out of business long ago—wasn't just an empty lot with no past. It had been a longtime dumping ground for mob hits. Several bodies had been found there in years past, most connected in one way or another to New England organized crime. But what the hell could that mean? Ronald LaSalle was hardly the kind of suit to be taken out by the mob. He was a meek, conservative money guy. It made no sense. What the hell could Ronald have been into to deserve a fate like this?

"Are you still there?" his father asked.

"Still here."

"I . . ." His father took a long time before finishing his sentence. "I need to ask you something."

"Go ahead."

"We'd like you to come up here. We'd like you to find out what happened."

"Of course. I'll do anything you want. Billy's very good at this, though."

"Yes. But . . . in a way, this is family. If you had heard Victoria—"

"Dad, when you said 'we,' did that mean you and Mom?"

"It meant Victoria, too."

"Did she say that specifically? Just now?"

"Yes. She asked me to ask you."

"I'll be up tomorrow."

"Can you do that? I thought you were too busy."

"Turns out I've got some free time on my hands. It's why I was calling you—to say I was coming up. I don't know how long I can stay, but let me see what I can do."

There was no thank-you, no expression of gratitude from Jonathan Westwood, just another lengthy silence, then: "I'll tell your mother to expect you for lunch tomorrow."

Before Jonathan could hang up, Justin mumbled, "Dad." He waited, not exactly sure how to proceed, then he took the last swig of beer and said, "You might also want to tell her not to read the papers tomorrow. Or at least not to believe everything she reads."

"I'll tell her," Justin's father said. "And I'll see you tomorrow."

Justin half smiled at the receiver he was left holding, then he placed it back in the cradle, thinking it wasn't always such a bad thing to have a father who didn't ask questions.

Ronald LaSalle, he thought. Murdered. Body dumped amid the rusted remains in Drogan's.

What the hell could this mean? What the hell was going on?

He didn't know how much time he could spend away from East End Harbor, not with what he'd promised Abby. And not with the fact that he needed to clear his own name. But he had to go up to Providence. He needed to see if his newly devised scheme would work, and he had to try to help Vicky. He could still see, all too clearly, the expression on her face when Alicia had been buried. He didn't want to see the new sadness that would envelop her now, didn't know if he could bear it. But he knew he had to. Providence had, for so much of his youth, been a shelter for him. Then it had become an inferno of pain and death. Lately he had come to grips with his past, had been able to dip in and not be overwhelmed by his memories and his loss. But now there was new pain to deal with. New loss. And he knew he had to go home.

Justin glanced down as he felt a throbbing in his hand. He wondered if he should put some cream on his blister, maybe a Band-Aid, then he thought, *Fuck it.* His thoughts turned next to one more bottle of beer. He decided against that, too. Then he looked at the half-full bottle sitting on the table next to him.

The bourbon was a different story.

14

The first twenty minutes Justin spent at his parents' house was not conducted amid great chatter. In fact, Justin thought he'd been to substantially noisier and more entertaining morgues.

The subdued silence wasn't just due to the shock of dealing with Ronald's death. His parents had also seen the papers. While the burgeoning Harmon scandal and murder was not quite the front-page, explosive story it was in New York and on the east end of Long Island, it had enough juice to draw a reasonable amount of attention in New England. The headline—way more tasteful than any of the New York tabs—on page five of the Providence paper read: EX-PROVIDENCE HERO INVOLVED IN SEX SCANDAL, MURDER PLOT. There was a photograph of Justin from several years—and twenty-five pounds—ago, when he was with the Providence PD. There were some damaging and pointed quotes from DA Silverbush, and there was a typical Billy DiPezio defense of his old protégé, the Providence police chief saying that Justin was certainly capable of having an affair with the wrong woman, but he was incapable of doing anything morally wrong. Billy reminded everyone that neither of the two people arrested—David Kelley and Abigail Harmon—had been convicted, and that Justin had not even been accused of anything except by snide innuendo.

When Justin walked into his parents' massive house, he had that sinking feeling he remembered having for most of his teenage years:

that, despite his bulk, he was too small for his surroundings. He felt as if he'd just walked in the door at 3 A.M., and his parents were waiting up to punish him for staying out past curfew. Justin wondered if one ever got too old to believe in one's mother and father as an intimidating pair of moral compasses. In a way, he hoped not. There was something reassuring in that unchanging and rock-solid superiority. On the other hand, he was confident in his own choices, in his own morality. He'd killed people and felt no guilt. And he'd befriended people who had done far worse things than he'd ever dream of doing—and made no judgment on them or at least did not let his judgment interfere with the relationship. He'd also ended relationships with people who did not live up to his standards. He'd done the same with others who couldn't deal with the complexity of the way he saw the universe. Perhaps the key was that complexity. In some instances, he saw the world in crystal clear terms of black and white, right and wrong. But many areas were also varying and distressing shades of gray. He did not believe in authority that demanded trust without proof of being trustworthy. He did not accept rules and regulations simply because they'd existed for decades or even centuries. He did not take kindly to anyone telling him what to do without an explanation for his actions. So usually he just wouldn't do it. As a result, he had over the past twelve or thirteen years been beaten, shot, hunted, and tortured.

Hey, nobody said he was a genius. But it came with the territory and he accepted that.

It came with the choices one made.

The thing is that he himself was an authority figure. And he often demanded the same blind obedience he abhorred. The problem there was that he was too aware of his own fallibility. He knew how wrong he could be. But when a decision had to be made—either for his own good or for the good of others—there was no one he could imagine making it other than himself.

No one.

Contradictions. Maybe that was why his view of life was so complicated. He saw so many wrong things done by so many people who thought they were right.

Justin shook his head at the meekness he felt in his own home. He did not have the need to conform to anyone else's code—and yet he did want his family to take his side. Or at least wait a reasonable amount of time before jumping over to the other side.

So he sat now with both parents, sipping iced tea in the den—the wood-paneled room that was nearly the size of Justin's entire East End house—waiting for Louise, their longtime housekeeper, to serve lunch. After perfunctory hugging in the entry hall, the silence had come quickly. Justin thought he might as well cut to the chase after his second sip.

"Look," he said, "maybe we should talk about my situation. I'm sure it's embarrassing for you."

"Is that what you think we're upset about," his father said, "that you've embarrassed us?"

"Not entirely. I know what happened to Ronald is shocking . . . and something you're not used to."

"Used to?" This was Justin's mother. Lizbeth's voice was higher pitched than normal, as if the tension in the room had grabbed her by the throat and didn't want to let her speak. "No, Jay, we're not used to people we know being murdered."

"I understand. And there's no way to make that any easier or more palatable. We'll talk about Ronald—of course we will, it's why I'm here—because I can help everyone deal with that. But what's going on with me is going to continue. What happened to Ronald is—"

"Over?" his mother asked.

"I know it sounds callous."

"Yes, it does," his mother said sadly. Justin couldn't tell if she was sad because of the finality of death or because her son was someone who was able, so easily, to move past that finality. He thought about telling her it wasn't ease, it was necessity, but he didn't have time because his father was already speaking.

"It might be callous but it's true," Jonathan said, and turned slightly to directly face Justin. He took a long sip of iced tea. Justin had a feeling that his father wasn't all that thirsty; the pause was very effective punctuation. "So what is it you want to say about things that aren't over?"

Justin exhaled slowly. He also knew how to punctuate for effect.

"Look, you read the paper. I'm involved in something messy. But what they're saying isn't true. I don't think that Abigail Harmon had anything to do with her husband's murder. And believe me, I certainly didn't."

"We believe you."

Justin rubbed his eyes. This wasn't for effect; it was to try to ward off the beginning of a headache that was rapidly approaching. "Thank you. But look at the two of you. I've never seen two people so tense—your entire *bodies* are clenched."

"And you think it's because we're embarrassed? Or because we don't believe you?"

"Dad, we don't have to go into this. It's a lot of things. I know that you blame me for certain things . . . for Alicia and Lili . . . We've never truly had it out about that—"

"We've dealt with that," Jonathan Westwood said.

"Sure we have. And I appreciate it. I know you've really tried to make it work between us over the past couple of years. But dealing with something doesn't always make it go away. I've dealt with it, too, I've dealt with it in every way I possibly can, and I still blame myself."

"Justin . . ." This was his mother now, and her voice was no longer high-pitched. She sounded calm. Still sad, but calm. "You're wrong about us. Both of us. We're not acting this way because we're embarrassed. And we're not acting this way because—because of what happened in the past. What happened with Alicia . . . what happened to Lili . . . However terrible it was and is for us, we know that it's been much more terrible for you. But that's not . . . that's not . . ." She didn't seem to know how to finish her thought, so her husband finished it for her.

"That's not why we hate what you do, what you're doing."

"Then what is it?" Justin asked.

Jonathan Westwood spoke slowly now. And, Justin couldn't help notice, rather kindly. "You could have been many other things, Jay. We don't have to rehash what your life could have been like. It's what it is, you do what you do. But knowing you've made this choice doesn't make us any less afraid."

"Afraid?" Justin said. "What are you afraid of?"

There was a long silence as Jonathan Westwood seemed to search for the right words. It was his wife who found them.

"We lost our grandchild because of the world you've chosen to live in," Lizbeth said. "We don't want to lose our child."

There was a long silence. Justin tried to pick up his iced tea, but his hand felt unsteady. He was just about under control when Louise stuck her head in the door and said the most welcome words Justin had ever heard: "Lunch is ready."

The dining table was eighteenth-century Spanish. Heavy and ornate and austere at the same time. The twelve chairs that were placed around the table were just as austere. The chair at the head of the table was larger than the others, more like a throne. In all the meals he'd had at this table, Justin had never sat in the chair at the head of the table. That was Jonathan's chair.

Justin had just put a small bite of Louise's perfect roast chicken into his mouth and was nodding with pleasure when his father said, "When I told you that Ronald's body had been found, how did you know where?"

"That place has a history." Justin finished chewing. He quickly cut another piece off the juicy breast and popped it into his mouth.

"What kind of history?"

"A violent one." Justin couldn't help but notice the expression on his mother's face now. Not anger or sadness or even confusion. It was one of wonder. When he finished chewing, he said, "Mom?" and she immediately understood his question.

"The things you know," she responded. "I remember when you used to know toys and TV and rocking horses."

"And business," his father added, "and medicine."

"Now," Lizbeth said, "you know murder. And places with violent histories."

There was a typical Westwood family silence. Justin used it to taste the roast potatoes and garlic, just as delicious as the chicken. He even managed to chomp on a few carrots. Then Jonathan asked, "So what are you going to do now?"

"Finish lunch 'cause it's the best food I've had since the last time I was up here. Then go see Vicky. And Billy. I'm going to do what you asked me to do, which is try to figure out what the hell's going on." And as something occurred to him, when he realized there was something else he needed to do first, Justin couldn't help himself: he allowed the tiniest line of a smile to cross his lips. "But first," he said, "I'm going to see a history professor."

Dolce was a small Italian restaurant in the heart of Providence's Little Italy. The tables all had red-and-white–checked tablecloths, most of the pastas came with a simple red sauce, the cannolis were the best in New England, and the espresso arrived steaming hot and joltingly strong.

As Justin sat toward the back of the room, sipping his second double espresso, he was the recipient of mixed responses from the twenty or so customers idling in the late afternoon. There were several middle-aged couples; one exhausted-looking skinny man in beige Bermuda shorts busily reading a Fodor's guide to Rhode Island; two women who were talking as if there were no tomorrow—both looked as if this was a much-needed hour break from husbands and kids. None of this crowd paid him any mind; they had never seen him before nor heard of him. Others were a little more attentive. Three men sitting four tables away were glancing over with a benign distaste. Justin had put two of them in prison and he'd attended the parole hearing for the third, attempting to dissuade the board from going along with an early release. The third man, whose name was Joey Fodera, had raped and murdered a professor of twentieth-century art appreciation at the Rhode Island School of Design. After she was dead, Fodera—his associates called him Joey Haircut—removed her sexual organs. His defense was that she'd reminded him of his first wife—who had disappeared several years before and never been found. The first wife had been so abusive, the defense attorney maintained, that seeing the professor involved in a heated conversation in a restaurant had triggered something in Joey: the memory of the rage and hatred he'd felt when his wife berated and humiliated him. The jury was hard to read—after four days of trial it could have gone either way—so both sides settled on a plea bargain of murder in the second degree and a twelve- to twenty-five-year sentence. After two and a half years in prison, Joey Haircut had ratted on another prisoner, looking to negotiate his way back onto the street. Justin's argument to the board wasn't enough to override the deal with the local DA and keep Fodera behind bars. Three days after the hearing, another sociopath was free and back at work.

Four or five other customers had also crossed paths with Justin back in the day. They nodded cautiously but respectfully when he walked in or as he sat and sipped.

Justin had just ordered espresso number three when the front door opened and a man who seemed nearly twice the size of anyone else in the room came inside. Along the way to the back of the restaurant, he stopped to shake a few hands. When Joey Fodera's hand met his, it held on a few seconds too long. Fodera quietly said something to the large newcomer, something that did not seem as friendly as, say, an invitation to come over and watch a ball game. The large man drew his hand back slowly and deliberately and he smiled at Joey Haircut. Justin, watching carefully, couldn't help himself. The smile made him shudder.

Then Bruno Pecozzi arrived at his destination. Before he could say a word of greeting, the waiter was at Justin's side and Bruno ordered two double espressos, three cannolis, and one sfogliatelle. Then he turned to Justin and said, "Sorry I'm late. I had to do a little bobbin' and weavin' on my way over here."

"Somebody following you?"

"Hey, it's almost an insult these days if somebody ain't followin' me." He stuck his hand out and Justin shook it firmly. "So to what do we owe the pleasure?" Bruno asked. And then followed up his own question with, "Who am I kiddin'? It takes your fuckin' brother-in-law gettin' whacked to get you back home? What's the matter with you?"

And then Bruno drew Justin closer, dragging his chair along with him, and gripped him in a tight bear hug.

"Who we gotta kill?" the professional hit man said, and when Justin managed to give a quick shake of his head, Bruno looked disappointed. "What, this is just a social call?"

"Why don't you shut up and listen," Justin was able to say.

Bruno released him from the hug. "Good thing I like you," he said.

Justin watched the huge man sit down as his two cups of coffee and several desserts were now placed in front of him. He visualized the chilling smile plastered on Bruno's face when he'd stared into Joey Haircut's eyes.

"Yeah," Justin agreed, and slid his chair back to its proper place at the table. "Good thing."

If someone asked Bruno Pecozzi what he did for a living, he would reply that he was a consultant in the movie business. If that same some-one went on to ask on what subject he consulted, Bruno would elaborate slightly and give out the information that he was hired on films that dealt with criminal personalities and their world and that his job was to enhance the reality of that world for directors, actors, and writers. If anyone pressed the giant man further, wanted more detail on Bruno's knowledge of that world, he would simply give a stare that wouldn't quit until the interested party would finally wither under the scrutiny and shrink away in embarrassment. And fear.

Bruno's assessment of his own career was, to a degree, accurate. He'd consulted on four different Hollywood pictures so far. On the very first one he quickly became a legend when the director—a temperamental three-time Oscar nominee who thought he was a genius and went out of his way to be crude and super macho to compensate for the fact that he was only five feet five inches tall—was trying to shoot a scene near JFK Airport in Queens. The scene kept getting interrupted because planes kept taking off and landing, ruining both the aesthetic of the shot and the sound. The director was working himself into a frenzy when Bruno disappeared for a few minutes. He returned, tucking his cell phone into his pocket, tapped the hysterical director on the shoulder, and said, "Okay, you can finish the shot now."

The director continued his rant, only now he began berating Bruno, telling him he might think he was a big-shot fucking hoodlum but to stay the fuck out of stuff he didn't know a fucking thing about. Bruno let him rant for maybe a minute or so, just long enough for the entire crew—including the director—to realize that suddenly no planes were landing or taking off. Everyone grew quiet, and the director said to Bruno, "What did you do?"

Bruno said, "I made a call."

There was another lengthy pause, then the director asked, "Who did you call?"

And Bruno quietly said, "If I told you that, then you wouldn't have to hire me next time, would you, you piece of shit, ass-munching little dwarf?"

The director nodded his head, said, "Thank you," and the shoot went on.

Bruno got hired in quick succession on three more movies; made very good money for talking to the writers and the actors, giving them some details that did indeed enhance the reality of the world they were trying to re-create. And best of all he didn't have to cut back on his regular job.

Bruno's regular job was chief enforcer and hit man for the head of the largest New England crime family, Leonardo Rubenelli, known to close friends and associates as Lenny Rube, Ruby, or Leo Red. By Justin's count, Bruno had killed twenty-three people over the years while in Lenny Rube's employ.

And one at Justin's request.

That last hit was one that had no strings attached to it. Justin had no regrets about it—he'd have done it himself if he'd had the physical strength at the time—and Bruno never held it over Justin's head. It was a business transaction, plain and simple.

Both knew that that particular connection wouldn't stop Justin from doing his job if Bruno happened to be involved in anything Justin was investigating. And Bruno wouldn't hesitate to do anything necessary to carry out an assignment if Justin's job meant that Justin was going to be in the way.

Those were the unspoken rules of their relationship. They'd never been defined, but they didn't have to be.

Both men understood the reality of the world in which they were living. No enhancement was necessary.

"You look good," Justin said. "Where'd you get the tan?"

"Lyin' on the most gorgeous beach in the world." When he saw that Justin was waiting for a further explanation, he said, "The old country, my friend."

"It agrees with you."

"White sand, blue water, red wine. Throw in some fresh pasta and an iced limoncello and you got yourself a good vacation."

Justin's lip curled into a smile. "Somehow I don't think of you as the vacation type."

"Can't work all the time, you know what I mean? Especially when you start gettin' a little older. You gotta take it easy every now and again. Get away. It's why I like goin' back home. Everybody's friendly, you sit around and drink espresso, you get in touch with yourself—you know what I'm talkin' about?"

"Yeah. It sounds a lot like right here."

"All right, you keep makin' fun. But I'll give you a tip, 'cause you look like you can use some relaxation yourself. You wanna get away, you let me know. My aunt Lucia, she's got what you might call a little villa, up on a cliff, overlookin' the Mediterranean." Bruno touched his fingers to his lips and blew a kiss. "You spend a week there, you bring a girl, you'll feel like a new man. I'll get you a good price."

"When I feel like being a new man, I'll take you up on it."

Bruno stretched his long legs out under the table, took a cigar out of his pocket and stuck it in his mouth. He didn't light it, just chewed on it as if it were a pacifier. "So tell me why we're having this extremely pleasant dining experience," Bruno said to Justin. He finished half of a cannoli in one bite just moments after he finished his sentence.

"You already know about Ronald LaSalle?"

Bruno nodded. The nod said, *What am I, some schmuck? You think I'm not gonna know what goes on in my own backyard?*

"So what can you tell me about it?" Justin said.

"That's really why you're here? You think I know something about this guy's—whaddyacallit—demise? Jay, I been tellin' you, I was away on vacation."

Justin shrugged. The shrug said, *What, you think I think you're just some schmuck who doesn't know what goes on in his own backyard?*

"I'm not here in an official capacity," Justin said wearily. "I'm not necessarily looking for a who. I'm looking for a why." And when Bruno's eyes narrowed, trying to figure out the angle, Justin said, "I'm looking for something to tell my ex–sister-in-law."

"Tell her she shouldn'ta married a crook."

"*Was* he a crook?"

"You know another reason these big-money guys get whacked? You ever hear of an honest one windin' up the way this guy did?"

"What did he do?"

"Maybe he just knew the wrong people."

"Got anyone specific in mind?"

Bruno didn't answer. Justin couldn't tell if he was thinking about an answer or if he was just enjoying the cannoli he was biting into slowly and deliberately.

"So what's happenin' back in your sweet little hometown?" Bruno asked eventually, deciding to ignore the last question. "I miss that place." A year earlier, Bruno had spent several weeks in East End Harbor, consulting on a movie that was shooting there. He and Justin had reconnected after not having seen each other for several years. Justin had been in the midst of a difficult case, and Bruno had helped out. If killing a man could be said to be helpful.

"You read the papers?" Justin asked.

"I don't have to. People tell me stuff."

"Then my guess is somebody told you what's going on back in my sweet little hometown."

"You're a good guesser, Jay. I heard somethin' about it. That guy who bought it, your girlfriend's hubby . . . another scumbag money guy."

"There are a lot of 'em."

Bruno nodded, as if considering the number of nasty rich people populating the world.

"Bruno," Justin said, "Ronald LaSalle's body was dumped in Drogan's lot. It kind of swings the odds in favor of one of your associates being involved."

"Or someone who knows that Drogan's is our location of choice for doin' business. It's not the best kept secret in the world, you know."

"You can give me a starting point. I know you can."

Bruno chewed on his lower lip for a moment. "Okay. You know what I'd do if I were you?"

"I'm all ears."

"I'd check out where this Ronald guy worked. What the fuck kind of name is Ronald, by the way? It's like that fuckin' hamburger clown."

"I'll ask his parents at the funeral what the hell they were thinking, okay? You mind staying on the subject! What is it I should check out at his office, Bruno?"

"The usual stuff. Who he worked with, who he did business with. You know, that kind of shit."

"This just your insight into police work or is there someplace you're trying to move me toward?"

Bruno downed his next espresso in one quick gulp. Then he leaned forward, put one elbow on the table and his hand under his jowly chin. In a softer voice he said, "Jay, I can't help you here. To be honest, I shouldn't even be havin' this little snack with you."

"Why not? What makes this one so special?"

"I got a few problems of my own I should be takin' care of."

"What kind of problems? They connected to what happened to Ronald?"

Bruno shook his head. "You know me, I'm not big on sharin'. I kinda like to internalize."

"What the hell aren't you telling me?"

Bruno choked back a laugh. "Almost everything that's ever happened to me I'm not tellin' you."

"So why *are* you having this little snack with me?" Justin asked.

"'Cause when did I ever strike you as a guy who gives a fuck about what he's not supposed to do?"

Justin smiled thinly. And as he did, he caught a movement out of the corner of his eye. One of the customers—one of the ones who had paid no attention to either of them, who had no connection to either of them, the skinny guy in Bermuda shorts and a brown polo shirt—was heading toward their table. At least Justin thought it seemed like that's what the guy was doing, and he tensed in his seat, his cop sense putting him on edge. But no, the guy in the shorts was just on his way to the men's room. As he passed by the table, the man smiled an abstract but polite hello, just a nod to two strangers, and Justin relaxed, embarrassed that he'd overreacted. The guy was past them now, and Justin was about to say something to Bruno, ask a question about Ronald's business, but then his Spider Sense was tingling again and he realized the guy in the shorts had stopped walking. Still smiling and nodding, the guy was reaching into the front of his shorts. Justin saw it, saw the glint of metal, and he immediately began to move, was throwing his chair back and scrambling over the table, and managed to knock the gun off course before a shot could be fired, and then Bruno was moving, too. Justin was amazed at the huge man's speed. And also his strength, which he felt when Bruno swatted him out of the way. The gun was still in the man's hands, was being raised again for a shot, but Bruno's hand wrapped around the guy's forearm, enveloping it. And that was the end of the gun's movement. Justin was close enough to hear the snap, like a twig being broken in two—the sound of an arm bone breaking. Justin saw the look of pain in the guy's eyes, but he didn't utter a sound, and he never stopped struggling, never stopped trying to get the gun up and pointed and ready to fire. But there was no longer any chance of that. Bruno's hand swept along the side of the man's head, and the guy in the shorts went down hard. Two other men came from nowhere, were pinning the man down on the floor. Justin looked at the man's face. He no longer looked like a vapid and tired tourist. His eyes were hard. Cold and deadly.

"You should get the hell out of here," Bruno said, looking up at Justin.

"I think you have it backward," Justin said. "I'm the cop."

"Not from what I hear. I hear you're a suspended cop."

"I can wait until Billy's guys get here. Suspended or not, they'll want to hear what happened from another cop."

"Billy's guys aren't gonna get here," Bruno said quietly. "Nobody's gonna call 'em. So there ain't gonna be nothin' for anyone to tell or anyone to hear."

Justin looked around, realized that the place had emptied out. The only ones left in the restaurant were him and Bruno, the man in the Bermuda shorts, and the two men pinning the guy in shorts to the floor. Justin also realized that the curtains had magically been drawn along all the windows. Nothing happening in the room could now be seen from the street. The guy on the floor was conscious, but he wasn't saying a word, wasn't struggling. Justin realized he was looking at a pro. A pro who knew what was about to happen. "What the hell is this?" Justin said. "What the hell is going on?"

Bruno made sure the two men had the situation under control, then he stepped over to Justin, steered him a few feet away, and spoke quietly so no one else could hear what was being said.

"I told you I couldn't help you, Jay. Especially not here."

"Then where?"

"When you goin' home?"

"Home to East End?" And when Bruno nodded, Justin said, "I don't know."

"I'll find you in a few days. Somewhere. It'd be better there."

"And when you find me, what are you gonna tell me?"

Bruno looked down at the man in shorts, still lying motionless on the floor. "I don't know," he said. "Part of it depends on what I find out here."

"Bruno," Justin said, "you switch jobs? Or at least change bosses?"

"No," the big guy said. "I wouldn't screw around with my pension like that."

"Then who the hell is gonna mess around with you?"

"I told you I had a few things to work out. I'm not as popular as I used to be, hard as that is to imagine."

"Tell me why this guy was trying to kill you."

"That's where it gets a little tricky," Bruno said.

"Tricky how?"

"You gonna see Billy DiPezio while you're up here?"

"Yeah."

"How 'bout your girlfriend in the FBI?"

"Wanda Chinkle? I wasn't planning on it."

"What happened here stays here. You don't pass it to either of 'em. No matter what you think."

Justin thought about whether he was capable of keeping quiet about what he knew was about to turn into a murder. The skinny guy on the floor knew what he was doing. He knew the risk he was taking. And he was willing to commit a murder of his own, if he was quick enough and good enough. He wasn't. So he had to suffer the consequences. That was the world he'd chosen to live in. But Justin was a cop. He wasn't supposed to allow that world to exist in quite those terms. But then Justin thought, *I'm not a cop at the moment. Larry Silverbush took care of that. Bruno's right—I'm a suspended cop.* So he nodded at Bruno, decided he and his conscience could live with the choice, and said, "If that's what it takes."

"That's what it takes."

Justin waited, but Bruno didn't speak. "Bruno," Justin said, staring at the man pinned to the floor, starting to get impatient and sounding it, "why was this pasty-faced asshole trying to kill you?"

Bruno let his teeth show, something akin to a smile. "There are a few possibilities," the big man said. "One is he may think I've got somethin' he wants back."

"What?"

"This ain't a quiz show, you know. I'm tellin' you what I can tell you. And it don't matter what it is. All that matters is he's wrong, I don't got it."

"What's the other possibility?"

"Two others. And one is simple: he's pissed at something I did."

"But you won't tell me what."

"Again, it's on a need-to-know basis."

"What's the third choice?" Justin asked.

"You ain't gonna like this one, Jay. The third choice is that he didn't want me talkin' to you."

"What? Talking to me about what?"

"You're gonna have to wait a little bit on that one."

And when Justin looked at him, a *what-the-hell-are-you-talking-about* look, Bruno said, "You might wanna be a little careful while you're up here in friendly New England, pal. You might want to think about watchin' your back."

Justin thought about watching his back the whole time he was walking out of Dolce. He was thinking about it when he passed by the table where the skinny would-be assassin had been sitting, and he was thinking about it when he surreptitiously used a napkin to scoop up the Fodor's Guidebook the skinny guy had been reading. And he thought about it the entire twenty minutes it took him to drive to his next destination. He thought about nothing else.

But it still didn't make any sense to him.

15

Justin had not seen Victoria LaSalle since Alicia's funeral, and he was startled when she opened the door to let him into her home. She was as beautiful as ever. Her thick, dirty-blond hair fell down to her shoulders in waves, perfectly framing her pale face. Her skin was smooth and unlined, unmarred by contact with the sun. She was tall and slim and wiry; in her jeans and tucked-in collared shirt, she revealed the body of a teenage girl. And her hands were exactly the way he remembered them—long, tapered fingers; no polish on her perfectly manicured nails; hands that were delicate and gentle but also strong. In the more than seven years since he had last seen her, she had aged not a bit. But that was not what startled him.

What threw him, and what rendered him momentarily speechless, was that as she'd gotten older she'd come to look more and more like her sister. His wife. When he stepped into her foyer, it was as if he were staring at Alicia.

Victoria's neck was taut, and her eyes were angry. Those were the only indications of the strain she was under and the unhappiness that had to have enveloped her.

She made no movement to kiss him hello or even shake his hand. Just a curt nod and—ever polite in the way of all Providence upper-class housewives—a murmured "Thank you for coming."

She was alone, which surprised him. No one around to comfort her.

As if she could read his mind, as they reached the living room she said, "There were several people here. I asked them to leave."

He nodded and said, "Okay."

Feeling the need to elaborate, she went on: "I didn't feel comfortable talking to you in front of them. And some of them wouldn't have felt comfortable having you here." She hesitated; and he got the strong sense it wasn't a polite hesitation, it was meant for emphasis, meant to be harsh. "My parents."

"I understand."

They reached the sofas. She sat first, directly in the middle of one couch, making it clear he was meant to sit opposite her, on the other side of the fabric-covered ottoman that served as coffee table. He did.

They sat in silence until he said, "I'm sorry about Ronald."

And almost instantaneously she replied, "I don't really know why you're here."

"I'm here because my father thought I could help you."

"Yes, he told me. And how is it he thinks you can help?"

"Well . . . at first he thought I could help find Ron."

"He's been found."

"Yes," Justin said. "I think the idea is that now I might be able to find out what happened to him. And why. If you want me to."

Victoria didn't answer. He didn't mind; he was content just to look at her, to fool himself for these few moments that he was looking at Alicia. As hard as he tried to resist, his mind drifted away into the past. To the day he'd met Alicia on campus. It was summer and her legs were bare. But it had also turned cool, and she had goose bumps running up and down her calves. It was the way he had always thought of her, for years, if they were apart and he conjured up her image: tanned, bare legs, a line of goose bumps. That ended when she killed herself. Since then, when he thought of her, the image he conjured up was of his wife sprawled on the floor, bloody, one side of her face gone from the self-inflicted gunshot wound.

Again, it was as if Victoria read his mind. Justin remembered that she'd always had that knack. In some ways, even when she was just a kid, she knew him better than Alicia did. She teased him with references that

Alicia didn't understand. She always seemed to know what he was think-ing about, particularly when he was thinking about things he wasn't supposed to be thinking about. He smiled at the memory, picturing her as a fourteen-year-old girl, kind of a tomboy, wanting to hang out with him and her older sister because they could do cooler things: drink and go to dirty movies.

"I look like her, don't I?"

Justin nodded. The word "yes" came out like a quick, sad sigh.

"I see it every day. I see her every time I look in the mirror."

Justin closed his eyes for a moment. It made it easier to talk with his eyes closed. "You and I, we used to be good friends, didn't we?" And when she was the one who nodded this time, he said, "It's weird. I don't let myself miss too many things. It's too dangerous. But I miss you."

"Well, I miss my sister," she said. There was an iciness to her voice, a meanness that he would never have thought her capable of. Her words were like a slap to his face, and he sat up straighter and tried not to let the hurt show.

"Is there anything you want to tell me about Ronald?" he asked.

"What should I tell you?"

"Vicky—"

"I'm Victoria now. People call me Victoria."

"Okay," Justin said. "Victoria. Do you want me to find out what happened to Ronald? Or do you just want me and it to go away?"

It was Victoria's turn now to close her eyes. When she opened them, she said, "I'm pregnant."

Startled, Justin said, "I didn't know. No one told me."

"No one knows. Six weeks. That's all. We were waiting before we said anything, to make sure everything was all right."

"It's hard to know what to say. Congratulations doesn't seem to be the right thing, but I'm happy for you."

"If it's a girl, Ron and I agreed we'd name her Alicia."

"I'm glad. It's a nice thing to do."

He could see her lower jaw trembling. Whatever it was she wanted to say was extremely difficult.

"I don't want to know what happened to Ronald. I don't care what

he did or who did it or why. All I care about is that he got himself killed."
Her whole body was trembling now, beginning to shake violently as if a
fever were running through her. "That's all that matters to me. First my
sister, now my husband. How can such a thing happen?"

"Vicky . . ." He moved to go toward her, but she held up her hand,
stopping him in his tracks.

She steeled herself. The trembling didn't stop completely but it less-
ened considerably. It looked as if she might burst from the effort of
keeping herself still. "But I'm going to have a child," Victoria now said.
"A child who is never going to know his father. And I have to be able to
tell him—or her—something about Ron. So I don't want to know the
truth . . . but I need to know the truth."

"Then let me help you."

There was another silence. And finally Victoria nodded.

"Tell me about Ron," Justin said quietly.

"What kind of things do you need to know?" She was calm now. She
sounded the way some people sounded after a good cry: both drained
and relieved, weak but resolved.

"Remember, I knew him slightly when he was a kid. I didn't know
him as a grown-up. I don't really know anything about him. But let's
start with work. What did he do?"

"Mostly he was a financial analyst. He did work for your father
sometimes."

"What kind of work?"

"He did a lot of things—research, analyzing various kinds of
companies and products. For potential investors. To see what their
upside was."

"Or their downside."

"Yes. Of course."

"So if he gave a bad report to an investor, someone could have been
unhappy."

She frowned and shook her head. "I suppose. But not really. For
one thing, companies don't really know who's checking them out. And
it would be hard to pin it on one person if, say, a fund manager decided

not to invest in a specific company. A lot of people have input into those decisions."

"Was there a specific area he specialized in?"

"No. Whatever interested him or his clients. He didn't always do research for other people. Lately he'd been investing OPM as well, for his firm." She stopped when she saw the faint smile on his face. "Something funny?"

He wiped the grin away. "No, of course not. It's just that I haven't heard that phrase in a long time. Other people's money. And I guess I'm not totally used to you as a thirty-year-old. So it's odd to me to hear you talk like that. I'm sorry, I'm a little bit stuck in the past up here."

There was no humor in her voice, no easing up on him, when she said, "Well, I'd prefer to stay in the present, if you don't mind." And when he nodded his assent, she continued as if there'd been no interruption. "There were things he was better at, areas he was more knowledgeable about. He was very good at his job; there was nothing he couldn't dig into."

"How about recently? Anything different or interesting going on with his business?"

She shrugged. "He'd spent more time traveling lately."

"How lately?"

"Over the past year, the last six months or so in particular."

"Where was he going?"

"Wherever he had to. California . . . Europe. He spent some time in South Africa over the past month or so for clients." He saw her eyes water briefly, but she pulled herself together immediately. "I kept telling him he'd better come back with a diamond."

"Would you say he was an honest person?"

He knew as soon as he said it that he should have phrased it better. The water was definitely gone from her eyes now, replaced again by anger. "Are you trying to make him responsible for what happened to him? Is that how you handle things, drag people down into the gutter?"

"No," Justin said. "And I apologize for being so blunt. I know things are raw. But if I'm going to find out what happened, I have to know as

much as I can. About Ronald, about his work, about the people he surrounded himself with. And I have to ask questions. I'm not looking for
any particular answer—I just need to ask the questions, if for no other
reason than just so I can eliminate something. I'm starting with a blank
canvas and somehow I've got to come up with a finished picture."

She nodded curtly. Didn't acknowledge his lengthy explanation, just
said, "He was honest with me. He was honest about us. That's the only
way I knew him, so I'd have to say yes, he was an honest person."

"Did he deal with a lot of powerful people?"

"He dealt with rich people. If money makes them powerful, then,
yes, he did." She inhaled deeply. "I know what you're trying to do. See if
he crossed a line with someone, see if he did anything foolish or careless.
He didn't. Ronald was the least foolish or careless person who ever lived.
He didn't drive fast; he always wore a seat belt; he kept an umbrella in
the car at all times. He was safe. It's why I married him, because I knew
nothing bad could happen around him. And now—now . . ." The tears
began to stream down her cheeks. "Goddammit. I wasn't going to cry."

"There's nothing wrong with crying," he told her.

Her anger and her stiffness and her sorrow now erupted in sudden
rage. "Don't tell me how to grieve!" she spat. "Don't tell me about crying
and sadness. My sister's dead! My husband's dead! Don't tell me it's okay
to cry. Does crying bring them back? Does crying make the rest of my
life safe and happy . . . Does it keep people like you away from me?"

"No," he said quietly. "It doesn't do that." He waited until her tears
were done and her breathing was back to normal. "Do you want me to
stop?" Justin asked.

She shook her head. "No. I want you to ask what you have to ask."

"Do you have a list of his clients?"

She exhaled deeply, as if frustrated that, now that it was too late,
she knew so little about her husband. "His assistant would have that,
I'm sure. Or one of the analysts who worked for him. There were a few
social occasions where we'd go out with clients—Ron would entertain
them—but I never had much contact with them."

"Did he have his own firm?"

"Yes," Victoria said. "For the last year. Maybe a little more."

"All right. I'll get the client information from the people at the company, if that's all right."

"I'll call them, tell them to cooperate with you. Is there anything else?"

"Not right now. If I think of something, is it all right if I call you?"

She nodded and he stood up. As he took his first step toward the entryway, she said, "It's come full circle, hasn't it?"

His foot stopped in midair and he turned back toward her. "What has?"

"Your wife was murdered because of something you did. Now you murder someone's husband—he dies because of something she did. Full circle." When he didn't answer, she said, "Yes, I cry while I'm grieving. But I can also read the paper."

Justin stood there frozen, agonizing for what seemed like hours but was merely seconds. He said, "I'll call you if I need anything." Then he found his own way to the front door, leaving her on the couch, back straight, legs crossed, unbending and not moving. When he stepped outside, for a moment he thought he was going to be sick, and he doubled over. But he wasn't sick. Not physically. So he stood back up, rubbed off the beads of sweat that were soaking his forehead, got in his car, and drove away.

He didn't think he'd be back for quite some time.

16

In keeping with the rest of his day, Justin's conversation with Billy DiPezio did not start out as a raging success.

Billy was not much on exchanging pleasantries—Billy was not much on pleasantries in general—so the first thing he said to Justin was, "You look like shit."

"I can't imagine why," Justin said. "The last few days have been so pleasant and stress free."

"What do you want?" Billy said. Then, "No, never mind. You want whatever the hell I know about Ronnie LaSalle's murder."

"I want a couple of things. But that's a good place to start."

"No problem," Billy said. "Here's every single thing I know." He held up his index finger so it touched his thumb, forming a circle. "Zero. Zilch. Nada. You beginning to understand what I'm saying?"

"Not such a good start then," Justin said.

"I've had better."

"You got a theory?"

"You've known me a long time, Jay," Billy said. "I got theories on everything. On life, on Ronnie LaSalle . . . you want my theory on why you came up here?"

"No," Justin said.

"'Cause you think if you solve this little crime, then the colder-than-fuckin'-ice Vicky LaSalle is gonna forgive you for something you don't need to be forgiven for."

"What part of 'no' don't you understand?"

"I'm just givin' you some free advice, my friend. Whatever you do, you aren't gonna change the look in Vicky's eyes. You don't deserve that look, and the sooner you accept that, the better. But you ain't gettin' rid of it."

"Victoria."

"What?"

"She calls herself Victoria now. Not Vicky. She's a grown-up."

"But she still thinks like a kid when it comes to you and Alicia."

"Shut up, Billy. I'm not kidding. End of conversation."

"You want to talk about somethin' else, name your subject."

"Let's try to stick to Ron LaSalle. You got any of your famous theories on what happened?"

"Yeah. He was screwin' around and someone thought they could take him for big bucks. His girlfriend, his girlfriend's boyfriend, somebody. Somethin' went wrong somewhere and Ronnie winds up in Drogan's lot."

"Who leaves his house before dawn, with his wife still in bed, to go see a girlfriend? Or a blackmailer?"

"Shit, Jay, who leaves his house before dawn for any reason?"

"That's my point. You don't. Unless you have to. And unless you don't care if your wife finds out you're doing something screwy."

"So maybe he didn't care. Maybe he was leaving her."

"Billy, it's not the way people like that work. Somebody like Ronald leaves like that because he has no choice. Because he doesn't see any other way. The alternative—say something or just stay—is worse."

"You know rich people better than I do, Jay, I'll grant you that."

"With all the graft you've taken, I'll bet your bank account's bigger than most of the people paying you off."

"I resent that." Billy grinned his best wolfish smile. "But I wouldn't take the bet."

"So you gonna stick with your borderline-insane theory or are you going to follow this up and see what really happened?"

"You ever know me to let a murderer get away with something in my town?"

"No," Justin said. "Never. Unless he paid you enough."

"They couldn't pay me enough on this one."

Justin cocked his head. Billy sounded serious. "And why's that?"

" 'Cause this one's nasty."

"How nasty?"

"The ME said most of LaSalle's organs were crushed." When Justin winced involuntarily, Billy said, "Yeah, I know. It had to be excruciating. And slow."

"Beaten to death?"

"Except hardly any marks on him."

"That doesn't make sense."

"Tell me somethin' about murder and death that makes sense," Billy said.

Justin took a sip from the small glass of single malt scotch that Billy had put in front of him when they'd sat down. Most conversations in Billy's office were conducted over a glass of single malt. Didn't matter whether it was morning, afternoon, or night. "Were you this philosophical when you were young?" Justin asked.

"I was never young," Billy DiPezio said. "You and me, we were born old. We're just gonna die young."

They sat in silence for a moment, pondering the truth of Billy's statement. Justin finally said, "You do talk a lot of bullshit."

"Yes, I do," Billy said. "And why are you carryin' around a Rhode Island guidebook? Doing some sightseeing while you're up here?"

Justin held up the book, still partially wrapped in the white and red cloth napkin from Dolce. "Can you run this for fingerprints?"

"I can do anything I want. What's it about?"

"Nothing connected to Ron LaSalle. Just something to help me out."

"Always happy to help you out, Jay. But am I missing something? Don't you have a little police station of your own with, you know, all those modern accoutrements?"

"I've been suspended."

"What a bunch of assholes."

"No argument there. Will you run the prints?"

"If you tell me you're not bein' an asshole, too. We don't lie to our friends, do we?"

"No, we don't. This has nothing to do with Ron LaSalle."

"All right. I'll run 'em."

"And, Billy . . ."

The Providence police chief shook his head. "What else do you want?"

"Are you kind of shorthanded these days?"

"I'm always shorthanded. Why?"

"You interested in a pretty good cop who needs a job?"

"Talk to the goddamn politicians. They control the budget."

"Luckily, I don't need the money," Justin said.

"You? You want to come back here?"

"In a way," Justin said.

"What the hell kind of way?"

Justin told him. It was what he'd come up here to say, why he'd come back home. When he was done explaining, Billy had the biggest smile on his face that Justin had seen in a long time.

Justin was feeling extremely clever. He'd gotten Billy to agree to pay him the princely sum of one whole dollar a week. For that sum, he was now a consultant to the Providence PD and, as such, had an official way in to the murder of Evan Harmon. And, as a side benefit, of Ron LaSalle as well. Larry Silverbush could go to hell. Justin was going to get to H. R. Harmon and Lincoln Berdon, the head of Rockworth and Williams, and anyone else he wanted to reach. And Silverbush couldn't stop him now. The only thing Justin was feeling a little bad about was that he hadn't planted a big kiss on the top of Billy DiPizio's silver-haired head. He'd just gone ahead and shaken his hand and said thanks.

As Justin was walking down the imposing cement steps from the station house, he was enjoying his own cleverness. And he was picturing breaking the news to DA Silverbush. That was the reason he didn't see the man walking up quickly behind him on his left. The man's eyes were hidden by Ray-Ban sunglasses and he was wearing a lightweight gray suit. As he came upon Justin, the man in the gray suit said, quietly, "Just keep walking." And when Justin instinctively hesitated, the man said, just a little bit louder, "Don't stop. Walk. There's someone who wants to talk to you."

Justin glanced to his left, took the man in—the dirty blond hair in a near buzz cut; the thin, wiry nature of his body; the fact that he was probably in his late forties or early fifties; that he was in good shape; looked confidently strong. Justin also saw the gun that was sitting in the man's shoulder holster, tucked neatly under the lightweight suit. He heard Bruno's warning in his head: *You might want to think about watchin' your back*—so he nodded; took one more step in compliance with the man's wishes; and as he did so his left elbow came up hard, very hard, and connected with the man's jaw. Justin saw an ugly, thin stream of blood fly out from the man's mouth and he saw the man already reaching inside his suit as he began to topple over, but Justin's hand was there first. When it emerged, Justin's right hand was holding the pistol that had been holstered. With a quick motion, he slashed the gun across the side of the man's head, sending him sprawling. The man in the suit tumbled two or three steps, used one hand to stop himself from falling any farther. As the man lay there, Justin turned the gun on him, told him not to move. And that's when Justin heard the shouts. Men screaming: "Drop the weapon! Drop the fucking gun!" Justin could see maybe a dozen cops—all of whom had been coming in or out of the station, catching a quick smoke, buying a coffee or a hot dog from a street vendor—dotting the entire plaza in front of the building. Guns were drawn, pointing at Justin, who was now yelling back at them, "I'm a cop! Don't shoot, I'm a cop!" And the man in the suit, still stunned and sprawled on the steps, was also screaming: "I'm a federal agent! Put your fucking gun down!"

Justin considered his options, saw the dozen or more guns pointing straight at him, threw his left hand high in the air and with his right tossed the gun a few feet away, watched it skitter down the cement steps. He raised his right hand high in the air to match his left. He was swarmed upon by the surrounding cops, two of whom were helping the man in the gray suit up to a standing position. The man in the suit stepped over to Justin, said, "You asshole," but he didn't say it very well because his jaw was out of whack and already swelling up, and then he swung at Justin, punched him hard on the side of his head. Justin went down, stunned. And he offered very little resistance after that as he was escorted down the steps by two cops and the man in the gray suit. In less than a minute, he was sitting in the front seat of a beat-up Honda. Sitting beside him was Wanda Chinkle, the head of the New England branch of the Federal Bureau of Investigation, whose first words to him were, "Jesus, Jay, can't you do anything without screwing it up totally?"

Justin sipped from a small bottle of warm Fiji water. Wanda kept a supply in the backseat of her car. After his first sip, Justin asked her if she'd ever heard of a cooler. He offered to give her ten bucks so she could buy a nice Styrofoam one. Wanda didn't answer or even acknowledge his offer.

They were alone, parked on a small street around the corner from the station. The man in the gray suit, who was indeed one of Wanda's agents, Norman Korkes, had been taken to the nearest hospital. At the very least, his jaw was sprained and he'd lost one tooth. The jaw probably wasn't broken, although Justin decided he wouldn't be overly sorry if it was.

"You make friends wherever you go, don't you?" Wanda said.

Jay took another sip of water. His head was still not completely clear after the punch he'd taken. "Just a little quirk of mine—I'm not crazy about people with guns who try to force me into cars." After another sip, he said, "What the hell were you thinking? You have my cell number. Why didn't you just call up and go, 'Hey, can we meet?' What is it with you people? Everything has to be cloak-and-dagger. Well, that's how people get hurt. If you're looking for me to say I'm sorry, I won't. 'Cause I'm not. Next time I'll drive the son of a bitch's jaw into his brain. If he has one."

"You done with the macho spiel?" Wanda asked. She didn't take his bait. She showed very little emotion. Mostly she sounded exhausted.

"Yeah," he acknowledged. "More or less."

"I'm not looking for an apology, Jay."

"So what are you looking for, Wanda?"

Wanda Chinkle was not a particularly appealing-looking woman. Her features were fairly plain, even harsh. And she didn't have one of those smiles that covered for her plainness. She rarely smiled, in fact, and when she did, it was more of a grimace than anything that revealed pleasure. Wanda was not someone who experienced a lot of pleasure. Nor did she think she deserved much. She worked, that's what she did. She worked and she thought about work and she slept. That was pretty much her life. At the moment, her life was revealed on her features, making her look even harsher than usual. She appeared not to have had much sleep lately, and tension lines were drawn deep into her forehead and under her eyes.

"I don't think I have to explain myself," Wanda said, "but there is a reason for the cloak-and-dagger stuff. Pretty minor cloak-and-dagger, considering your excessive response." He said nothing, just waited, so she went on. "It's not the smartest thing for me to do, to be seen with you. You come with a lot of baggage, as far as the Bureau is concerned."

"Is that right?"

"Yes, that's right."

"Oh, excuse me," Justin said. "Crazy me. Of course I do. I mean, let's see, first there was the agent who tried to kill me and then put the entire law enforcement community on my tail as if I were a wanted criminal. And then wasn't it you guys who planted an agent on me, who set me up to be killed? And wait, wasn't there an agent who actually let me get sent to Guantanamo where I had the shit tortured out of me . . . Oh, sorry, wait again, no, that wasn't just some agent, I believe that was *you*." This time it was Wanda who stayed silent. "*I* come with baggage?" Jay said. "Go to hell, Wanda. You *owe* me."

Her voice was quiet when she said, "Yes, I know I do."

"So what are we doing in your car?" he asked. "You want to shoot me just for fun?"

"I've heard worse ideas. But, no, I'm trying to do you a favor."

"Because we're such close friends?"

"I don't know how close we are anymore. But I like to think we're still friends."

"What's the favor?"

"You should leave these cases alone."

He was genuinely puzzled. "What cases?"

"The murders."

"Ron LaSalle and Evan Harmon?"

"That's right."

"Why?"

"I can't get into specifics, Jay. But you have to trust me. You don't understand what you're dealing with. I'm just beginning to see what's under the surface here."

Now he was more than puzzled. He was shocked. "Are these murders connected?"

"I'm not here to give you information, Jay. I'm trying to help you out."

"Why the hell are you involved in either one of them? What makes them federal cases?"

"Look . . . I've been keeping track of Harmon for a while . . ."

"For what?"

"It doesn't matter. What matters is that you're better off staying out of it."

"Better off how?"

"Better off by not ruining what I've got going. And better off for your own safety."

"Now you're concerned about my safety?"

"Yes, goddammit, I am."

Justin snorted in disbelief. "Is this coming from Silverbush?"

She looked disgusted. "Give me a break. Larry Silverbush doesn't know his ass from his elbow. But I'm telling you, you should listen to me on this one, Jay. Nothing good is going to come out of it if you force your way in."

"What have you got going? Tell me how the two murders are connected."

"I'm not telling you any such thing. I'm trying to keep you out of trouble, not drag you in."

"This is bullshit, Wanda."

"It's anything but."

"Prove it."

"I don't have to prove it. But I'll prove that I know a lot more than you give me credit for."

"Let's hear."

"You should stay away from Bruno Pecozzi, too."

He thought about what Bruno had said to him, that he had to watch his back. "Have you been tailing me?"

Wanda didn't answer.

"Is Bruno connected to all this?"

Again, not a word from the FBI agent. The silence hung in the car like a cloud of cigarette smoke, thick and unpleasant. Justin knew better than to try to pry more information out of her. And she had to know him well enough to know her words weren't going to keep him from doing what he wanted to do. So the question was: Why was she saying all this to him? What was her goal? What was her angle?

"I hope you don't think this is payback" is what he finally said.

"What I'm telling you just might keep you alive," she said. "So, yes, I think this counts as payback."

"A warning to mind my own business? That's not good enough."

"If you listen to me, you'll thank me."

Justin shook his head. "You're a long way from payback," he told her, "and you know it."

"The only thing I know is that you're a stubborn damn idiot. Which I knew all along, so I can't say I thought you'd really pay attention to me. But you can't say I didn't try," she said.

"I wouldn't dream of it."

"Then you're on your own now, Jay."

"It always does seem to come down to that, doesn't it?" he said. Then he opened the door to her car and stepped out into the Rhode Island sunshine. Half a block away, he saw the first thing he'd seen in a while that brightened up his day. An absolutely stunning woman walking toward him. She was tall and moved like a dancer. There was something overwhelmingly sensual about her. Her dark, straight hair rustled in the slight breeze. Her bare shoulders rose and then sloped perfectly, and her arms were muscular and beautifully tapered. Her legs were long and, like the rest of her, perfect. But it was her eyes that grabbed him the most. He caught only a glimpse of them as they passed each other in the street. She had perfect eyes: the color, the shape, the way they seemed to devour her surroundings. She was Asian. Chinese, he thought. The light brown of her eyes seemed to glow against the polished, darker color of her skin. He smiled at her, couldn't help himself, and she turned her head in his direction. Just the slightest of turns. Not really welcoming his silent greeting but not ignoring it, either. Just accepting it as if it were her due. Neither of them slowed down as they passed each other, going in opposite directions, and Justin forced himself not to look back at her. As he kept walking, he felt as if he were leaving a little part of himself behind. And when he knew she would be out of sight, this heavenly creature, he realized that the temperature had turned colder than it was supposed to be. And the sky was grayer. The summer weather had stopped making sense.

Like everything else, Justin thought. *Just like everything else.* And he headed back to his car.

17

At first she thought, *Shit, I did it again,* thinking she'd twisted her knee and torn her cartilage. She'd done it two years before, just walking down the street. The operation wasn't bad, but the recovery was a bitch. Then she realized, *No, this is worse. This pain is much, much worse. What the hell did I do?* And then she saw the Asian woman—a beautiful woman, breathtaking really—and she wondered why the woman looked so happy, how could someone be so happy when she was in so much pain, and it wasn't just her leg now, it was her back, and then her neck—and then she didn't see the Asian woman anymore or anything else. Her eyes closed and she felt herself falling, and then the pain was gone.

For the moment.

Li Ling wondered what it must be like to go through life being as unattractive as this woman. Her body was toned but had no real shape. Her legs were thick from ankle to thigh. Her hair was thin; there was no pleasure in touching this hair. This woman's hips were wide and her breasts were small. Her skin was dry and colorless and cracked, not soft and touchable like Ling's own lustrous skin. Li Ling looked down at the naked woman and all she felt was curiosity. Did this woman have lovers? Did men stare at her and lust after her and want to fuck her? Did women?

Ling was alone with the woman now. Togo had gone to get the transportation. They no longer needed the woman; they had gotten the information they'd needed from her. It hadn't been easy. She'd been tougher than the man. Stronger. It had taken Togo's best effort to get what they'd needed. But of course they'd gotten it. They always got what they needed. The naked woman had given them more names. And more information. She had put them one step closer to their ultimate goal.

Ling admired this woman. She was impressed by her strength. As physically unappealing as she was, that strength made Ling want to touch her, to caress her, to have some physical contact other than the pain she'd helped inflict.

The woman wasn't moving, but Ling knew she was still alive. She bent down, put her hand on the woman's forehead. She ran her fingers down the woman's neck, gently stroking it. The hand moved farther down her chest, to her left breast. Ling let her hand rest there, rubbing the breast softly. She bent farther down, put her mouth on the woman's nipple. Ling's tongue snaked out and she tasted the nipple. It was salty from the woman's sweat. It tasted good.

She put her mouth up against the woman's mouth, put her lips against her lips. She could feel the soft breaths coming in and going out. She kissed the woman, very slowly, then she pressed harder and harder still. She could feel the woman stir ever so slightly.

Ling thought that perhaps she was making the woman happy. She deserved happiness.

Li Ling believed that all people deserved happiness before they died.

She was aware that someone was touching her. It was as if she were dreaming. And perhaps she was. The touch didn't feel real, but it felt comforting. A caring touch amid the terrible pain. Perhaps she was at a doctor's. Perhaps the miracle she'd been praying for had occurred. Perhaps someone had saved her.

She felt movement on her cheek and then the gentle touch slid downward. She felt warmth on her breast. And she wasn't sure, but she thought the same warmth was somewhere near her mouth. Then the warmth and the light pressure of the touch stopped. And she felt as if she were being transported. For a moment she thought, *I'm on a stretcher, yes, I have been saved.* But that flash of happiness didn't last long. Because something else occurred to her. What if she wasn't on a stretcher? Maybe it was something else. *Maybe this was what death was,* she thought. *It was hands picking you up and moving you to the afterlife.*

She felt nothing for some time after that. No hands, no warmth, no movement.

She did hear a steady drone, though. So she was still alive. Maybe this was what you heard when you were flying toward heaven. It was the noise generated by the world of the living, slowly fading as you went to a quieter place. Quiet was appealing. Quiet sounded nice. But suddenly she was overcome by a yearning for noise.

The drone stopped—she had no idea how long it had been going on; the line between conscious and unconscious was way too blurry for her to conceptualize the passage of time—and then she felt hands on her again. And more movement. Yes, she was being carried once more. She had a brief moment of panic as she began to suspect that she was not being lifted toward heaven. She was not going upward; she felt herself falling now.

She began to realize that she was far, far from heaven. And even enveloped by the pain and the darkness and the jumble that her senses had become, she understood that heaven was not a reality for her. Not now. Now she was being dropped straight down into hell.

Li Ling knew what her instructions were. And she had no real problem carrying them out. Togo had left the killing to her, knowing how much pleasure it usually gave her. But this time she did not feel the glow that normally accompanied a kill. She felt a touch of sadness that such a strong woman was disappearing. Ling could tell the woman was struggling to live. She had no chance, of course—it was a battle she could not win; one that Ling could not let her win—but still Ling felt she deserved the chance to fight and to die on her own terms. She put her two fingers on the pulse that was beating ever so faintly in the woman's neck, but she didn't press down and still the pulse. She kept her fingers there until she felt the pulse begin to slow naturally. Then she turned and walked away.

There was no need to make the kill.

The unattractive woman with the will of steel would be dead in seconds anyway.

There was no noise at all now, nothing at all really, no sense of movement around her, no warmth or even cold. She couldn't tell for sure, but she felt as if she were alone. As if she were the only person left in whatever world she was in.

She didn't know if she was able to move, but she thought that perhaps she could. She felt some connection to her arm and to her fingers. She tried moving her hand, and it seemed to work.

It also brought the pain back.

It was so strong, so overwhelming, that she almost willed herself to die on the spot. She understood where she was now. It made perfect sense. And she understood, too, that she did not have long to remain on earth and that it seemed so much easier to die without all the pain.

But she knew there was something she could do before she died.

No, not could do. *Had to do.*

She had to make things right. That was what was important to her. Finishing her job. And making things right.

This thing especially.

Her hand moved enough to touch her own chest. She almost passed out from the sharp stabs that seemed to plunge themselves into her arm. But the pain didn't matter; she understood that now. Living was important. Dying was important. Pain was something in between that ended and was forgotten. She knew that her pain was very close to being over. So she forced her arm and her hand to move and that's when she realized she was naked. That was okay, she thought. It didn't matter. She could make things right *using* her nakedness. Her eyes opened now, just a slit of an opening—it was all she could manage. It wasn't really relevant anyway; she couldn't really see. The pain was already disappearing; she could feel it fading the way she could feel the life fading from inside her. Her hand moved to the ground again, felt around. She needed something. Something sharp. She didn't know if she could even tell the sensation of sharp anymore. Then she felt it. Something with an edge. She pressed her finger against it and there was a different warmth than she'd felt from whatever had been touching her body. This warmth was not as pleasant. But it made her happy, happy enough to move her lips into a simple and glorious smile.

Yes, she could do this, she was positive. She could make things right.

She *would* make things right.

And then, she hoped, if she was lucky, she'd die with the smile still on her face.

18

The OGM on Abigail Harmon's cell phone was the same as the one on the answering machine in her New York City apartment. Neither was in Abby's voice. Justin could assume only that a housekeeper had either been recruited for the task or had taken it upon herself to make sure that the message was singular rather than plural, or at least no longer made reference to the deceased Mr. Harmon: "You've reached the Harmon residence. Please leave a message and your call will be returned as soon as it's convenient."

Justin left the same message on both machines: "I'm in Providence. I'm just making sure you're okay. Nothing much to report . . . just checking in."

He hung up, feeling unsatisfied. He had a discomforting feeling that it might not be convenient for his message to be returned for quite a while.

Glancing at his watch, he looked up at the ten- or twelve-story glass building he was now facing. He had a few minutes yet before he had to be at his appointment. He decided to loiter and make believe he was savoring a smoke. That lasted thirty seconds or so before he decided his imagination was not what it should be. Pretending didn't provide much satisfaction.

He hoped the meeting he was about to have would provide a bit more.

*   *   *

In keeping with the safe and conservative personality that Victoria LaSalle had extolled, her husband's company was simply named the LaSalle Group. The name held no promises of riches or glory. No sense even of what services the company provided. Unfortunately, it also held no key as to why its founder and president had been murdered.

Justin appeared exactly on time and was ushered into a small conference room by Ronald's assistant, an attractive but grim-faced woman wearing a conservative gray skirt suit and white shirt and who appeared to be in her late twenties. They were quickly joined by two men, also seemingly in their late twenties or early thirties and also dressed in crisp gray suits with white shirts. Justin was only a few years older than they were, but they all made him feel old and tired and out of shape and somewhat soiled.

Justin thanked them for coming into the office. It was Saturday, and already six-thirty in the evening, but Justin had wanted to meet there, to get a feel for the surroundings. He also was expecting them to provide material and information that might be available only in the office files or on the office computers. He didn't want to wait to get that information. They all murmured that it was no problem, that they'd like to help in any way possible, that they often worked late and on weekends anyway. They said they'd all spoken to Victoria and she had instructed them to give Justin absolutely anything he needed. He thanked them again, then he did his best to tell them what he needed. He began by explaining what he was looking for and why.

One of the men—his name was Harry Behr and Justin took him to be the highest up of the three—explained how Ronald LaSalle had operated his business.

"He was a good teacher," Harry said. "He believed in discipline and intellectual . . . I'm not sure of the exact word I'm looking for here . . ."

"Integrity," the woman said. Her name was Ellen Loache.

"Yes," Harry said, and looked pleased. "He believed in intellectual integrity. One of the reasons he started his own company was that he said he always felt that when he worked at a large firm he was letting external sources control his time and his thinking. He didn't think that was the best way to get the right results."

The other man nodded and spoke up now. His name was Stan Solomon. "Ronald liked the freedom this place gave him. He said he used to spend his mornings taking phone calls, his lunchtimes listening to other people telling him what they thought he should do, and his afternoons meeting with analysts and strategists who did nothing but talk *at* him."

"What he used to drum into us," Harry said, "was that he wanted us to give him facts, not opinions. He didn't really care if we saw anyone or talked to other people; he wanted us to read newspapers, trade publications, magazines, corporate reports, legitimate financial analyses. He wanted to ignore the junk—and there's a lot of junk in this business—and try to dig for the reality. Ronald always said you couldn't really trust people but you could trust ideas and facts."

"And results," Stan added. "He believed in the Bill Parcells school of economics. You are what your record says you are."

"Okay," Justin said. "I've got the theory he lived by. But what did *he* do during the day?"

"Mostly the same as what we did," Stan said. "He read, he researched, he focused."

Justin nodded and scratched at his half day's growth of beard. He wondered how the two guys in the room managed to stay so perfectly clean shaven. "And you didn't notice anything different over, say, the last few months?" he asked.

"Different how?" Ellen Loache asked.

"I don't know. Different behavior on Ronald's part. Different business practices. Different in any way."

"Well," Ellen said, "things definitely changed about six months ago, but that was only natural."

"Why?" Justin asked.

"The nature of our business changed," Harry said.

Justin didn't have to say anything. He just moved his fingers in a "come on" motion. Harry continued talking.

"Originally we were basically just a research company, providing services for other companies. That's mostly what Ronald did at the Rock."

"The Rock?"

"R and W. Rockworth and Williams."

"Wait," Justin said. "What does Rockworth and Williams have to do with Ronald?"

"That's where he used to work before starting TLG."

"He used to work at Rockworth?"

"Sure. He pretty much *was* Rockworth up here. He ran the Providence office. Ellen and I worked for him there."

"He brought me over from Citibank," Stan said, "in Boston."

Justin held his hand up, motioning for them to be quiet. He didn't know what the Rockworth connection could possibly mean, but it was too strong to ignore. The one thing that had popped up at every turn so far was the financial institution of Rockworth and Williams. Justin decided that he sure as hell was going to find out what that connection meant.

"Okay," he said after a few moments. "Go on. How did the business change?"

"We began doing a lot more of our own investing, dealing directly with clients rather than only working through Rockworth."

"And this changed things how?"

"A lot more personal service for one thing. When you're dealing directly with clients, you're at their beck and call." That was from Harry. He clearly didn't like being at other people's beck and call.

"A lot more travel for another," Ellen said. "Particularly for Ronald. He was spending a lot more time out of the office dealing with clients."

"Do you have a list of the clients and the places he traveled to?" Justin asked.

Ellen nodded and handed over a folder. "Mrs. LaSalle told me you'd be wanting that, so I already prepared it."

"This is everyone?"

"Certainly everyone I knew about."

Justin picked up on her hesitation. "Is it possible there were clients you didn't know about?"

Another hesitation. "I don't think so," Ellen Loache said, "but . . ."

"But Ron seemed like he was becoming more secretive about things," Stan said.

Harry shot Stan a sharp glance, but Justin turned to face Stan and asked him to be more specific.

"It's hard to really be specific," Stan said. "I just got the feeling he was doing something he didn't want to discuss with us. Or with me, anyway. To be honest, I thought maybe it was because he didn't think I was doing a great job."

"That's ridiculous," Ellen said quickly.

"Well, I mean, I know that," Stan said. "I had a great year. But still, he just didn't seem to want to include me sometimes."

Justin turned to Harry Behr. "Did you think the same thing? About you, I mean, not about Stan."

Harry also hesitated, then nodded. "Yes," he said. "It was weird. But not so weird that I felt like I could say anything."

"That's exactly the way I felt," Stan said. "It was subtle."

Justin had a few more questions but before he could ask anything else, Ellen said, "It's crazy, isn't it? Ronald and Evan Harmon . . . having this happen so close together. It creeps me out."

Justin managed to keep his voice calm and quiet. "Ronald knew Evan Harmon?"

"Sure," Harry said, "from Rockworth."

"Did they do business together?"

"Some."

"Recently?"

"Pretty regularly," Ellen said. "Particularly since we expanded the business."

"Was Ascension one of your clients?"

"One of our biggest," Stan said. "Maybe *the* biggest."

"Do you know the specifics of what they were doing together?"

"We did a lot of research for Ascension. Evan and Ronald talked a lot," Harry said.

Ellen indicated the folder. "Whatever I have is on that list. I tried to make it as thorough as I could."

The conversation went on for another twenty minutes or so. But Justin had run out of questions. He was staying because it was easier to sit there and talk with the three younger people than it was to get up and move. But he could tell that they were becoming fidgety and impatient, and it was Saturday night after all. He thought about taking them to dinner, having a few drinks with them. It would be nice. But he realized it would be nice only for him. They didn't want to spend their big night of the week drinking with a melancholy cop immersed in a murder case. They wanted to go home to their spouses or lovers or even their pets and TV sets. Dining with him would be way down on their list of desirable things to do. Maybe number 101 out of a hundred. So he thanked them one last time, and told them to go and try to enjoy themselves. They said that they'd do their best.

His parents had waited to have dinner and Justin appreciated the gesture. He was starving and bone tired and it was nice to relinquish control, even if for only a couple of hours. He made himself a perfect vodka martini with three olives, exactly the way his father liked his drink fixed, and his father joined him. Then Jonathan opened a superb bottle of Châteauneuf du Pape and they sat at the table and Justin did his best to fill them in on his day. He left out details he knew they wouldn't want to know—what had happened at Dolce, his encounter with the FBI agent on the steps of the police station—but he gave an in-depth accounting of the time he spent at Victoria's house. As he spoke, he could hear his words tinged with disappointment, even anger.

"Her grief is very raw right now. And even if weren't, people deal with grief in different ways," Jonathan said. "Some people are afraid of it."

"And some people wallow in it," Lizbeth added. "It took you a long time to get over yours."

Justin looked up from his wineglass. "Do you think I'm over it, Mother?"

She smiled softly. "What I think is that when we suffer loss and pain, it makes us a different person. It's like a physical wound. When you break your leg, you're not the same afterward—you're left with a scar or a limp or an ache whenever it rains. At some point it heals—the scar is barely seen, the limp is hardly noticeable—but your body is still different. Altered. Not necessarily worse, I suppose, but still different. And at some point you accept the fact that this is your new body; you realize you can still run, just maybe not as fast or as long; and you move on. It's the same when we grieve, except no one can see the scar, not when it's raw and not when it heals. But it changes you just as much, and the change is permanent. And at some point you accept the change and realize this is the new you. Emotionally battered and bruised and maybe even forever heartsick, but you move on."

"I'm not as sure as you are that I've moved on."

"It doesn't mean you've forgotten. And it doesn't mean you're not still sad. Of course you are. The scar is permanent. But I've seen enough of you now . . . you've become a different person. And I think you've accepted this new you. I'm very glad about that."

It was the longest speech he'd ever heard his mother utter, and he loved her for it. He started to thank her, to tell her he hoped she was right, to say he thought she just might *be* right, but his downtime had ended. He hadn't gotten two hours; he'd barely gotten a full sixty minutes. He hadn't even finished the salad that Louise had made. Didn't matter. His cell phone was ringing, and when he pulled the phone out of his pocket and glanced at the caller ID, he knew he had to answer the call.

"Can I call you back?" Justin said. "I'm in the middle of dinner."

He got the answer he was expecting.

"I think your dinner's over," Billy DiPezio said. "Wrap the rest of it up to go."

"What's going on?"

"I'll pick you up in fifteen minutes. I'll tell you on the way."

"On the way where?" Justin asked.

"Drogin's lot," Billy said.

19

Billy DiPezio pulled his new Mercedes inside the wire mesh fence that surrounded the several acres of overgrown property known as Drogin's lot. As they stepped out of the car, Justin noticed that the night sky was particularly dark. There were few stars and the moon was hidden by fast-moving clouds. He was surprised to find that it was nearly nine-thirty. The slivers of moonlight that reached the ground gave the property an ominous feel. Not just the property, Justin thought. The world.

They were met by an FBI agent who didn't bother to introduce himself but led them toward two other agents. One of those agents was Norman Korkes, the agent whose jaw Justin had dislocated earlier that day. Agent Korkes nodded curtly at Justin but didn't speak. It was the other agent who spoke, after Billy introduced him as having just flown in from Washington, D.C.

"It's not a nice sight," Special Agent Zach Fletcher said.

Justin nodded but said nothing. Then he was led over to where Wanda Chinkle's body lay. She was unclothed and her skin was covered with severe bruises. Her chest and stomach were covered in swirls of blood, as were her right hand and her left shoulder. Justin inhaled quickly and deeply. His exhale was slow and uneven.

"You saw her earlier today," Agent Fletcher said.

Justin nodded again. He still wasn't quite ready or able to talk.

"What were you meeting about?"

"Do we have to have this conversation right here?" Justin finally said, looking down at Wanda's still form.

"Unfortunately we do," Agent Fletcher said. "At least for the moment. Look at the markings on her body."

The unnamed agent flicked on a flashlight and fixed the beam on Wanda. Justin let his eyes focus on her now. He had never seen Wanda naked when she was alive, and it seemed particularly obscene to have her exposed this way in death. He forced himself to survey her entire body until it began to seem less a real person than an inanimate object—the same mental exercise he used every time he covered a homicide. He was able to study her with a slightly clinical eye now, and Justin saw that what, at first glance, he'd taken to be smears of blood on her breasts, stomach, and one arm were, in fact, words. The writing was difficult to make out—the letters were not very clear, the blood had dripped and coagulated and mixed with dirt, and the writing was anything but smooth—but he could finally make out what it said. And when he had, he looked up at Agent Fletcher in disbelief.

"How do you read that?" Fletcher asked.

"Who wrote this?" Justin asked.

"We think she did. Look by her hand."

The flashlight beam moved several inches over and Justin saw a jagged piece of broken glass in the ground by Wanda's right hand.

"There're plenty of broken bottles and cans scattered throughout the whole lot. It looks as if, right before she died, she used that piece of glass to cut herself and do the best she could to write this message on the only canvas she had available."

"Her own body. Using her own blood."

Fletcher nodded. "Must have been pretty important to her." Then he said again, "Tell me what you read."

"It looks like 'JW,'" Justin said. "Then it looks like the word 'payback.'" "Payback" had been written in a combination of capital and small letters. Wanda had left out the *c*. "The next word looks like 'Hades.' Then 'Ali.'" "Hades" was also spelled using a combination of capital and small letters. "Ali" was straightforward. The *A* was capitalized. The *l* was just a straight line. The *i* was also a straight line, but smaller. It tailed off from the first two letters. It looked as if it was the last thing Wanda had managed to write. Justin repeated the whole thing aloud: "JW, Payback, Hades, Ali."

"Yup. That's what I see, too," Fletcher said. "You know what it means?"

Justin was still looking down at the body. He didn't look back up at Agent Fletcher. "Maybe," he said. "At least some of it. JW are my initials. She knew she didn't have a lot of time, so it could just be a shortened version of my name."

"We agree. That's why you're here. How about 'payback'?"

Now Justin looked up. "It's part of what we talked about earlier. When I met her in her car. She owed me something. At least I thought so. We talked about what the appropriate form of payback would be."

"Payback on whose end?"

"On hers."

"How about on yours?"

Justin shook his head in quiet disbelief. "You think I killed her? As payback? That's what you think this means?"

"You want to convince me otherwise?"

"Can I?" Justin asked.

"What was the topic of conversation when you met with her today?"

Justin decided there was no point in holding back. There were too many things he didn't understand about the murders of Evan Harmon and Ronald LaSalle and now of Wanda Chinkle and how they were connected. He wasn't really worried about FBI suspicion of his involvement. That would take care of itself. He wanted to know what the hell was going on. And the only way to begin to get any answers was to speak on the level.

"I came up here at the request of my father and my sister-in-law, Victoria LaSalle," Justin said. "I'm sure you know why."

"Her husband's murder. What was she expecting you to do?"

"I don't know. Basically, find out what happened."

"And what have you found out?"

"So far, not a thing," Justin said. "I've just begun talking to people.

Before Billy picked me up, I was at Ronald LaSalle's office, talking to the people who worked for him."

"Looking for something in particular?"

"Looking for absolutely anything that I could tie together. Just throwing a lot of shit against the wall and seeing if anything'll stick."

"What did Wanda tell you about the murder?"

"Nothing. In fact, she went out of her way to tell me nothing. She wanted to meet with me to tell me to stay away from the investigation."

"Why?"

Justin sighed. "For my own good."

Fletcher looked at him curiously.

"Look," Justin said. "We had a complicated relationship. We were friends, but we also had our differences. Sometimes our goals were not exactly in sync."

"You blamed her for the time you spend at Guantanamo last year."

"I didn't blame her," Justin said. "I knew she'd allowed it. Possibly even manipulated things so it would happen."

"And you didn't like that."

"No, I didn't. Would you?"

"So you killed her as payback."

"I told you. 'Payback' refers to our conversation today. She thought she was doing me a favor by warning me off Ronald LaSalle's murder." Again, Justin decided there was no point in holding back. Agent Fletcher had the look of someone well aware of what was going on around him. "And not just LaSalle. I'm involved in investigating the murder of Evan Harmon down in Long Island."

"You're involved in more than the investigation from what I hear."

"Whoever you're hearing that from doesn't know what he's talking about. Wanda knew the truth. She was telling me to back off that one as well."

"Because they're connected?"

"She wouldn't say. But it seems like a logical conclusion."

"And what was your response to her payback?"

"I told her it wasn't even close."

"Not good enough?"

"That's right."

"So you don't think she was pointing the finger at you?"

"I know she wasn't. I think she was trying to finish the job she started this afternoon." He looked down at her body. "What she did to herself isn't *about* me, it's a message *for* me."

"Hades and Ali. That's her payback to you."

"I think it might be, yes."

"Then what do they mean?"

Justin shook his head. "I don't have any fucking idea," he said.

He spent nearly two more hours with Agent Fletcher and Billy DiPezio back at Billy's office at the station house. First they made him go over his movements so they could verify Justin's whereabouts every second of the day from the moment he left Wanda's car. They examined every word that Justin could remember about his conversation with Wanda. They hammered away at the meaning of the words "Hades" and "Ali" with absolutely no luck or new insight. They went over every possible thing Justin could add to their understanding of Wanda's murder, and Justin was as cooperative as he could possibly be. He told them everything, except for one detail. He made no mention of his meeting with Bruno Pecozzi that afternoon. He wasn't sure why. It wasn't just to protect the big man, although he didn't feel any great desire to simply throw Bruno to the wolves with no cause. The truth is, he thought there might be cause. Wanda had insinuated that Bruno was playing some kind of role in all this. Justin decided he needed to know what that role was before he gave up any more information.

Somewhere around 12:30 A.M. Fletcher finally told him he could go. As he was leaving, Billy told him that they'd speak soon. Fletcher said, "Wanda's advice was solid."

"About not getting involved," Justin said.

"That's right."

"I'll keep it in mind," Justin said.

"But you're not going to follow it, are you?"

"No," Justin said, "I'm not."

"Then I need a favor," Agent Fletcher said.

"You want me to do the FBI a favor?"

"All right," Fletcher said. "Let's consider it an offer more than a favor."

"I'm listening."

"Work with us."

Justin tried not to let his surprise show. "I think my hearing must be bad. You want to repeat that?"

"Wanda Chinkle was by the book. She was as straight as it got. But there are things that don't add up here. That aren't strictly by the book."

"Like what?"

"You met Agent Korkes. Well . . . you did more than just meet him, but let's save that. Wanda was his superior and she told him to contact you off the record. She didn't want the Bureau to know she was talking to you. Why was that?"

"She told me I came with a lot of baggage. That the Bureau wouldn't be happy that she was talking to me."

"That's bullshit," Fletcher said.

"It's what she told me."

"Yeah, yeah, I believe it's what she said. But it's total bullshit. You've had some run-ins with us, yeah, and maybe you've stuck it to us once or twice. But you think we actually go around thinking 'ooohhh, big, tough, scary cop from little tiny town on Long Island, we better stay away from him'? You don't have to answer, I'll tell you right now: No, we don't. You're not on our radar."

"So why would she say it?"

"You said she knew you well, knew how to manipulate things. I think she was jerking you around again. She tells you to stay away from something, what's that do to you? I mean as the big, tough, scary cop that you are."

"All right. I get your point," Justin said. "She tells me to stay away, she knows that's not going to work."

"No. It means you're going to do the opposite: jump right into the center of the action."

"But if she wanted help, wanted me to do something, why wouldn't she just ask? Why the secrecy and the manipulation? It's an investigation I was already involved in."

"I'm not sure. But if I had to guess, it's 'cause there was something she didn't want us to know. Her reports on this investigation were not detailed. She had sources we weren't aware of. She was working on her own, which wasn't what Wanda did. So I'd say there was something she was worried about internally."

"Like what?"

"Don't know. Maybe leaks. Maybe political bullshit. We have a lot of ways we fuck up."

Justin was starting to like Agent Fletcher. Well, no, he thought, that was an exaggeration. But he was beginning to trust him a little bit. "So what is it you want me to do?"

"Wanda was a great agent. And she thought there was something you could do that we couldn't. I don't have a clue what that is, but whatever it is, why don't we work together and try to find out?"

"Work directly with you?"

"Partly. But I'm going back to D.C. We'll assign an agent to partner with you." When Justin hesitated, Agent Fletcher barreled on. "You asked Billy here to give you some kind of bullshit title so you could link yourself to the murder investigations. Well, I'm offering you more than that. I'll give you FBI backing. And we'll make it clear to anyone who gets in your way that you are working with us and have our support."

"That does have a certain amount of appeal."

"Yeah," Fletcher said. "I once met Larry Silverbush. I thought it might."

"Do I get some kind of cool badge?"

"I guess this conversation's over," Fletcher said. "We'll have an agent contact you over the next couple of days. And I know it goes against your nature, but this time try to play well with others, okay?"

Agent Fletcher stuck out his hand and Justin shook it. Even Billy looked impressed by the result of the conversation.

Justin went home, found his parents waiting up. He told them what had happened to Wanda. He saw his mother go pale, saw his father's hand go to her back to pat her, to comfort her, to support her. He saw his mother regroup quickly. Both of his parents told him to go on, so without giving them many details, he told them that he thought Wanda's death might be connected to what had happened to Ronald. Possibly even to what had happened to Evan Harmon. He told them to say nothing to Vicky, told them, in fact, to say nothing whatsoever to anyone. He told them he was exhausted and needed to get some sleep, said they should do the same. And he told them he'd be gone by the time they woke up the next morning, that he'd be on his way back to East End Harbor.

His mother kissed him on the top of the head. His father shook his hand. They both went off to bed.

As tired as he was, Justin didn't go right to sleep. He sat in his parents' living room for another hour or so, drinking two large snifters of brandy and piecing together the day's events, replaying them over and over again in his mind.

At three in the morning, he called Vicky LaSalle. As soon as she answered the phone, he knew that he'd awakened her. The thick sound of sleep was in her throat.

"Vicky, it's Jay. I'm sorry if I woke you up."

"What time's it?"

"It's late. It's too late to have called but—"

"Took a pill. Took a pill to sleep."

"I'm sorry. That's good. You need sleep. But I wanted to let you know that I'm going home tomorrow. Back to New York. But I had to tell you . . . Seeing you . . . Jesus, you look so much like her . . . It was like talking to her again . . ."

"You're drunk." She sounded more alert now.

"No. I'm not."

"Been drinking."

"Yeah. I've been drinking, but I'm not drunk. I just want you to know . . . I know what this means to you. I know what you're feeling. I'm not going to let you down. I'm not going to let *her* down again. It's important to me. *You're* important to me. I just want you to know that."

He waited for a response. There was none. It took him a few seconds to realize that she'd hung up. He had no idea what she'd heard or hadn't heard. And he realized it didn't really matter.

Justin went to bed a little after three-thirty. Woke up at six, showered, and headed for the airport, where he'd arranged for a small private plane to take him directly back to the East Hampton Airport, just a ten-minute drive from his home in East End Harbor.

At nine-fifteen on Sunday morning, he walked into his East End house.

At nine-twenty, he called Leona Krill, told her he was no longer on suspension because he was resigning from the East End Harbor PD. She actually tried to argue him out of it, but he told her that he already had another job. He didn't tell her what it was, just told her that she and Silverbush would be seeing him around.

He went into the kitchen, made a pot of strong coffee, helped himself to a three-quarter full mug, and poured the rest into a white thermos he kept by the stove. He took the mug and sat in his living room. Justin wrote the words "Ali" and "Hades" on a yellow pad. He sat and stared at those two words. His only movement was to go back to the kitchen from time to time to refill his mug.

At noon he still didn't have the faintest clue what the words meant. But he did have the beginning of a plan.

Wanda had come to him because she had wanted something. And even as she was dying, Wanda was trying to get what she wanted. She had mutilated herself and spent the last minutes of her life in what had to be an excruciating exercise in order to give him a clue as a way of telling him how to get to the bottom of all this. She knew what he wanted as payback. What he always wanted. The truth. Of that much he was certain.

He knew what he was going to do.

He was going to get his payback.

He was going to find the truth.

He was going to solve this goddamn puzzle and he was going to help the woman he'd been sleeping with who was accused of murder; the woman who blamed him and hated him for the death of her sister; and the woman who'd just been murdered, whose last moments on earth were spent trying to communicate with him.

That's what he was going to do.

Justin wanted a drink.

He decided instead to stay sober.

He went to the kitchen, found an open can of Coke in the fridge. He took a sip—it wasn't much on fizz, but it was cold and sweet, so he took a long swig. Without thinking he rested against the stove and then instantly jumped back. He'd left the damn burner on again and had burned his palm. Swearing, he went upstairs to his medicine cabinet and put a Band-Aid on the already forming small blister.

Justin went back to the kitchen, finished the flat Coke in one more gulp.

Then he decided it was time to go to work.

PART TWO

20

It was early Sunday evening by the time Justin was organized.

The pace frustrated him because the process was so slow, but he knew the value of being thoroughly prepared before moving on to the next step: action. So he spent his day reading and rereading everything he had, as well as new material he took off the Net. He made lists of people and places and tried to get an overall sense of the chronology of the events. It was the most effective way to reveal the patterns he was seeking. It's the way he worked. First, find the patterns. Next, find the motive. Finally, find the passion. At some point, all three elements would intersect. They always did. And when that happened, he'd have his murderer. He'd have the truth he was seeking.

He had now read, in much closer detail, the pages he'd already printed out giving the history of the Harmon family. He'd gone through the information that Ellen Loache had provided for him. As he read he'd taken notes, kept track of any potential links and connections between all the disparate parts that were making up this complicated whole. When he was done, he entered it all into his computer—the simple act of repetition and transferring information helped to clarify and focus things in his mind.

Wanda had been keeping tabs on Evan Harmon before he'd been killed. She'd told him that while they were sitting in her car. Justin had a good memory for dialogue—he'd trained himself to remember specific words in conversations rather than simply the general tone or information, knowing that nuance and accuracy could make all the difference when going back to interpret something. She had said that "I" had been tracking Evan. She had not said "we." That probably meant that the investigation into Evan's activities was not official and that the Bureau knew relatively little about this. That jibed with what Fletcher had said—that she was holding information back. It meant there was something politically sensitive involved, possibly some kind of internal corruption or compromise. Justin needed to know why Evan had come into conflict with the Feds. That was essential info. He was expecting an agent to contact him soon. He'd get that info, he hoped, from his new "partner." Justin didn't have any illusions as to what the working relationship would be. Special Agent Zach Fletcher might be better than most, but that didn't mean Fletcher was dealing without keeping an ace, or even two, up his sleeve. The Feds might indeed be wanting to use him to do some of their dirty work, Justin knew. But by bringing him inside and assigning someone to work with him, it meant they could also keep an eye on him. Keep him under control. Maybe even find out if he was involved in this weird triangle of death in a deeper way than he was admitting.

It was a trade-off he was willing to accept: access for limited freedom. But he had to take advantage of that access for this to work. So first up: Find out what the hell the Feebs wanted with Abby's husband.

But there was more to Evan Harmon than whatever he'd been doing recently to attract attention. People did not operate in vacuums. They were shaped and formed by family and friends and events. Justin needed to know what had shaped Evan so he could understand the way the man thought. It wasn't just action that formed patterns, it was thought processes. Justin understood that he needed to know a lot more about the first victim.

Next on his agenda: Ronald LaSalle.

Ronald was linked to Evan. They communicated regularly and they did business together. Justin had to find out exactly what the business was. In Ellen Loache's folder were names of people and businesses that had to be checked out. Someone on that list would prove to be a critical connection between the two men and the three murders. He also had to find out if Ronald had been involved in Evan's illegal activity. And if so, how deeply. Was he a peripheral player who had stumbled onto something by mistake or could he have been involved at the very core?

Third on his list to explore: Rockworth and Williams. The firm was the single element in this entire mix that appeared repeatedly and had tentacles that reached out to all parties. Justin had learned an important lesson as a homicide investigator: People killed for love or money. It's what everything boiled down to. In this case, Rockworth and Williams seemed to be the source of—or at least the common link to—all the people who were involved. Evan Harmon had worked there. His father had worked there. Evan's company, Ascension, used Rockworth as its primary broker for its hedge fund investments. Forrest Bannister, Ascension's CFO and the man who found Evan's body, had connections to Rockworth. Ellis St. John was R&W's link to Ascension, and he had disappeared.

Justin had to get inside Rockworth and Williams. Had to talk to H. R. Harmon and Lincoln Berdon. Most of all, he knew he had to find Ellis St. John. Right now, St. John's disappearance made him the prime suspect in Evan Harmon's murder and possibly the other two as well. But Justin knew the fact that he was gone had other ramifications, too. St. John might have fled because he was afraid. Or he, too, might have suffered the same fate as his two fellow Wall Streeters. Justin understood that if he did find Ellis St. John, he might not find him alive. Right now, though, he had to work as if the R&W employee was on the lam. And involved in the murders.

Then there were the two official suspects. Justin knew he couldn't overlook them. He did not believe in Larry Silverbush's solution to the crime: that Abby and Dave Kelley had committed a crime of passion. Or even one of convenience. Right after Evan's body had been discovered, it had been a plausible theory. But now it was too myopic a view. The case had expanded, gotten more complicated. There were too many other angles that had overtaken the DA's quick fix. And too many other deaths. Right now, Justin had one big advantage over Silverbush and his investigative crew: It was unlikely that they had any suspicion that the two murders in Rhode Island were connected to Evan Harmon's slaying. That probability made all the difference in the world. Nonetheless, Justin knew that he couldn't dismiss Abby's and Kelley's involvement. Just because things had gotten more complicated didn't mean that they weren't involved at some level. He didn't believe that they were, but he couldn't ignore the possibility. He couldn't afford to ignore anything right now.

Justin also knew he had to talk to Bruno. He was still waiting for Billy DiPezio to send him the results of the fingerprint search he'd asked for—a search that would, Justin hoped, identify the man who'd tried to shoot Bruno. The big man was another piece to this strange puzzle, and Justin had to find out where that piece fit. Bruno had said he'd appear once Justin was back in East End Harbor, and Justin knew that Bruno was, in his own way, a man of his word. So he could wait for Bruno to keep his word. At least for a little while.

And finally, he had to find the meaning of Wanda's message to him.

Just for the hell of it, he had googled the words that Wanda had managed to scrawl on her body: "Hades" and "Ali."

Hades had 9,850,000 mentions on the main page. There were 176,000 different references to the use of the word "Hades" in song lyrics; there was a Hades computer software program; paintings of the god Hades in museums all over the world; poems and books about Hades dating back hundreds of years; food products named Hades and a Hades Bloody Mary mix. It was impossible even to begin to sift through the various choices. The only thing he knew about Hades was the mythological aspect: it was the name, in Greek mythology, for both the underworld and the god of the underworld. So what Justin did was to pick the very first and easiest Google reference and enter it into his computer. He didn't really know why he bothered, except he liked the sound of it, and including it in his file—seeing it whenever he went back in to refer to his notes—would work to keep his anger about Wanda fresh and present and alive. He decided to title the entire casebook document *Hades,* and he typed in the following from something called the "Hades homework page": "HADES: Zeus's brother and ruler of the underworld and the dead. Also called Pluto—God of Wealth."

Justin thought it was fitting. The god of wealth and the ruler of the dead. Sounded like a god whose path he might cross one of these days.

Googling the name "Ali" produced 216,000,000 mentions. He managed to scroll through about forty of them—one-line descriptions of sites for info on Muhammad Ali, Ali G, NASA's advanced land imager (acronym ALI), Ali Baba, and an actor named Ali Suliman who was in the film *Paradise Now* (which, oddly enough, Justin had gone to see with Abby Harmon at the old-fashioned, arty East End Harbor movie theater that always smelled of grape drink and disinfectant). Justin gave up fairly quickly on this second search, deciding it was a reasonably safe bet that neither Muhammad Ali nor Ali G had anything to do with his murder investigations. He found absolutely nothing there he deemed worth adding to his lists.

Restless, he reached for his cell phone and dialed Abby's number in the city. She had not returned his calls from yesterday. He got her answering machine again, left a briefer message than his last one. "It's Jay. I'm in East End and I'd like to talk to you." She knew his number, so he didn't bother leaving it. The fact that he even considered leaving it made him realize that the relationship had shifted and was already different. So after a very brief pause, all he said was, "So call me. Bye." He then called her cell, which also immediately went to voice mail. He repeated, almost word for word, what he'd left on her home machine. Then he hung up, dissatisfied.

He paced around the room, not exactly sure what was fueling his impatience. At 7:30 P.M. Justin forced himself to sit back down at the computer. He made a short To Do list: an abbreviated version of everything he'd already entered, now turning them into specific tasks, in order of priority. This final list read:

1. Evan Harmon—background; Fed investigation
2. Ronald LaSalle—business connections to Harmon
3. Hades
4. Ali
5. Rockworth and Williams—Ellis St. John, H. R. Harmon, Lincoln Berdon

6. Billy DiPezio—print results
7. Dave Kelley
8. Abby
9. Bruno

There was nothing more he could realistically get done tonight except perhaps for some more reading, so he began to think about dinner. He had nothing in his fridge or freezer—and the lack of anything even remotely domestic in his house made him think about the differences in the life he led from the one led by his parents. Right about now Louise would be setting a delicious meal and an excellent wine on the table before Jonathan and Lizbeth. No one was going to serve Justin the bottle of Pete's Wicked Ale and the shitty Chinese food he was about to go out and get and eat straight out of the cardboard carton.

Choices, he thought. Everything was about choices.

He'd made his. Maybe he should have made some different ones along the way.

Maybe it wasn't too late to make different choices for the future.

Then again, maybe it wasn't about choices. Maybe it was about fate. Or randomness. Maybe it was just about doing the best you could to control the uncontrollable.

His thoughts were interrupted by a knock on his front door. Three knocks. Two were rather soft and tentative. The last one was harder, more forceful, as if whoever it was wasn't really sure about wanting to come in, then gathered up some courage and decided it was okay after all. Justin didn't know who could be showing up unexpectedly. He was not exactly Mr. Sociable. He supposed there were several people who wouldn't mind talking to him at the moment. Larry Silverbush. Leona Krill. Maybe even Bruno. So he rose from his chair—not without some effort; another reminder that he'd better get to the gym sooner rather than later—and went to open the door.

If there was one person he was not expecting to see—now or ever again—it was the woman standing in his doorway.

"Are you going to invite me in?" the woman said.

Justin didn't answer. He just stared. At first it was a stare of surprise. But the longer it went on the harder his eyes turned.

"You're going to have to let me in sooner or later," she said. "After all, we're partners."

Justin's first words to her in over a year were: "What the hell are you talking about?"

"They didn't tell you?"

And from the look on his face, the stunned silence, she saw that he hadn't been told, that they'd left all this up to her, so she met his hard stare with a softer one of her own and broke the news to him herself.

"The FBI," Reggie Bokkenheuser said. "I'm the agent assigned to work with you."

Her hair was blonder now; it had been darker when he'd seen her last. It was more natural this way; seemed to fit her better. She'd let it grow some; it had gotten a little wilder looking. And she'd lost some weight; she looked stronger than she used to look, leaner and more muscular. Her blue eyes were the same, though—clear and lovely, if a bit sad, and her skin was smooth and tan, her neck short and not thin but somehow elegant. Her mouth had the same touch of sadness that her eyes had, but it also had the faint trace of a protective smirk. Her mouth and that smirk gave away the fact that she had a sense of humor. But they also kept the world at a distance. Yes, it was definitely the same woman who'd been planted on Justin in the East End Harbor police department a little over a year ago and whom he'd taken into his confidence and to whom he'd made love and who'd led him into a trap that saw him wind up in Guantanamo's prison. The same woman who'd shot and killed Ray Lockhardt, the manager of the local airport, under orders from her superior at the FBI. The same woman he'd arrested for that murder.

And the same woman he realized—looking at her standing on his doorstep, her lips parted slightly, her thin smile hopeful and nervous and, as always, lopsided—could still make his stomach flutter and make his knees buckle ever so slightly.

Damn her.

Damn them.

Damn, damn, damn them all.

He didn't let her in. At least not immediately. Justin went into town to get Chinese food and insisted she come with him. He didn't say it, but he didn't want Regina Bokkenheuser to stay alone in his house. Even for the twenty minutes it took him to get some fried rice and sesame chicken and cold noodles with sesame sauce. Even if it had taken one minute. He didn't know what she would do. What she might look for, what she might plant.

They didn't say one word while they were in the car or while they waited in the small take-out place for the food to be prepared. He wasn't ready to speak yet, and she followed his lead. His silence was fueled by anger. Hers was more placid—it was just a reaction to his, and it annoyed him even more that she knew him well enough to wait for his mood to change rather than challenge it.

When they returned to his house he set the food—dropping it, still in the brown paper bag—on the small dining table that sat in his living room. He went into the kitchen and when he returned with two bottles of beer she had already removed the food cartons from the bag and placed them on the table. He put one beer on the table in front of her.

"Thanks for remembering," she said.

"Fuck you," Justin said.

"Well," Reggie said, "at least we're talking."

He turned and went back into the kitchen, emerging moments later with silverware and two plates. He put the plates on the table and served himself some food. He made no effort to serve Reggie, just pushed the white cartons closer to her.

They ate slowly and silently. She was halfway through the food on her plate when she looked up and said, "Are you ready yet?"

"For what?"

"For a conversation."

"No," he said. Then, putting his fork down, he said, "I thought you were in prison."

She shook her head. "No."

"How is that possible?"

"I told you, Jay, or I tried to tell you, you just wanted to see me in jail so bad you wouldn't listen to me."

"You belonged in jail."

"I was doing my job."

"Nice job. Killing an innocent man."

She winced. "Yes. Something I'll have to live with the rest of my life. And it won't be easy. But I thought I was doing it for national security reasons. I thought the orders were coming all the way from the White House. I was lied to, and I have to stay awake at night knowing I believed the lies. I was manipulated, and maybe I was stupid, but I did what I was trained to do and what I hope I could do again if I had to for the right reasons."

Justin didn't say anything, even when Reggie said, "You've killed people before. People who didn't deserve to die." And when he looked up sharply, ready to respond in anger, she said, "You think we don't know what happened to Lieutenant Colonel Warren Grimble, military intelligence?"

Justin went silent for a moment. Grimble had been the man in charge of his interrogation at Gitmo. Justin had managed to learn his identity. And then he'd done more than that. He was too weak to act himself, so he hired Bruno to do the job. Lieutenant Warren Grimble had disappeared. Justin knew that the disappearance was permanent. Bruno was good at his job.

"He was not what I'd call an innocent man," he said.

"Maybe. But what he did to you, he was doing because he thought it was the right thing to do, because he was under orders to do it."

"No," Justin said quietly. "There are no orders that would cover what he did to me."

"Jay," Reggie said, just as quietly and just as urgently, "after you arrested me, the FBI got me released from custody almost immediately. It wasn't even a question. The slate was wiped clean. The fact is, they examined what happened as thoroughly as it was possible to examine a case. I don't have to tell you what the ramifications were after everything that occurred. They thought I did a good enough job that not only was

I exonerated, they assigned me to New York. That's where I've been the last year."

"You did a good job," he said. "I'd never deny that. You did one helluva job."

"I saved your life," she said. "Or are you forgetting that?"

"I haven't forgotten anything."

"I wanted to come see you," she told him. "Almost every day for the past year, that's pretty much all I thought about. But I knew you wouldn't want to see me or hear anything I had to say."

"You're right on that one."

"I asked for this assignment. I want you to know that. When word came down, I asked for it."

"And they *gave* it to you?"

"Sometimes God works in mysterious ways."

"I don't believe in God."

"Neither do I. So I guess it's the FBI that's pretty mysterious." Reggie finished off the bottle of beer in front of her and said, "I wanted this job because I care about you. No matter what you think of what I did or what you think of me, I care about you. And I think I owe you something. I'd like to make it up to you—what I did and what happened."

"All of a sudden I've got a lot of people trying to make things up to me."

"I know. That's one of the reasons why they agreed to send me here."

"I'm not following."

"The people I work for aren't as dumb as you like to think they are. They can be pretty insightful. And pretty manipulative."

"I still don't follow."

"They think you'll trust me."

He just laughed. A quick, harsh burst of a laugh.

"Because of what happened to Wanda. And with us. Because of what happened . . . what's happened in your past. They think you'll trust me because you'll want to trust me. And maybe want to help me and protect me."

"Out of guilt?"

"I said they can be smart and manipulative."

"And what do you think, Reggie? Do you think I'm going to go along with this because I feel guilty about other women in my life?"

She did her best to draw on her lopsided smile. "I'm hoping you'll go along with it because of my natural charm." And when he said nothing, didn't change expression, just stared at her with that hard stare of his, she said, "Then how about the fact that I've already called Larry Silverbush and told him that you're working with me and that we expect him to give you his full cooperation?"

"Full cooperation with someone he's looking at as part of his murder investigation?"

"Not anymore. I told him we've cleared you of any involvement."

"And is that true?"

"The 'we' part probably isn't. But I'm the agent in charge now, so it's my call. And I don't think you're involved in any way."

"Why not?"

"I don't think you'd kill anyone or anything because of a woman. Hell, I know you were falling for me just a little bit . . . and you tried to send me to prison."

"What is it you don't think I'm capable of? Falling in love or killing someone out of love?"

"I don't know, Jay. I didn't get to know you well enough to make that call."

She closed her eyes once, opened them quickly, did it again. He remembered that she did that—batted her long lashes and widened her already large, round, blue eyes. She thought it made her look irresistible. The thing of it was, it did make her look pretty goddamn irresistible.

Justin swatted at the plate of food in front of him and sent it flying off the table. When she jumped, he anticipated her move, reached out, and grabbed her by her collar, pulling her closer to him over the table.

"Reggie, let's get a few things straight." His voice was low and ragged. "I don't trust you. I doubt that I ever will. And I won't be charmed by you, no matter how many times you blink those blue eyes at me. I don't feel guilty, and even if I did, it wouldn't make one fucking bit of difference. And I'm sure as hell not going to sleep with you or fall in love with you, not even a little bit."

She didn't look frightened or even surprised at his outburst. She just gave him that lopsided smile. "But you'll work with me?" she said.

He loosened his grip on her collar. "Yes. I'll work with you."

"Why?" Reggie asked.

"Because right now I need you to get information and to get inside the investigation. And I can use you to help me figure out what the hell's going on."

"And that's the only reason?"

"That's the only reason."

"It's a start," she said. "Now . . . shall we clean up the mess you made?"

The thing is: they worked well together. They had in the past and they did now. Reggie was meticulous and tireless, and while her instincts weren't quite as acute as his, they were fine. And she could cut through the bullshit to make a point when it needed making.

He printed up his notes and gave them to her to read. As she pored over them, she looked up from time to time to ask him questions: about Evan and Abby, about his relationship with Abby, about the conversations he'd had on his one visit to Rockworth and Williams. Her questions were sharp and clinical and on point. When she was done looking at his lists and written comments, he handed over the various folders of information he'd collected and told her she should go through it all over the next twenty-four hours. She said she would, and he knew she'd have a worthwhile take on what she read. He told her what his plans were for the next day and he told her what he wanted her to concentrate on. She agreed.

"Now," she said, "what do you need from me?"

He told her he wanted to know everything that Wanda knew about Evan Harmon's business. He wanted to know why Evan was being investigated.

"We don't have a lot," she told him. "And what we have isn't all that firm. Wanda wasn't reporting on a lot of what she was doing. And one of the problems is that Evan Harmon came in through the back door. He wasn't who we were investigating."

"Who were you looking at?"

"Leonardo Rubenelli. Your friend Bruno's boss."

"I know who he is. You guys have been trying to get something on him for most of my lifetime. What is it now?"

"Money laundering."

"And what the hell is the connection between Evan Harmon and Lenny Rube? How'd they even cross into the same world?"

"Come on, Jay. You should be able to come up with that one. Who could link a New York hedgehogger with the head of the New England mob?"

Justin shook his head. "Ronald LaSalle? I don't believe it. Just because he was a money guy in Providence? My *father's* a money guy in Providence."

"You should check with your pal Bruno."

"Since he's not here, why don't you tell me what he'd say?"

"I don't know what he'd say. I don't have the same high regard that you do for his character," Reggie told him. "But I know he's been dealing with LaSalle. We have the two of them meeting several times over the past year. And we know that Bruno was here in East End Harbor for several weeks last year. Hell, you and I know that from personal experience. It would have been easy for him to cross paths with Harmon."

"Do you have proof of any direct contact between Bruno and Evan?"

"Only according to Wanda's reports. But they weren't incident specific."

" 'Incident specific.' Nice phrase. I like that," he said.

"We don't have an eyewitness—is that better? At least none we know about. It seems as if Wanda did. But we can't ask her."

Justin frowned. "Evan and Ronald were laundering money for Lenny Rube—and Bruno was the go-between? It just doesn't add up."

"Why not?"

"From everything I've been told, Ron LaSalle was as straight as they come."

"And who did the telling? The people who worked for him? His wife? Maybe they have a lot to gain by making us think that."

"It's possible." He was thinking about sitting in Vicky's living room, listening to her talk about her husband. She wasn't lying. She might have been duped, but she wasn't lying.

"What else doesn't add up?" Reggie asked.

"Bruno. He's not exactly the go-between type."

"That's right. That's why we think he's involved in a lot bigger way."

"You think Bruno killed them?"

"We think it's a good possibility."

"I like the way you use the all-protective plural, Reggie. Do you ever think something all by yourself?"

"I've been out of the loop on this case, Jay. I was brought in at the last minute, so I can't even say I'm fully briefed. I'm just telling you what I've been told so far. The more involved I am, the more I'll learn and be able to think for myself. And the more I'll be able to tell you."

"All right, so give me some more groupthink on Bruno."

"We know he was dealing with LaSalle on a regular basis. And we know he was using LaSalle to invest millions of dollars. Some of the investments were corporate investments. LaSalle was dealing with Bruno as if he were an institutional investor."

"Bruno?" Justin had to smile. "He's not what I'd call the corporate type."

"Our point exactly. One of the companies investing has Rubenelli on its board."

Justin sighed. "So you started investigating, looking for a way to get to Lenny Rube."

Reggie nodded.

"I still don't see the link to Harmon," Justin said.

"I told you, we don't have it firm. But it exists. We know from Wanda's notes that some of the Rubenelli money was going through Harmon's hedge fund."

"If you know that, why don't you have it firm?"

Reggie looked embarrassed. Finally she just shrugged and said, "You know what it's been like since 9/11. If it's not terrorism related, no one actually gives a damn. At least at the top levels. We've had a lot of our resources taken away from us. So we haven't been able to make a financial paper trail."

"So good old mob crimes and killings don't really matter anymore?"

"Not so much, no. But Wanda wouldn't let go of this. She thought it was big. And she was working on making the connections."

"Which is why she got killed."

"That's what we're assuming. And that's why we've moved this to high priority."

"Come on, even Lenny Rube's not stupid enough to off a federal agent. Bruno certainly isn't that dumb."

"Again, you have a higher regard for your friends than we do."

"I wouldn't exactly call Lenny my friend."

"And Bruno?"

" 'Friend' is too strong a word. But just because we're on opposite sides of the fence, I don't underestimate him." He was still shaking his head. "It makes sense on the surface, but it's off. For one thing, even the way the murders were done. It's not Bruno's style. One thing you can count on, he wouldn't have left Wanda alive long enough to do what she did."

"Nice that you know his modus operandi so well."

"It may not be nice, but it's meaningful. Especially if your theory's based on the fact that Bruno was killing for the family."

"Am I missing something? Isn't that what he does for a living?"

Justin sighed and said, "Look, I didn't tell your guy Fletcher everything when we had our little chat yesterday."

Reggie said nothing. There was just the cock of her head to the left and the fluttering of her eyelashes.

"I'm still not sure I want him to have this info. So I want to know if it'll stay with you," Justin said.

"I work for them."

"But you're partnering with me."

"That's not fair, Jay. You're putting me in an untenable position."

"Sure I am. And what do I give a shit about fair? You want me to trust you, tell me that you'll keep this between us."

"This is a test?"

"Pass-fail. One time only."

She chewed on her lip for a moment, did her blinking thing, then she nodded.

"You lie to me, our partnership's over," he said.

"I get it. You're not exactly subtle."

"Okay," Justin said. And he told her what happened at Dolce when he'd met with Bruno.

When he was finished, she said, "Who was it?"

"I don't know yet. I got prints and I asked Billy to run 'em before anything had happened with Wanda and before I'd talked to Fletcher."

"You're unbelievable. How did you get prints off this guy?"

"He was reading some travel guide at the table, part of his cover. I took it on my way out. When I gave it to Billy, I didn't have any idea he might be connected to Harmon or even LaSalle."

"It was just you being curious."

"Just me being a cop."

"Most cops wouldn't have left that guy there to meet his fate."

"I did what I thought I had to do."

"Which is usually your choice."

"Yes," Justin said. "That's usually my choice. And one of my reasons was that Bruno said something that made me think I was involved."

"And that was . . . ?"

"He told me that there were people who didn't like that he was talking to me."

"Why?"

"I don't know. But that was reinforced when I saw Wanda. Or at least I thought it was. She knew I'd talked to Bruno. I thought it was because she was keeping tabs on me—I thought that was all part of her warning me away. Now I realize she was following Bruno—tailing him, not me. Or bugging him, more likely."

"What have you gotten back from DiPezio?"

"Nothing yet," Justin said. "I kind of downplayed it. Didn't really want him getting overcurious." And then he said, "Oh, screw it," and went to the phone and dialed.

"What?" Billy DiPezio said when he answered the phone. "You want a raise to two dollars a week?"

"I'm checking up on the fingerprints I asked you to run," Justin said. "I know you're a half-assed department, but I thought maybe you could do something on time."

"Kinda late for you to be calling, don't you think?" Billy said. "Especially on a Sunday. And especially for something that didn't seem too important yesterday."

"It might be a little more important than I thought," Justin admitted.

"Why don't you have your hot-shit Fed friends run it, now that you're workin' so closely with 'em?"

"I would if I hadn't been a moron and given the thing to you."

"You got no gratitude, you know that," Billy said. "But I'll get you the results in the morning. And don't blame me if you don't like 'em."

"What?" Justin said. "You already know something?"

"Hold on a second, will you?" Justin heard the sound of glass touching glass and a woman's voice, laughing. No. Giggling. Definitely giggling. Billy had been married for something like twenty-five years and Justin was fairly sure his wife didn't giggle like that.

"Billy," Justin repeated, "you know something about this guy already?"

"I don't know shit," Billy said. "But I figure the way your life's goin', you're not gonna like the results whatever they are."

Justin hung up and looked at his watch. Past midnight. He didn't know how Billy did it. He'd be out drinking until two or three this morning and he'd be sharp as a tack and on the job by seven-thirty. Justin was finding that harder and harder to manage. Hell, he was finding it harder just to stay awake past ten at night. As if on cue, Reggie yawned.

"I think we might have to finish this conversation tomorrow," she said. "I'm pretty beat."

"Where are you staying?" he asked.

"No house this time around. The drawback to not being undercover. I've got a room at the Fisherman. Cheap but really, really ugly."

There was an awkward silence. They both stood facing each other, maybe two feet apart. The distance felt a lot farther at the same time it felt a lot closer.

"You need a ride?" he asked.

"Got a car."

"You want one more beer before you go?" He heard his voice go dry for just an instant. *Idiot*, he thought. *What are you, in high school? Stay away from this one. Don't go there.*

She said quietly, "Do you want me to stay and have one more beer, Jay?"

"No," he said. "I don't."

"Then good night."

"Good night," he said.

He watched her from his living room window as she walked to her car parked on the street. It wasn't anything fancy. Maybe a VW. He kept watching as she got in the driver's seat and then drove away in the direction of her motel.

He took a deep breath. Went to his phone and dialed the number for Abby Harmon's cell phone. He got the same voice message he'd heard over the past two days. When the message ended and he heard the tone, Justin didn't say anything. He just stared at his receiver and then hung up.

He picked two songs to play on his computer, "Ends" by Everlast. And "Things Have Changed" by Dylan. He turned the volume way up.

The rap music was strangely soothing to him. And equally disturbing. He closed his eyes and got caught up in the sad rhythm of the song as he thought about what they were saying, how everything seemed to be about the ends.

Sometimes kids did indeed get murdered for the ends.

And he wondered if the all-wise Bob Dylan was right once again.

People were crazy. And people were strange. Justin knew that he used to care, too. He just wasn't sure if things had changed.

He took another deep breath.

Then he put both songs on again and went and had a beer all on his own.

21

Ling stared at Togo. His face was impassive. She thought she knew everything about him, thought she understood every nuance of his body language and each and every tic, grimace, stare, or smile he was able to muster. But she couldn't tell now if his complete lack of emotion was because he had been humiliated earlier and was angry, because he was trying to save face in front of her, or because he was trying to hide the fact that he found the woman they were watching—the blond woman coming out of the policeman's house—attractive.

He had never indicated to her that he had ever desired another woman. But she could see that this one fascinated him. She was so American, so confident looking, so casual in her sexuality.

Ling realized that she was wet between her legs. She didn't know if it was because she was thinking about Togo and this other woman or if it was because she was remembering the way he'd been humiliated, thinking about how vulnerable he had been in the big office building.

She was the reason for his humiliation.

And knowing that made her even more aroused.

They had been summoned to give a report, an update on their activities. They went to a big glass building that seemed to rise nearly to the sun. They had never met there before, it was a new place for them, and it was nearly empty. Almost no one was working on the summer weekend. A security guard had instructions to send them up in the elevator, and when they got out on a high floor, they were met by another security guard and shown to a wonderful room, with thick carpeting, many television screens built into the paneled walls, and a black marble table that shone like polished glass.

They were kept waiting before the familiar man had come into the room. Ling knew his name. And she knew that he was rich and had much power. That was all she really knew about him. Except that he was old. But even at his age, he stood straight, and his face was so chiseled it looked as if it were made from stone. There was something about this man that made her want to obey him. She did not understand why, although she had a vague inkling that the kind of power he possessed was comparable to hers, possibly even greater. Whenever he needed them, they were told where to meet. They were told to do whatever he asked, to follow his instructions exactly as he gave them. And he usually gave them in Chinese. He spoke Cantonese and it was quite good. Not perfect but reasonable. And he spoke it confidently. During their meetings he never said much. He asked several questions, told them what they were to do next. That's all. But she was always impressed with the way he communicated with them. He used their native tongue far more often than he used his own. She assumed that was for Togo's benefit; her English was far better than his. Sometimes Ling actually believed that Togo didn't speak English. She knew he understood it. She spoke to him in English sometimes, and, although he always responded in Hunanese, he knew what she was asking or saying. But sometimes this man spoke in English and Togo never acknowledged comprehension. So when the man spoke in English, he usually spoke to Ling.

This time she remembered he spoke to Togo in Cantonese. He ignored her almost completely. "Tell me how it went with the FBI woman," and Togo had said that everything had gone well. That's when the man pulled out an American newspaper. He showed them the headline. It was all about the unattractive woman, the one that Ling had left to die with dignity. She saw nothing wrong with what the paper said, but the man said the woman had lived long enough to send a message. He told her what the paper did not reveal: that the woman had used her own blood to write words on her body. He told them the words—he said them in English, he did not translate—but they meant nothing to Ling. She did not know if Togo understood their meaning because he said nothing and did nothing. But according to the man, what the unattractive woman had communicated was not a good thing. It meant she knew more than she was supposed to know. What she had done could cause them problems. Severe problems.

As the man spoke, he grew angrier. He shoved the paper in front of Togo's face. Togo didn't flinch. His eyes never even shifted. And when the man said, "What happened?" Togo didn't answer. He still did not move.

The older man then moved to Ling. He said, "I know it was not him. He would not leave someone alive to do this. But to you it is a game we are playing. It has always been a game for you."

She wondered what he meant by the word "always." Had he known her for so long? Had he been watching her since she was young? She wondered if he was too old to desire her. She could not tell from his eyes. He did not let his eyes ever linger on her.

He walked back over to Togo, stood inches away from him, said, "Are you so weak that you let her play games?" Then he suddenly slapped Togo hard across the face. The noise reverberated in the spacious room but still Togo did not move or respond. "It is your fault," he said to Togo. "She may be playing a game, but you are the one who is supposed to be in control. You are the one we trust to understand the stakes."

For one moment, Ling thought that the man standing in front of them was going to kill Togo. Pull out a gun and put a bullet in his brain. She knew that even then Togo would say nothing, would never acknowledge that what had happened had been her fault. He loved her too much to ever betray her.

But the man did not shoot anyone. She realized he was not the type of man to use a gun. That's not the way he controlled people. Instead, he just turned his back on them and said, "What's done can't be undone. We must try to learn from it and move on." He faced Togo and pointed at the newspaper and said, "What did you learn from her?"

Now Togo said his first words. He quietly explained that they had learned more names. Names that would bring them closer to what they were searching for.

"What names?"

Togo told him. The man nodded as if the information was not new. Still, he seemed pleased.

"You must be particularly careful now. The people on this list are more important than the others. And more dangerous. I want to learn what they know and where they go. They may be helpful, and if they are, use them. If they are not, you may leave them alone. But if they get in your way, if they stop you from doing what you must do, you do whatever is necessary. This is most definitely not a game. Do you understand?"

Togo nodded. And said the first words she'd ever heard him say in English: "I understand."

When the man turned away, Ling smiled.

And she was smiling again as she stood outside the house of one of the men on the list. The man the unattractive woman had said was a policeman.

Justin Westwood. That was the name. Ling could remember the way the woman had hissed the two words, almost as if speaking the name aloud would be her dying breath. Seeing him now, she recognized him. She had seen him on the street. He had been in the unattractive woman's car. She had seen his eyes that day and she had liked what she'd seen. He looked strong. And angry. Maybe a little bit careless.

He looked like he would, at some point, be fun to kill.

And so would the blond woman. The woman Togo was staring at so intently. Ling saw his chest rise and fall, the way it did after she had made love to him.

Togo was not thinking of saving face. He was not thinking of his anger. Not now.

He was thinking about the blond woman coming out of Justin Westwood's house late at night.

Ling wished she could stay in this Long Island town and see what happened to the policeman and the blond woman. They looked as if they would be very entertaining. But Togo had claimed them for himself. She and Togo were going to separate, that's what he'd told her after they left the man's office in the glass building. They needed to be apart so they could do their work more efficiently and more quickly.

Li Ling took a last look through Justin Westwood's window.

She did not want this to end too quickly. She was in no rush for this to end at all. And she decided she would not obey the old, chiseled man, not totally. Not one hundred percent.

This has been a very fun game, Ling thought. *And getting to be more fun all the time.*

22

Nowhere more than academia did people look upon cops with suspicion and distrust. It was because, Justin thought, there was a type of so-called intellectual who could not deal with the black-and-white world that cops often had to live in. Academicians lived in a far grayer world, where actions often had no consequences, where theory did not have to relate to reality. Reality was not something this type of person particularly cared about. Reality was too physical, too harsh; so it was best to separate from it. In the real world, one's mind could take one only so far before strength often took over. It was like being in the jungle and coming face-to-face with a lion. You might be a lot smarter than the lion, but the lion had far sharper teeth. And was probably hungry.

Quentin Quintel, the dean of Melman Preparatory Academy, fell most definitely into this category, Justin decided. He was a man frightened of bumping into sharp teeth. He fell into another category, too: superobnoxious, asshole snob.

Justin sat in the head of the school's book-lined office, listening and doing his best to smile pleasantly as Dean Quintel lectured about Melman's high academic standards and spotless reputation and then began rattling off the list of illustrious alumni who had attended over the ninety-eight years it had been sheltering and educating the best and the brightest the world had to offer. As the bow-tied man in the tweed jacket spoke, Justin let his eyes shift toward the window and take in the rolling Connecticut grounds and ivy-covered stone walls and all the accoutrements that helped keep the place so spotless. When he decided he'd let the dean pontificate enough to satisfy even his own outsized ego, Justin said, "It's a very impressive place, all right."

Dean Q beamed. "Thank you."

"How long have you worked here?"

"It's a funny thing. People always ask me that question and almost always ask it the same way. But I don't even consider what I do to be work. I consider it a privilege."

"Okay," Justin said, "how long has it been your privilege to oversee the lives and curriculum of those also privileged to attend?"

Dean Quintel's eyes narrowed, both in surprise at Justin's ability to articulate the question with a reasonable degree of sophistication as well as in suspicion that the question was not entirely sincere. But he couldn't find a flaw in the phrasing and he was not secure enough to argue with the tone, so he just said, "I've been dean for three years now. I was the youngest dean in Melman's history."

"Congratulations. I'm looking for information a little before your time, then."

"What exactly are you looking for?"

"I need some information about the period when Evan Harmon was privileged enough to attend."

"Evan Harmon?" The dean immediately looked uncomfortable. "Wasn't he . . . I mean, wasn't he . . ."

"Murdered. Yes."

"That's why you're here?"

"That's right."

"But—but he was at Melman so long ago. In the eighties."

"I know."

"Then I don't see how I can possibly help you."

"I assume you have records of all the students who've been here."

"Of course."

"Academic records as well as anything that might have been no-table—extracurricular activities, suspensions, anything out of the norm that might have required staff awareness."

"Yes."

"I'd like to see Evan Harmon's records."

Dean Quintel shifted uneasily in his seat. "I—I don't think I can do that."

"Then maybe there's someone else who knows how to access the files."

Quintel couldn't help himself. He gave Justin the kind of pitying look he'd give a dumb puppy. "I know how to access the files. I meant that the information in those files is privileged."

"Like you."

"I'm sorry you feel the need to deride my attachment to Melman. And I'm afraid we can't let anyone simply come in and rummage through our students' histories."

"First of all, I'm not anyone. I'm a member of the Providence, Rhode Island, police department and I'm working directly with the FBI on this case."

"I don't see how that changes anything."

"Then allow me to explain it to you." Justin leaned a little bit closer to the dean, putting his hands on top of the dean's dark mahogany desk. "I kind of know a lot about this sort of place." He told the dean where he'd gone to prep school in New Hampshire—a school that had a superior reputation to Melman, with even higher academic standards. Quintel didn't do much of a job hiding his shock at hearing Justin's academic credentials. "I know, it's surprising that the old alma mater would produce a cop. Actually, it produced two, although I guess you'd have to say the other one isn't just a regular cop, he's the number two guy at the CIA. But I digress. The point is, I know how things work here. So if you don't show me the records, I'll get a court order, which I can do very quickly. And it won't be to just look at Evan Harmon's history. I'll demand the phone numbers of every single parent of every single boy who's currently attending this place. And I'll call every single one of those parents and talk to them about what we're afraid is going on in the dormitories. And as someone who lived in very similar dormitories, I know that things aren't quite as pure and spotless as all the bullshit you've been spouting, so I can pretty much assure you I'll be talking about drinking and drugs and fairly serious homosexual activity. All the stuff they know about but don't really want to think about. Or discuss with federal agents. And since it's summer and a lot of your students are home right now, I'll bet a pretty decent percentage of them won't be coming back after I have these conversations."

Justin smiled even more politely and watched as Dean Quintel used his intercom to signal his secretary. When he answered, the dean leaned toward the phone and said, "Will you please make a copy of the complete file for Evan Harmon, please, Robby. Everything we have on record. He was one of our students, attended in the early to mid-eighties."

The dean leaned back in his chair, not smiling back at Justin, and several minutes later his door opened and a thin, athletic-looking young man came in carrying a manila folder. He started to hand it to the dean, but Quintel nodded his head in Justin's direction, and the assistant quickly swiveled to hand him the folder.

Justin riffled through the school records, stopped, and frowned.

"There's material missing."

"I doubt that," Dean Quintel said.

"Evan Harmon left here when he was a junior. He spent his last year and a half at Madden Prep."

"So?"

"There's no mention of why he left. There are two pages missing, the page numbers are off sequence. Then there's a handwritten notation that he transferred out. This isn't the page with the original information."

"If that's what's there, that's all we've got."

"There are no records at all of his last six months here."

"It's an old file. I suppose they just weren't as diligent then as we are now."

"Or the file's been tampered with."

Dean Quintel didn't answer, nor did he seem concerned by the accusation.

"Are there any teachers still here who were here when Evan Harmon was?"

"I really don't know."

Justin stood up. "Listen," he said, "I don't have time to screw around.

So let me try to be as clear as I possibly can: I can make your life a living hell. I wasn't kidding about the court order. If I have to close the school down, that's what I'll do. And believe me, I'll really go out of my way to dog you personally. You're gonna look in your mirror while you're brushing your teeth and you're gonna see my reflection. So unless you haven't so much as taken an extra five dollars on your expense account, just give me the information and make your life a lot easier."

Quintel didn't even hesitate. "Leslie Burham. Miss Burham has been teaching here for over thirty years. And Vince Ellerbe. He runs our math department."

"How long has he been here?"

"As a teacher, just about eight years. But he was a student here in the eighties. I believe he knew Mr. Harmon."

"Is that it?"

"Yes. Those are the only teachers with ties to that period."

"Where can I find them?"

"Miss Burham is taking her summer vacation in Turkey. I believe she'll be back in another three weeks."

"Swell. How about Vince Ellerbe?"

"He's not teaching for the summer term."

"Where is he? Afghanistan?"

"No. I believe he's home."

"Okay," Justin said, "I'll bite. Where does he live?"

Dean Quintel couldn't hide his disappointment. "Approximately fifteen minutes from here," he said.

"Evan Harmon was an asshole then and I'd be willing to bet a year's salary he stayed an asshole," Vince Ellerbe said. "I mean, I'm sorry he's dead, I guess. Oh hell, no, I'm not. I wouldn't wish him dead, let's put it that way, but I don't really care one way or the other."

"Sounds like you two weren't exactly close," Justin said. He was sitting on a lawn chair in Ellerbe's backyard. The math teacher's wife had poured them both some lemonade—Justin would have preferred a beer but decided decorum called for a yes to the lemonade—and their eight-year-old daughter brought out a plate of chocolate chip cookies she'd helped her mother bake the night before.

"Very few people were close to Evan in those days."

"Why is that?"

"He wasn't a guy who invited people to *get* close. He had a very superior attitude, as if he were a different breed from most of us. And he was a bully. You know the type: his friends were mostly sycophants. He usually found one or two brainiacs who were frightened of him and that's who he spent time with. He'd get them to do some of his work for him and run errands for him—that kind of BMOC shit. I never understood it, but there were definitely a few of those kinds of kids who looked up to him and were almost in awe of him. Not to mention terrified."

"So you didn't know him all that well?"

"I knew him well enough. We were in the same grade. We were on the baseball team together—he was a pretty decent first baseman—and the track team . . . You know, there's a good example. It's a little thing, but when we were on the track team, Evan signed up for long-distance running, five and ten K races. At the beginning, we were kind of running partners. We were the same basic skill level, so we paired off well together for pace. So it wasn't so monotonous, we didn't just run on the track, there were a couple of country runs the coaches mapped out. After two or three sessions, Evan decided he hated running. But he couldn't quit. His father had been a long-distance runner back in the day and there was all sorts of weird family pressure, which is why I used to cut Evan some slack. Anyway, after a couple of practices, what he used to do was wait until there was a break in the running line—he'd deliberately fall behind or sprint ahead until he could do this without being seen—and then he'd duck out of the run and sneak off and have a cigarette or get a soda or whatever and then he'd just kill an hour or so, wait until we'd be heading back, wait until there was a natural break, and then get back in and run the last quarter mile back to school."

"Never got caught?"

"No. He really had it down pat. He'd cover himself with water so it looked like he was sweating up a storm, and he'd pant like crazy as if he were exhausted. I knew he was doing it, but no one else did. Evan was funny about stuff like that. I think he had to let someone know he was cheating—or it wouldn't have been worth it. Someone had to be aware that he was beating the system or I don't think he would have done it. I think he would have just kept running with the rest of us."

"How'd he do in the races?"

"That's the thing about Evan. He did fine. He didn't need the practice. He'd finish third or fourth or fifth. If he'd actually run hard and worked at it and trained, he could have finished first. But he didn't care enough to do it. He liked the cheating better. He was just basically dishonest."

"Is that why he got thrown out of school?"

Ellerbe thought long and hard about this. Took a swallow of tart lemonade, then another one. "No, I don't think so." He spoke slowly and carefully. "I think there were always problems with his grades—cheating on papers and exams, I mean. He got caught a couple of times, but somehow he was always able to weasel out of it."

"So what was it?" Justin asked. He wondered if it was safe to ask for a beer yet. Decided he should just stick with what he had and not rock the boat.

"Look," Ellerbe said, "the family's gone out of their way to keep this quiet. And I don't even know if it's true. I only got this secondhand."

"From who?"

"Evan was friendly with a guy named Bart Peterson. B. P. was another guy who liked to play a little fast and loose with the rules, also kind of an arrogant kid. Evan told him about this and B. P. told me."

"And now why don't you tell me?"

"What Bart told me was that Evan needed some money and his parents had cut him off. So he got another kid here to stage a fake kidnapping. I think Evan even got a TA to go in on it . . ." He saw the brief look of puzzlement in Justin's eyes, so he said, "Teaching assistant, sort of a faculty member in training. That was also one of Evan's—um—talents. He could always get people in authority to look the other way, to break the rules just for him. What B.P. told me was that Evan tried to get a hundred thousand dollars from his parents. But the whole thing got botched pretty quickly and Evan was transferred out."

"How'd the Harmons manage to keep this so quiet?"

Ellerbe rolled his eyes and said, "Do you really need to ask that question? Money."

"Enough money to get the school to expunge any record of Evan's behavior?"

"I do know for a fact that almost right after this supposedly happened, Evan's father donated a few hundred thousand dollars . . . I heard half a million . . . to Melman for the music building. The H. R. Harmon Music Building."

"Would have been cheaper to pay off his son."

"But not the Harmon way. You protect your children, but you don't reward them."

Justin pondered this last comment, then asked the amiable math professor, "Do you have a yearbook from the last couple of years you went to school with Evan?"

"I live twenty minutes from the school. I still teach there. I usually buy clothes that match the school colors. What do you think?"

Justin smiled thinly, then waited as Ellerbe went inside. It didn't take him long—his school-day mementos were clearly not packed away in some box in the attic—before he returned with two yearbooks. He handed them over and said, "I'd like them back, please. When you're done."

Justin promised. Took a long sip of the lemonade, and said, "Let me ask you something. Do you believe it? You think that's a true story, the one you just told me about the kidnapping?"

"Yes, I do. Two reasons. Bart Peterson was too dumb to make something like that up, so it had to come from Evan directly. And I think that, at heart, Evan Harmon was a crook. He liked to steal and he liked to lie. He just liked it."

Justin nodded. "And he was the kind of guy who did what he liked, is that right?"

"You got it," Vince Ellerbe said. "And I'll bet he was that way right up until the moment he died."

"I'll go you one further," Justin said. "I'll bet you it's exactly what got him killed."

*   *   *

Justin decided to take the ferry back from Connecticut to Long Island. The ferry was about twenty minutes into its voyage when Justin's cell phone rang. It was Billy DiPezio.

"You got an ID on my prints?" Justin asked.

"As a matter of fact, I do. And so do you. The results should be in your e-mail."

"Anything good?"

"No idea. The guy's meaningless to me."

"Connections to Lenny Rube?"

"Not that I can find."

"Rival mob?"

"I'm not sayin' no, Jay, but this guy ain't on my radar. His prints are on record, but I don't see any arrests, any suspicion, anything but the guy's name, which is all that's in the system. But that's not why I'm calling."

"Shit," Justin said. He knew that tone in Billy's voice and he felt goose bumps running down the back of his neck. "What happened?"

"The offices for the LaSalle Group were broken into last night. Files were taken."

"What files?"

"All sorts. But we do know that the lists that LaSalle's assistant made for you—"

"Ellen Loache."

"Yeah. Her hard copy of that is definitely gone." When Justin didn't say anything, Billy said, "Somebody sure seems to be very interested in what you're doin' and beatin' you to the punch."

"I just wish I knew what the hell I was doing." Justin sighed. "Was there any damage?"

"Only if you count the human kind."

"Oh Christ."

"One of the guys you met with, Stan Solomon."

"What the hell was he doing in the office on a Sunday night?"

"He was puttin' in some overtime, I guess you could say."

"What happened?"

"Had his windpipe broken. According to the witness, never knew what hit him."

"The witness? What witness?"

"Ellen Loache."

"She was there?"

"Yup. Ms. Loache . . . or I should say Mrs. Loache . . . is married. Looks like she and this guy Solomon liked to work together when no one else was around, if you know what I mean."

"Yes, Bill, I get the drift. I picked up on that when I was with them. Kind of thought there was something going on."

"Well, there was. And he was quite the valiant guy. When they realized there was an intruder, he told her to hide."

"But he didn't?"

"Nope. Not macho enough, I guess. And according to Mrs. Loache, when he saw who the intruder was he just kinda threw caution to the wind. Figured there was no danger."

"Who was he?"

"It wasn't a he, Jay. It was a she."

"A woman broke his windpipe?"

"Apparently one quick motion. Bam. That was it."

Even in the summer heat, Justin's skin turned cold as he flashed on the women who might possibly be in Ron LaSalle's office. Vicky, he thought. Then he thought, no, couldn't be her—she wasn't capable of doing that. And then he thought: Reggie. Could she have gotten up there and back down in time? Christ, was it Reggie?

"Okay, who was *she*?"

"We don't know. Ms. Loache didn't recognize her. Didn't even get a great look at her, she was too afraid, especially after she saw what happened to her boyfriend. All we got was that she was Asian."

"Asian?" He let his breath out in relief. "That's it? Nothing more specific?"

"Nothin' that's a giant help."

And then Justin saw her. It came as a sudden flash, something out of a movie, an image barreling into his brain. She was walking down the street, passing him by right after he'd left Wanda's car. Floating down the street was more like it.

"Billy, did Loache say anything else about her? Tall, really good-looking?"

"You got it. She said tall and beautiful, but she wouldn't recognize her again if she fell over her."

"It's okay. I would."

"You know her?" Billy DiPezio asked incredulously.

"No. But I saw her. I saw her when I got out of Wanda's car the other day. She was right there."

"Jay, there are a lot of good-lookin' Asian women walkin' around these days."

"It was her. I know it. I'm telling you, I can feel it."

There was a pause, then Billy said, "I've known you too long not to at least listen when you get a feelin'. What else can you tell me about her?"

"Let me think about it for a little bit, see if I can conjure up more. I'll get back to you and give you whatever details I remember."

Billy agreed, then he said something he'd never said to Justin before. "You be careful, okay?"

Justin nodded, realized Billy couldn't see the nod. "This is a weird one, huh?"

"There's somethin' goin' on here, Jay, and I don't like it. And, worse, I don't understand it. There're usually dots and the problem is connecting 'em. But I don't even see the dots on this one."

"You be careful, too, okay?"

"Later," Billy said, and Justin clicked his cell phone off.

Billy was right, Justin knew. He'd put his finger right on the fat of the problem: People were dying all around them. Something was happening. But where were the damn dots?

Justin sat in his car and, as the ferry churned forward, he stared at the dirty blue water stretching out ahead for miles and miles. The water looked as if it could go on forever with no land and no end in sight, and Justin realized he might not mind all that much if it did.

23

Reggie had heard the news about the break-in and murder from Agent Fletcher by the time Justin had called to say he was about half an hour outside East End Harbor. By the time he was pulling into his driveway, she was waiting outside his front door.

The first thing they did when they were inside was use Justin's computer to go online and open the information that had come from Billy DiPezio. The shooter's name was Pietro Lambrasco, and the reason his prints were in the system was because he'd recently come into the country, visiting from Italy, and had gone through customs. The norm was now to fingerprint anyone entering the country. He was visiting for pleasure rather than business, and his business was listed as salesman. There was nothing else of any use. Reggie immediately processed the name and the prints through the FBI system, which had a far wider range of links than did the Providence PD. She told Justin they'd have results within an hour.

He ran down what he'd learned at Melman Academy and from Vince Ellerbe, and when she asked about the yearbooks he dropped on his beat-up coffee table, all he said was "Can't explain it. Just wanted to know more about the guy's past."

"Well, I'm pretty much blind by now," Reggie said. "I've been going through all the LaSalle info you got from his office. I've also been trying to narrow down the search on Hades and Ali."

"And?" Before she could answer he said, "Hold on. Let me get a couple of beers. I spent the day drinking lemonade and it almost killed me."

He disappeared into the kitchen, came back with two open bottles, handed one to her. "Okay," he said, once he took a pull off the Sam Adams.

"Well, I don't have enough cross-references to come up with anything useful for either Hades or Ali, so that was a total bust. What I was able to do with the LaSalle info was try to break it down and see if it made any sense."

"Did it?"

"Not to me. But there are enough unique aspects to it that it will to somebody. We just have to find someone who can recognize the patterns, I think, or something else to match it all up against." He indicated for her to go on, and she pulled out a yellow legal pad that had pages of nearly illegible markings and scribbles.

"Jesus," he said, "your handwriting's worse than mine."

"So shoot me. No, forget I said that. Not a good phrase to use around you."

"Just tell me what you've got."

"More than anything else, it's the travel spots. I can't make sense of them. Ron LaSalle did very little traveling up until a year ago."

"That's about when he started his own company."

"The company started four months before that—that's when he left Rockworth. So for four months he's pretty stable at home."

"Could be just overseeing a new business. Recruiting, hiring, all that."

"No question. But then things really start escalating. Look, the first month he went to Florida, flew directly to Palm Beach. Comes back to Providence two days later. Then, not long after that, he goes to Holland, flies into Amsterdam. He makes two trips there. Then, gradually it picks up. First he goes to Canada, to Vancouver. Then he's out in Northern California. And then he really starts traveling heavily: to South America, Colombia. And New Zealand, Australia, Alaska, and Russia. The past three months, he made three trips to South Africa. He's gone almost every seven to ten days. And then it all stopped about three weeks before he died. He's home."

Justin nodded, absorbing the geographical locations. "They don't mean anything to me."

"Me either. If there's a connection between all those spots, I don't see it."

"Did you see who got billed for these trips?"

"Yup. I cross-checked every one of them. The two trips to Amsterdam were billed to Ascension. So were the ones to California and Colombia. Which means we've got a direct financial connection. But then no more Ascension. After that, all the trips are billed to different companies. Seven or eight different names."

"Did you—"

"Yup, I tried finding them, but so far no luck."

"Not one of them?"

"No. I've requested an expert in this area, but I haven't heard back yet. I just don't have the know-how. And there are federal channels. I can't just go and try to get the SEC to do my job for me."

"How do we try to cut through all that?"

"I don't know. I told you, as hot as this is, we're still not the highest-level priority. And every time a bomb goes off in the Middle East—or anywhere, for that matter—we go lower on the priority list."

He indicated the papers she'd put together, organizing the information. "So what do you need to try to make sense of all this?"

"I need more information. Something I can compare it to. Why'd he go to all these countries, who was he talking to, what kinds of businesses, who was paying him after Ascension stopped? I'd also like to know if there's any matchup on the Ascension side."

"Such as?"

"Business crossovers, for instance. I'd like to see if Ascension does business with any of the other companies paying for LaSalle's trips. And I'd like to see if any of the places match up to any trips made by Evan Harmon or his associates."

"What else?"

"If we're being thorough, we should try to check the same things to see if anything matches up with Ellis St. John or even David Kelley or . . ."

"Or who?" he asked as her voice trailed off.

"Or Abby Harmon," she said.

He barely missed a beat in the rhythm of their conversation. But he was well aware that he did indeed miss it. "Meaning Abby could have been doing her husband's dirty work?"

"Or doing whatever she was doing behind his back, without his awareness. We have a connection between LaSalle and Harmon. It's tenuous, but it's there. Right now, it seems to be purely business and, until we know more, there's no reason to think it's anything but legal. But might as well check out whether there's a more personal connection, too, and that might come between LaSalle and Mrs. Harmon. She seems to connect to quite a few people."

"Okay," he said.

"Just okay?"

"Just okay. You have any ideas on how we can get any of this info?"

"Some. I'd like to make an in-person visit to the Ascension offices to begin with."

"It's too late now. Set it up for tomorrow morning. No, set it up for tomorrow afternoon if you can."

"Why afternoon?"

"Because I want to see if I can get a date in the city tomorrow night. So I can just stay in."

"Have you lost your mind? A date, Jay?"

"This one'll be worth it," he said. "And besides, we can go see somebody in the morning out here."

"Another social occasion or could it be work related?"

"The morning's definitely work related."

"Who we going to see?"

"Dave Kelley."

"The big rival?"

"I'll tell you what, Reggie. You might want to think about knocking that stuff off. You haven't earned the right to flirt and make comments on my personal life."

She looked stricken. It was the look of someone who'd forgotten she was on probation and had way overstepped her bounds. "I'm sorry," she said. "I mean it. I apologize."

He nodded. "Okay," he said. Then, after a brief pause: "I guess we can't do much more today. At least right now. Would you like to go get dinner?"

He got that crooked smile from her. "Do you *want* to have dinner with me, Jay?"

"No," he said. "Not really."

"Then I'll see you at what, nine A.M.?"

"Make it eight-thirty. We've got to go to Riverhead and there'll be traffic."

"Eight-thirty it is. I'll be ready."

For the second night in a row he stood at his living room window and watched Regina Bokkenheuser and her lopsided smile head out to her car and drive off into the town and away from him.

He thought about the last time he'd touched her. He remembered the way she felt. And the way her hair smelled. And he remembered his lips lightly kissing the little tattooed butterfly nestled in the small of her back. She used a soap on her body that had the slightest hint of vanilla and even now he could almost taste it.

He thought about the little dots that made up the butterfly.

It's all about the dots, he thought.

Justin took a deep breath because he knew he was going to hate himself for what he was about to do, then he went to his desk, looked up a phone number he'd added into his notes on the Hades file. He picked up his phone and called Belinda Lambert, Ellis St. John's assistant at Rockworth and Williams. When Belinda answered, Justin identified himself and said that he'd like to get together. As soon as possible.

"Really?" she said. "You mean, like, in the office or something?"

"No," he told her, and he remembered the vague air of desperation she had about her. And her willingness to be used. "I was thinking more about dinner."

"You're asking me out to dinner?" Even over the phone Justin could hear the combination of pleasure and surprise. But there was something else, too. There was also a certain amount of satisfaction. As if she some-how knew that he'd call sooner or later. He thought that came from being around the hounds on Wall Street. There's no question she had a certain amount of sex appeal. It might be obvious and it might be a bit cheap, but it was there. And in her world, that meant that eventually she'd be a target for somebody on the prowl.

"If you'll go," he told her.

"Well, sure I'll go," she said eagerly. "When?"

"How about tomorrow night?" he asked.

"Tomorrow? Well . . . I . . ." The hesitation wasn't genuine and it didn't last long. "Okay," she said. "Sure."

They arranged a time and a place—he asked her where she lived and picked a good restaurant within a reasonable distance of her apartment. He said, "I'll see you there."

She said, "This is cool."

He said, "Yeah, cool," and after he hung up, he felt like a total shit for a minute, maybe two.

And then he went back to his computer and began to work.

Justin was just about to call it quits. It was about ten-fifteen at night when the phone rang.

"It's me," Reggie said.

There was a strange air of familiarity in the way she said those two words. There was both a hesitancy to the greeting and a definite intimacy. It was the way an ex-wife would just say hi when calling after the split. It threw Justin a little bit. There was no question that intimacy was hang-ing over the two of them. He wanted it to go away. But at the same time he liked it. It evoked a certain warmth and, he had to admit, lust. He wondered if it was the same on Reggie's end and decided it had to be. He shook his head—he did not need such distractions at the moment. But he couldn't help picturing her on the other end of the phone, shoes off, sitting on the motel bed, wearing jeans and a T-shirt, one foot planted with her knee up, the other leg tucked under her. He knew that's the way she sat. And he also couldn't help wondering if this was a personal call or business and he realized he wasn't sure he wanted it to be all business.

But it was.

"I got a hit on your Rhode Island shooter."

"Let's have it."

"His name's Pietro Lambrasco, just as Billy said it was. And he's not mobbed up—"

"So what the hell is he?!"

"Let me finish. What I was saying is that he's not mobbed up *here*."

"Back in Italy?"

"Sicily, to be precise. The only reason we have it on record is that two of the guys in the Bureau were over there a couple of years ago to help with the murder of that judge who got blown up on the highway, the one from Rome. They exchanged a lot of info and computer files. This guy Lambrasco was in one of their files."

"What's his story?"

"A stone-cold hit man."

Justin stayed silent.

"You still there, Jay?"

"Still here." Another brief pause. Then, "Reggie, what the hell is a Sicilian hit man doing in Providence, Rhode Island, going after Bruno Pecozzi?"

"I was hoping you'd have the answer to that one."

Again, nothing from Justin.

"So what now?" Reggie asked finally.

"I'm going back to work on the dots," Justin said.

"Did you make your date for tomorrow night?"

"Yup," Justin said.

"You going to tell me what that's all about?"

"Nope."

"Then I guess I'll see you at eight-thirty."

"Yup," Justin said again.

24

David Kelley was not the brightest guy Justin had ever met. But the contractor was nowhere near the dim-witted lout as portrayed by the tabloids and the local news stations. It didn't take long for Justin to realize that he was talking to a competent blue-collar contractor who'd gotten in over his head—both professionally and personally. He had moved up to deal with the moneyed class and gotten caught up between the two worlds. He'd been exposed to a lifestyle so grand that he could never again look back at his own life and be totally content. But the people he serviced lived at a level he could never attain. Justin realized it was that very fact that made Dave Kelley such an appealing suspect for Larry Silverbush and his crew. Greed was usually a pretty safe motive. As was lust. Kelley was also a guy with a temper and a cruel streak. That was immediately apparent from the sneer on his lips and the anger in his voice. It was not a combination that added up to a very appealing personality. But Justin was convinced it also didn't add up to someone who had murdered Evan Harmon.

Staring at Kelley in his prison grays, Justin wondered what it was about him that had appealed to Abby. Maybe it was his crudeness. Maybe it was the fact that this was a guy who had never in his life dreamed of having a shot with someone like Abby, so maybe she liked the idolatry that came along with this relationship. It made Justin wonder what she had seen in him, what had made her search him out at

Duffy's that night. He wondered if there was any link between him and Dave Kelley.

Then he thought maybe there was.

Cruelty.

He shook the thought away as best he could, because he realized that Reggie Bokkenheuser was staring at him. He had a sneaking suspicion she knew exactly what he was thinking.

"Dave," Reggie said to Kelley, continuing the line of questioning she'd been pursuing, "what can you tell us about the stun gun?"

"What the fuck is there to tell?" Kelley said.

"Quite a bit," Reggie said. "It was used to torture a murder victim and certainly contributed to his death. And it was found in your possession after the murder."

"Yeah, I know where the fuck it was found. There's nothin' you're tellin' me or askin' me that's even the tiniest fuckin' bit new. I told everything to the lawyers and the cops and nobody fuckin' believes one fuckin' thing I say."

"Maybe it's because you're too eloquent and sophisticated for them," Justin said.

"Fuck you," Kelley spat back.

"Case in point," Justin said.

"Look, my own damn lawyers want me to plead guilty to somethin' I didn't do. You know how fuckin' insane that is?"

"Dave," Reggie said, "*we* believe you. Or at least we'd *like* to believe you. But you're not making this easy."

"Yeah," Kelley said and jerked his head at Justin. "I'm gonna trust this guy 'cause I know he's really rootin' for me since we're both bangin' the same bimbo."

"Dave," Justin said quietly and calmly, "let me try to explain it to you in a way even you might understand. I don't think you're an idiot, even though you're doing a really good impersonation of one. I think you're getting screwed—by the cops, by the DA, by your lawyers, and probably by the Harmon family. They all want to nail somebody—and they want to nail him quickly—and you're the prime candidate. But we know things they don't. And those things make us think that even though you're clearly a total asshole, you're an innocent asshole, at least as far as this murder's concerned. And as far as the bimbo's concerned, I don't think she's involved in this either. So the best way I can help her is to also help you. Even though I personally couldn't care less if you spend the rest of your life in jail or even if they stick a needle in your veins and put you out of your misery. But I don't want to see the wrong man—or woman—go down for this. So the way I see it, we're kind of your last hope. We're the only thing standing between you and twenty to life. Or worse. So what do you have to lose by talking to us without all the bluster and the swagger and the pretense?"

Kelley stared at Justin, his mouth slightly agape, and said nothing.

"Okay," Justin said to Reggie. "Let's go. This guy actually is as stupid as everybody thinks."

They both started to stand, but Kelley said, "Wait." And when they shifted back to him, he said, "What do you want to know?"

Justin and Reggie settled back into their seats across the small table from the imprisoned contractor.

"Tell us about the stun gun," Reggie said.

"It's mine," Kelley said.

"According to the arrest transcripts, you denied that at first."

"Well, what the fuck do you . . ." He glanced over at Justin and immediately he lowered his voice and softened his tone. "Yeah. I know. It was stupid. I was scared out of my freakin' mind and they were tellin' me it was the murder weapon, so I did the first thing I could think of and said it wasn't mine."

"Why'd you have one in the first place?" Justin asked.

"Animals. That's all, I swear to God. You know I don't just work out here—I do some work in the city and you start breakin' down walls and diggin' there and you got no idea what's gonna come out at you. Rats, bats . . . I hate fuckin' rats. So I got myself one of those things so I could torture the little bastards."

"You ever use it out here?"

"Yeah, sometimes. On raccoons and shit."

"You ever use it at the Harmons'?"

Kelley nodded. "Hey, you got a piece of gum or somethin'?"

Justin shook his head, but Reggie reached into her pocket and flipped a piece of sugarless Juicy Fruit across the table.

Kelley popped it in his mouth and chewed vigorously for a few seconds, then he said, "Yeah. I used it at the Harmons'."

"Keep going."

"Look, I kept it there sometimes. I kept all my tools there, so I just stuck it in with them. This was a big job for me, I mean the biggest I ever had. And I had a crew and everything, it was a lotta work, but sometimes I worked by myself. I figured why pay to get stuff done *I* could do, you know? So I was up there alone a decent amount of the time. Or alone with the two of them . . ."

"Abby and Evan?" Justin asked.

"Yeah. Or just one of 'em. Or with the greaseballs."

"You're referring to the housekeeper and butler?"

"Yeah. Great fuckin' butler—the guy could barely speak a word of English. You'd say, 'Hey, Pepe, can I get some ice water or somethin'?' and he'd stare at you like *what the fuck are you talkin' about?*"

"Did Pepe or his wife ever see you use the stun gun?"

"No."

"How can you be sure?"

" 'Cause I only used it once up there and they weren't around."

"You sure?"

"Yeah, I'm sure. They don't drive and I gave 'em a lift to that taco place in East Hampton, you know, that little stand. They were meetin' some friends there for their night off. Try ordering dinner in less than half an hour. Nobody in that fuckin' place speaks English either."

"So how'd you happen to use the gun at the Harmons' that day?"

"I dropped off the beaners, came back to do some work. I was puttin' in the pond, which is a hell of a lot of work, and I wanted to check some dimensions 'cause if you don't get that right, it's a disaster. Anyway, I was actually measuring some of the land that needed to get filled in and there were, like, rabbits all over the place. I kept the gun there for raccoons 'cause those guys can be mean as hell. But I thought, well, I'll have some fun with the little bunnies."

"The good times, huh?" Justin said.

"Hey, to each his own. But I got one of the little guys."

"What did it do to them?" Reggie asked.

"Well, with the raccoons, it really did just stun 'em, you know? They're big. But with the rabbits, they don't got a lot of fat on 'em. So it fried this little fucker, I gotta say. And I look up and Evan and Abby are there watchin'."

"What did they do?"

"Evan was pretty interested. He'd never seen one, I guess a lotta people haven't. He wanted to see if I'd do it again."

"Did you?"

"Sure. Got another little Thumper in about five or ten minutes."

"What was Evan's reaction?"

"I think he kinda liked it. Thought it was cool."

"How about Mrs. Harmon?" Reggie asked. "Did she like it, too?"

"Abby? Hard to know. She's not one to, like, show her emotions, you know?"

"Was she squeamish about it?"

"She ain't the squeamish type. I don't know what the hell she thought; she didn't say much."

"And nobody else saw you?"

"Nobody."

"You're absolutely sure."

"I'm tellin' you, there wasn't nobody else around. And that was the only time I ever used it up there."

"You know that the DA is saying he's got a witness that saw you use the gun there. Somebody called in the tip. That's how they found it in your house."

"I know. And I swear to God, the only two people who saw me were Abby and Evan. And I don't think Evan's gonna call nobody to report on the thing that fuckin' killed him."

"Actually, the stun gun didn't kill him," Justin said. "It didn't help him much, but his skull was crushed by a bat or some kind of blunt object."

"Well, they didn't find that at my house, did they?"

"No. They haven't found it at all yet."

There was a brief silence. Then Kelley said, "So what else do you want me to say?"

"Who called Silverbush and gave him the tip?"

"Either somebody's lyin' or it's Abby."

"Why would Abby implicate you if it weren't true?"

"Who knows? I'm not kiddin' myself I could ever understand anything she does."

"You think it's possible?" Reggie asked.

"I think anythin's possible with her."

"You know there's also a witness that says you told him that Abby talked to you about killing Evan."

"Yeah, I know."

"So? Did she?" Justin asked.

"You wanna know the truth? We hardly ever talked at all. And when we did, it was mostly me tellin' her about my other rich clients. She liked that. Liked to hear how impossible they were, the weird shit they used to do."

"The witness who said you talked to him about killing Evan, do you know who that is?"

"It's nobody. 'Cause I never said nothin' like that!"

"Dave," Reggie said, "how do you think your stun gun wound up being used on Evan Harmon?"

"You think I ain't been tryin' to figure this out? I don't know. The only thing I come up with is that somebody stole it, used it, and put it back. But I know how that sounds."

"It sounds ridiculous," Justin said. "But do you have any ideas of who could possibly have done it?"

"Look, I have plenty of friends who know I got one of those things. And some of 'em even know where I keep it. But why the hell would any of 'em use it to go and kill Evan? It don't make no sense. The guy was the money train. Why'd you want to stop it from comin' down the tracks?"

"It comes right back to you then. You're the only one with a motive."

"Which is what?"

"Mrs. Harmon."

Kelley turned away from Reggie to look at Justin. "I'm really not stupid. At least I'm not *that* stupid. Even if she told me she wanted to run away with me and spend the rest of our damn lives together, you think I'd believe that? Come on."

"*Did* she tell you that?" Reggie asked.

"No."

Reggie sighed. "Why don't you give us the names of the people who knew about the gun and we'll check them out anyway."

"Okay," Kelley said. "No problem. But I'm tellin' you, the only person who makes any sense for this is"—and now he looked directly into Justin's eyes—"that bitch. We both know what she is and what she can do."

"And what is it you think Abby Harmon can do?" Regina Bokkenheuser asked.

"Anything she wants to do," Dave Kelley said. "Which is why I'm fucked seven ways from Sunday."

Justin sighed, too, now. "What about the security system in the Harmon house?"

"It cost a fortune. And it's about the best there is."

"You install it?"

"Yeah. I started out as just an electrician. That's my real specialty."

"Sorry to hear that."

"Yeah, no shit."

"How does it work?" Justin asked.

"It's simple really. A thing of beauty. Everything's connected to a central computerized system. Evan wanted it wired to his computer in his office—"

"At Ascension?" Reggie asked.

"No. His home office. He had a room upstairs that he used, you know, when he had to work out there. The guy was always at his computer; he worked all the time."

Justin and Reggie both turned at the sound of a door opening. Justin made a noticeable sound of disgust and when Reggie looked at him quizzically, he said, "This is the esteemed DA Larry Silverbush." And to Silverbush he said, "Regina Bokkenheuser, FBI."

"Yes," Silverbush said, "I know all about Ms. Bokkenheuser. Seems like you two make an ideal team." He turned to Kelley and said, "Morning, Dave. Got a good story for these two?"

"We're just trying to be as thorough as we can," Reggie said to Silverbush. "Mr. Kelley is being very cooperative."

"I bet he is." Silverbush smiled. "Mind if I sit in the rest of the way?"

Justin turned to Kelley. "It's your call, Dave. Our conversation is unconnected to Mr. Silverbush and his investigation."

"But we're all on the same side, aren't we?" the DA asked. "Truth, justice—all of that."

"I don't mind," Kelley said. "I'm not sayin' nothin' he hasn't heard before."

"Excellent," Silverbush said. "Go right ahead, as if I'm not here."

"We were talking about the security system," Reggie said to Kelley.

"Right. It was wired to his home computer. That's where the system could be operated from."

"What if the computer went down?"

"No problem. It didn't change the system, I mean, if the computer lost power, it's not as if the security system did, too. You'd just lose the ability to control it from that computer while it was outta commission. But there were backups for the control. For one thing, it could all be done by hand at each control point. As long as you had that password."

"Different passwords for hand controlled and computer controlled?"

"Yeah. Different passwords for every computer terminal, too."

"How many hand control points were there?"

"There was one by the gate at the end of the driveway. One by the front door, one by the back door, one by the stereo in the living room that operated the inside cameras. And there was one by the pool house that operated the outdoor cameras."

"That's it?"

"Well, there were remote hookups, too. You could operate the whole thing from a laptop. Each laptop had to be specially designated as authorized to handle the controls and each user was given a password, you know, so anyone who was workin' away at the computer couldn't just access the Harmons' security system."

"Who had laptop access?"

"Evan. On the laptop he used to travel with."

"Abby?"

Kelley nodded. "But I don't think she really knew how to use it. She didn't have much interest in it."

"Anyone else?"

Kelley hesitated, then nodded again, this time with one deep, long movement of his head back and forth. "Me."

"Your laptop could access the Harmon security system?"

"Yeah. Evan wanted it that way. I knew the house, I knew the system; if anything went wrong, he said he wanted me to be able to, you know, see what the problem was."

"So you could get into the system anytime you wanted?"

"Yeah."

"To change the settings or disable it—whatever you wanted."

"Yeah."

"Let me ask you something," Reggie said. "When you log on to the system, does the system register who the user is and what changes are made?"

"Yup. It logs it in the main computer and on the individual computer that's used."

"Should I ask?" Justin said. And when Kelley frowned glumly, Justin said, "Who was logged on when the system was disabled the night of the murder?"

"I was," Dave Kelley said.

"On the main system and on your laptop both?" Reggie asked.

"Yeah."

"Did anyone else know your password?"

"Evan and Abby," Kelley said.

"Where's your laptop now?"

"Evidence room," Silverbush said.

"And where was it the day of the murder?" Justin asked Kelley.

Kelley sighed and said, "In my truck, I guess. That's where the cops found it." As Justin and Abby stayed silent, Kelley added, "See what I mean? Seven ways from Sunday."

Silverbush's smile now spread across his entire face. And it was still there as he walked Justin and Reggie outside a few minutes later when the interview was over.

"I'm glad we could all share this experience," he said and extended his hand toward Reggie. "Good to meet you." He didn't bother to push his hand in Justin's direction. He just said, "I know you're trying to drag in all sorts of complications. But you're way off base. This guy did it. There's no question about it. And if we find out he did it with your girlfriend, they're both gonna get a needle in the arm."

"Always nice to see you," Justin said.

Silverbush had the same annoying smile on his face as he said, "You screwed it up when you were just a cop; you're screwing it up again working with the Feds. It's kind of reassuring to deal with someone who never learns."

"So what do you think?" Reggie asked. They were in the car heading into Manhattan, just a few minutes outside Riverhead, where they'd talked to David Kelley.

"What do *you* think?"

"I think I can see why Silverbush is going to prosecute. Kelley's right about being screwed. There's a lot of evidence against him. And there's a decent amount that links your—that links Abby."

"Maybe. If we were looking at Evan's murder in isolation, I'd say you're right. But what's the link to the other killings?"

"We have to check it out and see if those links exist."

"They won't."

"They *might*. And if they don't, it's still possible they're really separate cases. Maybe it's all just a crazy coincidence. Harmon could have been doing something illegal and still gotten killed for jealousy or money or whatever this guy would kill him for." She shook her head in frustration. "There are obviously complications, Jay, but after hearing all that, it's hard for me to think that this guy and Abby Harmon aren't involved.

Silverbush might be right. The stuff in Providence might really be unconnected." When Justin frowned, she said, "You sure you're not letting your personal feelings interfere with your judgment?"

"I'm not saying anything definitively, Reggie. But as dumb as Kelley is, some things just don't add up."

"Such as?"

"Let's say you actually are capable of committing the kind of well-thought-out, sadistic kind of act that someone committed on Evan Harmon."

"Okay . . ."

"So would you have the presence of mind to ditch the murder weapon but keep the stun gun, which would probably implicate you more than anything else? Why get rid of one but keep the other?"

"What else?"

"Kelley's right—I don't see the motive. He's killing off his money source."

"Unless he thinks she's an even better source."

"Yeah, but he's right again. Even Dave Kelley has to realize that he's not going to wind up living happily ever after with Abby Harmon."

"So maybe she just promised him money and not true love."

"Granted, that might make sense from his end. But why would Abby want Evan dead? All she has to do is divorce him."

"You never know what people can do when they're in a relationship, Jay. Maybe he was abusive and she couldn't stand it anymore. Maybe she found out he was molesting little boys. You never know what sends someone over the edge." She looked at him when he didn't react. "But there's something else, isn't there?"

Justin nodded. "It's the phone tip that led Silverbush to Kelley."

"What about it?"

"It came early. I mean it came the day after the murder. And a lot of details hadn't been released to the press. In fact, the detail about the stun gun burns still hasn't been released to the press."

She began nodding. "But the tip wasn't just that Kelley was having an affair with Abby Harmon. It said he owned a stun gun."

"So somebody had to know how Evan was killed."

"Maybe somebody talked. One of your guys or one of Harmon's guys. Or even Leona. Hard to keep that kind of thing quiet. Word could have gotten around that someone knew that Kelley had that freaking thing."

"Maybe."

"But it does seem kind of strange, doesn't it? Kind of . . ."

"Orchestrated."

"Yes. Orchestrated."

"Kind of," Justin said.

25

Justin had never been in an office quite like Ascension's before.

He had been around money all his life; had been raised, more or less, in the banking and financial world his father inhabited. He'd dealt with Wall Street types and people who owned their own businesses and had their own planes. Money did not intimidate him or overly impress him. To Justin, it was something you had or you didn't have. It was something to be used well or poorly. Even the office of Rockworth and Williams—a company dealing with more money and brokering more real power than Ascension could ever dream of—was an environment he understood. Even as it made him shudder. Rockworth and Williams was corporate life with all its pressures and politics and game playing. To succeed there was a matter of survival, of protecting yourself at all costs.

This was different.

From the moment he and Reggie were ushered into the back offices of Ascension, Justin realized they were not in a world where survival or safety mattered. What mattered was domination. Power. Greed. What mattered here was size. What mattered here was *more*.

Risk was what this was all about.

This was a world where success could be equated only with ownership. And ownership mattered only when it was defined by the worth of whatever was owned.

There was no pleasure here. There was only winning. Or oblivion.

As they sat in Carl D. Matuszek's office, Reggie instinctively reached out for Justin's arm. It wasn't a gesture of affection. She needed something to hold on to. He let her hand clutch his left wrist. As they sat, waiting, he could feel her relax, and he made no acknowledgment of their contact when she finally let go.

Matuszek was sitting at his desk, on the phone, his back to them. He wore sand-colored linen pants, a light-blue button-down shirt, and a blue-and-white striped tie. No sport coat. He was peering out a sparklingly clean window at a magnificent view of midtown Manhattan as he spoke. He didn't bother talking into a receiver; he kept the whole conversation on speakerphone.

"Phil," Carl Matuszek was saying, "how many times do we have to go over this? We bought fourteen percent of your stock and it cost a cool twenty-four million. You know what we got for that? We got to be your biggest shareholders. And you know what we got for *that*? We got the right to tell you that *you* work for *us*."

"You cannot assess a company's record on six months' worth of business," Phil was saying. "Especially a business like this which we're not just trying to expand, we're trying to shift the entire paradigm. I don't understand how you can be that shortsighted."

Justin wasn't sure what business Phil was in, but he realized soon enough that whatever business it was, it wasn't doing well enough to suit Matuszek.

"Actually, we *can* make that assessment, Phil. We can and we're doing just that. What *I* don't understand is how people like you think you can get away with not making your numbers and then not having to face the consequences."

"Because the consequences you're talking about are ridiculous," Phil was saying. "This is a long-term project. We're changing the way kids all over the country are eating, for Christ's sake. We're remaking the entire school cafeteria structure, moving them from slop to healthy, well-balanced meals. That's why we've taken on employees and, believe me, the risk-reward value long term—"

"Phil, let's get something straight right now. We're not interested in long term. We're interested in value. Kids want to eat chocolate cake for breakfast, that's fine with me as long as we're making a profit on the goddamn cake."

"Carl, you do realize that's an inane statement, I hope."

"I'll tell you what's inane, my friend." Matuszek's voice, on the surface, stayed friendly and calm. But underneath that surface it turned to ice. "Thinking you can lose money and still run this company."

"What are you, firing me?"

"Congratulations. That's the first perceptive thing you've said since we've been doing business together. We're also selling you. To CafRite."

Phil seemed able to ignore the fact that he was fired. Justin, just from listening to this brief conversation, had a feeling that getting fired by Carl Matuszek would be a relief and a blessing. But Phil wasn't able to shake off the sale of his company. "You'll put about five hundred people out of work down here. And maybe another seven fifty to a thousand around the country. You can't do that."

"It's done, Phil. It's done. Someone from our end'll speak to HR and we'll work out your details."

"My details? You scumbag—"

"Bye, Phil."

Carl Matuszek clicked off the speakerphone and now swiveled his chair around to face Justin and Reggie. He had a perfectly placid expression on his face. The conversation he'd just had with Phil, the mysterious cafeteria person, hadn't left an iota of stress on Matuszek's face. "So what is it I'm actually supposed to help you with?" he asked.

"Quite a conversation you were having."

Matuszek shrugged. "I don't let it bother me anymore. I talk to guys like that three, four times a day now."

"Doesn't bother you messing around with people's lives like that?"

Matuszek shook his head. "First of all, I don't mess around with anything, certainly not people's lives. I don't have anything to do with people's lives."

"Firing someone doesn't count as anything?"

"People find their own level. They fail or succeed on their own. I might be the one who has to point out their failure or success, but I'm not responsible for their fate. I take businesses and make them stronger. That's all I do."

"Stronger meaning more profitable," Justin said.

"There's no other definition, is there?"

"Sounds like you don't just invest in companies. Sounds like you have quite a bit of control over them."

"If we invest heavily enough, we do. And that's the way it should be. You put up the money, you get to demand results. And if you don't get them . . ."

"You do what you have to do," Justin said, "to make sure you *do* get them."

"Bingo," Carl Matuszek said. "Want to come work here?"

"I'm afraid," Reggie interrupted, "we're already working. Can we talk about Evan Harmon, please."

"A tragedy," Matuszek said. He put as much emotion into the word "tragedy" as he would if he were discussing a problem he might have with a suit that didn't fit properly.

"Did you work with Mr. Harmon?" Reggie asked.

"Of course. He was my mentor as well as my boss."

"So you learned from him?" Justin said.

"Almost everything I know," Matuszek answered.

"And did you work closely with him? On a daily basis?"

"Oh yeah. As close as it's possible to work with someone. Hey," Matuszek said, and Justin was pretty sure he saw an actual wink, "you mind if I see your ID or some badges or whatever you people carry? I mean, I know you're who you say you are, but even so . . ."

Reggie took her FBI ID out and held it out. Justin held up a badge he'd bought in the East End Harbor five-and-dime. It said FBI on it in big letters. Matuszek found them both equally convincing. As Justin put his badge away, he could see Reggie staring at him incredulously.

"So you'd know a decent amount about Mr. Harmon's dealings for the company," Reggie asked Matuszek once she was able to recover from the sight of Justin's toy badge.

"Pretty much," Matuszek said.

Reggie shoved a piece of paper across the desk. "So, for instance, if I asked you to identify these companies, you could?"

Matuszek scanned the list in front of him. "Sure," he said. "I don't know every single one, but we do business with most of these guys."

"Meaning what?"

"We handle their money. Do corporate investments. Some of them we invest *in*."

"Can you tell me what they do?"

"Every company on the list?"

"If you can."

"I don't think I can do every one but . . ." Matuszek ran his finger down the list. "Penzine is an energy company, does that new shit with corn . . . Balbear makes ball bearings. Not very glam but incredibly solid business . . . CafRite manages school cafeterias . . ."

"That's the company you just sold Phil's company to."

"Phil?"

"The guy you were just talking to. The guy you fired?"

"Oh, right, right. Yes, we just sold it to CafRite."

"That's allowed? Selling one client's company to another client?"

"It's not just allowed, it's what we do. We invest for our clients. We buy and we sell. Doesn't really matter who we buy from or who we sell to, as long as it's profitable and there's no exchange of inside information."

"All right," Justin said. "Keep going down the list."

And he did. One company designed and built ice-skating rinks around the country; one company was a trucking and shipping line; one manufactured lightbulbs. One company made substrates—and when Justin asked what a substrate was, half expecting Matuszek to come up with some kind of idiotic punch line—he was told it was the key to auto exhaust systems; it's what allowed those systems to meet environmental standards around most of the world. A big business, Matuszek said. A big business. And a good example of the way they worked. They didn't just invest in substrates. The next company on the list was an auto parts company that made the exhaust systems that *used* substrates.

"One hand washing the other," Justin said.

"Washing has nothing to do with it," Matuszek said. "It's one hand taking money from one pocket and putting even more money in the other pocket. That's what we do."

Other than the link between the two businesses that dealt in auto parts, there was no rhyme or reason to the others being on the same list except that they all were involved in a transaction handled by Ascension. Matuszek explained that they weren't developing a core business. Nothing had to relate to anything else. Their core business, he said, was money.

There were several companies on the list that Carl Matuszek didn't know. And there were two he knew but had nothing to do with.

"And why don't you deal with those two?" Reggie asked.

"They deal in commodities. Not my area. If you want more info on them, you have to talk to Hudson Fenwick."

"That's my favorite Dickens novel," Justin said.

"What?" Matuszek said blankly.

"Nothing. Where do we find Hudson Fenwick?"

Matuszek didn't answer, just reached toward his phone, pushed a few buttons, and said, "Hud? You wanna come in here for a minute?"

And a few moments later, Hudson Fenwick walked through the door. Fenwick was more or less a thinner, less-athletic version of Carl Matuszek. Same short haircut; same button-down long-sleeved shirt; same slacks; and same striped tie, except his was red and black instead of blue and white. Fenwick also seemed nervous and fidgety. He immediately got more nervous and more fidgety when Matuszek told him the visitors were from the FBI. Justin went to pull out his badge, but Reggie managed to grab his hand before he could dig it out of his pocket.

"What—um—what can I do for you?" Fenwick asked.

"They're looking for some information on Menking, Inc. and—what's the other one?" He looked down at Reggie's list. "Right. Cates and Herr."

"What—what—what do you want to know?"

"What they do, for one thing."

"Menking—um—deals in precious metals. Trades. Buys, sells. Mostly platinum."

"Platinum?" Reggie said. She leaned forward, then realized it probably gave the impression she was a little too interested.

"Yes," Hudson said. "Something wrong with that?"

"No, of course not," she said. "Where are they located?"

"They've got offices all over the world. London, Belgium . . . I think their home office is in Canada."

"What about the other one?" she asked. "Cates and Herr."

"Um . . . mining, actually. Platinum again."

"Uh-huh," Justin said. "Where does one mine platinum?"

"They're in"—he coughed two or three times, then cleared his throat from all the coughing—"South Africa."

Before Hudson Fenwick could do any more hemming, hawing, or coughing, Forrest Bannister walked into Carl Matuszek's office. Justin couldn't help noticing that with five people in the office, the room looked a lot less crowded than his own living room with just two people in it.

"Chief Westwood," Bannister said. "I apologize for being late. Things are a little . . . out of the ordinary, as I'm sure you understand."

Justin said that he understood completely and he introduced Reggie. He was surprised at the difference in Bannister's demeanor from the night that he had found Evan Harmon's body and called in the murder. He was far more calm and collected now, which wasn't really surprising. But he was also much more commanding and assertive. He no longer seemed like the kind of guy who'd immediately come running a hundred miles when Evan Harmon called.

"I hope Carl and Hud are being helpful."

"Yes," Justin said. "Extremely so."

"What can *I* help you with?"

Justin glanced over at Reggie, so she told Bannister what she needed. She wanted a record of Evan Harmon's travel over the past fifteen-month period, everywhere he went and who he went to see. She also wanted the same information for any of the associates at the firm who might have traveled to Canada, California, Russia, South Africa, and South America. She also asked for records of any business transactions that had been done with the LaSalle Group in Providence.

When she was finished, Bannister smiled evenly and said, "Of course. Would you mind telling us what you're looking for specifically? That might make it easier for us to give you what you want."

"I'm afraid it doesn't work that way, Mr. Bannister. We'd like all the information in as complete a form as possible. We don't want you sifting through it or editing it for us."

"Absolutely. I wasn't trying to interfere. I simply thought it might help us be more efficient." He looked up at the ceiling for a moment. "Let me see . . . This will take some time—"

"We need this as quickly as possible," Reggie told him. "What would be the delay?"

"Well, the records aren't kept in the same place or by the same person. The travel plans, for instance, are made by each assistant individually."

"You don't use a central travel agent?" Justin asked.

"No, we don't," Bannister said. "And Evan's assistant will certainly have a record of some of his specific meetings but not every one. Evan did a lot of that himself."

"That—that's right," Fenwick chimed in. "He was kind of a con-control freak for his schedule."

"But I'll talk to Evan's assistant and see what she's got."

"And her name is?"

"Lisa."

"Lisa what?"

"Are you going to want to talk to her?" Bannister asked.

"Is that a problem?" Justin said.

"No, not really. It's just that she was so devastated by what happened. She really hasn't been functioning very well, and I don't know how she'd hold up to any kind of interrogation."

"This is hardly an interrogation," Reggie said.

"You know what I mean," Bannister said quickly. "I didn't mean that pejoratively. She's just very fragile right now. It's why we've given her some time off."

"Not a problem," Justin told him. "But I do need her last name for my records."

"Schwartz." This was Carl Matuszek who chimed in. "Lisa Schwartz."

"Thanks," Justin said. "Now how about the LaSalle transactions?"

"Now that might be a different matter," Bannister told them. When Reggie asked why that might be, he said, "Because there are questions of privacy. We can't simply open up our clients' financial transactions." And before Justin could get a word out, he went on, "Or our transactions on behalf of our clients."

"We can get a court order," Reggie said.

"I'm not sure that you can," Bannister said. "But you're certainly free to try. It's not that we don't want to do everything possible to help catch Evan's killer. Lord knows, we do. His death is the worst thing that's happened to this company and possibly the worst thing that's ever happened to me personally. But this company is also Evan's legacy, and I fear that releasing those kinds of documents could do us great harm."

"Totally understood," Justin said. "I don't blame you." He continued as Reggie stared at him in amazement. "And I think we've taken up enough of your time. If you'll just give us your cards so we can get in touch with you again and figure out how to get the travel info we need." He rose and took a business card from each man. Reggie hesitated before rising, too. As they were being escorted out by Bannister, who was going on again about the tragic loss of Evan Harmon, Justin saw a secretary working away expertly on her computer. He stopped as he passed the young woman's desk and said, "Excuse me just a second." He turned to Bannister and said, "Sorry, this doesn't have anything to do with Evan, but . . ." Turning back to the assistant, he said, "We're completely redoing our computer system at the police station. In fact, they've asked me to put together a recommendation for all of the various forces on the eastern part of Long Island. What kind of system do you use? We all want to be linked wirelessly."

She smiled, flattered that he'd picked her to talk to, and told him the system they were using.

"Mac or PC?" he asked.

"PC," she said and shrugged as if that wasn't her choice but what could she do?

He thanked her. Then he turned to Bannister and said, "You know, I forgot to ask you one thing: how involved is H. R. Harmon with the company these days?"

"He's not particularly involved."

"That's funny. At Rockworth, they told me that one of the reasons he left was to spend more time working with his son."

"Well . . . he has an office here, if that's what you mean. But he's hardly involved in our day-to-day operations."

"Even now? I would have thought he'd be very involved right now, making sure that things hold together."

"I'm . . . I keep him apprised of anything important, of course."

"So you're in touch with him?"

"Yes. But this is hardly his top priority right now."

"Of course. That's only natural." Justin smiled kindly. "Thank you. And I'm glad to see you're doing so much better than you were the other night."

"It still seems like a dream," Forrest Bannister said, "a nightmare, really."

"I'm sure it does," Justin said. "But the good thing about dreams is that everybody wakes up sooner or later."

"What was *that* all about?" Reggie asked. She waited until the moment they were out of the lobby and stepping onto the sweltering midtown sidewalk. "Suddenly you're Mr. Easygoing? Mr. Personality? Mr. Hey, Everything's Fine? What the hell—"

"Don't worry about me. What's with you and platinum, all of a sudden? He said the word, and I thought you were going to jump out of your chair."

She scowled. "I know. I'm sorry. It's just . . ." She made another face, scrunching up her mouth, then said, "The weirdest story of the year: Some state troopers in Texas found an overturned truck—there'd been an accident—and hidden in the back of the truck were platinum bars. A lot of them. Worth a few million dollars."

"You're kidding. What happened?"

"Nobody knows. It's not my case; I had absolutely nothing to do with it; I just read about it, and other agents were talking about it. The bars were unmarked, so not traceable. And even the driver wasn't traceable. He had a fake ID, there were no dental records, no prints. The truck had been stolen and we couldn't get any lead on that, either."

"Didn't anyone claim the platinum?"

"No. That's what's so crazy. There doesn't seem to be any theft involved—no one's stepped forward to say it belongs to them."

"Any idea where the truck was headed?"

"Into Mexico, apparently. But that's not much of a help."

"How could I not have heard of this? When was it?"

"About ten days ago. I don't know—a few days before Harmon was killed, that's probably why you didn't notice. It was big in Texas, I'm telling you. It made the paper here, a little story in the *News*. I saw it. I don't think it even made the *Times.*"

"If the stuff was stolen, why wouldn't someone want it back? And if it wasn't stolen, why go to all that trouble of hiding it and trying to smuggle it? I mean, if that's what they were doing. It doesn't make sense."

"I know," she said, "and I'm sure it doesn't have anything to do with this. It's just I hear the word 'platinum' and my ears perk up."

"Well, you hide it well. Every person in the building probably saw your ears perk up."

"All right, so I don't have a good poker face. But can we get back to your major suck-up job on Bannister? What were you doing?"

"Were you watching him?"

"Bannister? Yeah."

"Did you see his face when we asked him about the travel records and the travel agent?"

"Yes."

"He was lying. He was lying his head off the whole time."

"I agree. So what good does it do to let him get away without giving us any of the information we need?"

"He's never going to give it to us. And it's not going to be easy pressuring them. They'll have lawyers swarming all over us."

"So you just give up?"

"Don't worry about it," he said. "We'll get what we need."

"How?"

"We'll steal it," Justin said.

She began rubbing her eyes and forehead. "You know how hard it is to pull off that kind of computer break-in?" Reggie said. She was practically yelling now. "I bet there's maybe two or three guys in the FBI who could pull it off. And I won't be able to get them to do it now, not on this short notice, if I can *ever* get them to do it. Plus, we'll never get this without a warrant. And even you think it's going to be impossible to get a warrant."

"I know."

"So what are you talking about?"

"I know a guy," Justin said.

Justin asked Reggie to walk him up to Central Park. It was a twelve-block walk and when they got there, he steered her toward a bench in the shade. Sitting, he pulled out his cell phone and punched in a speed-dial number.

"Mrs. Jenkins?" he asked after a moment. And after another moment: "Yes, this is Chief Westwood. How are you? . . . Thank you . . . Yes, I'm sure everything will work out fine on my end . . . Listen, I'd love to talk to your son if he's around . . . No, I know Gary's at the station. I meant your other son, Ben. Would you mind getting him? . . . Thank you."

"Oh god," Reggie said while he was waiting. "This is your little fourteen-year-old, isn't it?"

"Don't be an ageist. And I think he's fifteen now."

"Jay, do you know how crazy this is? This kid can't—"

He held up his hand to stop her. And then he spoke into the phone.

"Ben? . . . Yeah. Listen, I need you to do something for me and I need it quickly."

He told Ben Jenkins what he wanted.

Reggie groaned aloud about halfway through the request. When

Justin was finished talking, she heard something indistinct from the other end of the phone, then she heard Justin say, "That's highway robbery." More words from the teenager, then, "Okay, okay. You got it . . . Yes, I swear. A flat-screen TV. Yes, I heard you—thirty-two-inch screen. It's a deal. Now shut up and listen."

Justin gave Ben the information he'd gotten at Ascension—the computer system and the various names and e-mail addresses. He also gave Ben a list of the companies they were interested in. He made sure Ben had his cell phone and fax machine numbers back in East End. Then he was about to hang up, but he stopped and said, "Hey, Ben, how old are you now? . . . Fifteen? . . . Well, I'm going to make this more interesting for you. I'm sitting here with an FBI agent . . . yeah, an honest-to-God real FBI agent . . . and she says no fifteen-year-old kid can do what I'm asking you to do. She says the top FBI computer experts couldn't do it. Got anything to say to that?" He listened for a few seconds, turned to Reggie, and said, "How much?"

"What?"

"Ben wants to know how much you want to bet?"

"I'm not going to bet money with a fifteen-year-old boy," she said. And when Justin raised his eyes, she went, "A hundred bucks."

He repeated the figure to Ben, saying, "I'm going to get in on this action, too. I'll take you for fifty . . . Right. Get back to me as soon as you can."

Then he hung up and said to Reggie, "Want to get a drink? I've got time to kill before my date."

He gave Reggie her choice—she could drive his car back to East End or she could take the train. She chose to drive, which was fine with him. He liked the idea of a late-night train ride. The quiet appealed to him. So did the idea of actually catching a couple of hours' sleep.

But first he had a woman to wine and dine.

He got to the restaurant a little early, went into the men's room, and cleaned himself up as best he could. He went to the bar, told the bartender to give him a splash of bourbon and a lot of soda, and then he nursed it until Belinda Lambert walked into the restaurant.

Justin smelled her perfume a split second before he turned to see her. It was sickly sweet, and there was too much of it dabbed on. And, he would be willing to bet, dabbed in too many and too intimate locations. The whiff wasn't overwhelming, just enough to be overdone. That's how he would describe the rest of her: nothing too extreme, but the effect was that everything was taken just one step too far.

Belinda was wearing a dress just slightly too dressy for the restaurant. It was red and white—and the red was just a little too red—and shoulderless. Spaghetti straps held the whole thing up. It was cut low— just a bit too low—and she was not wearing a bra, so when she bent forward to kiss him hello, the tops of her nipples were exposed. The skirt was—he couldn't help but note—too short; it didn't quite reach mid-thigh. She wore high-heeled, open-toe shoes with so many straps Justin thought it would have taken him half an hour to put the things on. The overall impact was, he was surprised to find, sexy. She was a big girl, but she was comfortable with her body. In fact, more than comfortable. She knew how to use it and was more than happy to draw attention to it. But there was also something sad about the complete picture. She was trying just a little too hard. And there was a hint of desperation in her eyes, the way she revealed her hunger.

He flashed her his best smile and made a bet with himself that when he asked her what she wanted to drink, she'd say a glass of champagne. Either that or a margarita with salt. He thought she'd really want the 'rita on this hot, humid night but would go with the champagne because she thought it would be classy.

"Our table'll be ready in a minute," he said. "What would you like to drink?"

"A glass of champagne," she said. "Is that all right?"

"For you?" he said. "The sky's the limit."

The dinner went about as he figured it would. He'd pegged her for a drinker and a talker when he'd met her at Rockworth and Williams, and she was definitely both. She liked to talk about herself, too, so he knew he could use her self-absorption to his advantage. He insisted she have a second glass of champagne while he nursed his watered-down bourbon, then he ordered a bottle of red wine with their meal. As they ate and she talked, Justin made sure he poured the wine, much to the waiter's annoyance. By the time they made it to the second bottle, he'd had about a glass and a half of the St. Estèphe and she'd gone through the rest. She talked about her college days and what she'd studied and how she never thought she'd wind up working with money because she could never even balance her checkbook. Belinda talked about old boyfriends and moving to New York from Pittsburgh, and as she went on and on he began to like her. She had surprising flashes of insight and she was more self-aware than he'd given her credit for being. So he listened attentively and nodded when he was supposed to and clucked sympathetically to show he was sensitive; and at one point he said, looking embarrassed, "You know, I hope you don't mind my saying this, I know it's not very professional, but you're extremely attractive."

She couldn't hide her pleasure. She came back with, "I'm really glad you think so."

He smiled shyly—or as shyly as he could manage—and gradually he was able to steer the conversation around to Rockworth and Williams and Ellis St. John. Soon she was leaning across the table and putting his hand in hers and, with her other hand, stroking his arm. He asked how people in the office were responding to Ellis's absence, and she said no one seemed too concerned on the trading floor. She didn't know about the big boys. All she knew was that Daniel French had come by to say that she shouldn't worry too much about Ellis, that Mr. Berdon had heard from him and that everything was okay. It was some sort of family emergency, he'd said, and Belinda thought it was strange because Ellis didn't have much to do with his family. Mr. Berdon had instructed Mr. French to tell her that she was doing a good job and that she should refer all of Ellis's clients to Mr. French when they called in if it was something she couldn't handle herself. They said that if the police questioned her any further, she should say that Ellis was away on family matters and say that's all she knew, which was true enough because that's all she did know.

Justin asked if she believed them—was Ellis really in some kind of family situation?—and she frowned and said, "Sure. I mean, I guess so. Why would they lie? And I'm just so relieved he's okay. I was really worried." But Belinda obviously wasn't too worried right now, because she immediately brightened up and said they told her that because she was handling the situation so well the R & W powers that be decided to accelerate her bonus for the year. She leaned farther forward—one nipple was almost completely out of her dress now—and told him that they'd given her a check for fifty thousand dollars. Justin told her he was impressed and said that she deserved it. He asked her how Evan's cats were, and was she still feeding them, and she was impressed that he remembered about the cats. He said he loved cats and even remembered their names: Binky and Esther. Belinda's eyes softened, and he saw her melt a little bit at the thought that he'd been paying such close attention to her when they'd first met. She said she guessed the cats were fine but she hardly ever saw them—one of them never came out when she was there—but she was feeding them before and after work. It wasn't too difficult because she lived on Second Avenue and Twenty-third Street and Ellis lived on Gramercy Park, so she could feed them when she went to and from the office.

The evasiveness she showed in their first meeting had completely disappeared, and she was more than willing to gab. Ellis was a strange one, she explained. He was very good-looking but very insecure about his appeal. He was gay but uncomfortable with his sexuality. She thought he was the kind of person who didn't really like sex—he liked to be in love. She made it very clear that she was quite different from her boss—Belinda Lambert liked love *and* sex. Justin gently probed her relationship with Ellis, and, as he suspected, she was intimately acquainted with a lot of the details of his life. He was very dependent on her. And he trusted her. But there was no one he liked and trusted more than Evan Harmon. Belinda looked like she might cry at the mention of Evan's name and when Justin asked why, she said it was because Mr. Harmon treated Ellis so poorly. What did that mean? Justin wanted to know. "Oh," she said, "he just wasn't nice to him. Evan knew that Ellis worshiped him—he really, really worshiped him. It was almost weird."

"Weird how?" Justin asked.

"Is this getting too boring for you?" she asked, her words coming out slurred. "I mean, here I am going on and on about my boss and you haven't told me anything about you."

Justin shook his head. "Not much to tell," he said modestly. "You're much more interesting."

"Liar," she said. "But such a sweet liar."

"Tell me more about Evan and Ellis. I'm really interested."

"Ellis used to stare at him whenever I saw them together. I mean, just *stare* at him, like he was some kind of god or something. And Mr. Harmon, he'd just kind of use Ellis. You know, get him to do his errands. And then every sho offern—every . . . so . . . often, he'd throw Ellis a bone."

"What kind of bone?"

"A trip somewhere good. Parish or someplace."

"Ellis and Evan went to Paris together?"

"No. God no, sweetie. Never, never, never. He'd just give Ellis a ticket and tell him to have a good time. If you ask me, he probably just gave Ellis what he got with frequent flier miles."

She excused herself to go to the ladies' room. He filled her glass with the last bit of wine from the second bottle and then ordered her a double brandy and himself a very watered-down version of the same. When the waiter stared at him disapprovingly, Justin slipped him a fifty-dollar bill and suddenly the look was a lot more approving. Belinda returned, and as she passed by his chair she wrapped her arms around him and gave him a big kiss. Her tongue quickly forced its way inside his mouth and his eyes met hers. She looked extremely happy.

The kiss didn't last long, just a couple of seconds. It also didn't take her long to sit back down and finish her brandy and tell him she thought they should go back to her place. He agreed instantly.

They made out in the taxi going downtown. She was practically crushing him against the cab door on his side of the backseat. The doorman in her building had obviously seen plenty of this kind of behavior—either from her or other tenants—because he didn't bat an eye. Justin was worried that she'd actually disrobe in the elevator, but she managed to keep her dress on and stay upright until they tumbled into her apartment. It was the perfect apartment for her—all the adornments were too cute or too colorful or too big or too small. There were few books in view, and the ones that were there were either chick lit or self-help. She had a decent number of CDs. He couldn't help but notice that she was a big Beyoncé fan. Before he could take in any more of her apartment, she dragged him onto the overstuffed couch, but he fended her off by pulling out a joint. She licked her lips and said she didn't know that cops smoked pot. He told her that cops did just about everything. He lit the joint, let her take a few drags. He took a hit, exhaled most of the smoke, handed the joint back to her. She sucked it in with relish. Within thirty seconds she was reclining on her couch, a tired and dopey grin on her face, and about a minute after that her eyes were closed. He waited until he was certain she was out before he gently lifted himself off the sofa and stood up.

Justin breathed a sight of relief. Jesus Christ, he thought, she'd had enough alcohol and drugs to put down an elephant. The youth of today. They were made of better stuff than he was.

He didn't have to search for her key ring. She'd tossed it on a table as soon as she'd managed to unlock her door. There were too many keys on the ring for him to figure out which one belonged to Ellis St. John's apartment. He figured Ellis's key had to be on the ring. She'd keep it there since she'd been going to feed the cats every day. He stuck the entire ring of keys in his pocket, decided he'd worry later about getting them back to her.

He looked down at the figure on the couch.

All part of the job, he thought. Taking advantage of a lonely, drunk girl.

She'd be hungover and depressed the next day. He knew the feeling, so he tried to think of something he could do that might make her feel a little better. Couldn't really come up with anything. Finally, he searched for and found a piece of paper. On it he wrote, *Don't worry. Will feed the cats and give them enough for the morning. Will leave your keys with your doorman.* He put the note down on her coffee table, then picked it back up, scribbled: *P.S. Thanks for a nice evening.*

He didn't think she'd really believe the P.S. On the other hand, she was the kind of girl who could and probably would convince herself of just about anything. At least temporarily.

On his way down the elevator, he decided he was sorry he hadn't seen her remove her shoes. He really was curious to see how long it would've taken.

26

Seeing Ellis St. John's apartment broke the roll that Justin thought he was on. It was nothing like he suspected it would be.

Justin had expected sleek and modern all the way: lots of shiny glass and black marble, something cold and impersonal and hard-edged. But the Rockworth and Williams employee lived in a prewar twelve-story building overlooking Gramercy Park. The building was elegant and not at all flashy. And St. John's apartment was equally elegant and subdued, filled with a combination of antiques—American painted furniture, mostly of the colonial era and in muted colonial colors—and well-crafted, comfortable, contemporary furniture. The four rooms—living room, master bedroom, a second bedroom that doubled as a den, and a small space off the living room used as a dining area—were furnished sparsely and tastefully. The kitchen was the only thing that broke with the rest of the decor—it was all new, top-of-the-line, stainless-steel appliances, with expensive knives and utilitarian tools displayed on hooks and magnetic holders. St. John was not a man who decorated for show or convenience. The apartment obviously was done to cater to his own taste; his own comfort; and, judging by the well-used chopping blocks on the kitchen counter and the oiled cast iron pans, to his own skill level. As Justin began to poke around, the setting struck a chord: it reminded him of somewhere else, another apartment, another house, but he couldn't put his finger on it. He stopped for a moment, closed his eyes to concentrate and focus. Then he realized what it was: Ellis St. John's apartment looked a lot like Abby and Evan Harmon's home. It was furnished in much the same style, although probably not as expensively. Yes, he thought, surveying the scene, there are definite similarities. Same style of antiques, same kinds of chairs and sofas, same color scheme.

Justin took his time going through the apartment. He didn't know exactly what he was looking for, he just wanted to look. The only thing he was certain of was that Ellis St. John was not off embroiled in a family emergency, as Belinda Lambert had been told. If St. John was involved in the murder of Evan Harmon, Justin was now convinced that so too were some of his superiors at Rockworth and Williams. At the very least, Daniel French and his bosses were involved in some sort of cover-up, protecting St. John. Or protecting the firm's good name.

It's all about self-preservation, he thought again. *Survival and safety of the corporate structure.*

Having surveyed the overall layout of the apartment, Justin headed into the master bedroom to poke and probe more closely. The closets there were meticulously organized. Ellis's shirts were perfectly and evenly spaced so no sleeve touched another sleeve, and they were organized by color, going from white to gray to black to blue to green. That was the extent of the color range. If it was a patterned shirt, the dominant color was what dictated its placement. Ellis St. John had eight sport jackets, all solid—four of them black, two gray, and two blue. His ten suits were all pin-striped except for one light-gray summer suit and a dark-gray flannel winter one. The most daring of the pinstripes had a touch of wine red running through the black-on-black stripes. All shoes were highly polished and perfectly aligned on metal shoe racks, wooden shoe trees firmly in place. Justin couldn't be sure, but he'd be willing to bet a lot of money that each pair of shoes was separated by exactly half an inch of space. The guy was definitely compulsive and obsessive. There was not a speck of dust to be found. And there wasn't one single thing in the room that was not put in an exact and orderly spot. Justin turned from the closet, then stopped. He turned back, frowning. Something in there, an image, had jarred his memory in some way. An image tried to fight its way into his brain, but the image was diffuse, fractured, not connected to anything that Justin could come up with. Then the brief flash was gone almost as instantly as it had come into his head. And it didn't come back. He shrugged. He knew he couldn't dredge it back up. That's not the way these things worked. It would either be there or it wouldn't.

He moved on. There was a rack with luggage on it, in the farthest closet to the right in the bedroom. Ellis, of course, had a matching set, all made of light-green canvas and brown leather. There was room for four bags. The largest—a normal suitcase size and shape—was on the left, then a medium-size duffel bag. Then there was an empty space—large enough for an overnight bag—and then there was a matching briefcase with a shoulder strap. Justin stared at the space for the missing overnight bag. Ellis had been gone for four days now. Why had he taken only such a small bag? Planning on coming back—but something had suddenly come up? Like murder? Or had he left in that much of a hurry, knowing he had to travel light and move quickly?

Justin exhaled deeply, moved on to an antique tiger maple chest of drawers. As Justin was going through the drawers, he came upon a photo album. It was clearly not meant for public viewing, tucked as it was under a slew of men's underwear—briefs that matched his suits and jackets. Justin pulled the album out and began flipping through the pages. Nothing but photographs of Evan Harmon. Some were candid shots, in and out of an office. Some were newspaper and magazine clippings covering the last decade. Some were prints of Evan in his Hamptons house—and studying the background of those photos, Justin could now see how closely this apartment really did mirror the way Evan had lived. It was a disturbing selection of shots. Ellis St. John was not just obsessed with neatness and order, he was obsessed with Evan Harmon. The question was: Was he obsessed enough to kill him? Justin was now more certain than ever that St. John was mixed up in all this. But he still didn't have a clue how or, more important, why.

Was it jealousy? He realized that there wasn't one photo of Abby in the book. As Justin looked through it again, he saw that in some instances she had to have been cut out of particular pictures. Deeply sick. It was as if Ellis couldn't stand the thought of Evan with another partner, having intimate contact with anyone else. But Evan had been married the entire time he'd known Ellis St. John. The jealousy couldn't have been anything new. But could it have reached new heights? Could Evan have possibly begun an affair with Ellis? If he had, Justin thought, well, that would certainly spark something.

He thought back to Abby denying that her husband had homosexual affairs. She had been convincing. But was she in denial? Was she humiliated by the thought?

What the hell was going on with these people, these connections? These dots?

Justin thought of the famous scene from *The Third Man*. Orson Welles's great speech to Joseph Cotten atop the Ferris wheel. Welles's character, Harry Lime, justifying his black market dealing in bad penicillin, telling Holly Martins to look down at the small dots below. The dots were people but barely identifiable from so high up. Welles saying, Tell me the truth, if someone offered you a ton of money for every dot that stopped moving forever, would you really care? Harry Lime didn't care. There were too many dots, too many insignificant specks walking around, meaningless in the grand scheme of things.

Justin Westwood did care, however. He realized he didn't much care about the grand scheme of things. Didn't really even believe there was a grand scheme.

But he did care about those specks.

Those dots.

He shut the photo album and put it back where he'd found it.

This latest scenario he'd been envisioning didn't feel right to Justin. He couldn't rule it out—it was certainly possible and logical—but it didn't fit with everything he knew about Evan Harmon. Evan was a star. Evan did not live by ordinary rules or even ordinary passions. He wouldn't have looked twice at Ellis St. John unless there was some way Evan could have used him.

Evan was a user. It's what Vince Ellerbe had said. He'd always been a user.

Was that it?

Had Evan used Ellis in some way? And had Ellis finally taken enough abuse from his idol?

Justin shook his head.

Absolutely no way of knowing.

Shit.

He kept prowling through the apartment.

Justin checked St. John's bathroom and medicine cabinet. It was well stocked and as neatly arranged as everything else in the place. It didn't feel as though St. John had been planning on staying away for a long time. Everything was too full, too orderly.

Something was off, but Justin just couldn't put his finger on it.

There were several items he'd been hoping to find but didn't: an address book (electronic or otherwise), a calendar, a BlackBerry or cell phone, hastily scribbled notes, or even interesting garbage. Justin hadn't really expected otherwise. That sort of thing happened only on TV or in Hitchcock movies. The hero finds a notepad and realizes that the piece of paper that had been on top had had an important address written on it, and so he deciphers the address from the indented marks left on the clean sheet of paper. Yeah, right. Never happens.

He went into the second bedroom and eyed a notepad left on the desk. Couldn't help himself. He looked for some crucial markings. Nothing. Whatever had been written on the pad, its secrets weren't going to be revealed now. Sometimes Justin wished life were a little more like Hitchcock movies. And a little less like Bergman movies.

This bedroom. It had been set up as a home office in addition to being a guest room. St. John's desktop computer was there, a sleek silver Dell, and various office supplies. Justin went to turn on the computer but suddenly realized the hard drive was gone. All that was left was the screen and the keyboard.

Justin wondered if Ellis had taken it with him. Hard to know. If Ellis had preplanned this whole thing and had information on his computer he knew he'd want to hide, then it was possible. Unlikely, though, the more Justin thought about it. If he was going away for a weekend, it's much more likely he'd take a laptop. If he wanted to have information disappear from his desktop machine, he could just erase it before

he left. It didn't make sense that he'd take a difficult-to-carry part that
wasn't useful on its own. No, much more likely that someone had been
in this apartment before Justin and had taken it.

Justin jumped, startled, as he felt something graze his leg. He looked
down—it was one of the cats. This one was solid gray with a fat stomach. He wondered if she was Esther or Binky. Didn't really matter. The
cat started rubbing up against him and meowing plaintively. Justin
decided that what mattered right now was that he should feed them
both as long as he was here.

He went into the kitchen and saw three cat bowls on the floor. One
was for water, two were food. One of the food bowls was empty. The
other was a quarter full. He opened the door to what he assumed was a
pantry. It was. He saw a couple of dozen cans of cat food in several even
stacks. He took one can, split it in half and put it in the two bowls. He
didn't bother to clean out the bowl that already had food in it. Let them
party hearty, he thought. He put fresh water in the third dish and, as the
gray cat began to pick at the new food, Justin went back to Ellis's den.

He stared at the desk where the computer had been. Then he noticed
a closet off to the side of the room. He opened it, saw that it had been
professionally organized with built-in shelves on the top and a double
rack for hanging clothes—shirts and pants—below that. The shelves
were filled with office supplies and remnants of things that didn't seem
to belong anywhere else—empty gift boxes and ribbons and wrapping
paper, some DVDs, framed photographs that didn't merit public dis-
play any longer. And Justin now also saw the other cat. This one was
black-and-white and was on the floor of the closet. She wasn't moving
or meowing. She couldn't. Her neck had been broken.

Justin stepped back. The question of whether or not Ellis St. John
had taken his hard drive with him seemed to be answered. And the
answer was no.

Someone had come into the apartment. Someone had taken the
computer. And someone had killed Ellis St. John's cat.

He took out his cell phone, called Reggie. She started to make some
comment about his date, but he cut her off, asked if she could get a

fingerprint guy over to Gramercy Park. She said she thought she could. He told her to do it, said he'd fill her in in the morning.

He waited in the apartment, and someone from the FBI showed up less than half an hour later. Justin told him he could concentrate on the desk where the computer had been and on the closet in that room. The FBI guy did a quick check of the dead cat, said there was no trace of prints or blood. Justin nodded, not surprised, then he went and found a black plastic garbage bag under the kitchen sink, picked up the cat, and put it inside the bag.

The FBI agent told Justin he knew what to do, no need for him to stick around. He said he'd get the results to Agent Bokkenheuser and Agent Fletcher as soon as he had any.

Justin thanked him and left. Out on the street, a quarter of a block away from Ellis's building, there were three trash cans left out for pickup in the morning. He opened the lid of one of them, put the cat inside.

All he had to do now, before catching his train home, was walk the few blocks back to Belinda Lambert's apartment. Earlier, he had decided he would leave her keys—and Ellis's—with her doorman. There was no reason she couldn't return to her routine now. She'd just be feeding one cat, but she probably wouldn't even realize that for a while. She said one of the cats never came out to see her. So she could do her duty, blissfully ignorant of what had transpired.

But the theft of Ellis St. John's computer made him realize there was something else he needed.

So when he got back to Belinda's building, he dangled her keys in front of the doorman and said he had to go upstairs to return them. The doorman wanted to call Belinda first, but Justin grabbed his arm, told him he was a cop, and said he'd prefer to do things a little differently. The doorman nodded, waved his hands to show that it was no problem whatsoever.

Upstairs, Justin opened Belinda's front door. She was still sacked out on the couch. It didn't look as if she'd budged so much as an inch. And he wasn't shocked to find out that she snored.

She didn't stir as he moved around her apartment, and it took him only a couple of minutes to find Belinda's BlackBerry and slip it into his

jacket pocket. If he were a praying man, he would have thanked someone or something for giving Belinda Lambert a big mouth.

Before leaving, Justin looked at the note he'd left for her earlier.
He picked it up, crumpled it in his hand. There was no need for her to
know that anything had happened now. So he wrote a new one. This
one just said, "Thanks."

Back on the street, as he began heading toward Penn Station, he
thought about the cat that had been killed. It saddened him and, as
always, he was surprised that he'd become inured to the death of human
beings but not to the killing of an animal. He supposed it was because
animals were, for the most part, innocent. And people were, for the most
part, anything *but* innocent. And he thought about how the murder of a
human being almost always had a purpose. A twisted purpose, but there
was an underlying reason, whether it was jealousy or greed or power.
Murder was always a distorted means to a desperate end. But killing an
animal. There was no purpose, no means, no end. To hurt a little animal
meant that all you had to be was one sick, mean son of a bitch.

He thought about how he'd tossed the cat into the garbage can on
the street.

Not much of a burial, Justin decided, not for something that only
gave pleasure to people.

On the other hand, he thought, it served its purpose as well as
most.

27

The only thing better than the quiet, late-night train ride back to Bridgehampton would have been half an hour in a crazy-hot steam room and a long, cold shower. But Justin was content to let the solitude and the relative quiet help wash the soiled feeling off his body. By the time he'd taken Fred's Taxi Service from the train station back to East End, he was relatively relaxed and guilt free.

He got into bed and decided he didn't even need a drink to help him sleep. Then he heard his cell phone. He'd left it downstairs and he'd also left it on vibrate, but he could hear the vibration as it resonated against the hard surface of his desk. He swung his legs out of bed and made it downstairs in time to catch the call. When he heard the caller's voice at the other end, he wasn't sure if he was glad or not that he'd moved so fast.

"Jay?" Abby Harmon said.

He didn't answer.

"Jay?" she repeated. "It's Abby."

"I know," he said.

"I'm sorry I haven't called you."

"Uh-huh" was the best he could muster.

"I wasn't allowed to talk to you. My lawyer forbade it."

"And what changed?"

"Nothing. I just wanted to talk to you."

"Okay," he said.

"You sound so cold," she told him. And when he didn't answer—what could he answer?—she said, "I don't know who's on my side anymore."

"I'm on your side," he said.

"Yes, I know you are. I do know that. But . . ."

"But what?"

"Everyone's telling me something different."

"What are they telling you, Ab?"

"I'm not supposed to discuss it with you."

"You're not going to fall for it, are you, if I ask you what it is you're not supposed to discuss?"

She breathed out the best laugh she could. "No," she said. "I'm not. But thank you for making me laugh. I haven't laughed since this all started. God, is it really not even a week?"

"Who else is telling you not to talk to me, Ab?"

"My lawyer. H. R. Everyone."

"You're talking to H. R.?"

"Yes. He's—he's been very supportive."

"So he doesn't think you actually killed his son anymore?"

"He never really thought that, Jay. He was just . . . He was upset. Evan's death was crushing to him."

"I didn't think he was crushable."

"I was wrong about him. He's—he's been a big help."

"Who else, Abby? Who else is helping you?"

"Lincoln."

"Lincoln Berdon?"

"Yes. He was always very close to Evan. He was his mentor."

"Abby, I'd really like to see you."

"I can't, Jay. It's not a good idea."

"Why not?"

"Because of the relationship we had. I'm still being investigated. And you're working with the FBI now. You're still investigating. My lawyers said I'm not allowed."

"How'd you know that?"

"What?"

"How'd you know I was working with the FBI?"

It might have been the very first time he'd ever heard her flustered. "I—I don't know. It was probably in the paper."

"It wasn't."

That was the end of her flustered tone. Her voice instantly turned sharp and distant. "Then I don't know, Jay. Someone told me."

"Who?"

"I don't know. Probably my lawyer."

"Abby . . . I need to talk to you. I need to know more about Ellis St. John."

"What does Elly have to do with this?"

"Elly's in this up to his fucking eyeballs."

"No, Jay, you can't be right about that."

"I am right."

"You're not," she said. "You weren't right about Ellis being missing, either. I just heard. Lincoln told me he had some kind of family emergency."

"Really?" Justin said. "What kind of emergency?"

"I don't know. But I know they've given him a leave of absence from R&W."

"How'd Lincoln happen to pass this info along to you?"

"I was surprised I hadn't heard from Ellis, because he and Evan were close. So I asked about him."

"Abby, I'm telling you. There's no emergency. He's got something to do with Evan's murder."

"I don't think so, Jay."

"Listen to me, Abby. Listen to what I'm telling you—"

"I can't." And before he could go on, she said, "I'm sorry, Jay."

"Sorry about what?"

"I know you're on my side. So . . . I'm just sorry."

"Abby . . ."

"Good-bye, Jay."

"Abby, I have to talk to you. Don't hang up."

"Bye."

"Abby . . ."

But she was gone. Jay stared at his open cell phone in frustration before snapping it shut.

What the hell had she done? What was she apologizing for?

He decided he needed that drink if he was going to get any sleep at all.

Justin found out first thing in the morning what Abby's phone call was all about. As soon as he stepped outside his front door to pick up the morning papers.

The headline on one tab was: WIDOW SPEAKS! The headline on the other tab was: TRUE CONFESSION: HE DID IT!

The stories were more or less consistent. Abby had spoken to the media the night before and what she'd basically said was: *I've been a bad girl. I cheated on my husband. And now it's caught up with me because one of the men I cheated with—David Kelley—murdered the husband I really loved despite it all.*

He sank back on the couch in disbelief and read more. There were several photos of Abby, many of them from her past, looking as glamorous and sexy as it's possible to look. Each paper had a similar shot of her from the day before: flanked by her lawyer and H. R. Harmon. She looked drawn and subdued and conservative.

Abby said she was speaking out publicly because she decided it was best to get the truth out in the open. She revealed that she and Evan had been having troubles for several years. There was never any question about their love for each other, but his business was so consuming that it seemed more important than their relationship. Abby confessed to being somewhat selfish and spoiled—that was by far the worst thing to which she confessed—and she said she was hurt when she realized she wasn't the center of his world. So she had affairs. Not many, but several. One of them was with David Kelley and that one got out of hand. Kelley wouldn't accept the fact that it was just an affair. He kept insisting it was going somewhere she knew it would never go. He talked all the time about how if Evan weren't around, they could be together. It never occurred to her to take him literally. Nor did she really take him seriously. It was just talk, she said. Even when she discovered that Evan had been murdered, it was inconceivable that Dave—she called him Dave by this point in the story—was involved. Then she found out that Evan had been tortured and that the means of torture was a stun gun. At this point in the story, one tab had her tearing up and becoming too emotional to continue for quite a while. The other tab just continued with the story line, which was that when she heard about the stun gun, she knew that Dave had to be involved. She didn't say anything for a few days, still not able to convince herself emotionally of the truth. Then the police came to her and told her that they knew about the gun. She told them what she knew: that Dave had one, that he'd even kept it at their house for a while. She said that she'd have to live with her guilt. She said that she thought she was doing something that she couldn't justify but still wasn't high on the list of evils—cheating on her husband. But she realized that all cheating and all lying had to be put high on the list of evils, because this is what the result could be.

H. R. Harmon hugged her at the end of her emotionally draining tale. Reporters peppered her with questions. One had asked her about the police chief in East End Harbor. Hadn't she been having an affair with him, too? And wasn't he still being investigated by the police to see if he was involved?

Abby said, "I did also have an affair with Justin Westwood, the chief of police of East End Harbor. I owe him an apology because, I realize now, I was using him as a kind of psychological crutch, a way to move away from Kelley. I know the police are investigating Justin. I'm sorry he's been suspended, and I can only hope to God that he had nothing to do with Evan's murder. But after what's happened this past week, I don't think anything will ever surprise me again."

Justin tossed the paper on the floor, disgusted. Despite the fact that he seemed to officially have been cleared of everything but professional misconduct, this story—and Abby's not so subtle insinuation, leaving his culpability as an open question—wouldn't help in his investigation. It certainly wouldn't make it any easier for him to get in to see H. R. Harmon or Lincoln Berdon. Now he kicked the paper across the room and when the phone rang soon after, he didn't say hello, just barked "What?!" The person on the other end was flustered, and Justin heard a nervous voice say, "Um . . . Chief Westwood? This is Ben Jenkins. I hope I didn't wake you up. I'm sorry for calling so early."

"Ben," Justin said, doing his best to soften his tone, although he knew it wasn't exactly what he could claim as actually soft. "I'm sorry. What's up?"

"I got what you wanted," the teenager said.

"What?"

"The stuff you wanted me to do. I did it."

"All of it? Already?"

"Yeah. It wasn't so hard."

"You got into Ascension's system?"

"Uh-huh. It was pretty easy. They have lousy security. Hey, did that agent really mean it when she bet me a hundred bucks?"

"Yeah, she did."

"How do I collect?"

Justin shook his head, amazed. "I'll tell you what—I'll get it for you, that way she can't weasel out."

"Really?" Ben said. "Gee, thanks."

"Ben, can you get the info to me now?"

"Yeah, that's why I was calling. I just e-mailed it. I wanted to let you know it was there 'cause it sounded kind of important."

"It is."

"And I'll get my TV, right?" the kid asked.

"I'll even pay for the delivery charge," Justin told him. Then, eyeing the gadget sitting on his desk, the one he'd taken from Belinda Lambert's apartment the night before, he said, "Ben, let me ask you something. I think I've got another job for you."

"Cool," Ben said. "I can use a DVD recorder. U.S. and European capabilities."

"Name your brand."

"Wow, this is great."

"Yeah, great. Listen. I've got a BlackBerry here. It's a secretary's, but her boss had it configured so all his corporate info automatically shows up on it. Can you come here and take a look at it? I might need you to recover some information."

"Well, if she's attached to his system, I can hack it."

"How about coming over now?"

"Gee, I can't now. I gotta get goin'."

"Where you going so early?" Justin looked at his watch. It was still a few minutes before seven-thirty. "What are you even doing up so early? Shouldn't you be staying out all night and sleeping till noon?"

"I got summer school," Ben said.

"Summer school?" Justin said.

"I had to pull my grades up, you know."

"Your grades? How the hell can you get bad grades? Ben, you're a goddamn genius."

"Yeah," Ben Jenkins said, "but my grades still stink."

"How is that possible?"

"My mom says I watch too much TV. Listen, I gotta go, okay, Chief?"

"Ben . . . I think we're talking about you skipping summer school today."

"I don't know. My mom gets pretty pissed off about stuff like that."

"I'll talk to her. Is she awake?"

"Yeah. She never sleeps. She gets up at like five every morning."

"Let me talk to her, okay?"

Ben put his mother on the phone, and Justin explained to her what he needed her son to do. He said it was very important. And he told her he'd talk to Ben's teacher and explain everything to her, so Ben wouldn't get penalized for missing any work. The clincher was that he told her Ben wouldn't just be working with the police department, he'd be helping the FBI.

"Honest to goodness?" she asked. "The FBI?"

He swore on his life and Mrs. Jenkins agreed. She said she'd drive him over in a few minutes. Justin then spoke to Ben again, told him precisely what he wanted him to do so if he was going to need any special tools or connectors he could bring them with him.

As soon as Ben hung up, Justin went to his computer. When he went on AOL, the lead news story was: BLACK WIDOW ADMITS TO AFFAIRS BUT NOT MURDER. Justin said, "Fuck me," and then signed on to his mailbox.

Sure enough, Ben's e-mail was waiting for him. He opened it, briefly scanned the info on the screen, then printed it. Two copies. He started to dial Reggie on his cell phone as he waited for the pages to print, but before he could finish dialing, there was a knock at the door. When he opened it, Reggie was standing on his doorstep. She was holding a newspaper, but as she peered inside his living room, she saw his papers scattered on the floor.

"I see you're already up on your current events," she said.

He told her to shut up and come in.

28

Reggie's mouth was open wide as she studied the info that Justin had printed. She stared over at Ben, who had arrived a few minutes after she had, and was busy clacking away at the keyboard of Justin's computer.

"You *are* a genius," she said.

"You owe him a hundred bucks," Justin told her, "and me fifty."

"You mind if I wait till payday?" she asked Ben.

"When is that?" Ben asked.

"Friday," she said.

The teenager looked at Justin, who nodded.

"Should be all right," Justin said. "But if you want, I'll pay you and she can pay me back. With interest."

"Nah," Ben said. "That's okay. I can wait." And he went back to searching through Belinda Lambert's BlackBerry, which he'd hooked up to Justin's computer.

"This is unbelievable," Reggie said quietly. "He got us everything we need."

"So let me get your take."

"Why don't we go through it separately? So we get separate takes. Then we can merge what we each come up with."

Justin agreed and they spent the hour or so—Justin on the couch, Reggie with one leg tucked under her as she nestled in the easy chair, as Ben worked, silently engrossed, sitting at Justin's desk—trying to organize the new mass of information. When they were done, they compared their lists and the connections they'd come up with. They winnowed out anything they both agreed was irrelevant—companies that didn't seem to have any possible connection to the investigation, names that popped up that also were removed from any personal or business dealings that might connect to the murders—but if one disagreed, the information stayed in. Then they merged everything they had onto a master list.

Justin turned to Ben. "How much longer you gonna be?" he asked.

"I'm done. I was just kinda listenin' to you guys. That's how you work, huh? Pretty cool."

"Were you able to get into St. John's computer?"

"Nope. Rockworth's security's good, much better than Ascension. They got a serious system."

"So nothing, huh?"

"Not exactly nothing. I mean, I couldn't get into any of the financial stuff, like I did with Ascension. I think I could if I had more time, but I don't think it'll do any good. At least for the guy you want. I don't think this guy St. John is still in the system. I think all his info's been wiped out. Once I downloaded all of this chick's stuff"—he nodded at Belinda Lambert's BlackBerry—"I could do a basic hack and get into his Outlook. But there's nothin' there."

"E-mails?"

"Gone. And I can't find 'em without having access to his hard drive. I can't recover that from outside."

"Did he have a calendar in the system? Maybe an address book?"

"Yeah. But someone wiped it, too."

"You're sure?"

"Definitely. A few days ago."

"So you can't retrieve any of it?"

"I didn't have to."

"I'm afraid you did. It's pretty important."

"No," Ben said. "That's not what I mean. I didn't have to. It's like you said—everything on his system was automatically carried over onto this Belinda person's computer. I looked at some of her stuff, too, and man, did she have some crazy e-mails. Is she hot?"

Justin ignored the last question. "The stuff on St. John's computer is still saved in Belinda Lambert's BlackBerry?"

"Yup."

"And you can access it?"

"Yup. Already did."

"Ben, I'm sorry, but I want to make sure I have this straight. When St. John's calendar book and address book were erased, that didn't erase what was transferred to Belinda's BlackBerry?"

"Yeah, I'm tellin' you, it wasn't erased. I mean it was, but whoever did it didn't understand the way this St. John guy set his work up. Everything entered into his Outlook system or anything sent to him on e-mail was automatically transferred to her name and became a separate entity. It was like it was automatically cc'd to her—you know what I mean? It didn't just put his system onto hers, it created a separate entity."

"And St. John had to have known this, right?"

"I think so. You said he's the one who set it up, right?"

"Right." Justin looked at Reggie. "It means St. John wasn't the one who erased the material. If he had, he would have figured out a way to erase Belinda's, too." He turned back to Ben. "Right?"

"Yeah. I mean, that's what I'd say. But I'm just the computer geek. You're the cop—you know what I mean?"

Justin smiled. The broadest smile he'd managed in quite some time.

"I transferred it all to your computer," Ben said. "Filed under St.John. It's a cool name. You want to see it?"

Both Justin and Reggie dashed over to the computer screen. They said "yes" in unison.

"What do you want to see first?" Ben asked. "How about his task list?"

"Sure," Justin said. "And then go to his calendar book."

Ben scrolled through Ellis's current task list and the past month's worth of his appointments. Nothing jumped out at either Justin or Reggie. His list of things to do was fairly mundane. And most of the names on his calendar were either unknown to them or seemed reasonable to be there. Until Ben got to the date that Harmon was killed. It was a Thursday. That morning's typed-in notation said "EH/EEH." In parentheses—even this guy's calendar was perfectly organized and arranged—it said "See directions/adbk."

Justin looked at Reggie.

"Too good to be true," he said.

She nodded. "EH. The guy had a meeting with Evan Harmon. In EEH. Right here in East End Harbor."

"Ben," Justin said, "I want to make sure of this. Go to the listing for Evan Harmon in the Outlook contact list."

Ben typed in the word "Harmon" and clicked on "search." There was no mistaking the notation in the date book. In the space reserved for "Additional Information" under Evan's contact listing were specific directions to Evan and Abby's house. Seemed pretty clear. Evan Harmon was murdered on Thursday evening, six days ago, on Justin's birthday. Ellis St. John was at Evan's house that day—or, at least, his date book said he was supposed to be there. Justin looked at the next day's calendar. For Friday, all that was marked was another "EH." Same for Saturday and Sunday. Justin shook his head.

"The secretary said he had plans for the weekend. Secret kind of plans. Said he couldn't be reached."

"This guy Ellis was spending the weekend with Evan Harmon?" Reggie was incredulous.

Justin shook his head. "Seems like. But I'm telling you, it doesn't make sense."

"Wow," Ben said. "Is this really about the Harmon murder? This is so cool I can't believe it."

"Ben," Justin said, "is everything you could find on St. John downloaded into my computer?"

"Yeah, but like I said, it's not much. It's mostly just the e-mails and calendar stuff that was shifted to that Belinda girl's system."

"I think you can still make a couple of classes today."

"You mean I'm done?"

"Call your mom to come get you. You're done."

"But you're the hero of the day," Reggie added.

"Yeah, yeah," Ben said, "but I'm still gettin' my money on Friday, right?"

"I'll hand-deliver it first thing."

The kid turned to Justin. "And my DVD recorder?"

"Get outta here, Ben."

"Lemme know if you need anything else. This is a sweet gig."

"You'll be the first to know," Justin told him.

Their computer whiz kid was finally out the door, and Reggie and Justin turned back to the screen.

"So what happened?" she asked. "Ellis got dumped and he went berserk? And killed Evan Harmon?"

"And then what?" Justin said. "He killed Ron LaSalle and Wanda Chinkle and hired a Sicilian hit man to take out Bruno and got a Chinese woman to kill that guy who worked for LaSalle, Stan Solomon? Come on. Ellis St. John's a gay Willy Loman. He's not a mass murderer."

"Well, as long as you're coming up with things that make no sense," Reggie said, "care to explain how David Kelley's stun gun figures into all this? You got a connection between Kelley and St. John?"

"I've got a better connection between Kelley and the man in the fucking moon," Justin said. "None of this makes any damn sense at all."

He paced tightly out to the living room, veered into the kitchen for a moment, then paced right back out. He pounded his hand against the wall, a short, furious punch that cracked the paint.

"That's not all that productive," she said, "but it's a little impressive."

"All right," he said, rubbing his knuckles. "Let's see what we've actually got from all the stuff that Ben gave us. Let's just look at it in black and white."

He spent a few minutes entering everything they'd culled through and organized into the Hades file in his computer. When he was done he printed up the lists and cross-references they'd made, as well as the sheets of information that Ben Jenkins had managed to steal, all separated into various sections. Ben had managed to tap into the Ascension travel records—and Forrest Bannister had indeed lied. All company travel was booked through one agent: conveniently enough, through the in-house travel agent for Rockworth and Williams—another service that primary brokers clearly provided. Records were also kept by Bannister's secretary for every single trip that every employee made. Ben had also gotten a list of every client who invested with Ascension, individual and corporate. Amazingly enough, he also had a record of how much the investment was. There were also pages and pages and pages (several hundred) that, as near as Justin could tell, were records of Ascension trades. He couldn't follow them in any kind of real detail, but he was amazed that the kid had managed to get them.

He and Reggie started their organizing with the names. The first group of names needed no descriptive heading. It listed the three people who had been murdered up to this point (they didn't include Stan Solomon because they both felt he wasn't a target; he was an incidental victim, someone who'd just managed to get in the way during the course of a robbery): Evan Harmon, Ronald LaSalle, and Wanda Chinkle. Under each name, they listed any other names—of people as well as companies—that had a direct connection and could be deemed relevant to the investigation. Then they listed names that had surfaced to which there was no known connection, trying to pinpoint any gaps in the various chains.

Next, because of the folder prepared by Ellen Loache and the work that Ben had done, Justin and Reggie were able to compare the companies that Ascension did business with that also did business with the LaSalle Group. There were fifteen overlaps:

Cates and Herr (mining company in South Africa)
Charles Chan & Associates
Eggleston Catalytic Converters
Flame Bros. Ltd.
Goldman, Inc.
Maroon Group
Menking, Inc. (international company that trades in precious metals, particularly platinum)
Myles Johnson International
The National Beet Growers Association of America Pension Fund

Noodleman America Corporation
Pinkney & Associates
Rossovitch and Sons
Scarlet Knight, Inc.
Silverado Jewelry Association
The Tintagel Group

Next, Justin and Reggie listed all the other names involved in the case, however tangentially, and lumped them together when connections were already known to exist.

So the first group listed was:

Forrest Bannister
Lincoln Berdon
Hudson Fenwick
Daniel French
H. R. Harmon
Carl Matuszek
Ellis St. John

The second group was smaller:

Pietro Lambrasco
Bruno Pecozzi
Leonardo Rubenelli

The third was smaller yet:

Abigail Harmon
David Kelley

And the final name wasn't even a name, just a figure that Justin insisted on adding to the compilation:

Unknown Asian woman (seen at LaSalle Group break-in)

Next, and perhaps most interesting, they traced the travel records of all the Ascension employees as well as Ronald LaSalle's movements. There was an early overlap: both LaSalle and Evan Harmon had traveled to Johannesburg, South Africa, and to Palm Beach, Florida. When Reggie checked the time line for both trips, she struck gold: the two men had traveled on the same dates to both places. A firm connection: On the third weekend in March the previous year, both LaSalle and Harmon had been in Palm Beach. Two weeks after that, they both went to Johannesburg.

More direct hits followed. While Evan Harmon had not done more traveling to any places that corresponded to LaSalle's travels—Evan had made two trips to Detroit that didn't seem to match up to any other information they had—Hudson Fenwick's travel itinerary was almost identical to Ron LaSalle's. Their dates did not correspond, but their destinations did. Both men had, over the past fifteen months, been to Moscow, Vancouver, Colombia, New South Wales, New Zealand, Australia, Anchorage, and San Francisco.

The only difference was that Fenwick's travels had been curtailed about five months earlier. Ron LaSalle had continued to travel, making repeat appearances in many of the cities, up until a week or so before he was killed.

Reggie and Justin then listed the people and things that were physically missing. This list wasn't long but it was daunting:

Murder weapon used on Evan Harmon (blunt, clublike instrument)
Ellis St. John's computer
Ellis St. John

Reggie had wanted to include Bruno on the missing list but Justin pointed out that he couldn't be truly considered missing because they had yet to make a concerted effort to find or even contact him. Reggie concurred, and they agreed to leave him off the list for the time being.

And finally they listed the things they just plain didn't know or understand and couldn't connect to any other facts or events:

Who stole Kelley's stun gun to use in Harmon's murder?
Meaning of Wanda's final message: Hades and Ali
Who is the Asian woman? What is her role?
Why was Wanda keeping her investigation of Evan Harmon and
     Ron LaSalle quiet within the FBI?
Why did Pietro Lambrasco try to kill Bruno?
Does Leonardo Rubenelli have a direct connection to any or all of
     the murders?
Who was Wanda's inside source on this investigation?

It was Justin who insisted on adding that last line. He knew Wanda well, he said. Knew the way she worked. She never attempted an investigation of this potential scope—something big enough to link organized crime to Wall Street—without having some sort of inside contact. He told Reggie he'd bet her everything he owned on it. She said, "No, but I'd like to bet a dinner." When he looked up, confused, she said, "If you're wrong you have to have dinner with me. My treat. I'll find someplace expensive where you don't have to wear a tie."

Justin smiled sadly—or maybe it was just kindly, Reggie thought—and shook his head. "No bet," he told her. "Sorry. But . . . you know what? I don't have to explain. That's just not going to happen, though. I appreciate what you're trying to do, but it's not necessary. No dinner, no socializing. Okay?"

She nodded, for the first time embarrassed in front of him. And then she did her best to recover, cleared her throat and said, "We've got to get somebody looking at the Ascension trades, see what the exchange of moneys is all about." He nodded in agreement; she thought he was embarrassed, too. Then she said, "And we've got to go through Ellis's e-mails. There are a lot of them, but they might turn something up."

"Why don't you take the e-mails?" he said. "I think I've got the right guy to examine the trades."

"Your father's guy?"

"Roger."

"Can he do it quickly?"

"I'll try to get him down this afternoon. If he can't, we'll see if your guys can help. But Roger knows a hell of a lot. And what he doesn't know, he'll research to death."

"And what about you?"

"I need a little time to think."

She cocked her head and both shook her head and grinned the smallest of grins. She couldn't help herself. "You've got something."

"No," he said, "just a few things nagging at me."

"What?"

"I don't know," he said. "I can't tell yet. Maybe nothing."

Reggie hesitated. She saw the quick look of discomfort cross his face; he was worried she was going to bring up a social dinner again, so she quickly said, "Listen, there's something I'm supposed to do, but I want to check with you first." He waited and she went on, "I have to report in to Zach Fletcher."

"Okay."

"Here's the thing. On this type of case, they like to work with the local authorities. So he'll tell Silverbush at least some of what we know."

"You're asking me because . . . ?"

"I'm asking you because I want to make sure it's all right with you before I do it. I don't know how you feel about information getting back to the DA. And I thought you'd want to tell me if there's some specific information you'd like us to hold back."

He thought about it for a moment. "Go ahead," he said.

"With everything?" And when he nodded, she said, "You sure?"

"Pretty sure," Justin told her. "Either his head'll start spinning when he realizes this case has moved so far beyond him, or he'll just go blindly on and dig his own grave."

"An even deeper one than he's already been digging, you mean."

"Exactly."

"If we bring him in, you realize it means there's a chance the link between Harmon and LaSalle and Wanda might become public."

He nodded again. "It's all right. Maybe it should now. Keeping it to ourselves hasn't helped us much. Maybe it'll bring something out we haven't been able to uncover."

Her head bobbed up and down a bit in agreement. Then she gathered up the stack of printed e-mails. "Might as well go over these at the motel, huh?"

He knew she wanted him to ask her to stay and work with him. But he didn't. So she said she'd check in later. Justin looked at his watch. 11 A.M. He went to the phone.

"Dad," he said when he was put through to his father's office. "I'm wondering if I can borrow Roger Mallone."

"You coming up?" Jonathan Westwood asked.

"I was kind of hoping he'd come down."

"When?"

"I thought I'd try to hire a plane to get him here as soon as possible."

"Today?"

"Right now."

"You paying him?" Jonathan asked.

"Aren't *you*?" Justin responded. And he thought he almost got a laugh. He didn't. But almost.

"What time do you want him there?" Jonathan said.

29

Roger Mallone was four or five years younger than Justin. Parts of him—his face, his ruddy complexion, particularly his eyes, which didn't have much sadness or much introspection—looked a lot younger than Justin. But Justin was surprised to see that his father's employee's body had started to look like an old man's. He'd put on weight, and his arms were looking heavy and fleshy. He couldn't yet be described as having gone to seed, but he was on his way. Since the last time Justin had seen him, just around a year earlier, Roger looked like he'd gone from being a tennis player to being a golfer. He was thirty-five and looked forty. Justin thought that, at this rate, Roger would be a forty-year-old who looked fifty. And at fifty he'd look sixty-five. Maybe this was the price of success. Justin sucked in his own gut and made a mental note that he'd get back to the gym as soon as possible. And maybe even start yoga lessons again.

Roger was Jonathan Westwood's chief financial officer. He had rapidly moved up the corporate ladder to become the elder Westwood's most trusted adviser at the banks Jonathan owned and ran. Mallone was as thorough as a money man could be and equally honest and hardworking. Justin figured the guy never slept because you could name any stock, any company, any business-related matter at all, and Roger could immediately give you the up-to-the-second latest information on the subject.

The one thing Roger Mallone wasn't was brave. Justin had brought him into a collision course with two earlier cases and, while Roger had proved invaluable both times, he was not happy with his proximity to danger. The first time Roger had been dragged in unwillingly—at gunpoint, in fact. And the gun had been held by Justin. The second time Roger had, more or less, volunteered; but he'd crossed paths with Bruno and, at their first encounter, a frightened Roger had done just about everything but piss in his pants. Justin was fairly sure that the man's bladder had not yet fully recovered.

This third time around, however, Roger was being as cooperative as it was possible to be. Perhaps it was because he felt safe this time—Justin had assured him that there was no immediate danger lurking around the corner. Or perhaps it was because Roger had, to Justin's surprise, been accompanied on this trip by Jonathan Westwood.

Justin's father was at the door when Justin opened it to welcome Roger. They shook hands warmly, gave each other a partial hug, then Justin had welcomed the two men into his living room.

"This is a surprise," he said to his father.

"I decided as long as you were paying for the transportation, I'd take advantage of it."

"My pleasure."

"I'm assuming this has to do with what happened to Ronald," Jonathan said.

Justin nodded. "And a lot more than that, too." He filled both men in on what had been happening. Not every detail, but anything he thought might be relevant, to take advantage of their financial expertise. Justin was not unhappy that his father was sitting in on the session. Jonathan Westwood had a clear and incisive way of looking at complicated problems. He'd helped Justin focus on potential solutions in the past. Jonathan was very good at weeding out extraneous information and zeroing in on the things that mattered.

Justin had reached the point in his tale where he could give the details of his visit to Ascension and tell them the various elements of Ben's computer thievery. Justin's father sat passively, taking it all in, but Justin could see Roger's eyes light up at the thought of poring over another firm's trading history.

When Justin had finished filling them in, Roger just said, "Give me everything and let me go through it."

"It's a lot," Justin said.

"I know it's a lot. So why don't you just leave me to it?"

"Don't you want us to do anything?" Justin asked.

"And what is it you think you can do?" Roger asked. And when Justin shrugged, Roger said, "This is going to be a lot of info to slog through, and a lot of it will be technical and boring. To you, not to me. So why don't the two of you get out of here? Come back in a few hours."

Jonathan looked at his son and raised his eyebrows, a look that said, *He wants it, let him have it.* The two Westwoods wished Roger Mallone luck, and headed out the door.

"Wait," Roger said just as the door was about to shut behind them. "You've gone beyond dial-up, right?"

"All the way to Wi-Fi."

Roger did his best Marv Albert impersonation: clenched his fist and hissed out a quiet, "Yessss."

"Go wild," Justin said. And this time he and his father actually got to leave.

Justin asked his father if they could walk awhile. He said he was glad that Roger had wanted to be alone. He had things he wanted to ask Jonathan, things he wanted to pick his brains about. Jonathan said he was more than happy to stroll. And he told his son to pick away.

"I had a strange reaction to the Ascension people and offices," Justin said as they began to walk in the direction of the center of the charming old whaling village.

"Strange how?" his father asked.

"I'm not naïve," Justin went on. "Anything but. You know I don't expect—well, the best, let's say—out of people. But these guys were different."

"Different from whom?"

"Different from you. Different from the kind of moneyed people I know."

"Hedgehoggers? They *are* different. They live in a different world. At least it's different from the one I live in."

"Talk to me about it."

"Tell me what you want to know."

"Everything," Justin said. "Anything. It's the way I like to work. Learn things, get a feel for the overall picture. Then I'll see if something specific sticks. See what fits into the puzzle . . . or see what doesn't fit. Sometimes that's just as important." He noticed his father was staring at him. "What?"

"That's the way I work, too. When I'm looking at a company that wants a loan, that's what I do. I learn about their business, I learn about the people running their business, I listen to them talk, watch them when they talk."

"Same thing, really," Justin said. "It's all about getting it right."

Jonathan came back with a "hmmm," and then he picked up the pace of their walk and said, "One of the first hedge fund managers I ever met—maybe ten, twelve years ago—his arrogance was astonishing. I remember him coming to a meeting and basically he was saying that if I didn't get him what he wanted, he'd just *buy* me. Buy the big business, take the small thing he wanted out of it, then dismantle it, sell off the spare parts. I remember he looked at me and said he didn't care about the way things used to be done, he was the new breed, the new thinker. He said he was a man with no history. I remember he actually said he was like a phoenix, that he'd risen from the ashes as a brand-new person. He told me he was a completely self-made man."

"What did you say?"

"I told him he must also be a very religious man because it was clear that he worshiped his creator."

"I bet he didn't like that."

"He couldn't have cared less. Too self-absorbed, too absorbed with money and greed to care about anything that anyone else said or thought."

"What happened to him?"

"Made half a billion dollars in about two years. Lost a billion the next year. I think he's working for his father now, somewhere in the Midwest." Jonathan Westwood took a deep breath. Justin was startled to hear a faint wheeze. The first indication of frailty he'd ever had from his father. "There are about seven thousand hedge funds in the United States now. Ten years ago, there were maybe three, four hundred. They control a lot of money. A *lot* of money. Right now, probably over nine hundred billion dollars. And they control it quietly and secretly."

"Ascension manages about two billion bucks."

"Small to mid-range," Jonathan said. "There are a lot of funds in the two- to five-billion-dollar range. That's small in this universe. But you know what you can buy with five billion dollars?" Before Justin could answer, Jonathan said, "Anything you want." Then he said, "The people who run these funds, they personally make sixty, seventy, a hundred million dollars a year."

Justin whistled in amazement. "I knew about it, of course. But somehow I didn't quite realize . . ."

"Very few people do. You know how it works?"

"I know a little bit, but keep talking."

So Jonathan talked. And Justin listened as they strolled. He listened as Jonathan told him that hedge funds were basically started for rich people who wanted someone else to manage chunks of their money. The funds were open only to wealthy investors, and even now the minimum you could invest to get into a fund he'd heard about was twenty-five thousand dollars, and many wouldn't let you in for less than a million. Because they were basically serving rich people, they didn't have the same government restrictions and oversight that, say, a mutual fund would, when small investors have their money at risk. Hedge funds and hedgehoggers could move into almost any area that attracted them. They could trade equities, currencies, and debt. They could make loans, buy companies, and control companies and run them if they thought they had the know-how.

"And how do these guys, guys like Evan Harmon, make their money?" Justin asked.

"They take a two percent fee off the top from their investors. And twenty percent of the profit. Ascension has two billion dollars to invest? That means they're guaranteed an income of forty million dollars when they wake up on the first of the year. That's if they *lose* money. If they make a ten percent investment profit on two billion, the fund has a profit of two hundred million. Twenty percent of that brings in forty million more dollars to the firm. That's a nice little eighty-million-dollar income right there. And without crazy overhead. If push came to shove, one person could probably manage a hundred million-dollar funds from his garage as long as he had a computer and a few phone lines."

Jonathan said that the kind of money people made managing hedge funds over the past decade had changed the whole world. Investors lost sight of the products—not to mention the people and the companies—that were being invested in. The only things that began to matter were the profits—and then what mattered even more were all the toys that could be bought with those profits: the Warhols and Picassos, the Gulfstreams and Falcons, the horses and the horse farms, and the tens-of-thousands-square-foot mansions bought on miles of private beaches.

Justin asked what could go wrong with these funds, how they could blow up. When his father wanted to know why he wanted to know, Justin explained that it's the way cops had to think: They have to look for the worst possible scenario. "It's what people do when things go wrong that keeps me busy," he said. "People don't do desperate things—like commit murder—when they're getting what they want."

"It's simple. Hedge funds blow up if they lose money for too long," Jonathan said. "Or even short term—if they lose too much too quickly." What happens, he explained, is what often happens with companies. Success breeds the desire for more success: the urge to get bigger and bring in more and more and more. The hedgehog business has gotten so competitive, too, they start to care about the appearance, and they build up overhead, and suddenly if you have a down period you're in way over your head. You start with a fancy office, a lot of midtown Manhattan space. Your fund's too big to manage by yourself, or even as a two-person team, so you've got to pay analysts and traders and accountants. And buy computers and Bloomberg terminals and research services.

"Soon you can't live on the fixed fee; two percent doesn't cover it. And you've bought your Gulfstream and the million-dollar memberships in several different golf clubs and the house in Palm Beach and your wife has her charity balls, and guess what? If you don't make a profit for two or three quarters in a row, people start pulling out their money. Once that happens, you're dead."

"Gotta sell the private jet, huh?"

"Unless the creditors come and take it away."

"Tell me about the people. The hedgehoggers."

"It's impossible to make absolute generalizations, you know that."

"Then just give me your general impressions. I promise I won't go around thinking that all hedge fund guys are evil sons of bitches."

Jonathan shook his head disapprovingly at his son's flippancy. But he said, "It's a different game than the one investment bankers play. It's about the thrill. And it's not even about making a score . . . it's about making a *big* score. The biggest score. If you want to play in this game, you've got to have some balls. And I mean some iron balls. They're not interested in small bets. You put five or ten million dollars into something, what's five or ten million against a billion? It's nothing. It's meaningless. But if you have a billion-dollar fund and you see your opportunity and you put fifty million or a hundred million down, then you've got something. You can shake things up. Have an impact. That's the way they think. They don't believe in protecting themselves. If they think they've got something good, they'll put ten percent of their assets down on it. Sometimes more. You realize what a gamble that is? They think like hot rollers at a craps table. The more you win, the more you bet. You get on a good enough winning streak, you break the bank. But if you crap out too many times, you're out of business. You're also probably a heart attack waiting to happen or you're an alcoholic or you can't sleep for an hour without popping a dozen pills." Jonathan took a deep breath now and, again, Justin heard a wheeze coming from within his father's chest. "Have I told you what you wanted to know?"

"It's a start," Justin said. "You still like meatball heroes?"

"Your mother doesn't approve of meatball heroes."

"Is she meeting us for lunch?"

Jonathan acknowledged his son's logic with a brief nod of his head. "Good hero place, is it?"

"The best," Justin said. And when Jonathan smiled wistfully, his son added, "It's on me."

It was the first time Togo had ever gotten his instructions by phone. The man said there was not time to meet, that things were moving quickly around them and they had to move just as quickly. Even quicker, he said.

Togo asked in Chinese what it was he had to do so quickly.

The man answered in Chinese: "The policeman. The one you've been watching. He's getting too close. He knows too many things now."

"I should wait for Ling," Togo said.

"There is no time to wait for Ling." And when Togo didn't answer, the man said, in English, "You are afraid if you don't have a girl to protect you?"

Togo said nothing. Over the phone, the only sound that could be heard was the heavy breathing of the two men.

The man said, switching back to Cantonese, "We cannot wait. Soon he'll be talking to people. He is already talking to too many people. Do you understand?"

"I understand," Togo told the man.

"Then tell it to me, so I know you hear what I'm saying."

"He will not talk to any more people," Togo said. "That is what you want."

"Yes," the man said. "That is what I want."

"I must say one thing to you," Togo said.

"Go ahead," the man told him.

"Now *you* listen carefully," Togo said.

"I'm listening."

And then Togo spoke in English. He wanted to make absolutely certain the man on the other end of the phone understood what he was saying.

"I am not afraid," Togo said slowly.

"Is that it?" the man asked.

"Yes," Togo said, still in English. "I am not afraid of anything."

"Good for you," the man said, also in English. And then he hung up.

Justin's cell phone rang as he and his father were approaching Justin's white with blue trim Victorian house. The meatball heroes had been delicious.

"Yup," he said into the cell phone.

"We have some movement on Ellis St. John," Reggie Bokken-heuser said.

"Tell me."

"He used his bank card to get some cash. Five hundred dollars."

"Where?"

"Massachusetts. A town on the Mass–New York border. We've got someone on it already. Fletcher sent someone down from Boston to check it out."

"Has the rental car been spotted?"

"No. But now I'll get APBs out in New England."

"Good," he said. "How go the e-mails?"

"Ellis may be the most boring writer who ever lived. But anything you want to know about who's screwing who at Rockworth, just ask."

"Nothing at all?"

"I wouldn't say that. I'm pulling anything that seems remotely relevant. A lot of it has to do with specific trades, so I'm not a hundred percent sure what I'm looking at. I'm flagging anything that has to do with any of the companies on our lists. Oh . . . and Jay . . . just for the hell of it, I e-mailed you the article in the paper, the one about the truck that turned over. With the platinum."

"A particular reason?"

"No. It's like one of your hunches. It just interests me. Something pops up in one mystery, the same thing pops up in another, I think it's better to assume it's not a coincidence. How's your pal Roger doing?"

"He needed a few hours. I'm just about to find out."

"Well, you let me know how that goes, okay?"

"I'll call you later," he said.

"Later," she told him.

Roger Mallone looked as if he hadn't moved since Justin and Jonathan had left two and a half hours ago. He was sitting on the living room couch, papers spread all around him—on the coffee table, on the couch, on the floor. When they walked in the door, he looked as engrossed as if he were reading the most exciting thriller ever written.

"We brought you a sandwich," Justin said.

Roger looked up, a look of confusion on his face, almost as if he didn't understand Justin's words. Then he said, "Oh—oh, thanks. I'm not hungry."

Justin waved his hand at the stacks of papers. "Is it that good?"

"It's fascinating," Roger said.

"Let me just make some coffee," Justin said, "then you can lay it all on me."

He went into the kitchen, turned one of his electric stovetop burners on high, boiled water, and made eight cups of strong coffee, filling his plunger-style coffeemaker to the brim. Roger was not normally the most stimulating teacher, so Justin figured he'd need the jolt. When it was ready, he poured the coffee into the thermos he kept by the stove. He yelled in to ask if anyone else wanted some and got two no's. Happy to have it all to himself, he poured a mugful and took it back into the living room.

"Ready," he said.

"Okay," Roger said, and Justin could hear him trying to rein in his excitement. "I can't say for absolute certain without a lot more studying and possibly even further access to their records, but there's something very, very strange going on."

"Is there a simple version?"

"I've tried to organize this as simply as possible," Roger said, "but if it was simple, they wouldn't be able to pull this off."

"What is it they're pulling off?" Jonathan asked.

Roger spoke to Justin now. "The way a hedge fund works is exactly the way the name implies. It's one large fund and if you put your money in, you're investing in that fund as a whole entity. The fund is split up so it can invest in as many different stocks and companies and commodities as it wants to. But it's one fund. That's key."

"Okay," Justin said. "I grasp the meaning of the word 'fund.' You going to define 'hedge,' too?"

"I am, as a matter of fact. I know you've got a business background, but I do remember that that part of your brain is a little, shall we say, rusty?"

"Sure," Justin agreed. "Let's say that."

"So 'hedge' is also exactly what it means when attached to a fund. It means that at any time you can hedge your bet. You think a stock is going to tank, you can short it." Roger beamed. He loved talking about his business and nothing puffed him up quite so much as explaining to other people how that business worked. Justin decided this had to be one of the greatest days of Roger Mallone's life. He got to snoop through another company's records *and* he got to explain it all to Justin. "When you short something you're betting that the price is going to go down. Let's say you want to short a thousand shares of Company X, which is selling for ten dollars a share. You think it's going to be selling for half price before too long. So you make a contract that lets you buy it at a later date when it drops to five and sell it back to someone for the ten-dollar price. The beauty of it—and the danger—is that you don't put up any money. Your broker borrows a thousand shares from someone else's portfolio. That person usually doesn't even know they're being borrowed. The broker just transfers those shares into your portfolio and then automatically sells them back to someone else at ten—and you've made your profit."

"And if it goes up instead of down . . ."

"Same thing, only in reverse. You short at five and it goes up to twenty. You gotta buy all thousand shares at twenty—you've lost your bet. I know people who've lost tens and tens of millions of dollars sinking money into stocks they *know* will come down. Only they don't."

"How does this apply to Ascension?"

"Well, if I'm reading this right, and I'm pretty sure I am, they're violating all the tenets of hedge fund management."

Now Jonathan leaned forward. "How so?" he asked.

"Again, I can't say this with one hundred percent certainty because I don't have access to all their accounting records, but it looks as if they're making separate trades for certain companies that are outside the main fund."

"Trading shares to and from the main fund?" Jonathan asked.

"Exactly."

"That illegal?" Justin asked.

Roger shrugged. "It's difficult to say what's legal or not when it comes to hedge funds. It's not *honest*. But it's for the SEC to decide if it's legal."

"It's not something that would make Ascension investors happy, however," Jonathan said. "It means they can pick and choose who makes money from their fund."

"And here's where it gets trickier," Roger said, tapping one stack of papers. "It looks as if they made some of the trades themselves—just transferring funds back and forth between different investors, in and out from one fund to another. And it looks as if some of the trades were made using an outside broker."

"Rockworth and Williams," Justin said.

Roger nodded. "That's right."

"Is there more?" Justin asked.

"There's a lot more. One is that what they're shorting isn't consistent at all with a lot of the other trades they're making."

"What are they shorting?"

"Platinum," Roger said.

"Are you sure?!"

"You want to see my MBA?"

"No, of course not, sorry. It's just . . . go on."

"Well," Roger said, "you're not wrong to be so confused by that. Considering their connections, especially. And their timing is very curious considering what's going on in the platinum market. And then I have to say, their luck is extraordinarily bad."

"What about the timing?"

"Well, I don't think there are too many people shorting platinum heavily these days. Not with what's happening in China."

"What's happening in . . . ?" Justin started to say, then stopped himself. "Cars. Cars are happening, right?"

"Very good," Roger said. "*Very* good."

"China's going into the car business in a big way," Justin said slowly. He could hear Daniel French saying to him, up at Rockworth and Williams: *The wave of the future. Chinese cars . . . Chinese everything.*

"And you can't go into it in a big way without platinum," Roger said. "Not if you want to crack the international market."

"Right," Justin said quietly. "Platinum for—what the hell is it— platinum for substrates. Substrates for exhaust devices. It's all about emission controls."

"You have definitely been paying attention," Roger said. "I'm extremely impressed."

"What was the first thing you were questioning, the connections? No, never mind," Justin said. "I understand that, too. They're tied to China because of H. R. Harmon."

"I know that Rockworth does an incredible amount of business with the Chinese. They're the envy of everyone on the Street because of their connections. They advise them, they trade for them, they've got access to business opportunities no one else can ever get close to . . ."

"And I'll bet they've put Chinese money into the Ascension hedge fund. Daddy taking care of his kid."

"I'd guess that they did. There are a couple of companies on your list that can probably be linked to China. But that's what doesn't make sense."

"What?"

"Again, I can't say for sure, but I think several of these companies are shells. I haven't heard of them and I haven't been able to trace them, which makes me think they're set up as part of a scam. Why would Ascension or Rockworth want to scam the Chinese government when it's such a big source of income for them? Or, on the other hand—" He stopped.

"On the other hand what?" Justin asked.

"If they're not *being* scammed, why would the Chinese government want to be *part* of a scam?"

None of them had an answer. So finally, Justin said, "All right. That's the timing and the connections. What about the bad luck?"

"Well, the platinum market shot sky-high recently. Because of the shortage."

"A shortage of platinum? Why would that be?"

"Because of the cargo ship."

"Roger, you've got to be a little more forthcoming. Miraculously enough, I might know about Chinese cars, but I don't know shit about platinum cargo ships."

"One of them sank. About three weeks ago."

"Where?"

"Coming up from South Africa. Off the coast of Sicily, I think."

"How much of a shortage was there?"

Roger blew out a breath. Meaning: a big shortage. "I don't remember exactly how much," he said, "but enough to alter the market. Maybe fifty, sixty million dollars' worth disappeared. Maybe more."

"And they can't recover it?"

"Yeah, they'll get it back eventually. But it'll take time. And in the meantime, there's a serious shortage."

"And when that happens?"

"Come on, Jay, it's like everything else. Supply and demand. There's a short supply, the price goes up. In this case, it went up a lot."

"Has it come back down?"

"Not yet."

"This is unbelievable," Justin said.

"It's totally believable," Roger told him. "It doesn't make any sense, but it's very believable. Especially when you look at the travel documents you gave me."

"LaSalle's and Harmon's travel destinations?"

"And the other guy from Ascension, whatever his name is. Fenwick."

"You've got something from that that ties in to what you're talking about?"

"Well, look at where they went." Roger had that tone that Justin recognized now: the one that couldn't hide the fact he thought he was talking to an idiot. He patiently listed all the cities and countries that Evan Harmon, Ronald LaSalle, and Hudson Fenwick had visited on business, as if he were talking to a child.

"What about them?" Justin asked.

"It's where they mine platinum. Every one of 'em. Platinum mines."

Justin shook his head. "San Francisco? Come on, who the hell mines platinum in San Francisco?"

"Nobody. But you go about two hours up north to the Trinity River . . . platinum. You fly to San Francisco and drive up. You want to see a map?"

"How about Palm Beach?" Justin said, almost frantic now. "Harmon and LaSalle were there together. They're mining platinum in Palm Beach now?"

"No," Roger said. "That's the only one that didn't make sense, I mean, in the scheme of things. Well, that and Mexico. And, okay, Mexico I can't connect. But I figured out Palm Beach."

Justin was incredulous. "What is it?"

"It's not that they went to Palm Beach. It's *when* they went there. The third weekend in March."

Jonathan began nodding his head slowly now.

"What am I missing?" Justin asked.

"No reason you would know this," his father said. "But the first weekend in March is about the biggest date there is for hedge fund managers."

"It's the Rockworth and Williams hedge fund conference," Roger said. "Every year. Third weekend in March, at the Breakers Hotel."

"What happens there?" Justin asked.

"It's where the money is," Jonathan explained. "Rockworth invites its top clients—and people it wants to woo as clients—so it's where the hedge fund guys go. They meet, they talk, they drink, and if they meet and talk and drink well, they come away with a lot of that money."

"Dad," Justin said, "does anyone keep a record of who attends this conference?"

"I'm sure Rockworth does. It sends out the invites."

"Do you know anyone there who can get me that list? Immediately?"

"I can call Lincoln Berdon and—"

"No," Justin said quickly. "Not that high up. You know a low-level person there, someone who'd be under the radar, wouldn't think it strange if you asked for the list? And wouldn't think to mention it to anyone?"

"Sure," Roger said. "I know plenty of analysts who owe me favors, and I'm sure they could get their hands on it, no problem."

"Do it."

"Now?" Roger asked.

"Right now," Justin said. "Please."

So Roger made his call. Schmoozed a bit with whomever he was talking to on the other end, then gave out Justin's fax number. Two minutes later the list was faxed through.

"About five hundred names on this," Roger said. "You looking for anyone in particular?"

"Not necessarily. But I'm hoping I know it when I see it." Justin took the paper out of Roger's hands, began scanning down the list. And then he said, "And I see it."

He picked up the phone, called Reggie Bokkenheuser. When she answered, he said, "I've got our connection to Lenny Rube." He also told her that her hunch about platinum seemed to be paying off big-time. He explained about the boat sinking and about the shortage of the precious metal in a competitive marketplace. He also told her about the links between all the travel destinations—once again tying into that platinum wheeling and dealing was somehow central to everything else that had gone on. She started to pepper him with questions, but he said he needed to get a bit more info from Roger and that he'd call her later. Then he said, "Wait," and when she said she was still there, he said, "I know we're low on the Feebie totem pole, but can you use Immigration and get some info about someone going in and out of the country? And while you're at it, check into a few specific destinations?"

"I think we're still able to do that," she told him. "Immigration, Customs, they still like us. Who am I checking on?"

He told her and she whistled in surprise. She said, "Will wonders never cease," and before he could get annoyed, she said, "Later," and hung up.

When he hung up on his end, Justin turned to his father and to Roger Mallone and said, "Leonardo Rubenelli, the head of the New England mob, at a hedge fund conference. And I thought I'd seen everything."

30

Justin spent another hour with Roger and his father as they explained in greater detail the trading aberrations that Roger had spotted going through the Ascension data. It was not incredibly complicated, but there were twists and turns and obfuscations. Roger had isolated companies that had shorted platinum and lost money. Then he isolated companies that had lent their shares to the shorter and had raked in millions of dollars of profit as the price of platinum rose. Early in the scheme, the companies that had taken a bath were Charles Chan & Associates and the Noodleman America Corporation. Roger was disgusted at the names.

"Hedge fund assholes. They think that kind of stuff is funny."

"Chinese companies, obviously."

"Yeah, but shells. I'd bet my life on it. They make up the companies and give them fuck-you names. They're so smug, they like to flaunt their dishonesty. You look at all the companies Enron created before it took its fall, it was the same kind of thing—same kind of stupid, arrogant names."

"So the Chinese shells are losing money. What about the companies making a profit?"

Roger listed them: "Flame Bros. Ltd., the National Beet Growers Association of America Pension Fund, Pinkney & Associates, Rossovitch and Sons, Scarlet Knight, Inc."

"Just as stupid," Justin said. And when his father and Roger looked at him, confused, he said, "Lenny Rubenelli. They also call him Lenny Rube. And Lenny Red. All these companies . . . they're red."

"But there's still something off here," Jonathan insisted. "The profits are switched over the past few months. The companies making money on the shorting change at a certain point. Lately the ones taking in the profit are Eggleston Catalytic Converters; Goldman, Inc.; the Tintagel Group; and Silverado Jewelry Association. And the Chinese companies are back to making money."

"Because they've had shares transferred to them in those companies," Roger said. "And those companies are making money. Lots of money."

"And Lenny Rube's companies are down," Justin noted. And as he pondered the impact of that statement, he said, "I think we should have some dinner. Or some alcohol, at least."

"Excellent idea," his father said. "I don't suppose you have a decent wine in the house? Or clean wineglasses?"

"Hello," Roger said, a stilted, suddenly polite lilt to his voice.

Both Justin and Jonathan looked up, wondering why he was saying hello to them. Justin was about to tell him that it might be time for him to take a lengthy break, but then he saw that Roger wasn't saying hello to them. There was a man standing in the kitchen doorway. A Chinese man. He was standing very still, and it didn't take Justin more than his first glance to understand that this man was not here for any reason that could possibly do them any good.

"Give me papers, please," the Chinese guy said in halting English.

"What papers?" Roger asked. Then he waved at the records from Ascension. "These?"

"Give papers," the man said.

And Justin said, "Roger, move away from him. Move behind me."

"What?" Roger said.

"Don't give him any papers and don't get any closer to him. Move away right now."

Roger began to walk toward Justin. Justin glanced toward his desk. His spare gun—the one he hadn't handed over to Captain Holden—was in the drawer.

"Don't try to reach gun," the Chinese man said, his voice calm and quietly authoritative. "You will not."

The room was very quiet now. "Dad," Justin said, "get out the front door."

"Do not move to door," the stranger said. "Do not try. Will not make."

Justin nodded and smiled and did his best to look as listless as possible, and then he dove for the desk drawer and the gun.

He did not come close. The little Chinese man moved so quickly and with such balletic precision that even Justin had to appreciate its beauty. The man's left foot planted, and he whirled and his right leg swung in a graceful arc, and Justin's appreciation of the beauty disappeared in a flash, replaced by a searing pain and the recognition that at least one rib was broken. He doubled over in pain, saw the man relax for an instant, and Justin reached over, grabbed a lamp off the nearest end table and swung it with all his might at the Chinese man's head. The pain in his chest was staggering, and it was made worse when he connected only with air. The Chinese man had moved effortlessly out of the way. Justin didn't even see the movement—it was as if he was in one place and then suddenly he was in another—and the man's leg lashed out again, catching Justin in the same spot in his ribs, and Justin thought he was going to pass out from the fire that seemed to envelop him from within.

He saw the Chinese man moving slowly toward Roger Mallone. Roger was frozen with fear; he did not even back away as the man approached. The Chinese man smiled, a gentle smile, and moved one hand on Roger's neck. Justin could see the pain in Roger's eyes. He didn't make a sound, just began to sag, and Justin did the only thing he could think of; he grabbed a brass floor lamp and swung it at the back of the Chinese man's knees. The man staggered and let go of Roger, who still had not moved, but Justin could see he was still alive. And now the Chinese man's legs were steady, and as he took one step toward Justin, his left hand jabbed at Justin's heart. Justin moved, diving backward, so he didn't take the hit full on, but it still felt as if the man's fist had penetrated his chest and grabbed his heart and squeezed. Justin saw the look of disbelief and terror on his father's face as the Chinese man was moving toward him now. Jonathan had no chance to escape—there was nowhere to go—and so Justin was moving again, despite the pain, and this time he grabbed the man from behind, used his heft to pick him up and heave him, the whole time screaming at his father and Roger, "Go! Go! Go! Get out!" The man landed on his feet, near the kitchen, and Justin didn't give him a moment to breathe. He charged headfirst and barreled into the smaller man, as they both were swept into the kitchen, slamming into the refrigerator and caroming off a cabinet. Justin shook his head to clear it and that was a mistake, a big mistake. The Chinese man's hand snaked toward him again in that one instant and caught him in the cheek, and Justin tumbled backward. He braced himself against the counter, clawed at a drawer, managed to yank it open, and had time to pull out a butcher knife. But it was in his hand for a second at most because the Chinese man's leg whirled again, and Justin's wrist felt as if it had been broken in two, and the knife was clattering along the kitchen floor.

"I kill you," the Chinese man said just as quietly and calmly as before. "I kill them. You stop. No fight more. Less pain."

"Fuck you," Justin spat. "Less pain," he gasped. "You like torturing people. Fuck you, less pain." He realized blood was pouring from a gash on his face. But he charged again, and for a moment his weight advantage seemed to mean something because he could feel the smaller man toppling backward, but it didn't last long. Justin felt another pain in his neck, this one almost paralyzing, and then he felt himself being propelled backward again. He banged into the stove, put his hand behind him to try to prop himself up, and now he felt a searing pain in his right hand, only the man was nowhere near him. What the hell was this pain? And Justin realized that, yet again, he'd left the burner on high, and he'd just scorched the hell out of his palm. He thought, *Goddamm it to hell, fucking goddamn hell,* and he was all set to charge again—he was going to charge until he was dead—but suddenly he stopped. He stood up and sucked air back into his lungs. *This can work,* he thought.

"Is good," the man said softly, seeing the way Justin had thought better about continuing the brawl. "Fight no help you. I kill men. Come back for you. No touch knife. It be bad for you."

The Chinese man turned toward the living room, and Justin thought, *Is it possible he's telling the truth, that he doesn't like pain, doesn't like torture? And, if so—if he's not the one who likes it—who does?* And hoping he knew the answer, he said, "Where's your girlfriend? You're gonna need her help to kill me, you motherfucker."

The man turned slowly back toward Justin. "How you know her?" He stared at Justin curiously, then shook his head dismissively. "You no know her."

"How do I know her?" Justin could hear how fast his breath was coming. "I fucked her."

The man didn't smile. Justin didn't think he *could* smile. Didn't think he had any range of emotion in him. But there was something on his face that showed amusement. As if Justin's last-ditch attempt to rattle was, if nothing else, entertaining. "You liar. You crazy."

"I fucked her in this house," Justin said. "Right here. On that table."

The Chinese man didn't smile now, didn't frown, didn't look amused or any different at all now. He was back to his robot persona. Justin's words had no apparent effect on him at all.

"You no know her. You no see her."

"No? Think I no see her?" Justin managed to say. The pain in his chest made it harder and harder to speak. And harder and harder to breathe. The burn on his hand was also beginning to throb as waves of heat seemed to be shooting up his arm. But he began to describe the woman he'd seen by Wanda's car, in as much detail as he could remember. He described her eyes and her hair and the clothes she was wearing. He described her skin and even her shoes. All the information he'd e-mailed Billy DiPezio, who'd asked him to put together a detailed description. "You want me to describe her pussy?" Justin spat. "Want me to tell you how I fucked her?"

And now he saw it. The flicker in the man's eyes. The first touch of genuine human emotion.

Anger.

Jealousy.

Fury.

And that's when Justin screamed, screamed so hard he thought he broke another rib. "Dad! Get the hell out of here! Go now!" And it distracted the man, just for a moment—no longer than that, he was too good to ever get distracted for more than a moment—but that was the moment Justin needed. He grabbed for the thermos and flung it, and the man had to move, to duck, and that took only another moment, but it was enough because Justin charged. He saw the man raise his arms, knowing he could easily fend off any blow, only Justin didn't try to hit him or throw him; he didn't do anything but grab the man, get him in a bear hug, and pull him close. He felt a knee come up and strike his thigh and a short jab into his broken rib, but he didn't feel pain anymore, didn't feel a thing; he just kept thinking, *I can do this, don't let go, I can do this,* and instead of fighting back, he just shoved the man toward the stove, never letting go, never relaxing his grip. He felt the man's head butt, a crack right into his forehead; but he didn't let go, just held on tighter, and the man didn't realize what was about to happen, didn't have any sense of urgency, and then Justin spun him and slammed him down on the stove. The Chinese man got his hand in front of him, was ready to use it to propel himself backward and immediately attack, but he yanked the hand away in surprise—he couldn't stop that instinct—as the burner seared his palm, and then Justin was on his back, pushing him forward with all his might, holding him down with all his weight, the man's face flat against the hot burner. And the man fought back as if he were a wild animal, kicked and squirmed and tried desperately to buck Justin off, but Justin wouldn't back off. He heard the man make a sound, not a scream, because he couldn't scream now—his lips were melting. Justin pushed down harder, had his hands on the man's neck, on the back of his head, holding him, shoving him deeper onto the scalding-hot burner. He smelled the horrible odor of burning flesh, heard the sizzling sounds of skin being seared, but he wouldn't let go, wouldn't move back, not an inch; and the Chinese man was twitching and jerking now, like a live lobster thrown on a grill—crazy, wild gyrations—and Justin knew he couldn't hold on for much longer. And then he didn't have to, because the man wasn't moving much, wasn't moving at all anymore, couldn't move anymore; and Justin let go, flung the body across the room, and he saw the man's face, or what was left of it, which wasn't much. Just a burned and melted and charred circle of flesh. And he watched as the man's body twitched and jerked again, a fish on a hook, nerves responding to overwhelming pain; and then the movement stopped. And then everything in the kitchen was completely still except Justin, standing by the stove, his breath coming in short, desperate gasps.

He looked up. Saw his father standing in the doorway. Justin's gun was in his hand. Jonathan, pale and trembling, stared at the faceless man on the floor. He walked into the kitchen, grabbed a towel from the counter, held it against his son's cheek to stop the flow of blood. Justin took the gun from his father, stepped back, turned, and vomited violently. Pain surged through his chest again and his ribs. Then he straightened up, did his best to smile weakly at his father, walked slowly past him, touching him lightly on the arm as he went into the living room. He saw Roger Mallone, standing now, propped up against a corner. Roger nodded, a sign he was all right, an acknowledgment of what had just happened. Just went to the phone. He picked it up and dialed.

When Reggie answered, Justin said, "You'd better get over here. And you'd better call your boss."

She heard his tone, didn't ask what had happened, just said, "Anything else?"

And he said, "Yeah. I think an ambulance might be a good idea, too."

31

Reggie was superb from the moment she walked in the door. She took in the scene in the living room, strode past the three men, saw the body in the kitchen, said nothing about it, came back into the living room. Assessing the situation flawlessly, she touched Justin on the back, let her hand linger there for just a moment—it's all she had to do to let him know she understood what had happened and what he'd done. She made Roger sit in the easy chair and found a blanket in which to wrap him. She also poured him a stiff scotch. She did the same for Jonathan; but when she saw that he was alert and lucid, she asked him if he was up to talking, and he was. He told her, clinically and completely, what had happened. She touched his hand, knowing human contact was important sometimes, could be more comforting than any words, and had him sit down, too.

She called the East End Harbor police station, got Gary Jenkins. She identified herself and told him to get over to Justin's house immediately. Gary was surprised to hear her voice, started to ask questions, but she cut him off, told him that with his boss on suspension, this was his decision to make, and only his, so he'd better make it fast. He arrived in five minutes.

Things were wrapped up quickly.

An ambulance took the body to the Southampton Hospital morgue, and Reggie arranged for fingerprinting to take place as soon as the body arrived there. She tried to get Justin into the same ambulance, but he wouldn't budge, didn't respond at all to her gentle urging other than to shake his head once, and she didn't press him. One of the orderlies took a look at him, said, "I think you should listen to her, sir—you don't look too good," but Reggie shooed him away and said she'd get him there on her own.

Officer Jenkins called the station and, after clearing things with Reggie, he and Mike Haversham cleaned up Justin's kitchen, putting everything back in place and even mopping the floor. Haversham got violently ill when trying to clean off the front burner—he realized almost immediately what he was trying to scrape off—but Gary Jenkins took a deep breath and did the job. When he was done, he too had to rush into the bathroom.

When they were finished with the kitchen, they also straightened up the living room. Justin just sat on the couch, saying nothing. His breathing had slowed down, but it was still coming in short gasps, and when he took in too deep a breath, he winced in pain. Jonathan, too, sat quietly; he appeared calm and in control, more concerned about his son than anyone or anything else. He, too, had made one quick attempt to get Justin to go to Southampton in the ambulance, but Reggie also waved him off and he stopped pushing.

Reggie spent fifteen or twenty minutes talking quietly to Roger. She talked to him about the shock of violence and how he was right to have been afraid. She spoke soothingly and calmly, and gradually he came around. His alertness returned and he finally looked at her and said, "Thank you, I'm fine now. I just never thought . . . I never saw anything like . . . I didn't know . . ."

"It's all right," she told him. "No one should know about things like that. No one should see things like that."

When the house was straightened up and everything was back in order, she went over to Justin. She took his hand and said, "I want to take you to the hospital now. I know you're fine, but you have some wounds that have to be looked at. I'll call ahead so you won't have to wait, but you need to go and we should go now. Okay?"

He nodded. She helped him stand and took him out to her car. She asked Jonathan and Roger to wait at the house, asked both young cops to wait with them. She said she thought they'd be back in a couple of hours.

In the fifteen-minute ride to the hospital, she told him she'd reported everything that happened to Zach Fletcher. She said Agent Fletcher was concerned about Justin's health, said that any conversation could wait until he was up to it. He nodded. In the car she asked him if he had any idea why this had happened. He didn't answer. Didn't nod or shake his head. He made no response at all.

It turned out that her two-hour estimate was off—they were back in East End Harbor in a little over an hour. Justin took twelve stitches in his cheek and four stitches to close a small gash over his left eye. He did have a broken rib, and the doctor in the emergency room wrapped him in a bandage that left him feeling mummified. Burn ointment was lathered on his hand and that was wrapped also. He was given a solid dose of painkillers and told to take them whenever he needed them. Justin didn't speak much during his treatment. He answered the doctors' questions with one- or two-word answers, and Reggie made it clear that the doctors were not to ask too many questions.

When they arrived back at Justin's house, both Justin and Reggie were surprised to find out it wasn't yet 8 P.M.

"I think the plane should take you both back tonight," she said to Jonathan Westwood. "I called the pilot from the hospital. He's waiting at the airport. Gary or Mike can take you."

They were all surprised when Justin said, "We're going with them."

She turned to him and said, "Jay, that's not a good idea."

"Doesn't matter if it's good or not. And if you don't want to go, that's fine. But I'm going up there now." She said nothing, simply tilted her head—that was the way she asked the question—and he said, "I think I'm beginning to understand what's going on. And if I'm right, we need to see Lenny Rube. In person. I don't think he'll be taking my calls."

Jonathan started to argue, to say that they could all go up the next morning, but Justin waved him off. Looking at Reggie, he said, "We can see him and come straight back. But we need to see him tonight."

She looked at Jonathan and shrugged.

Ten minutes later they were on their way to the East Hampton Airport.

* * *

The airplane ride was short and relatively quiet. Roger had recovered enough to go over some of the fine points of the various stock deals he'd uncovered. Talking about it seemed to help him regain his strength. Reggie was hearing most of this for the first time, but she caught on quickly—asked a few questions for clarification, mostly kept quiet and absorbed what she was listening to.

When they landed in Providence and were disembarking, Jonathan handed the pilot a thousand dollars and asked him how long he could wait to take Justin and Reggie back that night. The pilot said, "As long as you'd like, Mr. Westwood."

On the ground, Justin touched his father on the shoulder, said, "I'm sorry you had to see that tonight. I'm sorry you had to be there. I would never have put you in danger like that if I had known."

Jonathan only said, "Thank you for saving our lives." And then: "I love you."

They smiled at each other. When Roger shook Justin's hand he, too, said, "Thank you." Then he did his best to grin and said, "I'm hittin' your dad up for one major bonus."

Jonathan had arranged for two cars. One for him and Roger. One for Justin and Reggie. Justin and Reggie's car took them about thirty minutes from the airport, into an area of Providence called College Hill. It was a clean, suburban-looking neighborhood with expensive, colonial-style houses.

"Looks like a place where wealthy businessmen should live," Reggie said as the car pulled into a gated driveway.

"They do," Justin said solemnly. "You're about to meet one of the wealthiest."

"How do you know where he lives?" Reggie asked.

"Every cop in Rhode Island knows where Lenny Rube lives," he said. "They've all been here for dinner."

The driver stopped at the intercom before the gate and dialed up to the house. When a man's voice at the other end said, "Who is it?" Justin leaned over and said his name. There was a fairly long silence, then a woman's voice said, "We're having a dinner party, Mr. Westwood. I'm afraid this isn't a good time. We're just starting our dessert."

"Is this Mrs. Rubenelli?" he asked.

"Yes, it is."

"Ask your husband if he'd rather talk to me in private right now or if he'd like me to drag him out of your dinner party by his hair and arrest him in front of all your guests."

There was another silence. Then the gate slowly began to open. The car drove up the long driveway, dropped them off in front of the house, and Justin asked the driver to please wait. He said they wouldn't be long.

They were ushered into the Rubenelli house—the parlor was nearly as big as Justin's house in East End—and asked to wait in a den off to the right. As they were led to the smaller room, they could make out the dining room and a large table with perhaps twelve guests seated around it. There was lots of laughter and good cheer emanating from the room. Justin was willing to wait exactly five minutes before going into the dining room and putting a damper on all the fun. But with thirty seconds to go, Leonardo Rubenelli joined them in the den.

"You were always a rude bastard," Lenny Rube said. He looked at Justin and said, "Jesus Christ. What the hell happened to you?" Justin didn't bother to respond. Lenny Rube raised his eyes, a look that said, *Okay, if that's the way you want to play it,* then he saw Reggie and said, "Excuse me. Leonard Rubenelli." He extended his hand, and she shook it.

"Agent Regina Bokkenheuser," she said. "FBI."

"What do you want?" Lenny Rube said.

It was Justin who answered. "I want Bruno."

"What, you don't know how to get in touch with him?"

"He seems to be out of touch at the moment."

Lenny said nothing for a minute, as if he was pondering the request, then he said, "You know, I never liked the fact that you and Bruno were so friendly. It's always made me uncomfortable. Other people, too."

"I wouldn't overestimate our friendship so much if I were you, Len. This isn't a social occasion. I want you to tell him to talk to me."

"I'll tell him when I see him. That it? That's what's so pressing? Can I go back to my guests now?"

"Not yet," Justin said. "You might want to sit down for this."

Rubenelli waited long enough to convey that it was his choice whether or not he was going to stay, but when the decision was made, he sat in a large, overstuffed chair with a multicolored, flower-patterned, quilted fabric. Justin began to talk. He told the Mafia boss almost all of the financial details he'd learned from Roger, down to the profits that Rubenelli's various red-named companies had been making—as well as their recent losses. He explained as much as he needed to about Evan Harmon's shorting scheme and financial sleight-of-hand artistry.

Rubenelli said nothing until Justin was finished. Then he pulled a pack of cigarettes from a drawer. To Reggie he said, "You mind if I smoke?" She shook her head and he said, "My wife, she don't like me to smoke in the house. But I think I need one—you know what I mean?" He offered one to Reggie and Justin; they each declined. "You always were a good cop," he said to Justin. He lit up, took a quick drag. "It's why you're so unpopular."

"I'll take that as a way of saying you're not disputing what I just told you."

"Take it however the fuck you want." Rubenelli took a deep drag. "I'm seventy years old and I smoked my whole life. Since I was ten. Probably live to be a hundred. Makes you wonder, doesn't it?"

"Not that much," Justin said.

"So what do you want from me?" Rubenelli asked.

"We want you to fill in some gaps."

"And I'm doin' this just out of the goodness of my heart?"

"You're doing it because I can make a really good case that you're responsible for the deaths of Evan Harmon, Ronald LaSalle, and Wanda Chinkle. It's good enough to take to court, and right now I'd say it's at least fifty-fifty it's winnable. And if that happens, you'll be smoking behind bars for those last thirty years of yours."

"What's stoppin' you from making your case?"

"I think there's something bigger going on."

Rubenelli smirked. "What, you're sayin' I'm innocent?"

"You're the least innocent guy I've ever met, Len. I'm just saying I'm not convinced you're guilty. At least of these murders. But if we release this information, and tie you to everything I know we can tie you to, everybody else is going to think you're guilty as hell. Of a whole bunch of things."

"Ask," Rubenelli said.

"You met with Evan Harmon and Ronald LaSalle down in Palm Beach at the Rockworth and Williams hedge fund conference."

"Yeah. I have a house down there. Right on the water. I use it in the winter. Bunch of snobs, you know, but you can't beat the fuckin' weather in January."

"How'd you hook up with them?" Reggie asked.

"You're not gonna believe me."

"Try us."

"Bruno. He was usin' LaSalle as a broker."

"As a legit broker?" Justin asked.

Lenny Rube laughed. "Totally legit. Bruno got interested in the market. He started to play around. LaSalle made him some dough. A lotta dough, if you wanna know the truth. So he came to me and said I oughtta check this guy out."

"Len," Justin said, "you're telling me that you were using Ron LaSalle as your personal, legit broker to play the stock market?"

"How much of this conversation is off the record?" Rubenelli asked.

"Unless I'm wrong and you ordered these hits, it's all off the record. I wish you nothing but success with your moneymaking schemes."

"Off the record, it started legit. As kind of a test. Then we went to him and said we wanted to invest some—uh—corporate funds. We wanted him to be a kind of funds-to-funds guy."

"Funds to funds?" Justin said. "What are you, going to business school?"

"Hey, scumbag," Rubenelli said. "A lotta what we do's legit now. And we gotta play it legit. And it wasn't just my dough, our dough. We got a few . . . outside investors."

"Other families?"

"I'm talkin' to you about my business. I don't have to bring in other people's business. I'm just sayin' my investors got money to invest and we got people to look out for and we're like anybody else—we like to hire good people to watch over our money."

"So LaSalle started investing your money in various hedge funds?"

"Yeah. Until . . . well . . . he kinda figured out we weren't interested in dealin', you know, a hundred percent on the up-and-up. I mean, we were makin' dough, but we decided we weren't makin' enough dough."

"He backed out?"

"He wasn't stupid. He *asked* out. I liked the guy. He did his job for us. I said fine. Just get me a good replacement."

"Evan Harmon."

"A greedy fuckin' guy."

"You put your—okay—corporate money into Ascension."

"We made a deal."

"Which was?"

"He wanted our dough and he wanted it bad, this guy. We told him we'd go with him. But we wanted a guarantee." Rubenelli paused. Justin knew it was for dramatic effect, so he gave him his moment in the sun. Then Rubenelli continued. "Twenty percent."

"Guaranteed on your investment?"

"That's right."

"And he agreed," Reggie said.

"He agreed happily. I think your friend LaSalle told him he was crazy. But like I said, this Harmon was one greedy fuck."

"You know how he did it? Guaranteed you that kind of return?"

"I wasn't dealin' with him too directly. But I heard a few things and I had my suspicions. Now I pretty much know for sure, thanks to you." Rubenelli stubbed his cigarette out in an ashtray. He went into a small bathroom off the den, tossed the remains in the toilet and flushed them away. When he came back he said, "My wife. I'm not kiddin'. She'll bust my balls big-time if she sees I'm smokin' in here." He looked longingly at the pack of cigarettes. But he put it back in the drawer. "You know, I'm gettin' kind of philosophical in my old age."

"How's that?" Justin said.

"I been thinkin' how things change. I been in this business a long time. Since I was a kid. And I seen a lotta changes. In the way we work, the way we think. People got the impression that we're like the movies. We sit around some table and do whatever the fuck they think we do. But we're a business now. We're in a lotta legit businesses. Our kids are legit. It's different. It changes things, sometimes make you cautious. Kinda philosophical even."

"Jean-Paul Rubenelli," Reggie said.

"Whatever. But I'm tellin' you, even the politics are different. When I started, you talk to a lotta the family heads, they were Democrats, you know. They didn't care so much about the niggers, but they liked the whole underdog thing. We could relate to it. And we had some clout. This was the Hoffa era, you know. The Daley era in Chicago. I heard stories, back to Kennedy and Nixon. The West Coast wanted Nixon, they had their hooks in him. But we told 'em to back off. It wasn't his time. We had to send people down to Florida—what the hell was that guy's name, Nixon's money guy. Stupid name. Rebozo. Bebe Rebozo. We had to send a couple guys to his house, meet with him and Nixon, tell 'em this wasn't their year—you know what I mean?"

"You should write a book, Len. But is this going anywhere?"

"I'm just sayin' it ain't like that anymore. Guys got rich. Guys got fat. Guys got houses like this one. We used to deal with unions. With businesses, small businesses. Now we deal with Wall Street, with investors, lobbyists. Much more genteel. Not as much fun."

"So the mob's a bunch of Republicans now—is that what you're saying?"

"I'm sayin' that things change. We got different connections, we got different friends. The whole way of thinkin' has changed. But some people don't change. I don't change. I mean, somewhat—you know? I adapt. But not that much. I like the old ways."

"And Bruno doesn't change."

"Bruno? Nah, he don't change at all. He does what he does. Always has, always will. And some guys like it, some guys don't. Am I done now?"

"I just want to get this clear: You didn't know about the platinum shorting?"

"What are you, gonna keep me here all night on this shit? I thought you wanted to talk to Bruno."

"I do."

"Then let him tell you what he knows. I took you about as far as I can go. 'Cause I didn't go to fuckin' business school, you smart-ass."

"How do I talk to Bruno?" Justin asked.

"He'll be in touch."

"When?"

"Soon," Rubenelli said. "Very soon. Now can I get back to the table? My wife's relatives. I'll be lucky if they left me one fuckin' cake crumb."

32

Reggie worked her BlackBerry on the short ride from the East Hampton Airport back to Justin's house. He sat with his head leaning back and his eyes closed. But when she told him the reports she'd requested had come through—all the information he'd asked for, and more; she'd gone ahead and put through searches on her own—his eyes opened and, although his head didn't move, the eyes did, shifting toward her. She read what had been sent to her. He blinked once, showing he understood, showing that the information was as stunning to him as it was to her.

When the taxi pulled up, she insisted on walking Justin into the house. He resisted but not very hard. And when they were inside he spoke in the same monotone he'd been using since she'd arrived at his house earlier. He was tired, said he wanted to go to bed, and she said, "I know. But I'm not leaving."

"Reggie . . ." he said, but then he stopped. He didn't have anything more to say.

"I'll sleep on the couch. I don't think you should be alone right now."

"I'm fine," he said.

"You killed somebody today, Jay. And it was horrible and brutal and it's not over yet, you know it's not over yet, so you can't be fine."

"Okay," he said. "Maybe I'm not fine."

He leaned back on the couch, and as he did she saw the physical pain he was in. She got up, got his bottle of single malt scotch and poured them each a glass. He took a small sip, recoiled as if the liquid were burning his lips, but then he closed his eyes in satisfaction, and when he opened them again he took another sip.

"You're a strange man," she said. He didn't answer, just probed with his eyes. "You smoke dope; you'll sleep with married women; I know from personal experience you won't say no to kinky sex."

He took another sip of scotch, this time a bigger sip. "So far I sound like any other guy except luckier."

"And you've killed people."

"So have you," he said slowly.

"But I don't sleep at night," she told him. "Do you?"

"Yes," he said. "Things wake me up in the middle of the night, but they're other things. Not that."

"You're a cop," Reggie said. "You enforce morality. And despite everything, I think of you as honest and moral."

"I don't enforce morality," Justin said. "I enforce the law. Two totally different things."

"So you don't think in terms of morality," she said.

"Of course I do. Constantly."

"And do you think you live a moral life?"

"I don't really think like that."

"I don't believe you," she said. "You're too driven, too fixated on what you do."

"Maybe," he agreed.

"Then do you? Live a moral life? This isn't multiple choice, it's yes or no."

"Okay, yes. Comparatively. Yes."

"Then define it."

"Morality? I can only define it for me, I think."

"Go ahead."

"Discipline."

"Say what?"

"For me it's discipline. I do what feels right or good until it doesn't.

Until it feels as if it's going too far. And then I'm disciplined enough to stop."

"And if it never feels wrong?"

"Then I don't stop."

She leaned over and kissed him lightly on the lips. He didn't kiss her back. But he didn't pull away. And he didn't close his eyes.

She kissed him again, tasting him. And this time he did respond. His hand came up behind her head and he gently pulled her closer to him. He could feel her warm breath on his lips, smell her sweat commingling with her perfume.

"I'm not feeling very disciplined," she whispered.

"Good," Justin told her. "Because I don't feel like stopping."

She had to help him upstairs and into bed.

She made sure he was comfortable, gently pushed him back so he could lie down, and then she began to kiss him lightly, careful not to touch his ribs or the bandage on his hand or the stitches on his face. She kissed his neck, his cheek and his lips. She kissed him deeply now, her tongue inside his mouth, and they began to make love. She took his clothes off slowly, saw the deep bruises from the battering he'd taken earlier. She removed her clothes just as slowly. She wanted it all to be slow; she wanted to please him as much as possible. She let him look at her naked, came back onto the bed, and let him run his good hand over her face, her neck, down her back. They kissed again and she got on top of him, and as they began to move she heard him groan. His eyes told her he was okay, so they moved together, and it didn't take long for either of them. When it was over, she was drained, realized how much she'd wanted him, how much she'd needed this, needed it with him. She looked down, wanted to tell him that, but she saw that she'd hurt him, that it had been too much for him, and she said, "I'm sorry, oh god, I'm so sorry," but he pulled her closer, using his bad hand, and he said, "It's all right, it's all right." And she said, "I don't want to hurt you. I don't want you to be in pain." She reached to the side of the bed, where she'd put the pills the doctor had given him. She went to open the bottle, but he took it. And he tossed it across the room. They heard the bottle roll and come to a stop as it hit the wall. He kissed her on the side of her head, and said, "Again." She looked at him in surprise, started to shake her head no, it wouldn't be good for him, but he said, "I want to make love to you again." And he began to move, slowly, and she could see how much it hurt him, but could also see how much he wanted it, wanted her, so she began to move slowly again, too, on top of him, and as they were making love, and as she was watching him, the passion not quite overriding her concern, he rose up a bit, and pulled her down to meet him, and he put his lips up against her ear.

"Pain is good," he whispered. "It means I'm still alive."

They woke up together, found they were entwined. Her face was in his chest, her legs curled over between his. His arm was around her, covering her. They were naked.

He looked at his alarm clock, saw it was 5 A.M. They both wondered why they were awake, felt that maybe they weren't, maybe this was some kind of mutual dream, then she sat up and so did he.

They knew why they had awakened.

Someone was downstairs.

They listened, heard a rustling noise, then a quiet cough, the sound of someone shifting position. Justin did his best to swing his legs out of bed, but he couldn't, and also couldn't stop the grunt of pain that escaped from his lips. She was out of bed quickly; she went to his bathroom door and grabbed his robe off the hook. She slipped it on, then she knelt down, ran her hand across the floor until it touched the gun that she'd left there. She had discarded it at the same time she'd taken her clothes off. But before she could grip it, she heard him whisper, "Drop it." She looked up and he was pointing his own gun at her. He shook his head, one quick jerk back and forth, and said, "Don't touch it. Move back," and then she realized what was happening—what he thought was happening—and she thought her heart might break. The first time they had made love, that very first time a year earlier, it had been a setup. *She* had set him up, or at least had agreed to it. Men had barged in on them in the middle of the night, had drugged Justin and taken him away. He had suffered enormous pain—emotional and physical—as a result. She could see in his eyes he thought she'd done it again. She shook her head, but he didn't waver. Reggie tried not to let her pain show, tried not to show that she was devastated, but she knew she wasn't doing much of a job.

He said in a hushed tone, "Get in the bathroom. If I hear the door open I'll shoot you."

She thought she was going to cry, but she didn't. She just stepped sluggishly—all energy sapped from her body—into the bathroom and closed the door behind her.

Justin was out of bed now, too. He had to struggle to pull on his pants. But he managed. He picked up Reggie's gun, stepped gingerly and silently down the stairs, his own gun held in front of him, pointed forward. As the living room came into view, so did the intruder. Justin yelled, "Freeze! Police!" The force of his voice made his ribs throb.

The intruder was sitting on the couch, leafing through one of the Melman Prep yearbooks that Justin had brought back from his meeting with Vince Ellerbe. He looked up, saw Justin, shirtless, wearing jeans, pointing the gun straight at him. He tapped the yearbook he was perusing, said, "Interesting reading."

Justin sighed and lowered his gun. Went back upstairs and opened the bathroom door. Reggie was standing in the middle of the small room, looking lost and despairing. He said softly, "You can come down now." She said nothing, only stared at him, and he said, "I'm sorry."

She shook her head, said, "How could you think that?"

He said, "I had to think that. I couldn't think anything else." And then he said, "I'll never think it again."

She said, "I understand. But I don't know if that's good enough." Then she stepped around him and headed downstairs. Justin followed her. When they both came into view, the man on the couch started shaking his head slowly.

"Unbelievable," Bruno Pecozzi said, looking at the two of them. "The more things change, the more they stay the same."

* * *

"So word reached me that you want to talk," Bruno said.

Justin wanted to ignore the big man, wanted to put his arm around Reggie, to kiss her, to make her understand what had happened, why it would never happen again, but he couldn't. He didn't have time. He had to focus and deal with what he had in front of him, so he faced the man on the couch. He was amazed that there was no difference between the Bruno who'd been sitting there with a loaded pistol pointed at him and the Bruno who was sitting there now, a beer in his hand. Justin and Reggie had quickly dressed; she had put on her outfit from the night before, and Justin managed to get a long-sleeved button-down shirt on. Bruno had taken careful note of Justin's injuries and asked about them. Justin told him what had happened. Bruno never changed expression. Violence did not faze Bruno or even interest him all that much. It was simply a part of his daily life; he had the same perspective on it that commuters had about their rush-hour train ride from and back to the suburbs.

"I thought you were coming to talk a while ago," Justin said. "Right after I saw you."

"I had to be a little careful," Bruno said. "Perhaps you might recall the circumstances under which we last met."

"I recall," Justin told him. "Pietro Lambrasco."

"Was that his name?" Bruno didn't seem surprised that Justin knew it.

"Yes."

"Well," Bruno said, "I didn't much care what his name was."

"You just cared why he was there." When Bruno nodded, Justin said, "And did you find out?"

"I told you, there were a few possibilities. Turned out, I'd done something he didn't like."

"Back in the old country, maybe? When you took your relaxing vacation?"

"Could be."

"Where you from again, Bruno?" Justin asked. "That place where your aunt has the beautiful villa, up on the cliffs? What part of Italy is that? I don't think you ever told me."

"The south," Bruno said.

"As south as Sicily?"

"As south as that, yeah."

"And this villa, does it happen to be on an island?"

"How official is this conversation?" Bruno said. "I'll talk to you"—
he jerked his thumb at Reggie—"but she makes me nervous. Bein' a Fed
and all."

"You should be nervous, Bruno," Justin said. "You killed Evan
Harmon. And I don't know how the hell you did it, but you sunk a ship
near Sicily. And Wanda Chinkle knew about it."

"Did she?"

"Yes, she did. She left me kind of a note about it."

"What kind of note?" Bruno asked.

"She left me the name of the boat. Reggie's associates just confirmed
it. Sometimes it's not so bad bein' a Fed and all."

"That right?"

"That's right," Justin said. He turned to Reggie. "You want to tell
him?"

"*Hades,*" she said. "You sunk a ship called *Hades* off the coast of the
Sicilian island Favignana. Named *Hades* because he wasn't just the god
of the underworld, or even just the god of wealth. Hades is the god of
precious metal. And the ship had a lot of precious metal on it. That's
what it carried on a regular basis."

"Platinum," Justin said. "On this trip, over fifty million dollars'
worth."

"You landed in Palermo five days before the boat went down,"
Reggie went on. Her voice got stronger as she spoke, although she still
wasn't looking at Justin. "You took a ferry from Trapani to Favignana.
And you left the island three days after the ship sank."

"Your visitor Pietro Lambrasco. He was here for something personal,
not just business," Justin took over. "We got the list of sailors working
on the ship. All present and accounted for. No deaths among the crew.
But apparently there was one stowaway. No one knows how he got on
board but he was there. A young kid. And he drowned. His name was
Angelo Tornabene. You want to know the name of Pietro Lambrasco's
wife? Her maiden name, I mean?"

"No," Bruno said. "I know it. Giovanna Tornabene."

"Angelo's older sister."

Bruno said, taking another long swig of beer, "You didn't answer my question. How official is this conversation?"

"It's official," Justin told him. "It's official on her part and on mine."

"How official is it if I didn't kill Evan Harmon?" the mobster wanted to know. "'Cause I didn't," he said. "I would've. No problem. But before I could, somebody else beat me to it."

33

Bruno drank his second beer and then his third while he talked.

He confirmed most of what Lenny Rube had told Justin and Reggie, but he was able to elaborate and provide more detail.

Bruno had indeed started going to Ronald LaSalle because of his stellar reputation as a financial adviser and money manager. He explained that he wasn't exactly in a business that provided long-term health care and retirement funds, so he wanted a legit place to stash his money—of which there was a considerable amount—and help it grow. He wasn't getting any younger, and he knew he couldn't depend solely on muscle forever. So he gave a couple of hundred g's to LaSalle, who did a hell of a job. Bruno made money, probably the first legal money of his life, he said, except once when he was a kid and he washed cars. Even then, as he thought about it, he used to steal anything inside the cars that wasn't nailed down—including once taking a spare tire from someone's trunk while the person was still sitting in the car—so he guessed that didn't really count.

He got Lenny Rube involved, he said. At first, just with the mob boss's own money. Also totally legit. And just as profitable as Bruno's initial investment. LaSalle had started his own business and was definitely looking for investors, so Lenny went to him and said they were putting together a fund and wanted LaSalle to handle it. This was Lenny's idea. Several families from around the country needed a place to put their cash; Lenny had the rep and the clout, so the other families knew he'd look after them. It was a good deal all around. Everyone made money; it was a good way to pay taxes and make everything look nice and tidy; and Len took a sweet little cut off the top for brokering with the broker. But then LaSalle began to realize what he'd gotten into. At first, he really believed that Lenny's businesses were legit. Then he was asked to do things, Bruno said.

"What kind of things?" Reggie asked.

Bruno said, "Things a guy like LaSalle wasn't used to. Doctoring profits, moving money around. Mostly he was asked to guarantee our investments. We got a monthly statement one time and the pot had gone down. Lenny didn't like it. LaSalle said he couldn't do that. Lenny told him, 'Sure you can.' Lenny figured that if LaSalle was taking an automatic cut of our investment, he could guarantee us a certain profit. LaSalle said, 'That ain't the way this thing works,' and the Rube said, 'That's the way it works now.'"

When Reggie asked why LaSalle went along with it, Bruno said, "We had him by the short and curlies. All I had to do was point out that he'd been doing business with some members of a known criminal organization. It didn't matter whether he knew about it or not, it wasn't gonna be good for his reputation. But the thing is, the guy had some stones. He still didn't go along with it."

"What did he do?" Reggie wanted to know.

Bruno told them that LaSalle came to Bruno and Lenny with a proposition. He said he'd find someone else who could do the job. Someone who'd go along with what they wanted. Someone who might fit in with them better. They could move their money from LaSalle's investment company into this new person's company. All LaSalle wanted was to untangle their business relationship. He had a wife and they were thinking about starting a family and he was too honest for this kind of work. It was because he was honest that he said he'd get them an acceptable replacement.

"I thought the Rube would never go for it. But he liked this guy. And, between you and me, I think he gets off now on bein' this kind of benevolent godfather type—you know? He's startin' to think he might actually be a respectable businessman, you know, with all his Palm Beach shit and joinin' country clubs and all that. So he said okay. With one condition. He said that for the first year, LaSalle had to keep his hand in and make sure whoever this new guy was wouldn't fuck up. Lenny said he'd make sure that the new guy hired LaSalle—so LaSalle wouldn't be doin' business directly with us but he could still look after our interests. And still make some money for his new company. And LaSalle agreed. Not that he had a lot of choice—you know what I mean. He knew he was gettin' a good deal."

"And so the person he came up with was Evan Harmon," Justin said.

"Harmon jumped at it," Bruno told him. "Len met him down in Palm Beach and said the guy had greed written all over him. So we cut a deal."

"The same kind of deal Ron LaSalle wouldn't go along with."

Bruno nodded.

"And what went wrong?" Reggie asked. "What happened?"

"You get in business with a rattlesnake, you can't be surprised when he bites you. And then you really can't be surprised when the bite turns out to be poison."

"Which side are you referring to as the snake?" Justin asked.

"I'll give you your point, but I'm talkin' about Harmon. He was the rattler."

"Give us the specifics," Justin said.

"It started out as a sweet deal. He did a lotta business with the Chinks. Family ties, business ties, all that shit. He was investin' a lot of money for 'em. And he knew what they were gonna be investin' in. He said the Chinese car business was gonna take off. The numbers were amazin'. I mean, we're talking huge. Puts us to fucking shame. I saw the numbers. They more than tripled the number of cars over there in the last five years—from somethin' like six million to twenty million. And that's gonna keep goin' up like crazy. They're sellin' a thousand new cars a day in Beijing. A thousand a *day*! I didn't even know that was a city! And you know what's gonna happen over here? We're fucked and

Europe's fucked and the Japs are fucked most of all. I'm talkin' good passenger cars for ten grand and an SUV for under twenty."

"Okay," Justin said. "You're hired. You can do the infomercial."

"I'm just sayin', this is a business that had our name all over it. Harmon said he could move a few things around, take our money and invest in platinum, which had to keep goin' up because all of a sudden China needed it—and needed a lot of it. They had to have it for all those fuckin' cars! It's makin' me crazy just to fuckin' think about it!"

"Try to keep your head in the game, Bruno."

Bruno did his best to calm down. "Yeah, yeah, all right. So Harmon said that if we put money in with his fund, he could arrange it so that we always made a profit. Other people could go up and down but we'd always stay up. He'd keep us strictly in platinum and slant cars."

"Why was he so willing to make that deal?" Reggie wanted to know. "His fund had plenty of money."

"It wasn't just our money," Bruno said.

"What was it?"

"It was our . . . expertise."

"Let's hear it," Justin said.

"Again . . . off the record. But it's not so complicated. Harmon's tied into China big-time. China doesn't want to just import cars and import car parts, they want to make their own fuckin' things, right? That's what they do. They take things over. They make 'em themselves 'cause that's where the money is. They're takin' over the whole world! So Harmon's helpin' them. He's shippin' parts to them on the sly. 'Cause Ford and Chrysler and nobody in the fuckin' U.S. governments wants to be helpin' them take over the whole car industry. So the exportin' is a little, let's say, dicey. I mean, they're gonna do it, you don't stop the Chinks once they get rollin', but the good ol' USA wants a share, right? They don't want 'em makin' all the parts we know how to make 'cause then what do they need us for?"

"So he lets you into his fund, he promises that you'll make a steady profit, and in exchange you provide a little smuggling expertise. For which you also get a share off the top?"

"Hey, we're a business just like everybody else."

"And where'd you smuggle the parts to?" Justin asked.

"Mexico. There was a plant there. Auto parts. The Chinese would fly their planes in there and Harmon could ship 'em whatever he wanted to ship 'em as long as he could get it to the plant."

"And how about your profits in the fund? Did they stay up?"

Bruno nodded. "Until recently."

"What happened?"

"He said that some of his other investors had gotten unhappy. And he said that a couple of people had gotten suspicious of the way he was playing fast and loose with their dough. I mean, I don't know exactly how he was working it, but he was basically taking profits from someone else and giving them to us."

"Did he say what people were suspicious?"

"He tried to keep things quiet but, you know, we're very inquisitive. I got the kind of face people eventually open up to."

"You are a charmer," Justin said.

Bruno shrugged. "He said it was his father. And a hotshot Wall Street guy. A guy who threw a lot of money his way, a guy connected big-time to China."

"Lincoln Berdon?"

Bruno nodded. "The guy who runs Rockworth and Williams, yeah. Berdon had put a lot of Chinese people, including the Chinese government, into the Ascension fund. He had a lot of Rockworth dough in it, too. And he wasn't happy with the results of his investments. Or the investments Harmon was making for his Chinese connections."

"Because a big chunk of the profits were going to you."

"Hey, he was givin' the Chinks what they needed—the platinum and the auto parts. He was just chargin' 'em top dollar and makin' a profit."

"So what did Evan propose to do about it?" Justin asked. "How was he going to deal with the pressure from his father and Berdon?"

Bruno raised an eyebrow. "He wanted to back off our deal for a while. Make sure a few other people got their big returns. He said he'd make it up to us in a few months. He swore it'd be bigger than ever. He said he had a scheme that would bring us into the whole Chinese car market, make us more than we'd ever dreamed about."

"And your reaction?"

"I told him we were capable of dreamin' pretty big. And I said, hey, it wasn't anything personal, we could talk about Chinese cars and shit all he wanted but we had a deal. Not for the future but for the here and now. And I explained that the people I work for like other people to respect their deals."

"So what happened?"

"I'm not exactly what you call a financial expert. But I know people. Harmon thought he could negotiate a deal with anyone. He was pretty surprised when he ran into someone who had a different kind of negotiating technique."

"Meaning you."

"Meaning me. And my technique is pretty effective. But I knew this guy Harmon was going to try to cheat us. And once that—how should I say this—once that bond of trust is broken, then we're not big on doing the repair work, you know what I mean?"

"Yes," Justin said. "I do. So what happened then?"

"We knew he'd invested us big-time in platinum. So before we . . . let's say severed our relationship with him . . ."

"You thought you'd make a killing. At least a figurative one. And drive the price of platinum way up."

Bruno nodded. "That's pretty much it."

Reggie stared at him openmouthed. "You sunk a ship with how many people on it? Fifty? A hundred? More than that? Just so you could make some money?"

Bruno didn't look as if he was offended. "I do what I'm paid to do," he said. "If you wanna know the truth, if things had gone right, nobody woulda died. I didn't know about that kid who'd hidden out."

"If you had, would you have cared?"

"You got me there," Bruno said. "I'm not really a sensitive kind of guy."

She couldn't sit still, couldn't look at the huge man sitting on the couch with a can of beer. Reggie got up, began pacing.

"Okay," Justin said. "You sunk the ship *Hades,* drove the price of platinum up, made whatever percent profit you made, and pulled your money out of Ascension."

"That's where it gets complicated," Bruno said. "We didn't get our money out."

"Why not?" Reggie said from across the room.

Before Bruno could answer, Justin said, "Because Evan sold all your platinum to someone else. He used you the way he'd been using his other investors. You didn't own it anymore because he'd shorted it so somebody else could make the profit."

Bruno quietly applauded. "Very good, Sherlock."

"Who'd he sell it to?"

"The bastard sold it to himself. He fucked us. We were buyin' the platinum and making money. But he'd bought the fucking company that was using all the platinum. The one we were selling to."

Justin said, "Bastard, is right. But he was a smart one." He remembered what he'd been told at the Ascension office. "Harmon bought the company that makes the filter device the cars need. And then he turned around and made an even bigger profit all for himself, by selling the devices to the company in Mexico that makes the final parts."

"The company he also owned," Reggie said.

"He had every base covered."

"You guys are pretty good at your job, I'll give you that," Bruno said.

"One thing throws me, though," Reggie said. "If he'd stiffed you and stolen from you, why were you still smuggling for him? Why agree to keep shipping the platinum to Mexico?"

"We weren't. And we didn't."

"But the truck that crashed . . . that had to be Evan's platinum."

"It was."

"But . . ." Reggie squinted. Her lips turned up in that crooked smile. "He'd started doing it on his own."

Bruno nodded. "He mighta done it legally at some point," he said, "but he starts moving it into Mexico on a regular basis, we're gonna know about it. So he had to keep smugglin' it in. He couldn't let us know what he was doin', takin' our goods and makin' a fortune."

"So when word got around about the truck—" Justin started to say.

"He knew Bruno and Lenny Rube would realize what was going on," Reggie finished. "He could have paid them back and even kept up paying them a profit on their investment. But they never would have realized what he was doing. Double dipping—giving them the small profit and taking the big one for himself and his other partners."

"Once the platinum was found in the truck," Justin said to Bruno, "Evan realized that you and Lenny would figure out exactly what he'd done: played you for suckers and taken you for a lot of money." He gave a half laugh. "And it would have worked, at least for a little while longer, if whoever was driving that truck in Texas hadn't gotten drunk and turned the thing over."

"Like I said," Bruno added, "I woulda killed the little prick. But somebody beat me to it."

"So we're back where we started," Reggie said. "Who killed Evan Harmon? And why?"

"Reggie," Justin said abruptly, "we have to see H. R. Harmon. And Lincoln Berdon."

"Jay, it's impossible. Their lawyers have blocked us every step of the way. Berdon's in and out of the country and Harmon's lawyers just keep talking about how he's so grief stricken. We haven't been able to get near them. We've been trying. They'll go right up to the attorney general, if need be—they've got a lot of clout and they're using it to keep us away from them."

He turned to her, his head cocked. "Say that again."

"What?"

"What you just said."

"I said they've got a lot of clout and they're using it to get off our backs."

"And they'll go up to the attorney general if need be."

"I'm sure they can even go higher than that."

Justin smiled bitterly, said, "Or lower." And when they both turned to stare at him, he said, "We have to see Harmon and Berdon. And we have to see them soon."

"I can't help with this," Reggie said. "You can't get in officially."

"Then we'll get in unofficially." Justin turned to Bruno. "You in the mood to do a little research?"

The three of them went through everything that Justin had printed up on H. R. Harmon and Lincoln Berdon.

Reggie said, "I don't see a way to do it, not in any way you're going to get them to talk. You're not going to be able to barge into their office and bully them into a confession."

And then Bruno said, "Wait a second. Go back to that golf thing. The club he plays at, it's in Westchester?"

Justin flipped through the papers on his desk. "Yup. In Westchester. Every afternoon at four."

"What's the name of the club?"

"Tilden," Justin said, glancing down to make sure he had it right.

"Tilden," Bruno repeated. And then he said, "I think we got our in."

"You want to explain this?" Justin said.

"The caddy master at Tilden. Good guy, nice guy. Name is Eddy Braniff. Never met a football spread he didn't like. Same for college hoops."

"Okay, so you know the caddy master, good for you."

"Hey, it's not like I go around socializin' with the guy. We don't go out for fuckin' high tea. The guy owes. And he owes big."

"How big?" Justin asked.

"Thirty-five grand."

Justin smiled and nodded. "I think we've got our in," he agreed.

34

H. R. Harmon was always surprised that golf was considered a morning game. What could be better than heading out on the links on a summer afternoon? The weather had usually cooled off; deer would flit across some of the expansive fairways; the timing was perfect, at the end of the round, to have an ice cold beer or, better yet, a tall gin and tonic. As usual, he thought, people had it all wrong. They did things backward. They went out when it was the hottest and most crowded because they were sheep. They were afraid to go against the norm. Frightened people making bad decisions. Even about something as simple and pleasurable as a game of golf.

H. R. smiled at the thought. And he realized his caddy thought he was smiling at him. Which wasn't the case. The caddy was kind of a screwup: couldn't find a ball on the second hole, told him to play a seven iron when he needed a six, was way off on the yardage on the fourth hole.

"You're new here," H. R. said.

"Yes, sir," the caddy said.

"Caddied around the area before?"

"Not so much," the caddy said. "It's kind of a new profession for me."

H. R. looked the caddy up and down. "A little old to be starting life as a caddy, don't you think?"

"Well, sir, it takes some people longer than others to find their lot in life."

Some lot, H. R. thought. *Spend your whole life trying to figure out what to do and this is what you come up with—carrying around someone else's golf bag.*

Frightened sheep, he thought.

H. R. teed off from the blue tees on the fifth hole. His Pro VI went about 220 yards down the right side of the fairway. H. R. still had good eyes, and he thought he saw the ball trickle into the right short rough. If he had a decent lie, he'd be in good shape. A solid rescue club knocked up toward the front of the green, a chip, and a one or two putt for a par or bogey. Easy. Except the caddy wasn't heading for his ball. The idiot was steering the cart off to the left, over toward the woods on that side.

"You gotta get yourself some glasses, son," H. R. said. "You're heading to the wrong side."

The caddy didn't respond, other than to step harder on the golf cart's accelerator. H. R. spoke louder, saying, "I'm on the other side of the fairway. You're going the wrong way!"

The caddy turned his head to look at his passenger.

"I don't think so," he said.

The woods were thick and shielded them from the open expanse of the rest of the golf course. Justin knew they couldn't stay there forever; at some point someone would come by. They had to move quickly.

As he slowed the golf cart to a stop, he saw H. R. Harmon's eyes widen as he saw the size of the man who was waiting for them in the woods.

"Thirty-five grand this cost me," Bruno said to Justin. "I can't fuckin' believe I let that little weasel skip out on the whole thirty-five grand."

"It's for a good cause," Justin said. "It'll help keep you from going to prison."

"Let's get this over with," Bruno said, "before I lose my temper."

"Whatever it is you boys are doing," H. R. said, "you're making a very big mistake. You're not going to get any money out of me. And people will be here very soon to see what's going on over here."

"We've got plenty of time, Senator," Justin said. "More than enough time, in fact. And we're not looking for money."

He saw H. R. flinch a bit at the word "senator." *He realizes we know who he is,* Justin thought. *Always a little unnerving.*

"Here's a cell phone," Justin said to H. R. "Call Lincoln Berdon and tell him you need to get together right away."

"What is this all about?" H. R. said gruffly. "I'm not going to do any such thing. What the hell do you think you're doing?"

"I'll repeat it one more time," Justin said. "Call Lincon Berdon and set up a meeting for this evening. Tell him it's important."

"Go to hell," H. R. Harmon said and he began to yell out for help. Before a syllable could escape from his lips, Justin swung his elbow as hard as he could swing it into the aging ex-politician's mouth. A tooth flew out. And Harmon went down hard.

From his seat on the ground, a dazed Harmon spit out some blood, looked up and said, "You just made a big mistake."

"I'm afraid you're the one who made the mistake," Justin said. "My associate is not nearly as easygoing as I am."

Bruno now stepped over to the man on the ground and said, "Take one shoe off."

Harmon looked up, confused. "What?"

"Take one shoe off. It'll be a lot worse if I have to do it for you 'cause I'm already in a bad mood and I might take your whole fuckin' foot with it. Now take your goddamn shoe off."

Harmon reached down and untied his left, all-white golf shoe.

"Take your sock off," Bruno said.

Harmon did as he was told.

"Stand up," Bruno said, and Harmon pushed himself off the ground and stood up.

Bruno pulled out a pistol with a silencer on it. And now Justin could see that Harmon was afraid.

"He asked you twice, so I'm not gonna ask. I'm telling you. I'm gonna shoot one of your toes off. Then he's gonna ask you again. Each time you don't do what he says, I'll blow another one of your toes away.

You won't die. But it'll hurt like hell. And I hope you don't mind the sight of blood."

"Wait," Harmon said.

"Too late," Bruno told him. He bent down, and before Harmon could react, Bruno put the end of the barrel against H. R. Harmon's pinky toe and pulled the trigger. There was a quiet pop and the toe disappeared in a spray of blood. The old man fell back down, in shock and enormous pain. Blood poured out of the end of his foot.

"Ask him again, Jay," Bruno said.

Justin stood over the onetime politician and said, "Call Lincoln Berdon and set up a meeting. Set it up for right now. Please." He held his cell phone down toward Harmon, who had, in the past five seconds, aged twenty years. His face had gone slack and his skin had turned pale.

"My foot," he groaned. "My foot . . ."

"Stand up again," Bruno told him.

"Give me the phone, give me the phone," Harmon said quickly. He reached up to grab it out of Justin's hand. He punched in the required numbers as quickly as he could manage. He was so rattled it took him three tries to get the sequence right.

Harmon reached Lincoln Berdon immediately, said there was an emergency and they had to meet. Said he couldn't discuss it over the phone. His voice was shaky but over the phone must have just sounded urgent. It worked. He hung up and nodded. He stared up at Justin and Bruno, overwhelmed by pain and the stunning realization that he was in a situation over which he had absolutely no control.

Bruno tossed a handkerchief in the air and it fluttered down to the dirt by Harmon's shaking hand. "Here," the big man said, "tie somethin' around that before you bleed to death." He looked over at Justin, saw the look Justin was giving him. "What?" Bruno said. "You got what you wanted, right? Now you think I gotta start touchin' people's feet? Fugettaboutit. He can fix his own fuckin' foot."

*   *   *

H. R. Harmon's driver, Martin, was surprised to see his boss coming
up to the car with two men. He was even more surprised when he realized his boss was walking with one shoe off, and that his foot was bleed-
ing like a motherfucker. What surprised Martin the most, however, was
when one of the men, the smaller one, put a gun into his side and told
him to get behind the wheel of the limo and start driving.

Martin had no desire to get shot, so he said, "Sure," and, without
demanding any more information, headed back toward the city, which
is where the smaller guy told him to go. The bigger guy, the scarier one,
didn't go with them. That was more than okay with Martin. And more
than okay with Mr. Harmon—he could see that as soon as the big guy
left. At one point during the drive, Martin glanced in the rearview mirror, saw his boss leaning back with his eyes closed, and he asked him
if he was okay; but Mr. Harmon didn't say anything in response, so
Martin decided to dispense with all further questions.

The traffic heading into Manhattan cost them about twenty minutes, so the drive took a little over an hour. As Martin drove, Justin
reapplied the makeshift tourniquet to Harmon's foot. Martin found a
few Advil in the glove compartment of the limo and Justin forced the
old man to swallow four of them. Almost nothing was said the whole
way in. The only words spoken were when Justin's cell phone rang. It
was Reggie—Reggie who spoke to him as coolly as if they'd never met
before. He closed his eyes while she talked, envisioning her naked on
his bed, remembering making love to her. He realized he wasn't paying
much attention to what she was saying, so he interrupted her to say
quietly, "Look, we have to talk."

"Let's just finish our business," she said, her voice even. "Let's just
get through this and finish, and then we'll see if there's anything to talk
about."

He said okay, his heart pounding, and she told him what she'd found
out since he and Bruno had left East End Harbor. She'd run prints on
the Chinese man that Justin had killed. They knew his identity. When
she told him, he looked over at the wounded man sitting next to
him. He said nothing to H. R. Harmon, just spoke into the phone:
"Okay, I've got it." Then he said, "These are sick goddamn people."

She also said she'd gotten the records for all Larry Silverbush's phone calls. Justin had been right, she said—Silverbush had made the calls that Justin thought he'd made. He had a moment of self-satisfaction, then he told Reggie to hold on a second, and he said to Martin, "What's the number of this car phone in the backseat?" Martin didn't hesitate; he reeled off the number. Justin gave it to Reggie, asked if she could get a list of all calls made and received on it starting a week before Harmon's murder, and then he went, "Hold on one more sec." He said to Martin, "You have a cell phone of your own?" Martin said, "Yeah," and Justin said, "Give it to me." It didn't take the driver long to hand that over, and Justin flipped it open, got the number, and gave that to Reggie, too, again asking her to check all outgoing and incoming calls. He saw the look in H. R.'s eyes, knew he'd struck a little too close to home. Then he put his phone to his ear again. He and Reggie both stayed on the phone without saying anything. He could hear her breathing, and he knew she didn't want to sever the connection the same way he didn't. There was nothing they could communicate to each other, not right now, but he was glad she didn't want to be separated from him. Even if it was only temporary. He listened to her breathe, and then he finally heard her hang up.

They went over the Triborough Bridge into Manhattan, but they didn't drive to the Rockworth and Williams building, as Justin had assumed. When they reached the city, Harmon—whose rich man's tan had faded into a sickly-looking pale green color—gave an address on East 69th Street. They pulled up in front of a brownstone.

"What is this?" Justin asked.

Harmon's voice was weak. It had no resonance. Justin knew the old man had to be in serious pain. He didn't really care. "Lincoln's home."

"No," Justin said. "He lives on Park Avenue."

Harmon shook his head. "That's his family home. He keeps this as a separate residence. To use for private functions."

Justin turned to Harmon's chauffeur and said, "Pop the trunk." When that was done, Justin said, "Now get out of the car and get into the trunk."

"What?" Martin said.

"Get into the trunk," Justin told him. "You have five seconds."

Martin was there in four seconds. Justin closed the trunk, said to Harmon, "Try to remember to let him out when we're done."

Harmon nodded but didn't look as if that particular command was going to be a top priority.

Justin wondered if he'd made the right move by not bringing Bruno. They had decided that it would be better if Bruno took Justin's car back to East End Harbor. Justin did not expect this session to take long. And he'd been afraid that Bruno's involvement wouldn't be good or productive for anyone concerned. For all he knew, the FBI would be waiting inside the house, and that would not be a meeting Bruno would relish. But now he wished he had some company. Some large and intimidating company.

"All right, let's go," he told Harmon.

"I want to put my shoe on," H. R. Harmon said.

"It'll hurt a hell of a lot worse if you do that," Justin said.

"I'm not going into Lincoln's house looking like this. I have to put my shoe on."

Justin shrugged and watched as the old man grimaced and groaned but got his shoe on. He even tied it. But not too tight. And Justin was impressed: H. R. barely limped on the short walk from the car to the town house. Justin decided the old guy wasn't much on honesty or decency but he was hell when it came to dignity.

They were met at the front door by Lincoln Berdon.

He was wearing a black, three-piece pin-striped suit, and the expression on his face was as somber as his funereal-looking attire. He ushered the two men into his living room. The house was decorated all in black, white, and silver. The tables were stainless steel. The floors were painted black and white. Couches and chairs were either white with black pillows or black with white pillows. Justin wondered if they had black and white wine. But he didn't get a chance to find out since Berdon didn't offer him a drink.

"What is this about?" Lincoln Berdon asked.

"Do you want to know who I am?" Justin asked.

"No," Berdon said. "I know who you are. What I want to know is what you're doing here."

So Justin told him. He went through the events of the recent past step by step, beginning with the discovery of Evan Harmon's body. He left nothing out. He told them both what he knew about Ronald LaSalle's murder—and LaSalle's recent business history. He told them everything he knew about Evan Harmon's corrupt financial dealings, all the way through the overturned truck in Texas. At one point, Justin said, "I know that Evan arranged to buy platinum as low as he could and sell it at a huge profit to the Chinese government. That couldn't have made you happy—him cheating your most important client." Berdon didn't respond; he was well trained. Neither of the two Wall Street legends looked shocked at anything Justin had revealed up to that point. Harmon was following Berdon's lead, which surprised Justin a little. He'd expected their relationship to be on a more equal footing. This was Berdon's show. Berdon's world. H. R. Harmon was a supporting player.

Justin then talked about Wanda: what she'd told him when they'd met in her car, what he knew about her death. When he told them about the words she'd managed to scrawl before she died, Lincoln Berdon didn't so much as blink. But this time Harmon looked startled. He glanced quickly at Berdon, who didn't return the look. Berdon's eyes never moved; they stared straight ahead at Justin.

"What else do you have to tell us?" Berdon asked. Justin felt as if he should compliment the man on having perfected his dismissive tone. But he thought he should hold off just a bit on any congratulations.

"I have a few other things," Justin said. He told them about the break-in and murder at the LaSalle Group and how they knew that the murderer was a Chinese woman. Harmon also seemed to blanch at that news. Then Justin told them about the Chinese man who came to his house. And he went through exactly what had happened. He spared no details.

He then said, "We know the man's identity now. The FBI ran his fingerprints, and we're aware of his connection to the Chinese embassy. We also know his place of employment. I guess I should put that in the past tense. We know where he *used* to work. It's hard to hold a job when your whole face has been melted away." The two men were silent. Justin said, "Don't you want to know where he worked?"

"Where?" H. R. asked.

"Rockworth and Williams," Justin said. "His name was Togo Lu. And he had a job in Rockworth's security division." Justin turned to H. R. Harmon. "You speak Chinese, don't you, Senator?"

"No," the ex–ambassador to China said. "It was way too complicated a language for me. Never learned more than four or five words." Harmon was turning paler by the moment. He turned to his longtime business associate. Then back to Justin. "But Mr. Berdon speaks excellent Chinese." He turned to look right into Berdon's eyes and said slowly, in a hoarse, raw voice, "How many dialects, Lincoln?"

Lincoln Berdon ignored H. R. Harmon as if he weren't in the room, as if he didn't exist. He spoke directly to Justin. "So far, all you've done is entertain us with stories. I still don't know why you're here. What is it you're looking for?"

"Something simple—the truth."

Berdon snorted. "What truth exactly? Which one?"

"That's the thing about truth," Justin said. "I find there usually tends to be only one."

"That's where you're wrong," Lincoln Berdon said. "If there's anything I've learned from being around Wall Street all these years it's that there isn't any truth, there's only perception. It's what people *think* is true that drives the world."

"Then maybe," Justin said, "you should hear what I think is true."

"I'd like to hear it," H. R. Harmon said.

Justin looked at H. R. and said, "I think that you raised a very devious son. So devious, he couldn't tell the difference between his friends and his enemies. So he cheated them both. And they both decided to do something about it. Only his friends got there first." Now he turned to Lincoln Berdon. "And they killed him. And then they killed Ron LaSalle. And Wanda Chinkle."

"And why would his friends do that?" H. R. asked.

"Because they wanted what Evan had taken from them. What he'd bought for himself. They wanted the platinum he owned. And the companies he'd bought to transform that platinum into something everyone needed."

Lincoln Berdon smiled. "You're a very interesting man, Mr.

Westwood. Quite surprising. But you don't have any proof and you will never find any proof to back up what you're saying. And the reason is because it's not true. In this case, perception does not equal reality."

"You have a computer in this house?" Justin asked.

"Of course."

"You mind if I use it for a minute? I'd like to show you something."

Berdon hesitated. But he couldn't resist. His curiosity got the better of him. He led both men into another room. A desktop computer sat on a large, antique, dark wood desk. Justin went to the computer, connected to the Internet, and found his way onto a Web site.

"This is Larry Silverbush's Web site," Justin said. "I believe you both know him. He's a Long Island DA, and he's running for attorney general." When neither man said anything, Justin went on. "Mind if I show you something in particular? It's a listing for one of Silverbush's recent fund-raisers. It was at a private apartment. At seven forty Park Avenue. Does that address mean anything to you, Mr. Berdon?"

"I have an apartment at that address."

"Not really such a coincidence. The fund-raiser was in your apartment."

"There is nothing illegal or out of line about raising money for a politician."

"No, there isn't. But I'm pretty sure if I keep digging, I'm going to find a few things that are illegal and out of line. You want me to tell you why? Because this isn't what I think, this is what I know. Silverbush was one of the first people who was told that Evan Harmon was murdered. Leona Krill called him right after I woke her up in the middle of the night to tell her. We've just seen the phone records, Lincoln, and they show that Silverbush called you immediately after he heard about Evan. I knew he had to have told somebody and you were the logical choice. You were his big backer. You were his ticket to eventually get him to the governor's mansion. So he'd want to curry favor with you. He knew about your relationships with H. R. and with Evan. He knew you'd want to know what had happened. What he didn't know was what you were going to do with that information. At least I hope he didn't."

"And what is it you think I did?"

"My *perception*? My perception is that as soon as you got the word that Evan was dead, you had your Chinese friends kill Ron LaSalle. And soon after that you had them kill Wanda Chinkle. You had one of them try to kill me, too."

"And why would I do all that?" Berdon said.

"I've already given you a few of my theories. I'm still looking for a few specifics. And you'll be the first to know when I prove them. But right now, the best I can do for sure is that you're a son of a bitch," Justin said.

Lincoln Berdon laughed. "That is very true," he said. "I am one mean son of a bitch. And so is Mr. Harmon here. Isn't that right, Herbert?"

"Yes," H. R. Harmon said quietly and seriously. "I am. But I'm not as big or as mean a son of a bitch as you."

"Then that's settled," Berdon said. "So if that's what you came to find out, Officer Westwood, you got your answer. And you can go."

"Not yet," Justin said. He said he needed to know how to get in touch with Ellis St. John.

"I'm afraid he's not reachable," Berdon said. "At least we don't know how to reach him. He had some sort of family emergency. We told him to take as long as he needed."

"And why would you be so generous?" Justin asked.

"Ellis is one of our most valuable employees. We're like a family at Rockworth and Williams. We do what's best for everyone."

"Who's handling his clients while he's away?"

"Everyone's helping out. It's difficult but we're managing."

"You have all the answers, don't you?" Justin said.

"I just want to be as cooperative as possible," Berdon told him.

Justin exhaled a long, slow breath. "What the hell am I not seeing?" he asked. "What the hell is it that you two crazy old bastards know that I don't know?"

"The truth," Lincoln Berdon said.

And he started laughing again.

35

Justin let Martin, the chauffeur, out of the trunk. He decided he had the upper hand so, what the hell, he told the driver to take him back to East End Harbor. Martin said he had to ask Mr. Harmon and Justin said it was okay, he thought he could safely speak for Mr. Harmon.

Sitting in the backseat, he opened a crystal decanter and sniffed. Scotch. Nice touch. He poured himself a small glassful, leaned back in the plush leather upholstery, and called Reggie.

"It's right here in front of me," he said. "All I have to do is make sense of one or two things. But I just can't do it. I can't see it."

So she had him go over the whole thing again. Step by step. The murders. The connections. The path of the money. The corporate cheating. Lenny Rube's role. Bruno's role. *Hades.* The still unsolved meaning of the word "Ali" that Wanda had written. The limo was almost to the East End Harbor town limits and they were still on the phone when he said to Reggie, "I'm going to pick you up. Come over. We're too close to let this go." She hesitated and he said, "It's business, Reggie. You said we had to finish this before we could move on to anything else, so let's finish it. Now."

She agreed and the limo showed up at her motel a few minutes later. When they got back to his house on Division Street, Justin checked to make sure his car was back, saw that it was, then he told Martin he could head back to the city but to make sure that Mr. Harmon was billed for the extra time. They walked into the house, and Justin expected to find Bruno there, but the big man was not around. He and Reggie didn't waste any time. They started in all over again. From the beginning.

Justin sat down on the couch, absentmindedly picked up one of the yearbooks that Vince Ellerbe had given him, and began leafing through it.

"It doesn't make sense," he said. "I don't see the domino effect. If Evan Harmon was murdered, why does that mean Ron LaSalle had to be next? And why Wanda? And why weren't they just killed? Why were they tortured? What information did they have that someone wanted? That Lincoln Berdon wanted?"

"You're sure it's Berdon?" Reggie asked.

"It's the only thing that makes sense. He's the link to Togo and the Chinese woman . . ."

"Who we're searching for, by the way. We've got a bureau-wide alert out for her."

". . . and he's the only one who's connected to everyone else: LaSalle, St. John, H. R., now even Silverbush. But why? Why would he want Evan Harmon dead? He doesn't benefit by Harmon's death. He only benefits if Harmon lives and he gets to buy what Harmon's selling. He needs what Evan Harmon *has*—so why would he want him dead? Why would—" He stopped talking. He bit off the rest of his sentence and stared at the yearbook page in front of him.

"What is it?" Reggie asked.

"Oh my god," Justin said. "Oh—my—god."

She knew enough not to say anything. She didn't ask a question, she just waited.

He didn't say anything either, not immediately. He couldn't say anything, too many images were flashing through his mind. Too many pictures, too many bits and pieces of conversations. It was as if the pieces of the puzzle were raining down upon him.

And suddenly those pieces were forming themselves into a whole:

Vince Ellerbe talking about Evan Harmon: *"His friends were mostly sycophants. He usually found one or two brainiacs who were frightened of him and that's who he spent time with . . . He liked the cheating better.*

He was just basically dishonest . . . He could always get people in author-
ity to look the other way, to break the rules just for him . . . At heart, Evan
Harmon was a crook. He liked to steal and he liked to lie. He just liked it."

The talk he had with Reggie after they saw Dave Kelley.

". . . The tip wasn't just that Kelley was having an affair with Abby
Harmon. It said he owned a stun gun."

"So somebody had to know how Evan was killed."

"It does seem kind of strange, doesn't it? Kind of . . ."

"Orchestrated."

"Yes. Orchestrated."

Ellis St. John's calendar.

EH/EEH (see directions/adbk)

Reggie saying, "This guy Ellis was spending the weekend with Evan
Harmon?"

Him saying back to her: "Seems like. But I'm telling you, it doesn't make
sense."

The phone conversation with Abby Harmon.

"How'd you know I was working with the FBI?"

"I don't know, Jay. Someone told me . . . I'm sorry, Jay."

Him thinking: What the hell had she done? What was she apologizing for?

Lenny Rube, in his den in Providence. *"We used to deal with unions.*
With business, small businesses. Now we deal with Wall Street, with inves-
tors, lobbyists."

Dave Kelley, talking in the Riverhead jail about the Harmon security system.

Him asking Kelley: "Who had laptop access?"

"Evan. On the laptop he used to travel with."

"Abby?"

Kelly nodding, saying: "But I don't think she really knew how to use it.
She didn't have much interest in it."

Wanda. The horrible image of the words she'd managed to scrawl
on her naked body, words written in her own blood: The last word tailing off. The final thought she'd ever have. The last two letters barely
legible as her life was ending.

"Ali."

And now the yearbook in front of him. Evan Harmon's last year at Melman Prep. Photos of his classmates. Photos of one particular classmate. One classmate who'd conveniently not mentioned that he'd been a classmate.

Quentin Quintel. Now the dean of Melman.

Lincoln Berdon's town house.

Justin saying, "What the hell is it that you two crazy old bastards know that I don't know?"

Lincoln Berdon saying, "The truth."

And back to the crime scene. Back to the Harmon bedroom. Justin standing over the body.

The body that was beaten to a pulp, beyond recognition. Blood everywhere. Pools and splashes of red.

The wedding ring . . . the favorite sweater . . . the shoes.

He remembered looking into Ellis St. John's closet. And the image that refused to materialize. Now he knew what that image was.

The shoes that were shiny and new looking. The shoes on the battered body that didn't have a drop of blood on them.

And listening to Bruno when the Mafia hit man was sitting on his couch: *"Like I said. I woulda killed the little prick. But somebody beat me to it."*

And then again Wanda's body. The word she'd managed to write. The word Justin now knew she wasn't able to finish writing.

"Ali."

Justin looked up at Reggie Bokkenheuser. He still didn't say anything. Went to his phone, dialed the number of the Southampton Hospital, got the morgue attendant. Justin identified himself, told him it was an emergency, said he needed access to the morgue files immediately. The orderly put him on hold for a minute; someone else got on the phone, asked Justin what he needed.

"Evan Harmon," Justin said. "I want to know his shoe size."

"That's it?" the guy in the morgue said. "That's the emergency?" And when Justin didn't bother to answer, the guy said, "Nine and a half."

And Justin still didn't say a word to Reggie. He just dialed another number, this time got the Riverhead police. This one took a bit longer but eventually he got the evidence room and he told the sergeant on duty what he wanted, the information he had to have immediately. It took a few minutes but Justin waited, and then the sergeant came back and said, "I've heard you're kind of screwy and I think this proves it. But your corpse was wearing a ten-and-a-half shoe."

Justin thanked him and hung up. He turned to Reggie Bokkenheuser and said, "It makes sense now. Everything that didn't make sense before makes perfect sense now."

He grabbed a pad of paper and a pen. And he wrote down Wanda's last word: "Ali."

"I still don't get it," Reggie said.

He said, very softly, "She didn't finish. She didn't finish writing."

And so he finished for her now. He wrote down the first three letters: A . . . L . . . I . . .

And then he wrote the last two. V . . . E.

Alive.

Reggie Bokkenheuser's eyes opened wide.

"Evan did it before, when he was a kid," Justin said. "He staged his own kidnapping. Now he just upped the stakes. He staged his own death."

36

Justin didn't know how he knew, but it was suddenly as clear to him as it could possibly be. Maybe it was the photo he'd seen on the Net, the one of Evan Harmon playing in the celebrity softball game. Wherever the inspiration came from, he knew what the murder weapon was and he also knew where it was. He got Reggie to arrange for someone to dive into the Harmons' man-made pond. Somewhere in there was a baseball bat. A bat that would have traces of blood on it. Ellis St. John's blood. And fingerprints. Evan Harmon's fingerprints. Salt water would have erased the evidence, but the pond was freshwater. Freshwater would not erase the evidence. Justin didn't even bother to wait around. He didn't need to. He knew.

He asked Reggie to stay in East End Harbor. He wanted her to make sure arrest warrants were prepared for Lincoln Berdon and H. R. Harmon. He also wanted her to figure out if they had enough to arrest Larry Silverbush. Silverbush might have been led down the garden path by Berdon, but there was also a reasonable chance he knew he was preparing the prosecution of the wrong man. He told Reggie that he could handle what was still left to be done by himself. But he needed her to put everything in motion. He said he couldn't trust anyone else. She didn't react to the word "trust," but he knew she had to understand the deeper meaning.

As Justin drove to Connecticut, he ran over the facts and the chronology. There were no doubts in his mind now. He didn't know what could be proved, but it didn't really matter to him. This wasn't about perception. This was about one truth. One absolute, undeniable truth.

Evan Harmon was cheating the mob and, at the same time, cheating Lincoln Berdon and his own father. He could have kept the game going, at least for a little while longer, except an accident ruined his plans. When the truck crashed on the way to Texas with Evan's shipment of platinum, he was screwed. As soon as the contents of the truck made the news, Lenny Rube and Bruno were going to know what Evan was doing. And Evan knew who he was dealing with. He knew what their reaction would be. He knew they would come and get him. So he found someone who not only looked like himself—same color hair, same basic build, same type—but was in love with him. Someone who would do whatever he wanted. So Evan arranged for Ellis St. John to come to the house. Ellis must have come willingly and joyfully, thinking he was finally going to spend the weekend with his fantasy lover. The joy would have been short-lived, though, because Evan killed him. Battered him so his face was little more than pulp. Physically unrecognizable. But wearing Evan's clothes—down to the shoes, which were put on after the murder—and equipped with Evan's wallet and credit cards and Evan's wedding ring.

And Evan was ready to disappear.

Evan knew that Abby would be out that night. Probably even knew she'd be spending Justin's birthday with him. It was perfect—the housekeeper and her husband were given the night off, and Evan's wife would be well taken care of, guaranteeing an empty house. And if the fact that she was spending the night with her lover happened to cast some suspicion on either of them, the better it was. And if suspicion fell on the missing Ellis St. John, that would be fine, too. Especially once Ellis's body had been identified as Evan and disposed of.

But Evan already had someone on whom he could cast full suspicion. He knew about his wife's affair with the contractor. And he'd seen David Kelley's stun gun—the perfect thing to point the finger at Kelley. Justin didn't know how Evan managed to get the gun out of or back into Kelley's house, but it wouldn't have been too difficult. He probably could have planted it there himself right after the murder. All he needed was to set the finger-pointing in motion. Justin didn't know for sure who Larry Silverbush's source was, but he'd bet big-time that it was Evan's father. There were calls to H. R. Harmon's phone from Ellis St. John's cell phone—after St. John was dead—and they already had gotten back the report that a call was made from Martin the chauffeur's phone to a cell phone that Justin knew would soon link directly to Evan—Quentin Quintel's cell. It would not be hard to pay someone to say that Kelley had talked about killing Evan. It would not be hard for Harmon or Berdon to pay anyone to say or do anything.

The problems came fast and furiously for Evan once he'd disappeared. Silverbush called Lincoln Berdon and reported the murder. Berdon must have suspected something, because he immediately sent his two Chinese killers up to interrogate Ronald LaSalle. He knew that LaSalle was doing a tremendous amount of business with Evan—Berdon had to have access to the Ascension records. He'd become suspicious of Evan's illegal activities and was already looking for ways to solve the problem.

Justin wasn't positive what Berdon was looking for from Ron LaSalle, but he had a decent idea. He wanted one of two things: he wanted to know if Evan was alive or he wanted to know how to get his hands on the platinum that Evan had hoarded. Berdon had to keep supplying China with platinum, or he might lose his most valuable client. China was probably worth billions of dollars to Berdon over the long haul. Justin knew that billions of dollars were usually a perfectly good justification for murder.

If Justin had to guess, he decided that LaSalle knew that Evan was still alive. That he'd faked his murder. He remembered what Vince Ellerbe had said: that Evan had to tell someone when he cheated, otherwise the cheating didn't count. LaSalle was one of the few people Evan could tell. He'd need to tell LaSalle because LaSalle could continue a lot of Evan's business dealings while he was in hiding.

This also solved one other thing that had been puzzling Justin: Where was Ron LaSalle going that early morning when he'd slipped out of his house and gotten himself killed? Justin thought he had the answer. He had told Reggie that Wanda liked to work with an inside plant. He was pretty certain that LaSalle was Wanda's source. He was an honest guy who had tried to do the right thing. When he began to be pressured by Lenny Rube and Bruno, the right thing would have been to go to the FBI. Wanda had to have realized that LaSalle would be a brilliantly effective source. And LaSalle was just honest enough to go along with that. It's how Wanda knew to bug Bruno. It's how she knew so much about Lenny Rube's dealings. It's how she would have put various bits of information together to figure out what Bruno had done to the ship *Hades*. And what Evan Harmon was doing with his illegal trading. What she wouldn't have known—and what LaSalle wouldn't have known—was just how involved Berdon and H. R. Harmon were in Evan's scheme. If they had been involved, Wanda knew she'd need a lot of absolutely secure information to bring them down. She'd also have known not to play her hand too soon with her superiors. Berdon and Harmon could go high up in the administration; they could pull a lot of favors. Wanda had to keep this to herself at the beginning or her investigation would have gotten squashed flat. So she would have kept playing her best card—her inside source. Ron LaSalle had gotten murdered because he was slipping away to meet Wanda. Justin was positive about that. He'd gotten killed while he was trying to do the right thing.

The odds were that Ron LaSalle talked before he died, told his torturers that Evan Harmon was still alive. That meant that Berdon knew almost from the beginning. And once he knew that, he also knew he had two chances to get his hands on Evan's platinum dealings and car-related companies. He could find Evan and make a deal or he could find Evan and kill Evan—and make a deal with his widow, who would inherit all Evan's property.

Money and power.

And thus Abby's conversion to the dark side.

The rest was just a footrace: Berdon trying to find Evan, Bruno trying to find whoever had what the mob considered to be rightfully theirs, Justin trying to figure out what the hell was going on.

He wondered what H. R.'s role in all this had been. The old man knew that Evan was alive. The phone records proved there were several conversations. Was the father trying to protect his son? Or was he work-ing with Lincoln Berdon to gain control of the son's assets? Or both? Justin had a feeling he'd never know the answer to that one. But he knew which way he'd bet. He did not think that H. R. Harmon had much paternal love in him. The old man seemed fed up with his son as far back as prep school. He'd go for the money. He'd feel bad about it—maybe have to skip a few rounds of golf he'd feel so bad—but he'd go for the money. He'd have the veneer of respectability but underneath was the dirt he'd never been able to completely hide.

Justin was almost to his destination now.

He parked about a block away from the small house in the country. There was a long driveway, a fairly steep climb that led to what was basi-cally a charming cabin in the woods. Sitting in front of the house were two cars. One was the rental car that Ellis St. John had used to drive to East End Harbor and to his death.

By the time Justin walked past the car and got to the house, he was out of breath.

Definitely back to the gym, he decided.

He decided to try the door without knocking. It was open, so he stepped inside. As he did, he pulled his gun.

Quentin Quintel was cooking in the open kitchen. His back was to the front door, but he must have sensed Justin's presence because he put his mixing bowl down and turned slowly. He looked shocked to see Justin, then the surprise seemed to fade quickly, replaced by a look of resignation and, Justin felt, the tiniest bit of relief. Justin waved his gun, just to make sure that Quintel saw it, and he put his fingers to his lips. The dean's eyes shifted ever so slightly toward the stairway. Justin nod-ded and headed up the stairs.

Evan Harmon was in one of the two upstairs bedrooms.

He was lying on a single bed, not sleeping, just staring up at the ceiling, his hands clasped behind his head. Justin stepped into the room, his gun in his hand. Evan did not look shocked to see Justin. He did not look resigned or relieved, either. He just smiled and shrugged, as if a long game of chess had come to an end.

"I was wondering who'd figure it out," Evan said. "I have to admit, I didn't think it'd be you."

"I guess you were wrong about a few things," Justin said.

Evan stood up from the bed and he let Justin handcuff him without a struggle. Justin led him down the stairs and out the front door. As they walked down the driveway, Evan leading the way, Justin saw that there was an almost buoyant spring to the man's step.

He's not unhappy, Justin thought. *Now everyone will know what he did. Everyone will know the scam he almost pulled off. He's happy to be caught.*

And that's when he heard the noise. From the woods to the right of the driveway. A twig snapping, maybe. A footstep.

Justin turned. Saw a shadow, a massive shadow, but that's all he saw. The blow came quick and hard and Justin went down to his knees. The second blow caught him behind his left ear and things went fuzzy. He wasn't out completely, wasn't out for long. Maybe a few minutes. But his world was a blur for those minutes. While he was down, he heard a pop, quieter than the snapping twig, but closer. He couldn't get his eyes open to see what was happening. And by the time he was able to clear his head, to stagger up to his hands and knees despite the brutal pain radiating behind his eyes and at the top of his skull, it was too late.

Justin sighed and quietly said, "Oh shit," when he saw that Evan Harmon was lying on the driveway right next to him, a small hole in the back of his head, blood still pouring out of the wound.

Justin managed to turn his head but there was no sign of anyone else around. There were footprints in the dirt next to the gravel of the driveway. A man's footprints. Justin saw that the prints were embedded into the dirt and crushed twigs. The man was not petite. He was large and heavy.

Justin closed his eyes, but that was a mistake because he was overcome with dizziness, so he opened them, forced himself to forget about the nausea and the pain, and he picked up Evan Harmon's dead body, carried it down the driveway to the car, put it in the backseat, and drove back to East End Harbor.

37

The morning of Evan Harmon's funeral, Long Island District Attorney Larry Silverbush resigned his post. He publicly apologized to David Kelley, and both New York tabloids had a front page photograph of Kelley and Silverbush shaking hands outside the Riverhead jail.

Lincoln Berdon did not attend the funeral. The day before, Special Agent Zach Fletcher went to bring Berdon in for official questioning. He was told that Berdon had left the country. When records were checked at Teterboro Airport in New Jersey, the FBI was told that Berdon's private Challenger had gone to London. The plane never landed at Heathrow, however, and by the time of the funeral, Berdon's whereabouts were still unknown.

H. R. Harmon did appear at his son's service at the T. J. Klein Mortuary. Local police and the FBI were working with the New York City district attorney's office to determine if they had a viable case against Harmon. The initial determination was that they did not.

Attendance at the service was sparse. There were more paparazzi than mourners. No one from Ascension showed up. Nor did anyone from Rockworth and Williams.

H. R. sat next to Abigail Harmon. Abby wore a short black summer dress and her legs were bare. The day was way too hot and steamy for stockings. Justin, who sat with Reggie Bokkenheuser two rows behind and across the aisle from H. R. and Abby, noted that the widow Harmon always looked her best in black.

When the service was over, Justin stepped into the aisle just as Abby passed him by. H. R. ignored him, refused to even glance in his direction, but when Justin touched Abby's elbow, she turned and flashed him the faintest of smiles. She slowed enough to let him draw even with her and he said, quietly, "When did you know?"

She didn't say a word until they were outside on the street, and then she said, "The day before I called you."

"Not from the beginning?" he asked.

Abby shook her head. "No. I didn't know until Lincoln and H. R. told me. They came to my apartment, told me that Evan was alive. When I saw him . . . when I saw the body in our bedroom, I thought . . . well, I didn't know until they told me."

"And what did you do?" he asked.

"I did what I told you people like me always do."

"You made a deal," he said.

"I did what was easiest," Abby Harmon said.

She leaned over, kissed Justin gently on the cheek, said, "Good-bye, Jay," then she disappeared into her father-in-law's waiting limo.

That afternoon, he flew up to Providence. He met with his parents, told them as much as he thought they would want to know. He thought that, somehow, they both were dealing with him differently than they'd dealt with him over the past decade or so. He didn't know if they were more respectful or just softer, but there was something about the way they spoke to him and listened that touched him. When he kissed them both good-bye—maybe the first time in thirty-five years that he'd kissed his father—he said he would see them soon. And he meant it. And he was glad to mean it.

Justin drove to Victoria LaSalle's house after that. There were other people there when he pulled up. Justin didn't know any of them and, when he was ushered into the living room, he wasn't introduced to any of them. Victoria excused herself, took Justin into a den and closed the door. She didn't say anything, just waited for him to talk. All he said was "You were married to a very good man."

He told her what he knew, sparing her any ugly details of his investigation, focusing on her husband and his role. He told her that he had died through no fault of his own. And he told her that Ronald had been trying to do the right thing. The moral thing.

Vicky waited until he was finished. She said, "Goddamn him. He was a goddamn fool and damn him to hell." Then she started to cry. Justin didn't move an inch toward her. He just waited for the crying to stop. She used her sleeve to dry her eyes. She said, "Who killed Evan Harmon?"

Justin said he didn't know.

Victoria nodded at him and went back to the living room. She didn't thank him. She didn't say anything else to him.

He showed himself out.

Justin had told Victoria LaSalle that he didn't know who killed Evan Harmon. Even though he did.

Evan was killed by a man whose job it was to kill people. Whose job it was to kill Evan. Evan had stolen from the wrong people and when he was about to get caught, he'd run for his life. But the man he was running from was good at finding people. He'd used Justin to help him find Evan, even though Justin hadn't realized it. And he could have killed Justin at the same time he killed Evan. He probably should have. But he didn't. Which is why Justin knew who'd pulled the trigger in the driveway.

Justin had told Reggie that he didn't exactly put Bruno in the friend category. He didn't know exactly what category Bruno did belong in.

This didn't exactly clarify the situation.

Two days after he'd left Vicky's house and Providence, an envelope was delivered to Justin's home in East End. Inside were a key and a hand-drawn map. There was also a note that said: *You deserve a vacation. Enjoy my aunt's villa. Now I owe you one.*

There was no signature.

No signature was needed.

*   *   *

Three days after that, Justin Westwood and Reggie Bokkenheuser were on the island of Favignana.

The villa they were staying in was actually a fairly small house, but lovely and simple. Built out of ancient tufa with stone floors and thick walls. Even in the nearly hundred-degree heat, the house was cool and perfect. There were two bedrooms, a living room, and a small kitchen on the main floor. There was also a basement that was accessible only from outside the house. It was dark and even cooler down there. Upstairs the decor was bare and plain; beige and earth colors dominated. Downstairs everything was quilted with colorful, lush fabric. There was one oddity to the house, but perhaps not so odd they decided, considering who the owner's nephew was. In the smaller bedroom of the main house, there was a wall of antique weapons: guns, knives, and swords. Justin, out of habit, checked several of the guns. He told Reggie he didn't know if they would even fire, but they were loaded. She said she didn't care. She just wanted to know if *he* was ready to fire, and he said he was, and they made love.

Every day for a week, Justin and Reggie made love downstairs during the day and upstairs at night. They made love as often as possible and talked about everything they could think of. They drank ice-cold beer and Sicilian red wine and ate fresh tuna and lots of pasta with tuna roe. The third night, after a bottle of chilled Sicilian rosé, they made love on the very private patio. There was no one around to see them when they were outside. The house was a good seventy-five feet from the road in front, and it rested atop a cliff. There was a waist-high stone wall around the back of the patio. It was all that separated them from a three-hundred-foot plunge into the sparkling blue sea.

They were on the patio now, in the late afternoon, both of them already brown from the sun. Reggie was reading a Dean Koontz novel about a husband whose wife was kidnapped. Justin was content to lie next to her, bask in the sun, and think about the fish they might eat for dinner, his hand lightly rubbing against her bare leg. At some point she put her book down and said, "I've been thinking."

He smiled and said, "Big mistake." But then he said, "Okay, what are you thinking about?"

Reggie said, "I'm wondering if you're going to go back to the East End PD."

He stayed silent for a moment. "I don't know yet. I haven't decided."

She said, "Well, what I'm thinking is that, if you do, you never filled the opening you had from last year. You're still a person short in the department."

"I never found the right person," he told her.

"Maybe I'm the right person," she said.

He looked at her, shielding his eyes from the sun, and smiled. "You want a beer?" he said. And when she nodded, he stood up and went inside.

He was standing by the open refrigerator when he heard Reggie call his name.

"Jay?" she said. "Could you come out here?"

She sounded funny, there was the slightest quiver to her voice, and he called back, "I'll be right there. You want a glass or just the bottle?"

"Doesn't matter," she said, "but come out. I have to show you something."

"In a sec," he said. "Well, maybe two seconds."

It was actually a minute or two before he emerged, and when he did he was holding two bottles of beer in his left hand. His right hand was covered by two large white linen napkins he'd found in the kitchen. He looked over at Reggie's lounge chair, saw that it was empty. Then he looked toward the edge of the patio. She was standing in front of the brick wall. He could see the sea, deep blue and shiny, behind her. Standing next to her was a beautiful Chinese woman. The woman he'd seen near Wanda's car. The woman the FBI had been looking for. The woman who, right now, was standing next to Reggie, holding Reggie's hair pulled tight in one fist. In the other hand, the woman had a long, thin knife she was holding against Reggie's throat.

"I am Li Ling," the woman said. She let go of Reggie's hair. But the knife did not move away from her throat.

"Yes" was all Justin said.

"I have wanted to meet you," Li Ling said. "I have wanted to meet the man who killed Togo."

"You've met him," Justin told her.

"You are a good player," Ling said.

"Player?" Justin asked.

"Yes. Togo was excellent player. But you are better."

"I'm not playing," he said. "This isn't some game."

"Yes," Ling said. "It is game. I want to play with you." She nodded at Reggie. "I kill girl, as you kill Togo. Then we see who is better player."

Justin smiled calmly at her. "I don't think I'll play."

"You play," Ling said. "I fuck you. I kill you. It will be good game."

"When you put it like that," Justin said, "that does sound good. Okay."

And as he said okay, he dropped the two bottles of beer. Ling's eyes shifted downward when the glass shattered on the stone—she couldn't help herself. When she realized what was happening, it was too late. Justin's other hand, the one covered by the napkins, was coming up fast. The napkins fell off to the side, revealing an antique pistol, forty, maybe fifty years old, and without hesitating he fired.

It sounded like a cannon roar in the tranquil silence of the beach, and a large hole appeared in Ling's otherwise flawless forehead.

Reggie leaped sideways, falling to her knees on the stone patio, and just in time. Ling's hand, the one with the knife, swiped backward exactly where Reggie's throat had been.

Li Ling stood for just a moment, staring in disbelief at Justin, then her legs wobbled and the knife dropped from her hand, and she started to topple over backward. The brick wall held her momentarily but not for long. She bent at the waist and then went over. She did not scream. She couldn't. She was dead long before her body hit the rocks in the shallow water, several hundred feet below.

Reggie stood slowly. She felt a sting in her elbow, which had banged against the patio floor, and she glanced down at her scraped knees. She went to Justin, who slowly lowered his arm. She took the gun out of his hand and set it on the small patio table.

"I told you something once," he said. "And I lied to you."

"What was that?" she said softly.

"I told you that I didn't think about the people I'd killed. I told you that they didn't keep me awake at night."

"It's all right," Reggie said.

"I think about them all the time. And I think about all of them, not just the ones I've killed. I think about all the murders, all the deaths. I think about them day and night. I think about them when I'm awake and when I'm dreaming. I can never stop thinking about them," Justin said.

Reggie put her arms around him and drew him to her.

"I know you can't," she said.

And then she said, "It's time to go home."